SUCCUMBING TO THE ENEMY

His mouth, now just inches from her lips, lowered. This time there was nothing gentle in his kiss as he thrust his tongue inside her mouth and tasted her thoroughly. Before Gillian could bite him again, he sucked her tongue into his mouth, his tongue tangling with hers.

"What...are...you...doing?" Gillian asked on a gasp.

He raised his head. "Do you like it?"

"I...nay, I like naught you do to me."

"Liar."

Gillian felt her resistance slowly ebbing. What kind of man was the MacKenna to burrow through her defenses so quickly? What kind of woman was she to succumb so easily to her enemy? Her body felt heavy, sluggish, his kisses drugging. His mouth and tongue were doing things to her she never imagined possible. And now he was kissing her...again.

"MacKenna! Stop!"

Other *Leisure* and *Love Spell* books by Connie Mason:

A TASTE OF PARADISE
A KNIGHT'S HONOR
GYPSY LOVER
THE PIRATE PRINCE
THE LAST ROGUE
THE LAIRD OF STONEHAVEN
TO LOVE A STRANGER
SEDUCED BY A ROGUE
TO TAME A RENEGADE
LIONHEART
A LOVE TO CHERISH
THE ROGUE AND THE HELLION
THE DRAGON LORD
THE OUTLAWS: SAM
THE OUTLAWS: JESS
THE OUTLAWS: RAFE
THE BLACK KNIGHT
GUNSLINGER
BEYOND THE HORIZON
PIRATE
BRAVE LAND, BRAVE LOVE
WILD LAND, WILD LOVE
BOLD LAND, BOLD LOVE
VIKING!
SURRENDER TO THE FURY
FOR HONOR'S SAKE
LORD OF THE NIGHT
TEMPT THE DEVIL
PROMISE ME FOREVER
SHEIK
ICE & RAPTURE
LOVE ME WITH FURY
SHADOW WALKER
FLAME
TENDER FURY
DESERT ECSTASY
A PROMISE OF THUNDER
PURE TEMPTATION
WIND RIDER
TEARS LIKE RAIN
THE LION'S BRIDE
SIERRA
TREASURES OF THE HEART
CARESS & CONQUER
PROMISED SPLENDOR
WILD IS MY HEART
MY LADY VIXEN

Connie Mason

HIGHLAND WARRIOR

LEISURE BOOKS   NEW YORK CITY

A LEISURE BOOK®

March 2007

Published by

Dorchester Publishing Co., Inc.
200 Madison Avenue
New York, NY 10016

ISBN 0-8439-5744-1

The name "Leisure Books" and the stylized "L" with design are trademarks of Dorchester Publishing Co., Inc.

Printed in the United States of America.

HIGHLAND
WARRIOR

Chapter One

The clash of swords, the cry of the wounded, and the sharp scent of gore rose above the eerie mists swirling around the combatants. The blood feud over land, supremacy, and vengeance raged unabated in the glacier-scored valley separating MacKenna land from the MacKay holdings. The feud had had its beginnings a century ago, when Clan MacKenna won Ravenscraig Tower and the surrounding fertile lands from Clan MacKay; they had been bitter enemies ever since.

Laird Ross of Clan MacKenna, a fierce and courageous warrior, flexed the muscles in his bulging forearms as he wielded his claymore in his clan's defense. He fought side by side with his kinsmen, wincing every time one of them fell beneath a MacKay sword. Ross knew Clan MacKenna couldn't afford to lose another family member. Too many of his kinsmen had died feuding with the MacKays and their allies over the years. Constant warring had taken its toll. They

1

had seen their lands decrease and their resources dwindle.

Ross's own father and one of his uncles had fallen beneath a MacKay claymore, and so had his younger brother and several cousins. Ross knew this senseless killing had to stop, but he had no idea how to end it.

"Watch your back!" Ross's uncle Gordo yelled from behind him.

Ross whirled, his tartan swirling about his powerful thighs as he faced this new challenge. His eyes widened as a veritable virago bore down on him, red hair flipping about a delicate, fine-boned face, and a MacKay tartan flying about calves and thighs far too shapely to belong to a seasoned warrior.

Ross immediately checked the downward stroke of his claymore, a stroke that would have cleaved the lassie in two if he had followed through. But that did not stop the warrior woman from jabbing her claymore at Ross, nicking his thigh.

"Cease, lass!" Ross roared. "I doona kill women."

"Lass or nay, I'm a MacKay!" the woman shouted back. "Defend yourself or die!"

She came at him again, flame-red hair flowing behind her, gem-green eyes glittering. The wind caught the edge of her tartan, giving him a flash of a firm white buttock. The sight so mesmerized Ross that he nearly forgot to defend himself. But his senses returned in time for him to deflect her blow.

"Desist, I say!" Ross growled. "Who are you?"

"Your enemy," the woman panted as she ducked out of reach of Ross's sword.

"I doona want to kill you, but I will if you refuse to leave the battlefield."

"You can try," the woman taunted. "I trained with my brothers—you willna find me easy to slay."

Though Ross had to admit the flame-haired lass was adept with a sword, she was no match for a warrior renowned for his fighting skills. Ross continued to dodge and parry his opponent's efforts without inflicting too much harm, though he was growing weary of this child's play.

The day was waning. Wisps of mist peeled away daylight as the sun dropped behind the Cuillin Hills. It was no longer possible to distinguish the MacKenna red-and-black tartan from the MacKay green and blue. From the corner of his eye, Ross surveyed the battlefield. Men from both clans lay on the ground, while others helped their wounded comrades off to the sidelines.

Ross spotted the MacKay laird bending over a body that lay unmoving in the blood-soaked dirt. He heard the laird's anguished cry and saw him beat his chest. Obviously someone dear to the man had fallen.

Ross could scarcely see his opponent now for the dark mist that swirled around him. He cursed as the lass continued to hack away at him. Though she deliberately aimed for vital parts, her efforts were hindered by Ross's skill and the lengthening shadows.

Suddenly the MacKay laird appeared at the lass's side, his face contorted by grief. Grasping the lass's arm, he pulled her away from Ross's deadly sword.

"Gillian, what are you doing here?"

"Fighting," Gillian replied. "Let me go. I have the MacKenna laird where I want him. Let me finish him off."

Ross nearly laughed aloud. It would be a cold day in hell when a lass got the better of Ross MacKenna.

Tearlach MacKay glared at Ross. "I'm taking my dead home. Let the battle be over for now." So saying, he dragged the flame-haired warrior woman away.

"We'll meet again, MacKenna; count on it," the woman shouted.

"I'm looking forward to it," Ross returned.

Ross turned away, the woman instantly forgotten as he looked over the battlefield. Too many dead and wounded, he thought, shaking his head. The feud was killing men in their prime from both Clan MacKenna and Clan MacKay. But no matter how hard he tried to envision it, Ross saw no peace as long as Clan MacKay continued to demand the return of Ravenscraig and the fertile lands surrounding the tower.

"You'd best come, lad," Gordo said. "Your cousin Gunn is among the fallen."

Ross snapped his head around. "Gunn? He is but a lad, scarcely old enough to wield a sword."

"Aye, but wield one he did, and he is likely to die for his bravery."

"Take me to him," Ross ordered.

His body limp, his face pale, Gunn lay on the cold ground, his life's blood quickly draining from him. The boy, still a gangly youth despite his muscular body, opened his eyes.

"Och, lad, why didna you remain at Ravenscraig, as I asked you?" Ross choked out.

Somehow Gunn found the energy to shake his head. "I couldna remain with the women, Ross. Not as long as I am able to wield a sword. You taught me yourself."

Ross leaned close. Gunn's words were so softly spoken, Ross could barely hear him. "Hang on, lad. Old Gizela will fix you up as good as new."

A light rain began to fall, dampening spirits as well as clothing. Ross whipped off his distinctive red-and-black plaid and placed it over his cousin. He felt neither the cold nor the sting of rain; what he felt was a bone-deep sorrow. And anger.

"How bad is it, Gordo?" Ross asked.

Gordo knelt in the blood-drenched dirt and lightly touched Gunn's rapidly cooling flesh. "He's gone, Ross."

"Naaay!" Ross shouted up to the heavens. "'Tis not fair. Did you see which MacKay struck the killing blow, Gordo?"

"Nay, lad, it could have been any one of them."

"Even the woman," Ross said beneath his breath as he scooped Gunn into his arms and carried him back to Ravenscraig Tower.

Braemoor Castle

Gillian paced her chamber, waiting for her father to determine her punishment. She didn't regret joining her father and brothers in their ongoing battle with Clan MacKenna. She had been training with her brothers for years and felt competent enough to fight the enemy. She was of an age to make her own decisions, and joining the battle had been her choice. She had been willing to suffer the consequences; why was her father so angry?

The sheer exhilaration of actually wielding a sword in battle against the hated MacKenna laird had left Gillian too excited to rest. She replayed in her mind the exact moment she'd realized she had engaged Ross MacKenna in battle and was holding her own against him. If Da hadn't dragged her away, she might have driven her sword straight into her enemy's heart. What a grand day that would have been!

It was rumored that Ross MacKenna was nearly invincible on the battlefield. Bards sang his praises throughout the Highlands. From what she had seen, the man was certainly bonny enough. 'Twas said his clan was descended from the Norse Vikings who'd settled Caithness centuries ago, and Ross MacKenna lacked none of the renowned Viking fierceness.

Though the MacKenna's sky-blue eyes had glittered at her with malice, she could see why women spun tales about his prowess in bed. Admittedly, his muscular body might hold appeal for some women, but not for her. She preferred the more refined Angus Sinclair to a rough and violent man like the MacKenna. Gillian was as good as promised to the Sinclair laird, and was eager for the betrothal to be finalized.

Footsteps sounded outside her door. Gillian braced herself as her father burst into the chamber. Tearlach MacKay, a large, barrel-chested man in his middle years, wore an expression that sent Gillian's heart plummeting to her toes. Rage softened by sadness shimmered within the depths of his dark eyes.

"Name my punishment," Gillian challenged. "Just don't expect me to regret what I did. I can fight as well as Tavis. Why shouldn't I be allowed to raise a sword in the clan's defense?"

The MacKay's fists clenched at his sides. "Tavis is dead. He died on the battlefield."

Gillian's knees buckled; she stumbled to a bench and sat down heavily. Tavis was Gillian's younger brother by one year and dearly loved by her. "Nay, it canna be."

" 'Tis true, lass. His body is being prepared as we speak. Tavis is my second son to die by a MacKenna's sword; do you think I want to lose my only daughter in the same way?"

Gillian searched her father's face, frightened by what she saw there. Weariness etched deep lines around his eyes, and his hair seemed to have grown gray overnight. Damn the MacKenna for tearing apart her family. First Loren and now Tavis. When would it all end?

"I canna lose another bairn," MacKay lamented. "And you," he said, pointing a thick finger at her, "deliberately placed yourself in danger. A battleground is no place for a lass. You were mad to challenge the MacKenna. The man is heartless; he could have sliced you in two with little effort."

"But he didna, Da. I was holding my own against him."

MacKay shook his head. "Foolish as well as mad. He was toying with you, daughter. Never doubt that the MacKenna could have slit you from gullet to groin with one stroke."

He began to pace. "This killing has to stop. Deaths on both sides are destroying the clans."

"Nay, Da, we are in the right. Ravenscraig Tower belongs to us. Have you forgotten that one of MacKenna's ancestors kidnapped a MacKay lass on her wedding day? The poor woman jumped from the tower rather than submit to a MacKenna."

"I have forgotten naught, daughter, but the sad fact is that, one by one, the feud is taking my sons. First Loren and now Tavis." He peered intently into Gillian's eyes. Gillian could tell he had something in mind for her, and braced herself. "I should punish you, but my heart isna in it."

Gillian stared at her father, stunned beyond speech. He had ever been heavy-handed when it came to punishment. She had felt the sting of a switch often enough, along with her five brothers. It wasn't like her father to let her off so easily, unless grief had gotten the best of him. Tavis had been the youngest and favorite of his five sons.

Gillian began to weep silent tears, sadly aware that she was never going to see Tavis's mischievous smile again, or suffer his good-natured taunts. How could she bear it?

MacKay began to pace once more. Gillian could tell he was grieving, and hadn't the heart to interrupt him. If the MacKenna were here now she would tear him limb from limb. She hated the man. He might not have been the one to end Tavis's life, but she still held him responsible.

Gillian dried her eyes, leaped to her feet, and shouted, "We should attack the MacKenna, Da. We should storm Ravenscraig now, when he least expects it. Where is my sword?"

"Sit down!" MacKay roared, turning on her. "Bloodthirsty little wench." His pride in his only daughter was tempered by his anger at her. "I've come to a decision. I'm going to attempt to end the feud between our clans, if the MacKenna is agreeable."

"Nay! You canna do it, Da! The feud must continue until we regain control of Ravenscraig."

"Is that what you think Tavis and Loren would say if we could ask their opinion? I can answer that, daughter. They would want to live."

"I've never heard you talk like this before, Da."

"Losing two braw lads and watching my only daughter challenge a Viking berserker have taken their toll on me. I'm going to seek out the MacKenna and make my wishes known to him. Together we may find a peaceful end to the feud between our clans."

"Ross MacKenna is a bloodthirsty cur. He willna agree. What do Murdoc, Ramsey, and Nab say? I doona believe they will agree with you. We've been fighting Clan MacKenna too long to forgive and forget."

"I am still the laird, and your brothers will do as I say. Ramsey wants to go to court and canna leave as long as the fighting continues. Nab wants to go with him. Murdoc, my heir, is courting Mary MacDonald, and hopes to marry soon and raise a family. I doona want his sons to die because of a senseless feud."

"What about me? Does anyone care what I think?"

"You're only a lassie; your opinion doesna count. Besides, you're going to play a major role in my dealings with the MacKenna."

Gillian brightened. "I am? Am I to help my brothers attack and kill the MacKenna laird?"

MacKay made a clucking sound with his tongue. "Your sainted mother would turn in her grave to hear you talk like that. You didna get your warlike tendencies from her, God rest her soul."

"How am I to help, then?"

" 'Tis best you doona know until I've spoken with the MacKenna. But first, I need time to bury and mourn my son."

Ravenscraig Tower

A brimming tankard of ale in his hand, Ross sat brooding before the giant hearth in the great hall. A fortnight had passed since Gunn's death, and he still missed the lad. Missed his good-natured teasing, his laughter, his way with the lasses. But as much as he missed Gunn, he knew the lad's parents missed him more, just as he missed his brother, who had died fighting the MacKays a year ago.

"Laird Ross, beware."

Ross looked up at the old crone who shuffled into the hall. Though Ross thought the woman mad for claiming to see the future, he considered Gizela a miracle worker when it came to healing the sick and wounded. Still, he didn't want to deal with the woman today. He was still mourning the loss of his kinsman.

"What is it now, Gizela?" he asked crossly. "I've no heart for foolishness today."

"Call it foolishness if you wish, laird, but you had best listen to what I have to say."

"I suppose you're going to tell me you had another of your visions," Ross growled, more annoyed than he should be. Gizela was always having visions, most of which he ignored. Some called the hag a witch, but Ross didn't believe in witchcraft.

"Aye, and you had best heed me this time."

Ross sighed. "Verra well. You're going to tell me whether I listen or not, so go ahead. What dire event have you foreseen this time?"

"The news is not necessarily dire, laird. Make of it what you will."

Ross's patience was ebbing. "Are you going to tell me or must I guess?"

Gizela gazed past Ross toward the window, her eyes murky and unfocused. "The day approaches."

"What day? You're talking nonsense, Gizela. If you werena my kinswoman and a talented healer, I wouldna be so patient with you."

Gizela began to sway, as if in a trance. "The day approaches," she repeated. "I see the end of war. I see our clan at peace." She turned her unseeing gaze on Ross. "But for you, laird, there will be obstacles to overcome. A flame will enter our lives. You will be consumed by it if you are not vigilant. Or you can absorb it into your soul, become a part of it, welcome it. If you doona, your heart will know no peace."

"Begone, woman! Flame, indeed. As usual, you spout nonsense."

Gizella blinked. " 'Tisna nonsense, laird. A flame will arrive soon. You must embrace it."

"I willna live long enough to see the day our clan is finally at peace. As much as I'd like to see the feud end and the killing stop, 'tis utter nonsense to believe it will happen. The MacKays and their allies have been fighting MacKennas and our allies for generations."

Gizela shuffled off, muttering, "The flame will bring peace. Wait for the messenger."

Ross drank deeply from his tankard, his mood dark.

"What did Gizela say this time to upset you, lad?" Gordo asked, subsiding into a chair beside Ross. "You shouldna listen to her drivel. She's half-mad, you ken."

"I ken, Uncle, but she does more good than harm. She was spouting some nonsense about flames and lasting peace and a messenger that will be arriving soon."

Gordo shrugged. "Forget it. I just came from the village. Gunn's parents are taking his death hard. He was their only son in a family of five daughters."

"I'll find husbands for the lasses from among our allies," Ross promised. "They are all comely and will make fine wives."

A beautiful woman with flowing golden hair entered the hall and paused in the doorway. "Come to bed, Ross. I grow weary of waiting for you."

"Your leman is impatient," Gordo said quietly to Ross.

Ross glanced toward the woman and frowned. Though Seana McHamish made a delightful leman, her possessiveness had become cloying. "Leave me, Seana. I'm in no mood for a bedmate tonight."

Seana scowled. Apparently she didn't take rejection

well. "Come now, Ross. You know I can make you feel better."

"Not tonight, Seana. Find someone else to warm your bed."

Seana sashayed over to Ross, hips swaying, breasts jiggling beneath her thin bed robe, and planted herself on his lap. "Have I displeased you? Are you sure you want me to seek another man's bed? You know my father expects us to wed soon."

Ross sighed heavily. "I never promised marriage, Seana. When I wed it will be to strengthen alliances. Our clans are already allies; our ties are too strong to sever. You are here because you doona like your father's second wife and sought my hospitality and my bed."

Seana pressed her unfettered breasts against Ross and kissed him soundly.

"Mayhap I should leave," Gordo said. " 'Tis late."

"Nay, Gordo, doona leave." He pushed Seana from his lap. "There's something I wish to discuss with you."

Seana squealed and scrambled to her feet. "Mayhap your cousin Niall will welcome me in his bed," she threw over her shoulder as she flounced off.

"You shouldna treat the lass so callously, Ross," Gordo advised. "You might want her in your bed again."

"Seana is a smart lass. She kens there is naught between us but sex. Seana wasna pure when she came to Ravenscraig, and I ken I willna be her last lover. Forget Seana, Uncle. How long do you think we have before Tearlach MacKay regroups and launches another attack?"

Gordo scratched his thatch of graying hair. "Winter is nearly upon us. Mayhap peace will hold until spring."

"I pray you are right. Except for Gunn, our losses

werena severe this time, but who kens how many of our kinsmen will die next time? I doona want to think about more deaths."

Ross heard a noise and looked up, startled to find Gizela standing beside him. "Where did you come from? I didna hear you approach."

"I heard what you said, laird, and but sought to ease your fears."

Ross glanced around him. "Gordo and I were alone. You couldna have heard us speaking."

A small smile played about the corners of Gizela's lips. "I heard. Heed me well, laird. There will be no more deaths if you welcome the flame."

"You're mad, woman," Gordo spat. "All this talk of flame is annoying the laird. He has more important things to worry about."

"When the flame comes, remember and heed my words, for the flame is your destiny."

Chapter Two

Ross resumed training with his clansmen, aware that another attack could come at any time. Usually during the worst of the winter months, the MacKays and their allies remained in their homes, huddled around their hearths, but Ross dared not let his guard down, even though winter was fast approaching.

After a particularly grueling training session, Ross returned to the keep, eager for a hot bath and something more substantial than the bannocks he had eaten that morning before he left the hall.

He had just finished his meal of roasted boar and root vegetables and settled back to listen to Gavin, the clan bard, when a guardsman rushed into the hall, skidding to a halt before Ross.

"A messenger has arrived, laird. He waits outside the gate. Do you wish to speak to him?"

"A messenger?" Ross repeated.

"Aye, he says he is Murdoc MacKay, and that his message is for the MacKenna laird."

Ross stroked his chin. "Is he alone?"

"Aye."

"I wonder what MacKay wants?"

"There is only one way to find out, laddie," Gordo advised.

"You are right," Ross said, pushing himself away from the table. "I will speak with him. Open the gate," he told the guardsman. "But keep a watchful eye for any sign of trouble. I doona trust any MacKay." He turned to his uncle. "Will you stay and hear him out with me, Gordo?"

Murdoc MacKay was ushered inside. Ross did not invite him to sit.

"Say your piece, MacKay," Ross rasped.

Murdoc looked at Gordo and raised his eyebrows.

"You can speak freely in front of my uncle."

"I bear a message from my father."

"So I ken," Ross said, growing impatient.

"Father wishes to meet with you on the sacred ground of St. Tears Chapel."

"Alone?"

"You may bring five men with you. My father will bring the same number with him. They are to wait outside while you and my father meet in private inside the chapel."

"Is that all?"

"Aye, except the MacKay told me to stress that the meeting will be mutually beneficial to both our clans and our allies."

Ross searched Murdoc's face, his eyes narrowed suspiciously.

" 'Tis not a trick," Murdoc assured him.

"What think you, Gordo?"

Gordo shrugged. "I doona ken what the MacKay wishes to parley with you about, but it must be important to risk sending his heir with the message."

"I am thinking the same thing, Uncle. Verra well, Murdoc MacKay, name the day and time of the meeting. But keep in mind that I am no fool."

"I will relay your message to my father. The time set for the meeting is the hour of sext, the day after tomorrow. The place is St. Tears Chapel, as I mentioned before."

"Verra well, I agree."

Murdoc turned to leave. Ross motioned to his uncle. "Escort Murdoc MacKay to the gate, Gordo. See that no harm comes to him."

Ross sat in brooding silence long after the two men left. He had no idea what MacKay wished to discuss, and was more than a little wary. Though the MacKay wasn't above trickery, Ross seriously doubted even a MacKay would launch an attack on sacred ground.

"It has begun, laird."

Gizela had sidled up beside him while Ross was lost in thought.

"I wish you wouldna sneak up on me, Gizela," Ross scolded. "What did you just say?"

"It has begun," she repeated. "Didna I tell you a messenger would arrive? Your meeting with the MacKay is just the start. Changes are coming."

Ross narrowed his eyes. "How did you know about the meeting? You were not in the hall when we spoke."

Gizela sent Ross an inscrutable look. "I have no need to be present to know what passes."

Ross waved her off. "You know naught. You simply guessed what the MacKay's son wanted. Is that all you wished to say?"

Gizela's eyes held a shimmering light that Ross had never seen in them before. Though he wouldn't call it unholy, it was definitely unnatural.

"Doona fear the flame, laird. Embrace it, for the flame is your destiny."

Ross sighed heavily and stared into the fire dancing in the hearth. "As usual, naught but nonsense comes from your mouth. Stick to tending the sick and wounded, woman. 'Tis what you do best."

When Ross looked up, the healer was gone. Needing to be alone to think, Ross made his way to the solar and sank into a chair before the hearth, trying to make sense out of Gizela's words. Why should he fear the flame? Unless . . . Did someone intend to burn Ravenscraig Tower? The MacKay? Nay, that could not be. Gizela said he shouldn't fear the flame.

Ross's thoughts were still engaged when Seana entered the chamber without knocking, wearing naught but a bed robe. "After I learned Murdoc MacKay had visited, I thought you might have need of comfort," she cooed.

Ross grinned at his leman. Seana was exactly what he *did* need tonight, although any woman would have sufficed. He held out his hand to her. Hips swaying, she strolled over to him and placed her dainty hand in his. Ross rose and led her to his bed. Coyly, she dropped her robe and arrayed herself on the furs.

Ross stared at the lush charms he knew so well and quickly shed his tunic and hose. He knew the moment he joined her on the furs that something was wrong.

Even as he bent his head and suckled her nipple, he saw flames shooting up around him, engulfing the bed. He leaped up, seeking the source of the fire.

"Ross! What ails you? Have I offended you in some way?"

"Did you not see it?" Ross asked, shaking his head in wonder.

Seana glanced around, her eyes wide and frightened. "See what?"

"Flames. They surrounded us."

"I saw naught. Mayhap you saw the fire in the grate."

Ross glanced over his shoulder. "Nay, I . . . Forget it. Leave me, Seana."

Seana reached for him, trying to tug him back into bed, but Ross was as immovable as a stone wall. "Go away, Seana, I need to think."

"You need to think of naught but me, Ross. Come to bed. Let me ease you."

"Another time," Ross said as he walked to the hearth and stared into the dying flames.

Huffing indignantly, Seana launched herself from the bed, picked up her robe from the floor, and stormed out, naked as the day she was born. Ross neither noticed nor cared.

Ross subsided onto a bench, wondering why Gizela's words had unsettled him to such a degree. Clearly there were no flames, and his bed was not on fire. The only flames were in the hearth, right where they should be. Abruptly his mind carried him back to the recent clash with Clan MacKay and the flame-haired woman who had challenged him on the battlefield. Never had he seen a more aggressive fighter, except for himself, of course.

The woman had to be mad to challenge him in battle when she had no hope of winning. At least her father had had sense enough to drag her away, and Ross had let them go. His honor would not allow him to kill a woman, not even a MacKay woman. For some unexplained reason, he could not forget that vision of the woman's long red hair flowing behind her like a silken flame as she flew at him.

Flame.

Living flame. Could it be? *Nay* . . .

He shuddered and turned his mind to his meeting with the MacKay.

St. Tears Chapel

The MacKay had arrived first and awaited him beneath the spreading branches of a linden tree. Ross entered the churchyard cautiously, just as the church bells pealed noon. True to his word, the MacKay had brought five men with him. Tearlach MacKay dismounted and waited for Ross to do the same.

"Shall we go inside?" MacKay invited.

Ross nodded to his cousin Niall. Niall dismounted, drew his sword, and entered the chapel. He returned shortly. "'Tis no trap, Ross."

"Verra well, MacKay, lead the way," Ross said, gesturing toward the chapel.

A black-clad, rotund priest with tonsured hair, his arms crossed over his barrel chest, greeted them at the doorway. "You must leave your weapons at the door if you wish to enter the house of God."

At first Ross was reluctant, but when MacKay unbuckled his belt and let his sword fall, he did the same. Nevertheless, he waited until his enemy had entered the chapel before he followed.

Satisfied, the priest shuffled off, disappearing behind the altar. MacKay led the way to the tiny sacristy, where two benches, a small table, and a pitcher of ale awaited them.

Ross perched on the edge of the bench while MacKay poured ale into two mugs. He held one out to Ross. Ross accepted it but didn't drink until MacKay sampled it first. Only then did he take a generous swallow. MacKay sat down opposite Ross and inhaled deeply.

Ross glanced about him. "It seems you've laid the groundwork for this meeting, MacKay. Now tell me why I am here. What could two blood enemies have to say to each other?"

"We could pledge peace," MacKay ventured. "We have the power to stop the feud so that our children and our children's children willna die for our ancestors' sins."

Ross nearly dropped his mug. "You want to end the feud? Why should I believe you?"

The hint of sadness that dimmed MacKay's eyes intrigued Ross. "I had five braw sons, MacKenna, and now I have three. And I came near to losing my only daughter. I doona want to lose another bairn. Are you so bloodthirsty that you would see all my bairns fall beneath a MacKenna's sword?"

Ross shook his head. He was of the same opinion as MacKay. "I lost my father, a beloved brother, a cousin, and countless kinsmen. Still, I canna believe you want to end the feud. What assurances do I have that you willna take up the sword against me when I least expect it?"

"What I am about to propose will demonstrate my good faith."

Ross leaned forward. "What exactly *are* you proposing?"

"I want to unite our clans, and the union must be one that our allies will honor."

"Unite our clans?" Ross narrowed his eyes. "What are you suggesting?"

"Naught but a marriage can bring our clans together and end the feud."

Ross drank deeply from his mug and wiped away the remaining foam on his sleeve. "I have no sister, nor any cousin of an age to wed one of your sons."

MacKay banged down his mug. "Are you dense, man? I'm offering my wee lass Gillian to you."

"Wee lass? That sword-wielding, flame-haired hellion who challenged me on the battlefield? Nay, thank you. I'd sooner wed a wildcat."

"Aye, Gillian can be a handful, but I believe a berserker can tame a hellion. It must be you. No one else will do."

"Do you have another kinswoman you can offer?" Ross asked hopefully.

"None but my lass Gillian can unite our clans."

"Does she agree to this mad scheme of yours?"

"I am her father; she will do as I say."

Ross laughed. "Your daughter hates me. She demonstrated that on the battlefield. Besides, I canna believe you are giving up on Ravenscraig. Our clans have fought over those lands for generations."

"Your first son with Gillian will settle both our claims to the land. My grandson—your son—will inherit Ravenscraig Tower. Now do you ken why Gillian must wed you and not another MacKay?"

Though Ross understood, he was not convinced. He recalled Gillian's gem-green gaze piercing him. He had felt her hatred; his skin still burned with it. She would have hacked him to pieces had she the skill or strength to do so, and then she would have spit on his dead body.

"I ken that all your hopes of a MacKay owning Ravenscraig rest on Gillian giving me an heir." Ross chortled. "If I am any judge of women, I doubt she will let me bed her without a fight." And what a fight that would be!

MacKay cocked a shaggy eyebrow. "I wager you are up to the challenge."

Ross thought long and hard about the proposition MacKay had laid on the table. Like MacKay, he had long wanted to end the feuding. He cringed at the thought of his future children dying at the end of a MacKay sword. But marrying that flame-haired wildcat would bring him more grief than any man wanted. Still, the logic of MacKay's proposal appealed to him.

MacKay must have realized Ross was giving his idea careful thought, for he plunged on. "The wedding should take place soon. Friday is a propitious day for weddings, so shall we say Friday next? We will invite our allies and hold the ceremony and reception at Braeburn. But first you must promise to respect my lass and treat her well."

Ross's icy gaze pierced MacKay. "I doona hurt women. I could have killed your lass on the battlefield with one stroke of my claymore had I wanted to." His words held the ring of truth. "I will agree to your plan only if the wedding is held here at St. Tears Chapel and the reception at Ravenscraig. Have your lass at the chapel before the bell tolls sext."

MacKay considered Ross's words a long time before

nodding. "Verra well, but I intend to be present the next morning when you hang out the bloody sheet. A consummation must take place on your wedding night; there will be no grounds for annulment of the marriage."

"I agree, with one exception. If your daughter leaves me of her own free will at any time after we are wed, she willna be allowed to return to Ravenscraig, and the feud will resume."

"You strike a hard bargain, MacKenna."

MacKay offered his hand to seal the deal. Ross hesitated a moment, but in the end the promise of peace won out, and he grasped MacKay's hand.

Braeburn Castle

Gillian waited anxiously for her father and brothers to return from their mysterious errand. Angus Sinclair, chieftain of Clan Sinclair, had arrived shortly after Tearlach had left, and Gillian hoped he had come to finalize plans for their betrothal. He sat with her now, drinking ale, his eyes bright with admiration.

"When do you expect Tearlach to return?" Angus asked.

"He didna say, but he took no provisions, so I expect he will show up before the evening meal."

Angus leaned toward her and grasped her hand. "I think you ken why I am here, lass."

"I hope 'tis to finalize our betrothal," Gillian replied, smiling at the handsome Sinclair chieftain. "What took you so long, Angus?"

Angus squeezed her hand. "I am here now, so what does it matter? Your question is a bold one, but I like a bold lass, especially in my bed. Will you give me a kiss, lass?"

Gillian glanced around, saw that no one was about in the hall, and offered her cheek. But Angus would have none of that. He rose, grasped Gillian's shoulders, and pulled her up against him. Then his lips seized hers, forcing her mouth open and ruthlessly ravaging it with his tongue.

Gillian's first kiss wasn't exactly what she had dreamed it would be. She had assumed Angus's lips would touch hers sweetly, lingeringly. But the reality was something far removed from what she had expected. Angus's kiss was more like a frontal attack by the enemy than a lover's caress. The longer he kissed her, the more she found to dislike about it. His taste wasn't all that pleasing, and his hard lips and teeth were hurting her. She supposed she could get used to it, however.

When his hands slid around to cup her breasts, Gillian pulled away from him, a frown marring her smooth brow. She touched her bruised lips. "Angus, what are you doing?"

"You liked that, lass, did you nae? I ken you did by the way you responded. After we are wed, I will teach you all the ways to please me in bed."

Gillian tried to imagine such a thing but could not. When she pictured her marriage bed, she saw in it a wild Viking with bulging muscles. She shook her head to clear it of traitorous thoughts and smiled at Angus.

Angus returned her smile with a stern look and gave her a hard shake. "I heard about your foolishness on the battlefield, lass. Once we are wed you will not pretend you are anything but a docile wife. No more training with weapons; no more riding like a wild woman over the moors. You will learn your place if I have to pound it into you.

"Do you ken, Gillian? You will obey me in all things. I am sure your father will thank me for taking you off his hands. You have become too difficult for him to handle. I, on the other hand, am prepared to deal harshly with you."

Gillian thought Angus didn't mean half of what he said. All men wanted to be masterful, and Angus was no different. She was sure she could bring him to heel once they were wed. She placed a finger over his lips.

"Hush, Angus, and kiss me again. I know we will deal well with each other."

Placated, Angus pulled Gillian into his arms and ravished her mouth once more.

"Take your hands off my daughter!" a voice roared from behind them.

Gillian gasped and pushed Angus away. She smoothed her skirts down nervously as her father and three brothers entered the hall. Her father glared at her before turning his heated gaze on Angus. "What are you doing here, Sinclair, besides manhandling my lass?"

"Is that any way to greet your future son-in-law?" Angus gloated. "I've come to finalize my betrothal to Gillian and sign the marriage contracts."

"You are too late," Tearlach growled. "Gillian is to wed another on Friday next."

"I am to wed someone other than Angus in less than a sennight?" Gillian gasped. "Why would you promise me to another when I have known for years that I would wed Angus Sinclair?"

"No papers have been signed, and Angus didna come forward in a timely manner to finalize the betrothal."

Gillian marched up to her father, thrusting her nose into his face. "Just who am I to wed, Da?"

Tearlach cleared his throat and looked to his sons for support. Murdoc, the eldest, stepped forward. "Da made a deal with the MacKenna."

Gillian fell back as if struck. "You want me to wed Ross MacKenna?"

Tearlach's stubborn chin, so like his daughter's, shot defiantly upward. "I willna lose another son or my only lass as long as 'tis within my power to stop the feuding. 'Tis time for the feud to end. The only way to do that is to unite our clans."

"So I am to be the sacrificial lamb," Gillian spat. She searched her brothers' faces, each in turn. "Did you all agree to Da's mad scheme?"

Angus Sinclair chose that moment to toss in his opinion. "You canna do this, MacKay. The feud has been going on too long; too many lives have been lost to call it quits now. Our clans are allies. The Sinclairs have fought side by side with you against the MacKennas and their allies and lost as many lives as the MacKays. Why would you give in now?"

"For the reasons you just outlined. We canna afford any more deaths, and the MacKenna agrees. Do you intend to fight to the last man, Sinclair?"

Sinclair rolled his shoulders back. "If need be."

"I am laird of Clan MacKay and overlord of Clan Sinclair. If I say there will be no more feuding, then so be it."

"Gillian is mine," Angus snarled. "You canna take her from me now."

Sinclair's hand flew to his sword hilt. Immediately all three of Gillian's brothers drew their swords. Angus's hand dropped helplessly to his side.

"I doona ken why you want peace when we have always fought for what is rightfully ours," Angus said sullenly.

"I agree!" Gillian shouted. "No one asked me whether I wish to wed the MacKenna. I am your daughter and a MacKay. How can your conscience allow you to hand me over to a blood enemy? I am less than naught compared to your beloved sons."

Suddenly Tearlach looked older than his forty-five years. "I love you well, daughter. When I saw you on the battlefield challenging the MacKenna, my heart nearly failed me. 'Tis because I doona wish to lose another bairn that I sought an end to the feud."

"I canna believe the MacKenna agreed to wed me after what happened on the battlefield," Gillian argued. "How do you know he willna beat me, or treat me like the enemy I am? Is that what you want for me, Da?"

"The MacKenna gave his word. He said he doesna hurt women, and I believe him."

"Fool!" Sinclair snarled. "You are all fools. Just remember, Gillian, lass, if ever you need help, send word to me and I will come for you."

So saying, he stormed off. Gillian watched him leave with mixed feelings. After Angus's speech about how he expected her to behave, she wasn't as keen to wed him as she had been before his visit. But the thought of marrying the MacKenna laird sent a shiver of dread down her spine. Residing in the enemy camp would make her life a living hell. She had been taught to hate MacKennas from the time she was a wee lass. They had killed her brothers; how could she marry one? How could her father expect her to wed the enemy?

Gillian started when Tearlach placed a heavy hand on her shoulder. "Doona fret, lass. I wouldna give you to the MacKenna if I thought the man would hurt you."

"What makes you think you can believe the laird of a clan you've been feuding with your entire life? You said yourself the MacKenna is a berserker." Her firm little chin tilted upward. "You can make me wed him, but you canna make me stay with him."

Murdoc stepped in front of his father. "If you doona stay with the MacKenna after you are wed, Gillian, the feud will resume and you canna return to Ravenscraig. Those were MacKenna's terms."

"MacKenna's terms? Bah! Why are you so eager to side with Da? I canna believe it of you."

"I hope to wed Mary MacDonald, and doona wish my sons to die in a feud that was none of their doing."

Nab spoke up next. "We fight because it is expected of us, but each of us wants to end the feud for our own reasons. Ramsey and I want to go to Edinburgh, to experience life at court before we settle down to wed. You are the only one who can end the killing."

"You are all mad!" Gillian snarled. "Where is your courage, your fighting spirit? Why must I be made to pay for your happiness?"

" 'Tis not about happiness; 'tis about saving MacKay lives," Tearlach explained. "Stop and think about it, lass. Your bairn with MacKenna, my grandson, will become laird of Ravenscraig. Isna that what we have always wanted? To regain Ravenscraig for our family? You are the only one who can do that for us without resorting to bloodshed. 'Tis the perfect solution, Gillian."

"For everyone else," Gillian groused. "You are not the one who has to lie with the Viking, bear his child, and suffer his abuse."

"There will be no abuse; he gave his word. I swear, if

he abuses you, you can return home and the feud will continue."

"Do you mean it, Da?"

"Aye, daughter, I wouldna want you hurt. But for the good of our clan, I beg you to give the MacKenna no reason to abuse you. Make your peace with him and mayhap you will find happiness."

"The only way I will find happiness is if you let me wed Angus."

"Angus had all the time in the world to finalize the betrothal. He didna want you badly enough, lass."

"Not true!" Gillian cried, though she suspected her father was right. "I willna marry the MacKenna! I willna!"

Turning on her heel, she stormed off. But she found no peace, not even in her own chamber. She kept picturing the dark-haired, blue-eyed devil her father wanted her to wed. He exuded power, from his broad shoulders and thick warrior muscles to the brawny body that could have belonged to some long-ago Viking.

Gillian recalled the fire in his eyes when she had challenged him. His fierce gaze would inspire fear in lesser men. But Gillian did not fear the MacKenna. She loathed him.

Despite her violent protest, her raging anger, Gillian realized her entire clan would suffer if she did not wed the MacKenna. Gillian had known for a long time that Clan MacKay was being decimated by constant feuding. Now she'd been told that only she could save her father and brothers from falling beneath MacKenna swords.

It wasn't fair. Why were women expected to mindlessly obey, as if they had no opinions of their own, no feelings? If she had to wed Ross MacKenna, she was going to make sure she wasn't the only one made to suffer.

Ravenscraig Tower

"You heard what I said, Gordo: I am going to wed the MacKay lass."

"Aye, I heard, but I doona believe you. Isna she the lass who flew at you with her sword?"

"The verra same."

"I doona ken why MacKay would offer his lass to you."

"MacKay has lost two sons, Uncle, and we, too, have lost loved ones. He wants the feud to end in order to save his surviving bairns. I canna blame him. He offered his daughter as a means of uniting our clans."

"Wheesh, lad! Seana is going to throw a fit. She had her heart set on marrying you."

Ross stiffened. "Seana knew I had no intention of making her my wife. Forget her. I am to wed Friday next, and on that day the feud between the MacKays and the MacKennas will officially end. Will you notify our allies and invite them to the wedding? I want every clan chieftain to witness the marriage, and to be aware that as their overlord, I will tolerate no breaking of the peace."

"Aye, Ross, I will see to it, though it doesna give us much time to prepare. You had best speak to Cook and ask Donald to organize the servants. You should do the wedding up right; 'tisna every day that the laird of Clan MacKenna takes a wife."

"Aye, Gordo, we will make my wedding a celebration of magnificent proportions."

"Who is getting married?" Seana asked as she sauntered over to the two men.

"Ross. Congratulate him, Seana," Gordo said. "He is marrying the MacKay's daughter."

Seana tilted up her head and laughed raucously. "Stop jesting, Gordo. Ross would never wed the daughter of his enemy."

" 'Tis true, Seana," Ross confirmed. "MacKay offered his daughter to me as a means to unite the clans and end the feuding, and I accepted."

"You accepted? Where does that leave me? I have given you two years of my life."

"Aye, you have, but you were free to leave at any time. I promised you naught, if you recall. And did you nae make yourself available to others when I wasna in the mood?"

"I willna make your wife welcome," Seana replied, refusing to answer Ross's accusation. She sidled close to him and lifted her face. "A marriage between a MacKay and a MacKenna is a marriage made in hell. Never fear, Ross. I will be here to pick up the pieces."

The two men watched her flounce off.

"She is right, you know," Gordo warned. "I hope you enjoy taming wildcats, because you are going to have one in your bed, if you can get the lass there at all. I wish you luck, lad—you are going to need it."

Chapter Three

Ross arrived at the chapel well ahead of the ceremony. The day was cool and oppressively dismal, with dark clouds hovering on the horizon. Not an auspicious day for a wedding, even though it was a Friday.

Ross waited at the altar of the tiny chapel, which was filled to bursting with allies of Clan MacKay and Clan MacKenna. Outside the door the cotters stood in the cold, waiting for the bride to arrive.

Ross watched in consternation as the elderly sexton made his way to the bell tower. The hour of sext was approaching with nary a bride in sight.

"This could be a trap," Gordo whispered in Ross's ear.

"Nay, Uncle, mayhap the bride got cold feet. I doubt Gillian is eager to wed me."

The bell began to peal. Ross counted beneath his breath. One, two, three, four, five . . . Just as the bell tolled the final time, the chapel door opened, blowing the bride and her family inside in a gust of frigid air. Gillian paused regally in the doorway, her head held high.

Ross gawked like a green lad when he saw his betrothed standing in an errant patch of sunlight that had suddenly and mysteriously split the dark clouds. For a moment it looked as if her head had burst into flame, and he blinked.

She was still standing there when he opened his eyes. He noted that she was wrapped in the MacKay plaid, to annoy him, he supposed. But Ross was far from annoyed. His breath hitched, and his heart began to pump furiously in his chest.

Her head was uncovered; her red hair flowed down her back and framed her face in living fire. Ross saw naught else, not the ancient chapel awash in flickering candlelight nor the people gathered inside.

He saw tongues of flame. He blinked again, and when he opened his eyes the flames had disappeared, and in their place stood his redheaded bride-to-be. Suddenly he recalled Gizela's words and made a vow he intended to keep: He would not let the life force of Gillian's spirit devour him.

Ross's eyes narrowed on Gillian as she slowly started down the aisle with her father. Halfway to the altar her steps faltered; at one point she stopped and looked beseechingly at Tearlach. His face set in grim lines, the MacKay tugged Gillian forward, until they reached the place where Ross awaited.

Gillian was good and truly caught. She had tried every delaying tactic she knew of to stall the nuptials, but naught had worked. As a final act of defiance, she had wrapped herself in a MacKay plaid. Let Ross MacKenna make what he wanted out of her attire. With her father all but dragging her to a fate worse than death, Gillian knew there was no escape.

Finally she found the courage to look directly at the MacKenna, and the rawness of shock made her heart constrict. She remembered his fierceness on the battlefield, but she had never seen him like this. Though his face was impassive and difficult to read, the intensity of his blue eyes made her flinch. Did he hate her as much as she hated him? Was he marrying her against his will? Did he want peace badly enough to take a wife he could never like, much less love? Did she want his love? That thought startled her.

The expression in his eyes was a contradiction. She saw wariness, and beneath that a hint of admiration. For her? She doubted it. Then suddenly she was standing alone beside him. The priest cleared his throat.

Taking her arm, Ross pinned Gillian to his side. Gillian flinched away from his touch and bared her teeth at him. Another act of defiance, she knew, would get her nowhere.

She saw the MacKenna's kinsman lean toward him and heard him whisper, "Did you see that, lad? 'Tis a match made in hell."

"I assure you I am up to the challenge, Uncle," Ross whispered back.

Ross glanced down at Gillian. While Gillian tried to ignore his handsome face, the compelling authority emanating from him directed her gaze to his other attributes. His broad shoulders and muscular torso stretched the material of his white shirt and black jacket, and his legs, sturdy as rowan trees beneath his tartan, were muscular extensions of his powerful body. His fancy sporran and the silver brooch studded with gemstones that held his plaid in place were tangible evidence of his high rank.

The priest cleared his throat again, waiting for a sign

to begin the nuptial Mass. She saw the MacKenna nod, and when the priest turned toward the altar, Gillian whispered, "I hate you, MacKenna."

Though the MacKenna appeared not to have heard, Gillian could tell by the spark of anger in his eyes and the sudden tightening of his fists that he had. *Good!* Now he knew exactly where they stood and how their marriage would proceed. No matter what her father had promised, she would never be a true wife to Ross MacKenna.

The priest's voice droned on. Gillian was wound so tight, she felt ready to explode. This couldn't be happening to her. After what seemed like an eternity, the priest asked if she took Ross MacKenna as her husband. Her mouth clamped shut.

"Answer him, lass," Tearlach hissed from somewhere behind her.

Gillian was aware of the MacKenna watching her, of her father and brothers behind her, and then she heard a voice at the back of the chapel shout, "Stop the wedding! Gillian MacKay is my betrothed; she canna legally wed another."

His eyes bulging, the priest looked up from the holy book. "Who challenges the legality of this marriage?"

Gillian nearly fainted in relief when Angus Sinclair strode down the aisle. She would have run to him if the MacKenna hadn't anticipated her and circled her waist to hold her in place.

"Let me go!" Gillian hissed. "You heard Angus; I canna wed you. The marriage wouldna be legal."

"What say you, MacKay?" Ross asked as the MacKay laird rose from his seat to intercept Sinclair.

"No betrothal took place. No papers were signed. Sinclair is wrong."

" 'Twas a verbal agreement between friends," Angus insisted. "Ask Gillian—she will tell you the truth of it."

"There was no verbal agreement!" MacKay roared. "Sit down and let the good father continue."

When Sinclair continued to sputter and protest, he was forcibly escorted from the chapel by MacKay's three sons. Angus stopped short of the door, then turned and shouted, "You havena heard the last from me; this I swear!"

"Good riddance," MacKay muttered as Angus stormed off.

Gillian searched her father's face, sending him a silent plea, but Tearlach remained resolute.

"Continue the ceremony, Father," Ross ordered. "There will be no more interruptions."

The priest sent Gillian a pitying look. "Tell me the truth, lass: Did Angus Sinclair sign a marriage contract? Was there a betrothal?"

Gillian wanted to lie, but when she looked up and saw the statue of the crucified Christ staring down at her from the altar, the words refused to leave her lips.

"Nay," she whispered.

With a sigh, Tearlach settled back onto the bench, smiling benignly at his daughter.

The priest continued where he had left off. Though Gillian saw naught but darkness in her future, she mumbled through the rest of the ceremony and stumbled from the chapel on the MacKenna's arm, her only consolation the knowledge that her marriage would save MacKay lives.

Icy sleet hit her face like tiny needles. Numb and dazed, she felt naught as the MacKenna lifted her onto his magnificent stallion, mounted behind her, and grasped the reins. They were off to Ravenscraig Tower amid a chorus of cheers.

Ross felt the weight of Gillian against his thighs and tried to ignore the instinctive tightening of his loins. Though her weight wasn't substantial, the heat emanating from her was nearly unbearable. He was amazed at how good she felt in his arms. His hands tightened convulsively on the reins, which only brought her closer against him. She began to squirm, exacerbating Ross's condition.

"Hold still," he ordered.

Gillian turned her head to look at him. "Why did you do it? Why did you wed me when 'tis what neither of us want?"

"Did your father nae explain?"

"Oh, aye, he explained, but I doona ken why you would want to end the feuding. Our clans have always feuded. 'Tis a time-honored tradition."

Ross gazed into her green eyes and saw naught but anger shining from them. "What a bloodthirsty little wench you are. The killing canna go on forever, lass. Your da and I wish to have done with it."

"Why must I pay the price of peace?" The flare of fury within her intensified. "If you touch me, I will kill you." Her words, though spoken quietly, were rife with menace.

Ross sighed heavily. The lass was the fiercest warrior in her family. While he admired her courage, he couldn't support it. He hated the thought of breaking her, but he couldn't have her wreaking havoc in his household.

"I am your husband, Gillian," he said sternly. "In case

you havena been told, you will be sharing my bed, my table, and my hearth. Your father expects the marriage to be consummated this very night, and so it shall be."

Gillian went still, very, very still. "And if I refuse?"

"The choice isna yours to make. Doona make it hard on yourself, lass. I amna a monster."

"You are a MacKenna. 'Tis all the same to me."

Ross had opened his mouth to give Gillian a proper dressing-down when Gordo rode up beside him, forestalling his response.

" 'Tis comforting to know that neither of you has killed the other yet." Gordo chuckled.

"The day is still young," Gillian said sweetly.

"You'd best watch that one," Gordo said, his eyes sparkling with laughter.

"Thank you, Uncle; I intend to."

He felt Gillian's back stiffen as she leaned away from him in a futile attempt to avoid contact. But her heat and the imprint of her body remained. Forcing his mind in another, less distracting direction, Ross realized he had to start this marriage right if he was going to have any peace in his home. He had to show Gillian he wasn't going to stand for any of her shenanigans, trickery, or feminine wiles. He was her master, and it was best that she learn it sooner rather than later.

He heard Gillian gasp when Ravenscraig came into view. He tried to look at his home through her eyes as he spotted the tower rising above stone weathered to a soft, shimmering gray. Even under leaden skies and sleet, the tower, rising above the hall and adjoining buildings, appeared welcoming. The gate stood open, and he rode through it. The wedding party and guests entered behind him, some on horseback and others afoot.

Ross drew rein at the front entrance and dismounted. A lad ran up to hold the reins while Ross lifted Gillian down. "We are home," he said. "Welcome to Ravenscraig."

Home, Gillian thought incredulously. This was nothing like the way she had imagined entering Ravenscraig. She had always assumed her clan would defeat the MacKennas and victoriously claim Ravenscraig. Instead she had become its mistress by wedding the enemy.

"Smile," Ross said as he guided her up the stairs.

Gillian bared her teeth in a semblance of a smile.

"Ah, Ravenscraig at last," Tearlach said reverently as he joined his daughter. "You are mistress of Ravenscraig now, Gillian. 'Tis more than I could have hoped for. Hold your head high, lass."

"Heed your father," Ross advised. "Greet my people with a smile and they will treat you with respect. Hate them as you do me and your life here will be miserable."

The huge oaken doors opened. Ross and Gillian entered, followed by the wedding guests. Gillian was quick to note that the hall had been decorated in a festive manner. Since it was too late in the year for flowers, rowan boughs and other fragrant greenery had been strewn extravagantly on the rows of long tables and were displayed in tall vases. The rushes were fragrant with pine and dried herbs.

The hall was less drafty than Braeburn, heated by a huge hearth at one end. The walls were hung with tapestries depicting battles, and the windows were fitted with real glass, a luxury Braeburn Castle did not yet have. A gallery ran the entire length and width of the hall, reached by a stone staircase that wound up to the second story, which Gillian assumed was the solar.

The tables were spread with white tablecloths, another luxury, and servants waited to begin serving the midday wedding feast. Grasping her elbow, Ross guided Gillian to the high table, seated her, and sat down on her right. Her father sat on her left. Ross's closest kin and Gillian's brothers joined them. At Ross's signal, servants began carrying in trays of food and pitchers of ale. The head table enjoyed Flemish wine.

Gillian could tell a lot of thought and preparation had gone into the feast. It began with fresh oysters and continued with cock-a-leekie soup made with chicken, leeks, and rice; collops of venison simmered in a creamy sauce; fresh fish; smoked haddock; and other dishes too numerous to name. Gillian managed a few bites of each dish and even sampled the pudding.

"Are you enjoying the food, wife?" Ross asked.

"You have outdone yourself, MacKenna. Does your clan enjoy this fare every day?"

"Aye, though we are only moderately wealthy, we eat well. Today is special, however. I hope you appreciate all that has been done in your honor."

Gillian shrugged. She knew the work and expense that went into this kind of feast, but wasn't going to give MacKenna the satisfaction of knowing how impressed she was with Ravenscraig.

"If 'twas done for my benefit, 'tis a waste of time and energy. Ravenscraig is yours, not mine."

Gillian had meant to anger Ross, and she succeeded. His expression remained cool and composed, but she could see rage seething in the depths of his blue eyes. She suppressed a shudder. How far could she goad this man before he reacted brutally? Did she dare find out?

"You will mind your tongue, woman," Ross warned

through clenched teeth. "I will not allow you to belittle my people."

"What will you do, beat me?"

"Is that what you want me to do?"

"What I want you to do no longer matters. We are already wed, against my wishes."

Ross stared into Gillian's defiant green eyes and could think of many things he wanted to do with her, and not one of them had to do with beating her. Her tart mouth and acid tongue could be put to better use than nagging and complaining. Before this night was over he intended to have her purring with contentment.

"What are you staring at?" Gillian asked when Ross continued to gaze at her lips.

"You are a beautiful woman, Gillian. I canna wait to have you in my bed."

He saw her lips purse and knew precisely what she was thinking. He had been wise to ask Donald to make sure all his weapons were removed from the solar before he bedded his wife. His warrior bride couldn't be trusted. She would as soon skewer him as look at him.

Ross didn't want that kind of marriage. He had hoped Gillian would realize the importance of uniting their clans and reconcile herself to their marriage. Taming this woman was going to take a great deal more time and patience than he had expected. Fortunately, with winter nigh and the feud behind him, Ross had plenty of time to devote to his wife. He eagerly anticipated bedding his bride.

"Doona think I am going to fall into your arms, MacKenna," Gillian spat.

Ross laughed, leaned close, and whispered, "I am accounted a good lover, wife. I will please you well."

"And who, pray tell, accounts you a good lover?"

Ross's gaze found Seana, who was seated nearby, and quickly shifted away. "You will have to take my word."

Gillian hadn't missed the way Ross's gaze had lingered on a beautiful young woman seated at a nearby table. Was she Ross's leman? A pang of something akin to jealousy shot through Gillian, even though she tried to tell herself it didn't matter. She hoped his leman would keep MacKenna out of her bed.

While remnants of the meal were being carried away, Gillian studied the blonde beauty from beneath long, feathery lashes. She was startled to realize the woman was gazing longingly at Ross.

"What is that woman to you, MacKenna?" she asked, gesturing discreetly at Seana.

"Which woman might that be, Gillian?"

"Are you blind? The beautiful blonde who canna take her eyes off you."

"Ah, that one. Her name is Seana McHamish. Our clans are allies."

"Is she your lover?"

"I willna lie to you, lass. She was my leman before I took you to wife. However, I no longer need a leman."

"Doona send her away," Gillian advised. "I give her leave to take my place in your bed."

"Nay, wife, you will fulfill your duty in my bed and out."

Before Gillian could form a scathing retort, a group of entertainers entered the hall amid loud cheering. Tables were quickly cleared away to make room for the Gypsy musicians and dancers. Even Gillian clapped her hands. She adored music, especially wild Gypsy music.

"My uncle was fortunate to find a *compania* of Gypsies who hadn't gone south yet for the winter. I hope you like music."

"Gypsies are my favorite performers," Gillian admitted.

He grinned at her, the whiteness of his teeth startling her. Was there naught about the man that wasn't perfect?

"I am glad something I do pleases you."

The musicians began to play a lively melody while the dancers twirled and pranced about the hall. Swarthy men wearing dark clothing and brilliant-hued jackets, and women, their multicolored, bell-trimmed skirts swirling around their golden thighs, mesmerized Gillian with their energy and verve.

Entranced, she clapped along with the others when the performance ended. She didn't notice when Ross caught Gizela's eye and nodded. In fact, she was far from ready when the old woman came up to her and touched her arm.

" 'Tis time, lass. I am called Gizela. I will take you to the laird's chamber and answer any questions you might have."

Gillian skewered Ross with a look that would have turned him to cinders had he been a lesser man. "The celebration hasna ended yet."

Ross's gaze turned dark. " 'Tis finished for you, wife. We will long be abed before the celebration ends."

Gizela pulled gently on her arm. "Come along, lass."

When Gillian balked, Tearlach leaned over and said, "Do your duty, daughter. Your clan is depending upon your obedience to your husband."

Silently fuming, Gillian followed the old woman up the stairs to the solar, through a sitting room, and into the sleeping chamber. The chamber was too masculine for Gillian's tastes, but she hoped MacKenna would relegate her to lesser quarters once she did her "duty" to him and he replaced her with his leman.

"Let me help you disrobe and climb into bed, lass," Gizela said. "The men will be here soon."

"Men? More than one?" Gillian squeaked.

" 'Tis the custom. The laird's kinsmen will carry him up and put him to bed."

"With me?"

Gizela chuckled. "Of course with you." She turned Gillian around and began untying tapes until she had removed everything but Gillian's shift, slippers, and stockings. Then she led her to the bed. "Sit, lass."

The picture of Ross's kinsmen carrying him to bed was so ludicrous that Gillian obeyed without thinking. Gizela removed Gillian's slippers and stockings, but when she started to lift the hem of the shift, Gillian refused to part with it.

"Where is my night rail?"

" 'Tis your wedding night, lass; you doona need one. Lift your arms and I will have you tucked into bed in no time. Then you can ask me anything you like."

"I will keep my shift," Gillian said firmly. Her eyes darted about the chamber. The room was curiously bereft of weapons, highly unusual in a warrior's bedchamber. A warrior usually kept his sword close at hand.

Gizela shrugged. "Have it your way, lass, but you ken you will end up naked sooner rather than later." She lifted the covers. "In with you, now."

Gillian obeyed, if only to get rid of the old woman. But Gizela seemed in no hurry to depart. She found a hairbrush on a nearby chest and returned to the bed. "I will brush your hair for you, lass. Tomorrow you will have a proper maid, but the laird thought you should have someone to answer your questions tonight. So ask away while I brush."

"I . . . doona know what to ask."

"Do you know how the mating takes place?" Gizela asked bluntly.

"I've seen horses."

"Oh, aye, horses."

"The female screams and carries on when she is mounted, so I assume it will be painful for me as well."

"Only the first time, lass. But if I know our laird, there will be pleasure, too."

Gillian digested that while Gizela slid the brush smoothly through her waist-length hair.

"Your hair truly is a living flame," the old woman murmured. "I saw you and the laird surrounded by flames in a vision. I told him if he welcomed the flame, he would conquer it. If he failed, it would devour him."

Gillian shuddered. "Are you a witch?"

"A witch? Nay, I am a healer. If I say strange things sometimes, 'tis because of what I feel and see. You'd do well to heed me."

She ran the brush through Gillian's hair one last time and rose. "I vow you know all you need to know, lass. Trust your husband to show you the rest."

"I will never trust a MacKenna," Gillian maintained. In fact, she intended to jump out of bed as soon as Gizela left and meet the MacKenna on her feet, not lying helplessly on her back.

"I will leave you now, lass," Gizela said as she slipped through the door.

Gillian leaped from bed and fumbled about for her clothes.

"Are you going somewhere?" Gillian's head snapped

around toward the voice. She was surprised to see her husband's leman standing in the door opening.

"What do you want?"

"Do you know who I am?"

"Aye, you are the MacKenna's leman."

Seana appeared startled. "Did Ross tell you about me?"

"He did, and I wish you joy of him."

"What is that supposed to mean?"

"It means I want naught to do with your lover. You may have him with my blessing."

Seana preened. "You doona know what you are missing. Ross is an extraordinary lover. I have had none better. How many lovers have you had, Gillian MacKay? Is Angus Sinclair your lover?"

"If not for MacKenna, I would have wed Angus."

Seana glared at Gillian. "If not for you, Ross MacKenna would be my husband. Doona think I am leaving Ravenscraig because you have married the laird. Think you I will be replaced in Ross's affection by a woman not fit to lick his boots? Heed me well, Gillian MacKay: Ross is mine. 'Tis my comfort he will seek at the end of the day. Interfere with me and what belongs to me, and you will suffer the consequences."

Gillian's first inclination had been to be lenient toward Seana, but after hearing her out, Gillian changed her mind. Obviously the woman was a troublemaker. MacKenna's leman had made it perfectly clear that she would resort to violence to get what she wanted. Gillian was just perverse enough to want to thwart Seana's plans.

A commotion on the staircase alerted the women to the bridegroom's imminent arrival. Cursing beneath her breath, Seana made a hasty exit as Gillian, too flustered to face all those men in only her shift, dove into bed and pulled the sheet up to her neck. Scant seconds later, the door burst open.

The sight of the MacKenna being carried on the shoulders of his kinsmen almost undid her. She wanted to howl with laughter, but was too wary of what came next to succumb to the whim.

"Put me down, lads." Ross laughed. "I doona want to look foolish before my bride."

"You can carry him back out, for all I care," Gillian muttered.

Ross sent her a sharp look but said naught as he was set upon his feet and quickly divested of his clothing. Gillian gasped and looked away, but not quickly enough. She saw more than she wanted to see. His manhood, even at rest, was impressive. Gillian could not deny that everything about Ross MacKenna was magnificent.

If he wasn't the enemy, she might be more amenable to the marriage. But how could she welcome into her bed a man she had been taught to hate? The man whose clan had killed her brothers?

"In you go, lad," Gordo said as he lifted a corner of the bedcovers.

A round of laughter ensued as Ross slid into bed. Shocked when she realized a roomful of men were leering at her, Gillian scooted as far away from the huge, nude body as she could get. From the corner of her eye she noted that it wasn't just Ross's kinsmen who had gathered in the bedchamber. Among the MacKennas were a handful of MacKays, including her father and brothers.

Horrified, Gillian wondered if everyone intended to stay and watch Ross claim her. She knew of the barbaric custom and raged against it.

"Get out! All of you," she demanded.

"You heard the lass," Tearlach said as he shooed everyone from the chamber. "A wedding night is a time for privacy." Once the room was cleared, he retreated through the door and closed it behind him.

"You took the words out of my mouth," Ross said once they were alone. "No one needs to know what goes on in our private chambers."

Gillian sent him a speculative look. "Do you mean it?"

"Of course, did I nae just say so?"

"Then we really doona need to do what is expected of us, do we?"

Reaching over, Ross traced the line of her cheekbone with a finger. "Aye, we do. Your da expects to see the bloody sheet flying from the gallery in the morning."

She jerked away. "I will happily cut my finger to provide Da with the proof he needs." She held out her hand. "Give me your dirk."

"Nay, lass, do you take me for a fool? I made a promise, and I intend to keep it." He sent her a lopsided grin. "Besides, there isna a weapon in the chamber. I had them all removed."

"You doona trust me," Gillian accused.

"You've the right of it, lass."

Gillian tried again. "Mayhap you would prefer Seana in your bed."

Ross sent her a strange look. "Nay, I wouldna. You are my wife; you are the only woman who belongs in my bed. I doona think you will find the task burdensome."

He wound a lock of long red hair about his fist and tugged gently. "Come closer, lass."

Gillian had no choice but to obey, for resistance would bring pain. He kept tugging until she was pressed against him, the heat of his skin scorching her.

"What is this?" he asked, grabbing a handful of material.

"My shift," she said defensively.

"Och, lass, you've no need of it."

He ripped it down the front, tore it off of her, and tossed it to the floor.

"Much better," he said, leaning in for a kiss.

Chapter Four

Ross had just settled into the kiss when he felt a sharp pain and tasted blood. The wildcat had bitten his lip! He reared back, anger pulsing through him. Everything about Gillian was wild and untamed. The thought of subduing that wildness, of bringing it under his control, sent a shaft of desire through his body.

"Why did you do that?"

She attempted to shield her bareness from his gaze. "I canna do this. You are the enemy."

He pushed her hands aside and pinned them above her head. "You can and you will. I am your husband, not your enemy. Our clans are allies now. If becoming allies is good enough for your father and brothers, it should be good enough for you. Doona fight me, lass, for you canna win."

Ross's sensual gaze traversed the length of her body and back. "You have an extraordinary body." With one hand he drew a finger down her rib cage and felt her muscles contract. He watched her closely, trying to read her expression. Her bottom lip was caught between her teeth; he smiled when he heard the sudden intake of her breath. She wasn't as unmoved by him as she pretended.

Ross gently traced his finger down the silken skin of a surprisingly muscular thigh. "One doesna expect to find muscles in a woman," he murmured.

"I trained with my brothers," Gillian replied, trying to squirm away from his touch. "Do you find muscles repulsive?" she asked hopefully.

"I find naught but your belligerent attitude repulsive, wife. And I intend to change that verra soon."

He moved his hand upward, cupping the satiny weight of her breast in his palm and dragging his thumb across her nipple. Gillian closed her eyes and arched upward, as if fighting against Ross's attempt at arousal.

When he lowered his head and laved the nipple with the rough pad of his tongue, a raw cry burst from Gillian's throat. "What are you doing to me?"

Ross raised his head. "Making love to you, lass. Do you find it enjoyable?"

"Release my arms. I doona like being confined."

Ross didn't like holding her arms any more than she liked it. He wanted her to touch him. His body ached to be stroked, even though he couldn't imagine Gillian actually wanting to touch him unless she had a weapon in her hands. Nevertheless, he released her wrists. He preferred loving her with both hands anyway.

Immediately Gillian raised a fist to him.

"Doona do it, Gillian," Ross warned. "I doona want to hurt you."

His mouth, now just inches from her lips, lowered. This time there was nothing gentle in his kiss as he thrust his tongue inside her mouth and tasted her thoroughly. Before Gillian could bite him again, he sucked her tongue into his mouth, his tongue tangling with hers.

He felt her stiffen; then in slow increments her body softened against his. Ross's mouth left hers and slid down the slope of her neck, where he brushed teasing kisses against her satiny skin as his hands stroked the sides of her breasts. His mouth continued its downward trek to her nipple; he wound his tongue around it, suckling the tight little bud as his hand teased and caressed the other breast.

"What . . . are . . . you . . . doing?" Gillian repeated on a gasp.

He raised his head. "Do you like it?"

"I . . . Nay, I like naught you do to me."

"Liar."

He moved his hand again, skimming it over her ribs and flat stomach to the fiery curls below her belly, lightly stroking the inside of her thigh.

Gillian felt her resistance slowly ebbing. What kind of man was the MacKenna to burrow through her defenses so quickly? What kind of woman was she to succumb so easily to her enemy? Her body felt heavy, sluggish, his kisses drugging. His mouth and tongue were doing things to her she never imagined possible. And now he was kissing her . . . again.

"MacKenna! Stop!"

He ignored her as his fingers began pushing through the downy fleece at the juncture of her thighs, dipping into the damp cleft covered by red curls.

"Nay!" Her voice sounded thready, weak, as weak as her flesh, but not as weak as her resolve. When his finger dipped deep inside the moist heat between her legs, stroking, circling, relentless, she bit her lip to suppress a moan, but she feared she was fooling only herself. Ross's gaze darkened, intensified, as he watched her.

"Doona hold back, Gillian. Your body belongs to me; I can make it soar whether you wish it or not."

Gillian gritted her teeth against the pleasure Ross's hands and mouth were evoking inside her. She refused to give him the satisfaction of knowing she was feeling anything but disgust. Her hands clenched into fists to keep from touching him. But, oh, how she wanted to feel the texture of his skin, run her fingers through the dark hair covering his chest and . . .

She shook her head. Nay, thinking along those lines would be a betrayal of her clan. She was a MacKay, the only MacKay willing to uphold the feud so many had given their lives for. Her father and brothers had gone soft in the head. Didn't they know there could be no peace between Clan MacKenna and Clan MacKay? Sooner or later MacKenna would break the peace and the feuding would resume.

Her thoughts skittered away when she felt Ross's tongue touch a place between her thighs that was so sensitive, she nearly jumped out of her skin. The moan she had fought so hard to suppress slipped past her lips as her body arched up into the intimate caress. Never in her life had she felt anything close to this kind of pleasure. It stole her breath and made her body sing.

Gillian tried to buck Ross off of her, but he grasped her hips and held her in place while he worked his dark magic on her. She knew that what he was doing had to be witchcraft, for naught else could make her body feel things completely foreign to her nature.

And then she felt Ross's tongue dip inside her, in

and out, again and again, and Gillian lost the battle she had fought so hard to win. She cried out, letting her thighs fall open as her body thrummed in time to his thrusting tongue. Her hands began to twitch; she was no longer able to control them. Tentatively she touched his shoulders. His body tensed; she heard him groan.

Encouraged, she moved her palms over his back, as far as she could reach. His skin felt smooth and hot. Muscles rippled; tendons bunched beneath her fingertips. Never had she felt anything as arousing as Ross's skin.

Gillian felt her body hover on the edge of a precipice, a place she had never ventured before. She trembled; she quaked. Pleasure so exquisite it was nearly unbearable built to incredible heights. If Ross didn't stop what he was doing, she was going to soar off the bed and explode. She grasped his head between her hands to hold it in place, fearing he would stop before she found that exalted place she was reaching for.

"I want to be inside you when you come," Ross murmured as he removed his mouth from her and slid up her body.

Gillian cried out a protest and clung to him. How could he do this to her when she was so close? Though she had no idea what she was close to, she knew it would be spectacular.

She felt something hard and hot probe between her legs. She knew she was about to lose her virginity and stiffened.

"Relax, lass; 'twill hurt only this one time. And next time there will be naught but pleasure."

The pain that followed his words was no more nor

less than she had expected, but sharp enough to steal her breath. "Stop; you're hurting me!"

" 'Tis done, Gillian; I canna stop now."

Gillian wondered why his breathing should be shallow, his voice hoarse, when she was the one hurting. Just like horses, the pleasure belonged to the male while the female suffered the indignities of mating. Though she had to admit the pain was easing as she stretched to accommodate the length and thickness of him.

Then Ross began to move in and out, slowly, as if priming her for something grand, something unknown. She fought against it, fearing the loss of her soul if she succumbed.

"Stop!" She gasped.

"I can make this fast or I can give you pleasure. You choose."

Her eyes widened with disbelief. "You want to give me pleasure? Is that possible?"

He rose up on his elbows and gazed down at her. "You know naught about mating, do you?"

"I've seen horses and . . ."

He lowered himself until their bodies touched, meshed; her breath caught in her throat. She let it out in a slow hiss as his shaft drove deep inside her and one hand moved between them to a place so sensitive she lurched up against him.

"Aye, do you feel it?" Ross whispered against her lips. " 'Tis just the beginning, lass." Then he kissed her, a long, slow joining of their mouths, his tongue thrusting inside, searching restlessly, tasting, demanding.

She began to pant as the jolt of pleasure she felt in her nether regions spread throughout her body. Was this the pleasure MacKenna had promised? She wanted naught from him, especially pleasure, she told herself. But there was no help for it. Her body seemed to work separate from her mind. She felt the slow upward spiral of something unspeakably wonderful curl through her.

"Touch me," Ross said in a voice so raw it sounded as if his throat were bruised.

Her hands curled into fists. "Nay, I canna."

"Touch me," Ross asked again.

Gillian's hands twitched and then moved without her volition. Gillian loathed her lack of self-control, but she couldn't help herself as she touched his shoulders. His scorching heat caused her to jerk her hands away, but they soon returned to the smooth expanse of his back. Whether out of curiosity or the need to touch him, she moved her hands over his skin in a long caress.

She heard him groan, and then she lost the ability to think, overwhelmed with feelings and sensations utterly foreign to her. Her body responded spontaneously as he drove hard into her depths, and she arched up to meet his thrusts. Ross must have liked what she was doing, for he murmured encouragingly before kissing her again. His kisses became deeper, harder, more erotic, his tongue delving into her mouth, finding and capturing hers, sucking on it until she groaned wantonly.

Ross broke off the kiss and gazed at her. The fierce look in his eyes was intense, frightening. "Give it up, Gillian," he gasped. "Doona fight it. If you fall, I will be here to catch you."

Gillian had no idea what Ross was talking about; naught he said made sense right now. The only thing she knew was that she wanted. What she wanted wasn't clear. An air of expectancy surrounded her; her body vibrated with it. A thrumming began deep inside her; pleasure built; her skin burned.

Gillian saw a shimmering light high above her and knew it was hers for the taking, and that if she chose not to claim it, she would miss out on something earth-shattering. But if she took what she wanted, she knew she would never be the same.

Gillian waged a losing battle as she concentrated on the primal cadence of his hips thrusting and withdrawing, until she grew frenzied with need. She cried out as a white-hot flame snaked through her veins. She arched beneath the quickening rhythm of his thrusting loins and exploded into a thousand points of brilliant light, her body quaking beneath him.

Ross collapsed against her, shuddering, gasping for breath, his staff still embedded deep inside her. Shocked by her unreserved surrender and shamed by her response, Gillian tried to push him away, but Ross was having none of it. He rolled over, bringing her on top of him.

She pushed against his chest, expecting him to release her now that he'd gotten what he wanted. "You've had your way with me—now leave me alone."

"I knew you'd be as wild in bed as you are out of it," Ross replied. "We're not done yet."

She looked at him then, her eyebrows raised in surprise. "What more could there be?"

"You likened our loving to the mating of horses, so now 'tis your turn to ride me."

"But . . .'tis finished; I know that you . . . You canna . . .'Tis too soon. I mean, how can you expect that of me again?"

"Once wasna enough. Doona lie; I know you enjoyed what we just did."

"I hated it. I hate you."

"You may hate me, but you canna deny I gave you pleasure. I heard you cry out, felt your body shudder beneath mine. I tamed you once; I can do it again."

Gillian struggled to escape and then went still when she realized that her movements were affecting Ross in a very different way from what she intended; he was growing thicker and longer inside her. "No one named MacKenna can tame a MacKay," she spat.

Ross's hips jerked upward, filling her, stretching her. Gillian gasped as his hands cupped her breasts and he used his tongue and teeth on them, sucking them, flicking his tongue over the tight little buds. A surge of pleasure shot through her as he pushed his shaft high inside her. The man was insatiable. If he continued like this, he would kill her before morning.

But he wasn't killing her. The same nameless need she'd felt earlier rekindled within her. Try though she might, she couldn't stop herself from pressing down each time he pushed high inside her.

Ross could feel her sultry softness surround him, her muscles tightening against his cock, her thighs pressing against his hips, and nearly lost control. But since their first coupling had taken the edge off his lust, he maintained strict control, waiting for Gillian to find her pleasure before he sought his.

Ross was aware of the struggle going on inside Gillian's mind. He knew she believed that submitting her body to him was the worst kind of betrayal to herself and to her clan. He was beginning to realize that taming Gillian involved more than claiming her sexually.

Gillian's wildness spoke to him in ways he hadn't expected, ways he wasn't prepared to acknowledge.

When he heard her cry out, he grasped her hips and pushed deeper and deeper, spinning away from his thoughts, away from everything except Gillian and her wild gyrations on top of him. Whether she wanted to admit it or not, she had a wildly passionate nature, for which he thanked God.

"Damn you, MacKenna!" Gillian cried, baring her teeth. "Damn you to hell!"

Lost in a haze of blinding passion, Ross watched as she broke apart, a thin wail escaping through her clenched teeth. Then she collapsed against him.

Ross no longer fought against his escalating need to climax. His senses screaming, his body vibrating, he reached the peak and tasted heaven. With a MacKay lass, no less.

When he finally found the energy to move, Ross lifted Gillian's limp form and placed her on the bed beside him. Her eyes were closed; she was breathing hard. By the light of the dying candle, Ross looked his fill at his bride. Propping himself up on his elbow, he let his gaze travel slowly down the length of her and back to her face.

Her lips were swollen from his kisses, and her body was still flushed from their lovemaking. With her red hair tangled about her head, she looked deliciously disheveled.

His gaze shifted downward. Her body was magnificently proportioned and slightly muscular, which unaccountably pleased him. While most men preferred women with softer curves, he liked the fact that his wife's body had both softness and muscles. Instinctively his gaze was drawn to the fiery triangle at the base of her thighs, and the blood smeared there.

"Are you all right?"

She turned away from him. "Why do you care?"

Ross sighed. He hoped she wasn't going to return to her earlier belligerence. That didn't seem to be the case, however. Gillian seemed more lethargic than angry. He shouldn't have made love to her that second time, since she was so new to it, but his body hadn't been sated even though he'd reached a peak. Even now he wanted the flame-haired wildcat again. This time, however, he intended to ignore the clamoring of his body. Gillian already thought him an animal; he didn't want to confirm her belief.

"You are my wife," he said, remembering her question. " 'Tisna my intention to hurt you."

"Am I allowed to sleep now, or do you plan to abuse me again?"

Had Gillian been turned toward him, she would have seen the flash of anger in his eyes. "I doona abuse women, not even a MacKay with an acid tongue and hate in her heart."

He climbed out of bed, went to the washstand, and poured water from a pitcher into a bowl. He washed himself first, then dampened a cloth and returned to the bed. Though Gillian protested, he spread her thighs and cleansed away blood and spent seed.

"Now you can go to sleep," he said as he returned the cloth to the bowl and climbed into bed beside her.

Tears of shame flooded Gillian's eyes. How could she have enjoyed mating with Ross MacKenna? Beneath his touch, her body had soared. Was she abnormal? Would another woman respond as she had? Never in her life had she felt the sensations Ross MacKenna had made her feel; she hadn't even known they were possible. How he must have laughed at her for likening what they did to horses. But how could she have known that men weren't the only ones capable of feeling pleasure?

Gillian must have fallen asleep, for she awakened to thin threads of sunlight filtering through the windows. She glanced over at Ross and found him staring at her. She flinched when he touched her hair, ran his fingers through it.

"Flame," he murmured, pressing a bright strand against his mouth. "*You* are the flame, Gillian; I understand that now. Gizela wasna far off the mark with her nonsense."

He let her hair fall through his fingers and rose from the bed. Then he padded over to the hearth to rekindle the fire. Despite her initial reluctance to look at his nude body, Gillian's gaze strayed in his direction, and she nearly lost the ability to breathe.

His body, limned in a beam of sunlight, appeared more godlike than human. His warrior's body was honed to perfection; not an ounce of fat was visible. When he bent to feed wood into the hearth, displaying his taut buttocks, Gillian gasped aloud.

Ross rose and turned toward the sound, a smile playing at the corners of his mouth. "Do you like what you see?"

She turned away without answering.

"I certainly liked what I saw. I couldna be more pleased with your body. You were made for bed sport, Gillian. Giving you pleasure will be no chore."

"You mean we have to do *that* again?"

"Aye, if it pleases me to do so."

Gillian watched apprehensively as Ross approached the bed, bent, scooped her into his arms, then lowered her onto a bench before the hearth.

"What are you doing now?"

"Your father will be eager to return to Braeburn, but he willna leave until he knows our marriage has been consummated."

So saying, he whipped the bottom sheet off the bed. Bloodstains glowed vividly against the pristine white. Naked as the day he was born, Ross left their bedchamber with the sheet tucked under his arm.

"MacKenna! Nay!" Gillian cried. But there was no stopping him. She knew what he intended, and her cheeks burned with embarrassment.

Ross returned, strutting arrogantly. Cheers from those waiting below in the hall for evidence drifted into the chamber. "Did you have to do that?"

"Aye, I did. Even the priest waited below for proof. No one will doubt that we are well and truly wed now that they have seen the bloodstained sheet flying from the gallery railing."

Gillian shrank away as Ross stopped before her.

"You're not going to . . ."

"Nay, I'm going to see about a bath and food." He wound his plaid around his waist and strode off.

He sounded angry, but Gillian didn't care. She couldn't go through *that* again, not now and, she hoped, never. She refused to succumb to MacKenna's passion again. It shamed her to think that she had surrendered her maidenhead to an arrogant, lustful beast who reveled in her surrender.

Once MacKenna was gone, Gillian pulled the top sheet over the mattress, lay down, and yanked the blanket up to her chin. She turned her head into the pillow, determined not to cry. She was strong; she'd let no MacKenna turn her into a cringing coward. She'd show him that not every MacKay was a weak fool. For her the feud had not ended.

It had just begun.

A knock on the door diverted her thoughts. "Who is it?"

" 'Tis your da, Gillian. I've come to bid you good-bye."

"Come in, Da."

Tearlach entered the chamber and strode to the bed. "I had to see you for myself before your brothers and I returned to Braeburn. The MacKenna said you were fine, that he didna hurt you. Was he right? Was the MacKenna gentle with you?"

"Aye," Gillian murmured, though it hurt her to admit it. "He didna harm me."

"All is well, aye?"

"Nay, Da, all isna well. I hate the man, and so should you."

Tearlach sighed heavily. "Ah, lass, you grieve me sorely. Of all my bairns, you are the only one who refuses to accept that the feud is done, finished. Take my advice: Make your peace with your husband, lass. Despite our years of feuding, I believe MacKenna to be a good man."

"Are you satisfied, MacKay?" Ross asked as he walked into the chamber. "I told you Gillian was fine. She will remain fine as long as you doona break the peace."

Tearlach held out his hand. "Shall we shake on peace between our clans, son-in-law?"

Ross extended his hand. "Aye, to peace, MacKay."

"I'll be leaving now. Bring Gillian to visit before snow flies."

He turned to his daughter. "Remember what I told you, lass. You are a married woman now; trust your husband and all will be well."

Gillian held her tongue until Tearlach left. Then she

glared up at Ross and said, "Mayhap Da trusts you, but I doona."

"Cease your prattling, woman," Ross warned. "After last night, I am sure we will deal well with each other. Your bath will arrive soon. The water is heating. I've decided you should join me in the hall after your bath so we can break our fast together. The sooner my clansmen accept you as lady of Ravenscraig, the better for all of us."

A scratch at the door announced the arrival of the tub and bathwater. Ross sat on the bench as the round brass tub was filled and proclaimed ready by the maidservant he had ordered to attend Gillian.

"I am Alice, lady. Laird Ross has asked me to serve you. Your bath is ready. Shall I pin up your hair?"

Gillian sat up. "Aye, thank you," she replied as the attractive dark-haired maid fussed with her tangled hair.

Ross smiled inwardly as Gillian sent him a blistering look. "Do you intend to remain while I bathe?"

"Aye, I want to use the bathwater after you are through, so doona linger too long."

"Is Alice your . . ."

Ross knew precisely what Gillian was going to say and stopped her. "Alice is my kinswoman. She lives at Ravenscraig with her mother, Hanna, our cook."

"Oh," Gillian said in a small voice.

Using the sheet as a cover, Gillian slipped from bed and approached the tub. She dropped the sheet and lowered herself into the tub so fast, Ross saw naught but a small patch of creamy skin before she sank into the water.

Alice laid out Gillian's clothes as Ross sprawled nearby in a chair, watching Gillian bathe. Gillian glanced at him. Their gazes locked, held, but she quickly looked away when she saw no softness in his hard blue eyes. Fine, 'twas exactly how she wanted it. It was easier to hate a man who held her in little regard.

Gillian finished her bath quickly and called to Alice to fetch a drying cloth.

"I'll get it," Ross said. "You may go, Alice. I wish to bathe before the water gets cold."

Alice scooted from the chamber as Ross fetched the large square of linen and held it out for Gillian to step into. An angry flush suffused Gillian's face when Ross held the cloth low enough to allow him to look his fill of her naked body. Disgruntled, Gillian stepped out of the tub, waiting impatiently for Ross to wrap her in the cloth.

When no cloth was forthcoming, Gillian glanced over her shoulder. Ross's jaw was clenched; his eyes had darkened to the color of turbulent storm clouds.

"I'm waiting," Gillian prodded. "The drying cloth, please."

Ross's arms came around her, and with them the cloth. But instead of releasing her, he turned her to face him. His body was hard, so very hard. All over. Gillian felt his shaft poking against her stomach and wrested herself free.

"I thought you wanted to bathe," she said, carefully backing away.

"Aye, I do."

"Then you had best hurry. I'm so hungry my stomach is touching my backbone."

"I'm hungry, too, but not for food."

His look was hot enough to melt her, if she were of a mind to let him beguile her. "I'm not going to let you do *that* to me again," she said, placing herself on the opposite side of the chamber. "My duty to this marriage has been fulfilled, Ross MacKenna. 'Tis all you're going to get from me."

Ross gave a bark of laughter, though he didn't appear amused.

"Doona make fun of me, MacKenna."

"Ah, Gillian, lass, I can see the taming of you isna going to be as easy as I thought. I fear you're going to be disappointed, for we *will* do *that* again. And 'tis called making love."

"Why? There was no love involved."

Ross sighed heavily as he removed his tartan and stepped into the tub. "Will you scrub my back?"

"Nay. Shall I fetch Seana? I'm sure she will be thrilled to scrub your back."

"You try my patience, lass. Get dressed. We're expected in the hall."

Gillian waited until Ross turned his attention to his bath before scrambling into the clothing Alice had laid out for her: a fine linen shift, a dark green gown, and thick woolen stockings. As an afterthought, she fetched her MacKay plaid from the wardrobe and flung it over her shoulders. Wearing the MacKay plaid was Gillian's way of showing the MacKenna that she wasn't intimidated by him. Then she turned her back on Ross while he bathed and got dressed.

"I see you're ready," he said as he drew on a white shirt and pair of close-fitting trews fashioned out of the MacKenna plaid and fastened a wide belt around his waist.

Gillian headed for the door. Ross was there before her. "If you think wearing the MacKay plaid will anger me, you're wrong, lass. Our clans are allies now, though if you wore the MacKenna plaid, it would endear you to my kinsmen."

"I doona want to do anything to endear myself to you or your kinsmen. Remember that, MacKenna."

Grasping her arm, he pulled her against him. "Remember this, Gillian. Befriending my kinsmen will save lives, not just MacKenna lives but MacKay lives. Are you so bitter that you care naught for your father and brothers?"

Then he lowered his head and kissed her. The kiss was not gentle; nor was it meant to be, Gillian thought. Nevertheless, she was more aroused by it than she wanted to be.

Chapter Five

The moment Gillian and Ross entered the hall, the buzz of conversation came to an abrupt halt. Gillian flushed with embarrassment when she realized everyone was staring at them as Ross seated her at the high table. Raising her chin, she stared back, refusing to be intimidated by Ross MacKenna's kinsmen.

As if she didn't already feel uncomfortable, Seana entered the hall moments behind them. The attention of Ross's kinsmen sharpened as his leman sauntered up to the high table and chose a seat next to Ross. To Gillian's relief, Gordo arrived next and sat on her left. At Ross's signal, the servants began serving bowls of oats accompanied by bannocks and pitchers of ale.

Gillian nibbled at the bannock; oats didn't appeal to her and never had. She preferred to break her fast with eggs and a rasher of bacon.

Suddenly Seana leaned forward and said loudly enough to be heard by all and sundry, "I expected to see bruises and scratches this morning, but it appears you both survived your wedding night. I confess I am surprised you didna kill each other."

Gordo chuckled. "The absence of bruises is a good sign, lass. Our clan is better for the joining."

"Time will tell, Gordo," Seana replied. "I personally doona believe the truce will hold."

"Enough!" Ross growled. "Why are you still here, Seana? Why did you nae return home with the escort I offered to provide?"

Seana stared adoringly up at Ross. "I thought it would be fun to stay and see what comes of your marriage." She slanted Gillian a sly look. "Your bride doesna look pleased with you, Ross." She leaned close. "Nor you with her. When you have need of a real woman, I will be waiting."

Gillian popped a piece of bannock into her mouth and chewed thoughtfully, having heard Seana's provocative words. "Stay if it pleases you, Seana. It matters not to me." She turned to her husband, her expression bland. "What say you, MacKenna? Will you have need of Seana anytime soon?"

Ross slammed down his spoon. "Stop making trouble, Seana. My marriage is none of your concern. You should have left Ravenscraig."

"Niall asked me to stay, and I decided to accommodate him," she purred. "You aren't the only attractive man at Ravenscraig."

Ross scowled at his former leman; Gillian wondered if he was jealous of Niall.

"Do what you will, Seana," Ross said sourly. "Be forewarned, however, that at the first sign of trouble, I will send you home."

"You shouldna let the lass stay, lad," Gordo muttered. "Mark my words: Keeping a leman—even a former leman—and a wife under the same roof will cause trouble."

"Let Niall enjoy the lass, Gordo. I shall warn him to keep her away from Gillian."

Gillian had had about all she could take of this talking around her. "Seana doesna bother me, MacKenna. If you like," she said for Ross's ears only, "you may take her to your bed. I have no objections. 'Tis not as if I will be sharing your bed in the future."

"Find another place to eat," Ross told Seana, ignoring Gillian's pronouncement. "The high table is out of bounds to you. Gordo," he said, turning to his uncle. "Round up some men. 'Tis time we went into the hills to drive cattle down to their winter pasture."

Given no other choice, Seana sputtered indignantly but rose nonetheless and stomped off to join Niall. Gordo left at the same time.

"You didna have to send Seana away on my account, MacKenna," Gillian said. "One night in your bed was enough for me. Seana may take my place with my blessing."

Ross glared at her. "Doubtless your father would renew the feud if he learned I was keeping a leman. I told you before, Gillian, but I will tell you again so you willna mistake my meaning: You are my wife, and I expect to come to your bed whenever I choose."

"Where will you be when you do not come to me?" Gillian challenged, though she had no idea why she cared. If Ross wasn't in bed with her, then he wouldn't be demanding his marital rights. Naught hurt her pride more than the knowledge that MacKenna could control her body so easily.

"Where I will be is none of your concern," Ross replied. "But know this—it willna be in Seana's bed."

"Then whose—"

"I'll be gone most of the day," Ross said, cutting off her sentence as he beckoned to a man sitting nearby. The man rose and advanced toward the high table. "Donald will show you around Ravenscraig and introduce you to the cook and servants. You might as well become acquainted with your duties as my wife."

"Who is Donald?"

"A kinsman. He's been running Ravenscraig since my mother's death last year, but I'm sure he'll welcome the chance to turn some of his duties over to you."

Gillian watched Donald approach. Somewhat older than Ross, he had the body of a seasoned warrior.

"Donald," Ross greeted him, "my wife would like a tour of the tower. Will you do the honors?"

"Shouldna that be your duty, lad?" Donald asked.

"My duty is driving the livestock down from the hills to their winter pasture."

So saying, he strode off without so much as a goodbye. Donald scowled at his departing back before turning his scowl on Gillian. "Are you ready to see your new home, lass?"

"A moment, please," Gillian replied. "There is something I wish to do first. Wait here for me."

Without further explanation, Gillian strode off and mounted the stairs to the gallery, where the stained sheet still flew from the railing. She wadded the offending linen into a ball, returned forthwith to the hall, and flung it into the blazing hearth. She watched it catch fire and burn before she rejoined Donald.

"Now I am ready," she said. "But I have no intention

of taking over your duties. Apparently you have been doing a good job overseeing the everyday running of Ravenscraig."

"I've done what I had to do, but I willna be sorry to transfer some of the responsibility to your shoulders."

His coolness toward her did not escape Gillian. "You doona like me, do you?"

"I like you as well as you like me. You are the laird's wife. I will treat you with respect even though you are a MacKay. Come along, lass; we will start with the tower and work down, although I doubt you will wish to see the dungeons."

"Ravenscraig has dungeons?"

"Oh, aye, but they havena been used since the early days. Ross keeps the only key to the lower levels."

Donald strode off. Gillian had to hurry to catch up with him. She spent the next two hours exploring her new home. The tower room was unoccupied, but some of the chambers on the floors below were occupied by Ross's uncle, various kinsmen, and servants who worked and lived in the keep.

All things taken into consideration, the keep was in good repair. As with all castles, the corridors were drafty and the corners were draped with cobwebs, but at the end of the tour Gillian was duly impressed. The last place Donald took her was to the kitchen, where he introduced her to the cook and left her.

The tense silence that ensued prompted Gillian to say, "I doona intend to interfere with your cooking or menu. The kitchen is your domain, and so it shall remain. I know naught about cooking and menus."

Hanna visibly relaxed. "Did your mother not insist that you learn about such things?"

"My mother died when I was born. My father left me

to run free. My favorite activity was engaging in sword-play with my brothers."

"Oh, aye, I heard that you challenged our laird on the battlefield. That was foolish of you, lass. He could have slain you with a single blow."

Gillian bristled. "I was holding my own until my father interfered and called for a truce."

Hanna, a round woman with apple cheeks and rust-colored hair streaked with gray, chuckled. "If you say so, lass. Mayhap you should tell me if you have any favorite dishes so I can include them on the menu."

"If the wedding feast you prepared is an example of your skill, I vow I will like anything you cook." She worried her bottom lip, wondering if she should mention her breakfast preference.

"What is it, lass? Spit it out."

"I amna fond of porridge. I prefer to break my fast with eggs and a bit of meat, either bacon or ham. Would it be possible to—"

Hanna cut her off in midsentence. "Say no more, lass. I will personally fix your eggs every morning and cook your bacon."

Gillian grinned. "Thank you."

Hanna cocked her head, gazing intently at Gillian. Then she shook her head.

"What is it, Hanna?"

"You are nae so bad for a MacKay. I am thinking the laird did verra well for himself, although I am sure Seana willna agree with me."

"Thank you again. You are nae so bad for a MacKenna. And I like your daughter. As for Seana . . ." Gillian shrugged expansively, "I doona care what she thinks. This marriage isna what I wanted; nor is it what Ross wanted. If he prefers Seana to me, so be it."

"Methinks Ross will honor his marriage vows. He is that kind of man. Mayhap you should—"

"Doona give advice when you know naught about the flame, Hanna," Gizela proclaimed from the doorway.

Startled, Gillian whirled about. "Gizela, I didna hear you behind me."

Gizela shuffled over to Gillian and patted her hand. "Beware, lass: There are some at Ravenscraig who wish you ill."

"Almost everyone at Ravenscraig wishes me ill," Gillian replied.

"Oh, nay, I like you well enough," Hanna exclaimed. "And so does my Alice."

"Your flame burns bright, Gillian MacKay. You are strong, but so is the laird," Gizela proclaimed. "Be mindful of danger, lass."

"What kind of danger, Gizela?"

"Och, doona listen to her, lass," Hanna said. "No one here wishes you harm."

"So you say," Gizela muttered.

"Doona frighten the laird's new wife, Gizela."

The light in Gizela's eyes flared, then dimmed as she turned and walked off, muttering to herself. Gillian hastily crossed herself, certain that the old crone was a witch.

"Sit down, lass; your eggs will be ready in no time." Hanna placed a loaf of newly baked bread on the table and cut off a generous slice. "There's fresh butter on the table. Help yourself."

Since Gillian had left the hall hungry, she didn't hesitate to spread a thick layer of butter on the bread and bite into it. It tasted delicious. When Hanna placed a plate of eggs and ham in front of Gillian, she dug in unashamedly.

"Milk or ale?" Hanna asked.

"Milk, please."

Gillian ate with relish, savoring the milk, which was a rare treat. Most households saved the milk for their bairns. But there didn't seem to be any bairns at Ravenscraig.

Gillian cleaned her plate, thanked Hanna, and wandered into the hall. To her dismay, the first person she encountered was Seana.

"I've been looking for you," Seana cooed. "I thought we might share confidences about Ross. Did you nae find him a magnificent lover? He made me swoon with delight each time we mated."

Gillian wasn't as adept at exchanging barbs as she was at swordplay. Had Seana challenged her, she would have trounced her soundly. This kind of warfare was new to Gillian, but she was a fast learner.

"I doona have time for idle chatter, Seana," Gillian said coolly. "Since the weather is so fine today, I thought I would ride my mare over the moors. Silver needs the exercise."

"Och, doona be shy, Gillian. Did Ross nae please you in bed?" Seana persisted.

"What takes place in my bedchamber is none of your business."

So saying, she pushed past Seana and headed out the door. The weather was pleasant compared to the day before, when sleet fell to dampen her wedding. The sun was shining and the air mild enough for a brisk ride across the moors.

When Gillian found the stables and asked to have Silver saddled, she was told that her mare hadn't arrived from Braeburn yet. The small annoyance didn't bother Gillian overmuch. She blithely entered the stables and looked over Ross's stock. She selected a spirited black gelding named Raven and asked to have him saddled.

"I wouldna recommend Raven, mistress," the lad said, pulling his forelock. "He is a handful. No one but the laird ever rides him."

That made Gillian more eager than ever to ride the gelding. "Saddle him. If Ross can ride him, so can I."

Raven pranced about a bit when he was led out, but Gillian didn't think him particularly dangerous. She patted his nose, spoke softly to him, and soon had him gentled. With the lad's help, she mounted Raven, seating herself astride him. Then she urged him through the gate into open countryside.

Gillian maintained a slow gallop over the moors, which were still ablaze with heather, then gave Raven his head. The gelding didn't disappoint. He practically flew, his hooves barely touching the ground. Gillian threw back her head and laughed, her hair trailing loose behind her like a flaming banner. She hadn't felt this free in ages.

Gillian was still flying over the moors when she spotted a lone rider racing toward her. She slowed Raven to a more sedate pace. The rider began waving his arms, as if trying to attract her attention. When Gillian recognized Angus Sinclair, she drew rein.

"Gillian, what are you doing out here?" Angus asked when he reached her. "Riding alone in open country is dangerous, though I admit I am happy to see you."

"This land belongs to Ravenscraig," Gillian replied. "And beyond that lies MacKay territory. I am safe here. More to the point, what are you doing here, Angus?"

Did Angus still have feelings for her? Gillian wondered.

"I just left your father at Braeburn," Angus explained. "I know you were forced into marriage with the MacKenna, and wanted to ride to Ravenscraig to inquire about your welfare. But your father convinced me I amna welcome at Ravenscraig."

"As you can see, I am fine. But thank you for caring. If you hadna taken so long to sign the betrothal agreement, I would be your wife instead of MacKenna's." She stared into his eyes, wondering if she still cared for him as she had once thought she did. Had one night in MacKenna's bed changed her opinion of Angus? Surely not, she told herself. "I wish it had been you."

"I will regret the delay the rest of my life," Angus said. He moved his horse closer. "You doona have to stay with him, Gillian. The man canna be trusted. I wouldna be surprised if he broke the truce. He doesna want the feud to end. He will attack your family when they least expect it."

Gillian felt strangely compelled to defend Ross. "You doona know that, Angus."

Reaching out, he grabbed her reins. "Aye, I do know, lass. Come away with me now."

Gillian tried to jerk the reins from his grasp and failed. " 'Tis too late; I am already wed. Besides, you know what will happen if I leave MacKenna."

"Bride stealing is a time-honored tradition among the Scots. If you were mine, I wouldna let you ride about the countryside without protection," he said darkly, starting to lead her horse away.

"Stop! Are you mad? The feud will resume if I go missing. 'Tis as if you are eager to see the bloodletting continue."

Angus sneered at her. "Are you so eager to return to the MacKenna's bed?"

Gillian's cheeks burned. Returning to Ross's bed wouldn't be an onerous chore, even though she heartily disliked the man. "You know 'tis not that."

"Then I see no reason for you to stay with him. If the feud resumes, Clan MacKay and its allies will eventually rout the enemy from Ravenscraig and claim victory."

Gillian bit her lip. "I amna so sure 'tis what I want."

Angus did naught to control his anger. "I never took you for a traitor, Gillian."

Gillian bristled. "I didna want to wed MacKenna. 'Twas you I wanted. But I had no choice. Now I am a married woman and the feud is over. All I must do to keep the peace is remain at Ravenscraig. There is not even any need for MacKenna to bed me again, now that the marriage has been consummated. He keeps a leman. Seana McHamish can satisfy his base desires."

"If you were mine, I wouldna need a leman," Angus vowed. "You *will* be mine, Gillian. I doona care about your sham of a marriage."

Snaking an arm around Gillian's waist, he tried to transfer her from Raven's back to his own mount, but Raven shied away, forcing Angus to release his hold on Gillian.

Neither Gillian nor Angus heard the horse pounding toward them. Alerted by a shout from behind her, Gillian turned to glance over her shoulder.

It was Ross, and he was not sparing his horse to reach them. Angus cursed violently, but before he could turn his horse and race away, Ross was upon them.

Ross had been searching for livestock on a nearby hill when he recognized Gillian, clad in her MacKay plaid, riding below on the moors. He was startled and more than a little concerned when he realized she was riding Raven, whose disposition was anything but placid. But when he noted how well she handled the gelding, he ceased worrying. He was about to turn away when he noticed another rider approaching her. The moment he recognized the Sinclair plaid on the man, he started down from the hills.

Even from a distance Ross noted how intimate their conversation appeared, how Sinclair edged his mount close enough to embrace Gillian. His temper flaring, Ross dug his heels into his mount.

Surely the lass hadn't arranged this meeting so soon after their wedding, had she? His mouth flattened. With Gillian, anything was possible.

"Hold, Sinclair!" Ross shouted when Sinclair finally saw him and would have fled. Ross reined in sharply beside him. "I'll thank you to keep your hands off my wife."

"Our meeting was accidental," Sinclair replied, keeping a wary eye on Ross. "We were merely discussing old times."

Ross slanted a speaking glance at Gillian. "Why didna you tell me you wanted to go riding? I would have found you a proper mount until your own horse arrived from Braeburn. Go home, Gillian. We will discuss your behavior later."

Gillian stiffened her shoulders. "There is naught wrong with my behavior. As Angus said, we were merely socializing."

"From now on you will socialize in the hall, like a civilized person."

Gillian bristled. "Are you suggesting I amna civilized, MacKenna?"

"I am suggesting you are acting inappropriately for a married woman. Some might misinterpret your *accidental* meeting."

If Ross didn't know better, he would have sworn he saw flames shooting out of Gillian's head.

"You canna tell me how to act, MacKenna," Gillian charged. "Wife or nay, I will do as I please, and it pleases me to converse with Angus. If not for your agreement with my father I would be Angus's wife."

Ross clenched his fists at his sides to keep from reaching for Sinclair and beating him to a bloody pulp.

Angus backed his horse away. " 'Tis best you return to Ravenscraig, Gillian. I fear for your life if you continue to defy the brute you were forced to wed." He turned to Ross. "If you beat Gillian, MacKay will call off the truce."

Ross knew precisely whom he wanted to beat, and it wasn't Gillian, although a thorough tongue-lashing might ease his temper. "I have yet to beat a woman, but that may change verra soon."

"I'd like to see you try it," Gillian dared him.

Ross spared her a withering look. "Go home, Gillian. I want a private word with Sinclair."

Ross's fierce expression must have convinced Gillian, for she reined her horse around and galloped off. "Foolish lass," Ross bit out. "Raven is the devil's spawn. She shouldna be riding him at breakneck speed."

"You care naught for Gillian," Angus charged. "You wouldna keep a leman if you did."

Ross narrowed his eyes. He was seconds away from wringing Sinclair's neck. "Who told you I kept a leman?"

Angus smirked. "Gillian. Did you go to your leman after you relieved Gillian of her virginity?"

That did it. Ross leaped at Angus and bore him to the ground. The smaller man didn't have a chance.

Ross had his dirk out and pressed against Angus's jugular before Angus could reach for his own weapon.

"Go ahead and kill me, MacKenna," Angus goaded. "Killing me is one way to end the truce."

"Why are you so anxious for the feud to resume?"

Angus bared his teeth. "You stole my woman. I want you dead, MacKenna. The sooner you die, the sooner I can claim Gillian. If it takes a resumption of the feud to kill you, then that is what I want."

"The feud is done, over, Sinclair. Accept it. But heed me well: If you persist in pursuing my wife, I *will* kill you. Once MacKay is made aware of my reason for killing you, the truce will remain firmly in place."

Picturing Gillian in Sinclair's arms made Ross crave Sinclair's blood. Had Gillian yearned for Sinclair even as Ross was making love to her last night? His blood boiled at the thought. Gillian was his, and he intended to keep the flame-haired hellion.

Slowly Ross withdrew his dirk and rose to his feet. Angus inched backward across the ground before rising and dusting himself off. "That was uncalled-for, MacKenna."

"Take that as fair warning, Sinclair. I am the only man with the right to bed Gillian."

"Will you take her even if she is unwilling?" Sinclair challenged.

The corner of Ross's mouth curled up in a smile so charged with sexual innuendo that no one could mistake his meaning. "Do you really think Gillian is unwilling? She didna resist me on our wedding night. In fact, she ignited in my arms and burned to a cinder."

He leaped onto his horse, still smiling at Sinclair. "Think on that before you attempt to seduce my wife again." Digging his heels into his mount, he rode off, leaving Sinclair choking on his dust.

Fuming in impotent rage, Ross reined his sure-footed gelding back toward the hills. No matter how badly he wanted to return home to confront Gillian, it would have to wait until later. He needed to cool down first.

Gillian returned to Ravenscraig in a fury. How dared MacKenna embarrass her in front of Angus! It wasn't as if MacKenna held her in high regard. He barely knew her. Their marriage had been dictated by circumstances; he had no right to tell her whom to befriend. Why should he care what she did, when he had Seana waiting for his summons? The man was impossible, a veritable ogre: possessive and overbearing.

A thought occurred to Gillian as she rode through the gates into the courtyard. Would MacKenna really attempt to beat her? Angus had thought so. But the threat of a beating didn't bother Gillian in the least. She could protect herself as well as any man.

Gillian dismounted before the stables and tossed Raven's reins to the stable lad. By the time she strode through the front door, she was in no mood for a confrontation with Seana or anyone else. When Donald hailed her, she pretended not to hear and proceeded up the stairs to the solar. She went directly to her trunk, which had been delivered the day before, and flung open the lid.

Gillian had no idea whether Ross was angry enough to beat her but she wasn't going to take any chances. She rummaged amid the clothing in her trunk until she found the sword her father had given her. It was lighter than a claymore but sharp and deadly. Dismayed, she shook her head. She had been wed but one day and already felt the need to defend herself.

Gillian paced her chamber, waiting for Ross to return. She had missed the midday meal but felt no hunger pangs. Nor was she afraid to face the MacKenna. It was nearly time for the evening meal before she heard his footsteps approaching her chamber. She reached for her sword, hiding it in the folds of her skirt just as the door burst open.

Ross stormed into the chamber and halted before Gillian. Her defiant attitude was something to behold. Though he knew he shouldn't, he admired her spirit. "What have you to say for yourself, woman?"

"I wanted to go riding. There is naught else to say."

"Did you arrange to meet with Sinclair?"

"When, pray tell, was I supposed to do that?"

"I doona know. What did he want?"

"We were simply passing the time of day."

Ross's mouth flattened. "Doona lie to me, wife. He had his hands on you."

Gillian's chin angled higher. "Verra well, if you must know, he had wife stealing in mind."

Ross felt ready to explode despite his unnatural calmness. "You were wise to refuse."

"Who said I refused?"

Ross felt a burning sensation in the pit of his stomach. "Doona jest with me, Gillian. One thing I willna abide is an unfaithful wife."

Gillian glared at him. "What about an unfaithful husband?"

"I have no intention of betraying my wedding vows. Heed me well, wife. There will be no more 'accidental' meetings with Sinclair or any other man."

Gillian bared her teeth. "What will you do, beat me?"

He reached for her. Gillian must have thought he meant her harm, for she whipped out the sword she had hidden in the folds of her clothing, holding him at bay with the sharp tip.

"Damnation, Gillian, what do you think you are doing?"

"I willna let you beat me."

"What makes you think I intend to beat you?"

"'Tis what all men do when their wives displease them."

"Put the sword down, Gillian."

Ross had no idea if Gillian's intention had been to cut him as he attempted to grab the sword hilt at the same time Gillian started to withdraw it, but regardless of her intent, the sharp blade slashed across his palm.

Gillian dropped the sword instantly, staring at the blood welling from Ross's palm.

"Doona just stand there; fetch a cloth to stop the bleeding," Ross ordered curtly.

Gillian ran to her trunk, found a clean chemise, and pressed it against Ross's palm. "Shall I fetch Gizela? You will probably need stitches."

The words were no sooner out of her mouth than Gizela burst into the chamber, carrying a basket over her arm. "How bad is it, lad?"

"'Tis but a wee cut." He held out his hand. "Stitch away, old woman."

"How . . . how did she know?" Gillian asked with equal parts fear and awe.

Gizela removed needle and thread and an assortment of salves from her basket and placed them on a nearby table. "I know many things," she answered cryptically. "Sit down and give me your hand, laird."

Ross dropped down on a bench and held out his

hand. He couldn't believe what had just happened. He glared at Gillian, expecting to see her cowering in fear, but nay, not his wife. Gillian was staring at Gizela as if she expected her to sprout horns.

Ross didn't move a muscle while Gizela cleaned his wound and stitched it up. He fixed his gaze on Gillian and kept it there during the whole process.

After Gizela had bandaged Ross's hand and replaced everything in the basket, her penetrating gaze settled on Gillian. "'Tis just the beginning, lass. The struggle willna end until the flame consumes the warrior or the warrior tames the flame."

"What does she mean?" Gillian asked after Gizela had departed. "Is she a witch?"

Ross shrugged. "Who knows what she is? She has been Ravenscraig's healer as long as I can remember. Though she is strange, she means no harm."

Ross unfolded himself from the bench and stalked toward Gillian. Before he reached her, he scooped up her sword from the floor and handed it to her hilt-first.

"Doona ever raise your weapon to me again, lass. We will talk about your meeting with Sinclair later, after I devise a suitable punishment for your willfulness."

She backed up until the back of her knees hit the bed. "Punishment? You wouldna dare!"

"I dare much, wife."

Before Gillian could protest, Ross snagged her about the waist and pulled her against him. Then he lowered his head and kissed her.

Ross was wise enough to know he needed to subdue the flame before the flame consumed him. He might get burned in the process, but it would be well worth the effort.

Chapter Six

Attempting to understand Ross was driving Gillian mad. Instead of the beating she was expecting, she had received a kiss. She touched her lips, recalling Ross's kiss and how it had affected her. Was his kiss supposed to be a form of punishment? If so, it wouldn't change her behavior. Gillian didn't fear Ross's kisses. Then he had stormed out, leaving her more confused than ever.

Gillian walked to the window and gazed out. The chapel bell in the village was chiming vespers. Her stomach rumbled. She hadn't eaten since morning and was feeling the lack of food. Was she expected to join Ross in the hall for the evening meal, she wondered, or was he planning to ignore her?

Gillian decided that no MacKenna was going to ignore a MacKay as long as there was a breath left in her lungs. Squaring her shoulders, she walked toward the door, intending to take her rightful place at the high table in the hall.

Ross chose that moment to return. Gillian halted

midway between the door and window and glared at him. He glared back.

"I've come to escort you to the hall so we can sup together. It wouldna do for my clansmen to think there is dissension between us."

"I hope you are a good actor," Gillian replied.

She preceded him out the door. "I'm glad starvation isna the punishment you plan for me."

Ross bit his tongue to keep from responding. Anger still coiled deep inside of him. He had tried to forget the sight of Sinclair and Gillian together, but he couldn't dislodge the image from his mind. As for devising a punishment for Gillian, that had been mostly bluster. He had wanted her to spend the afternoon worrying about what he was going to do to her.

Ross almost laughed aloud at that thought. It would take a great deal more than threats to frighten his warrior woman, especially after he had chosen to kiss her instead of beat her.

Nay, Ross had more pleasurable ways in mind to tame Gillian.

With a hand on her arm, Ross urged Gillian down the staircase. "Smile, wildcat," he murmured when they reached the hall.

Ross wanted to shake Gillian until her teeth rattled when she lifted the corners of her mouth in a smile that fooled no one. They slid into their seats at the high table, and the meal began. Since the midday meal was usually more elaborate than the evening repast, the fare was light but delicious. It began with a flavorful potato soup, followed by flaky fish simmered in cream, and ending with pudding topped by toasted oatmeal.

Gillian, Ross noted, ate generous portions of everything. When he recalled that she had missed the midday meal, he felt guilty for failing to send something up to her. But not guilty enough to mention it. Instead he leaned back, sipped his whiskey, and watched Gillian eat. Each time she closed her lush lips over a morsel of food, he felt himself harden as he imagined her mouth closing over a certain part of his anatomy. He squirmed in his seat and looked away.

His gaze fell on Seana. She was staring at Gillian, her eyes brimming with hostility. Perhaps he should have sent Seana home. But since Ross had no intention of bedding his former leman again, he saw no reason to deprive his kinsmen of her favors.

"She is lovely," Gillian said.

Startled, Ross looked at Gillian. "What? To whom are you referring?"

"Seana, of course. Admit it: You want her."

"You are wrong, Gillian. I gave her to Niall and whomever else she fancies. She can return to her father's keep anytime she wishes."

"She fancies you. Were you promised to each other before my father interfered?"

"Nay, I was promised to no woman. Unlike you, I didna have another mate in mind when we wed."

Gillian flushed and returned her gaze to her plate. "It wouldna bother me if you bedded Seana."

"Naught you say will force me to set you aside, so stop your blathering, woman. Accept that men with higher goals than yours have found a way to make peace."

Though Gillian muttered something he could not understand, Ross was pleased that she had naught more to offer on the subject of Seana. He continued sipping his whiskey while Gillian scooped up the last spoonful of pudding. Ross waited until she dabbed daintily at her mouth with her napkin before saying, "Shall we retire, wife?"

Gillian sent him a belligerent stare. "Why, so you can punish me? I havena forgotten your threat."

"I think you will like the punishment I have in mind." He rose, bringing her along with him.

Others began to leave as well so the tables could be taken up and gaming and other activities could commence. With a hand on her waist, Ross guided Gillian from the hall. Suddenly Gizela appeared before them. Gillian yelped and jumped behind Ross. Laughing, he steadied her.

"The healer willna hurt you. What is it this time, Gizela?"

"Shall I change the bandage on your hand, laird?"

Ross flexed his hand. "Nay, 'tis fine."

The old crone stared intently at Gillian. "The laird has been waiting a long time for the flame to arrive."

"I doona ken," Gillian replied.

Gizela pointed a bony finger at Ross. "The laird kens." She smiled vacantly. "Enjoy your punishment, Gillian, lass." Then she ambled off.

"What is she talking about, MacKenna?" Gillian wanted to know. Ross shrugged. "Gizela rarely makes sense."

"Why will I enjoy being punished?"

"That I *can* answer. You will enjoy your punishment because I will make it enjoyable for you."

Gillian narrowed her eyes. "You're not talking about hurting me, are you?"

Ross snorted. "Hardly." He prodded her up the stairs.

"Ross, I'd like a word with you before you retire," a voice called from behind them.

Ross turned his head. "Gordo, canna this wait until tomorrow?"

"Nay, lad, it canna."

"Verra well." He turned to Gillian. "I willna be long, lass."

"Take your time," Gillian replied.

Gillian hurried up the stairs to the solar. She could well imagine the kind of punishment Ross had in mind, and wanted to be in bed and asleep before he arrived. Alice was waiting to help her undress. While Alice folded and put away her mistress's clothing, Gillian washed and put on a clean shift. Then she dismissed Alice and climbed into bed.

Her plan almost worked. She was hovering on the verge of sleep when Ross entered the chamber. He advanced toward the bed and stared down at her.

"You can stop pretending, wife. I know you are awake."

Gillian lifted her eyelids sleepily. "I thought you were meeting with your uncle."

Ross tossed back the covers and pulled her from bed. "Gordo told me Sinclairs have been spotted on Ravenscraig land. What mischief have you been plotting with Angus Sinclair?"

Gillian wrenched her arm free. "Give me some credit, MacKenna. While I doona think this truce between our clans will last, I doona wish to see another of my loved ones fall beneath a MacKenna sword. I planned naught with Angus. I am your wife."

Ross searched her face so long, Gillian began to fidget beneath his intense scrutiny. Suddenly his face softened and he pulled her against him.

"You are right. You *are* my wife, and I intend to have you, lass. Doona try to fight me. Gizela had the right of it." His mouth hovered scant inches from hers; she could almost taste him. "I can feel your flame scorching me. I must conquer it before it consumes me."

"Am I the flame?" Gillian asked.

He ran his fingers through her hair, holding the bright strands out for her inspection. "What do you think?"

"I think Gizela is mad, and you along with her. Release me. I am tired and in no mood to be conquered."

Ross grasped her chin between his thumb and forefinger and raised it to meet his mouth. "We are wed; if I am in the mood to conquer, you *will* be conquered."

Immediately Gillian twisted free. "Our vows have been consummated; we doona need to do *that* again."

Angry heat shimmered through Ross. "Are you suggesting that we forgo marital relations for the duration of our marriage?"

"Aye, that would be my preference."

Gillian looked so hopeful Ross nearly laughed aloud. "What about heirs? Am I to be denied children of my own?"

"A man like you must have countless bairns running about the countryside."

Ross's dark brows lowered. "I have sired no illegitimate bairns."

"I suggest you sire a son with one of your lemans and claim him as your heir," Gillian shot back.

Ross couldn't remember when a woman had had him as bewildered as his MacKay wife. Gillian seemed to hate all things MacKenna, especially the MacKenna laird.

Did she dislike him because he had made her respond to his loving against her will? Ross wondered. Though she had burned in his arms, she seemed to resent his ability to arouse a response in her.

"You try my patience, Gillian," Ross bit out. "Am I going to have to force you to perform your wifely duties?"

Gillian's chin shot up. "I willna do so willingly. I hate you!"

Grasping her arms, Ross shoved her backward. She landed on the bed hard. Surprisingly, he made no move toward her. He towered above her, glaring, his body drawn as tight as a bowstring.

"Verra well, wife, have it your way. I find no pleasure in forcing women, especially women who claim to hate me. While you enjoy your cold bed, you can rest assured that mine will be neither cold nor empty."

He stormed from the chamber before Gillian had time to register his words, decipher what they meant and how they would affect her. Did she truly not care with whom Ross slept? How did she feel about other women bearing his children? A frisson of something akin to jealousy swept through her. But how could that be? There was no reason for her to be jealous of the MacKenna. She hated him, didn't she?

One thing was sure:

Gillian hated the way Ross made her feel, the way her body responded to his. Naught had hurt her pride more than surrendering her body to Ross. Was she the last MacKay left with the courage to stand up to the MacKenna?

In the following days, Gillian took on some of the duties of the mistress of the keep and found them not too onerous. She had begun to feel a wee bit more comfortable in the MacKenna stronghold, thanks largely to Hanna and Alice. Donald and some of the others did not warm to her, but it mattered not. She wasn't trying to make friends. She was just waiting for the day the truce was broken and she could return home.

Gillian was pleased as well as surprised when she learned she was still allowed to ride each day. Her favorite mare, Silver, had arrived, and she tried to exercise the beastie every day. Gillian did notice, however, that she was never allowed to ride out alone. One of Ross's kinsmen always trailed behind her. Obviously Ross was taking pains to stop another chance encounter with Angus.

Gillian saw Ross rarely, the exception being at the evening meal. She had no idea where he was sleeping or with whom, although she was quick to note that there were many attractive women at Ravenscraig, including Seana. No doubt they were eager to satisfy the laird's sexual appetites.

Gillian had exchanged but a few words with Ross since he had stormed from their chamber, and was surprised one night when he turned to her at the table and asked, "How are you faring, wife? You look well."

Startled, Gillian replied, "I *am* well, MacKenna."

"Are you ready to welcome me back into our bed?"

Gillian's gaze wandered past Ross to Seana, who was smirking, as if she knew something Gillian did not. "When pigs fly," she said sweetly. "Have you tired of Seana? Mayhap I can suggest someone to take her place."

Though Ross appeared ready to explode, he kept his voice low. "Have you had your woman's time yet?"

Color slowly drained from Gillian's face. Did he think she was carrying his bairn? "Aye."

It was a lie she felt no guilt in telling. She had no reason to believe her woman's time wouldn't arrive when it was due. She peered at him through lowered lashes. Her imagination must be playing tricks on her, for he looked disappointed.

Ross turned away to hide his frustration. He had been hoping his seed had found fertile ground in Gillian, and that motherhood would mellow her. But his firebrand was as feisty as ever, and his hopes for an heir dimmed. Mayhap he should consult with Gizela. She might have a potion that would make Gillian willing to let him make love to her. It wasn't just heirs Ross wanted from Gillian. Nay, he desired her lush body, reveled in her response, no matter how unwillingly given; she aroused him as no other woman ever had. He had been walking around with a cock-stand since Gillian had refused him. For some unexplained reason, Ross had no desire to sate himself with another woman.

While Ravenscraig had no shortage of attractive women willing to bed with him, he wanted none of them. No one but his fire-haired warrior woman would satisfy him.

"What is wrong with you, lad?" Gordo asked when Ross continued to frown and shift food around on his plate. "You havena been yourself since your wedding. What has the MacKay wench done to you?"

Ross growled at his uncle. "The wench has done naught; that is the problem."

"I suspected as much. 'Tis common knowledge you havena been sleeping in your own bed. Doona let the lass turn you into a milksop, Ross. If you want her, take her, but whatever you do, doona moon over her."

Ross's head jerked up. "Is that what everyone is thinking? That I'm mooning over my wife?"

"What else are we to think? We all ken you havena

been the same since wedding the MacKay lass." Gordo shook his head. "Bed her, Ross. Doona give her power over you. No one here will say you nay, and I am sure even Tearlach MacKay would agree."

Ross stared down at his plate in moody silence. He had no idea what was keeping him from bedding his wife, unless it was his pride. If wasn't as if he didn't desire Gillian. His stupid notion of wanting her to come to him willingly was just that: stupid. He turned his head to stare intently at Gillian. She flushed beneath his scrutiny and pushed herself away from the table.

"I believe I shall retire. Good night," Gillian said as she rose and hurried from the hall.

"Go after her, lad," Gordo advised. "I'm for a breath of fresh air." He rose, stretched, and strode off.

Ross brooded over Gordo's unasked-for advice as he finished his second mug of ale and called for another. Damn Gillian for making him look like a besotted fool.

Mayhap, he thought, he *should* beat her. Her willfulness certainly demanded punishment.

Ross was so engrossed in his morose thoughts, he didn't hear Seana sidle up beside him. "You look unhappy, Ross. Isna your marriage going well?" She leaned over, brushing her breasts suggestively against his shoulder. "Let me help you. I can make you smile again."

Without waiting for an invitation, she plopped into his lap and wound her arms around his neck. "Do you nae remember how good we were together?"

"Are you trying to make Niall jealous?" Ross asked.

"Niall isna half the man you are. I doona belong to him. I am yours for the taking, Ross."

"Take her, MacKenna; you deserve each other." It was his wife's furious voice.

Ross jumped to his feet, spilling Seana on the floor. "Gillian, I thought you had retired for the night."

"I forgot my shawl," Gillian said, retrieving the garment from the back of her chair, where she had left it. "I hope you both enjoy your evening." She slanted Seana a contemptuous glance and walked away.

"Damn you!" Ross gritted from between clenched teeth as he started after her.

Seana reached up and grasped his leg, stopping him in his tracks. "The MacKay lass hates you. Doona make a fool of yourself over her, Ross."

Ross shook his leg free and lifted Seana to her feet. "No one, man or woman, makes a fool of Ross MacKenna." So saying, he took off after Gillian.

"Ross," Seana cried, "doona go to her!"

He paid her no heed.

" 'Tis no use, lass," Gizela told Seana. "Accept it. You have no power over the laird. He belongs to the MacKay lass. 'Tis the way of it, and there is naught you can do to change the hand of fate. The flame hasna won yet, and there is heartache to come, but I have seen the laird's future, and you have no place in it."

Seana gave Gizela a vicious shove. "Where did you come from, old woman? Go away. You know naught."

Spinning on her heel, she flounced off.

Ross was in a foul mood when he entered the solar and stormed into the bedchamber. Knowing that his kinsmen thought him a besotted fool made his blood boil. He had a wife, and she had damn well better begin acting like one. He stopped in his tracks when he saw Alice disrobing Gillian. Wearing naught but her shift, Gillian tried to hide herself behind her maid.

"Leave us!" Ross barked.

"Nay, doona go!" Gillian cried with equal fervor.

"Alice," Ross warned when Alice wavered.

Turning, Alice fled. Gillian reached for her chamber robe. Ross tore it from her fingers and tossed it aside.

"What do you want, MacKenna?"

"I should think that would be obvious. My kinsmen believe I am a besotted fool, that I am weak for letting you deny me my marital rights."

She backed away from him. "I doona think you are besotted with me—far from it. I think you are wise to realize we doona suit."

His face set in determined lines, Ross reached for her, bringing her against him. "I have been too indulgent with you. I was wrong to deny myself what I wanted."

Gillian struggled, but to no avail. "Why do you want a woman who doesna like you?"

His grin was not comforting. "I can make you like me. I can make you like everything I do to you. Have you forgotten our wedding night? You burned in my arms. You writhed and gasped and screamed with pleasure. Why are you denying yourself the joys of the marriage bed?"

"For the very reasons you just named," Gillian shot back. "I doona want to burn or writhe or scream. I doona want to feel pleasure with you. I am a MacKay."

"Foolish woman," Ross growled. Then he kissed her.

But Ross wanted more than just kisses. He wanted to touch her hot, wet center, to make her respond, to exult in sweet victory when she climaxed in his arms.

He wanted to conquer her, body and soul.

He wanted to burn in her flame.

Scooping her into his arms, he carried her to the bed and followed her down. Her shift came apart in his strong hands, and he tossed it aside. Then he rolled on top of her, sliding his uninjured palm along the smooth length of her thigh.

"You feel good," he muttered. "Better than I remember. You're a bonny lass, Gillian."

To Gillian's shame, she was enjoying the weight of Ross's body atop hers. All her senses seemed overwhelmed by him. She fought the feeling, but the moment his hand brushed her woman's hair and caressed lower, she feared she was fighting a lost cause. The MacKenna was too experienced for her.

He pulled away long enough to shed his plaid braies and shirt, and then he pressed his naked length along her quivering body. She burned everywhere they touched. When he dipped his head and spread kisses over her breasts and belly and outlined her navel with his tongue, she shivered uncontrollably.

"Do you like that, lass?"

The lie came easily to her lips. "Nay, I doona." The truth, were she to admit it, was that he made her feel wild, wilder than riding across the moors on Silver, wilder than engaging in swordplay, wilder than she had ever imagined she could feel.

Ross's intimate caresses were becoming unbearable. While her mind wanted him to stop, her body begged him to continue. Gillian had opened her mouth to protest when she felt his fingers slip inside her moisture. He sealed her lips with a kiss that stole her breath and drained her resistance. When his fingers began thrusting in and out of her, she sent a silent scream into his mouth.

Gillian closed her eyes, unwilling to let Ross witness the pleasure he was giving her. The world began to shimmer; reality faded. She gave a cry of protest when Ross removed his fingers, broke off the kiss, and stared down at her.

"Do you want me to stop, lass?"

Disoriented, her eyes glazed with passion, Gillian returned his stare. "What?"

"I thought not." He kissed her again, and rolled over to bring her on top of him.

"MacKenna . . ."

"My name is Ross. Say it."

"Nay."

He raised his head, took a distended nipple into his mouth, and began to suckle. The breath caught in Gillian's throat. She couldn't endure such sweet torture much longer.

"Ross . . ."

Ross grinned up at her. "Aye, lass, say it again."

"Ross."

Gillian could feel his sex throbbing against her intimate flesh, hot, hard, potent. She was past resistance now and well into the urgent need to take this to its ultimate conclusion. When Ross arched his hips and pressed forward, she felt his sex probe against a spot so sensitive she convulsed.

"Take my cock inside you, Gillian," Ross said on a groan.

Gillian no longer had a choice. Her body took on a life independent of her mind as she placed a hand around his sex and guided it to her throbbing center. His hips flexed, and he filled her completely. It was not painful like the first time, and she felt herself stretching to accommodate him.

"You are wet for me—do you ken what that means?"

Gillian shook her head. "Nay, doona deny it," he said. You want me as badly as I want you. Ride me, Gillian. Doona spare me, for tonight I am your stallion."

His words set off a firestorm inside Gillian. She rode him ruthlessly, tirelessly. When she heard him groan, she glanced down at him and saw that his teeth were clenched and his fists knotted in the bedsheet.

His eyes were open and he was staring at her. His intensity startled her. But she was too eager to find her own pleasure to concentrate on Ross's. Her flesh burned; her insides had turned molten. Pleasure spiraled upward from the place they were joined. She began to tremble; she moaned and thrashed atop him.

"Now." Ross gasped through clenched teeth. "Come now."

And then she shattered.

Ross rolled her over on her back and began thrusting hard, once, twice, thrice. Her climax strengthened, lengthened, held her suspended. As if from a distance she heard Ross's hoarse cry and felt his seed bathe her insides. Then he collapsed on top of her.

Gillian wanted to scream in frustration. What kind of woman was she to succumb to MacKenna with such wild abandon? On the other hand, what had made her believe she could resist him? He was a braw, bonny man with mesmerizing blue eyes and a hard body that any woman would want; that much she was willing to admit. But she had known other handsome men without feeling stirrings of desire. What was it about MacKenna that made her yearn for his attention?

His weight shifted off of her. Gillian inhaled sharply, suddenly aware that she could breathe freely again. She heard Ross sigh and waited with bated breath for him to mock her. She had insisted she didn't want him, and the arrogant man had proved her wrong.

"I canna recall when I've enjoyed making love more. You are wonderfully responsive, Gillian. Never try to tell me you doona want me, for I willna believe you. You enjoyed it as much as I did."

"Your arrogance knows no bounds, MacKenna. Aye, you made me feel pleasure, but I didna stand a chance. You are too experienced. Mayhap if I had someone to compare you to, I would be better able to—"

"Cease, woman! There will be no man but me in your bed. You would do well to remember that. You are mine, Gillian, mine. Mine," he repeated as he rolled on top of her and kissed her with renewed ardor.

Then he made love to her again, slowly, wringing a response from her. Before she knew it, she was panting with need, cursing Ross, cursing herself, and enjoying every minute of it.

"Tell me you hate me now," Ross said once his breath returned and he rolled away from her.

"I . . ." She tried again. "I . . ."

A knowing smile curved his lips. "I will listen to no more of your lies. Go to sleep, wife. We have both earned our rest."

Gillian turned away from him and closed her eyes. Why had the words of denial stuck in her throat? She did hate MacKenna, didn't she? That question remained unanswered as she drifted off to sleep.

Ross listened to Gillian's even breathing, wishing he could find sleep as easily as his wife. Mayhap sleep eluded him because he was having difficulty understanding the woman he had wed. She made love like an angel while professing to hate him. How could a woman who hated him find enjoyment in the marriage bed? Wouldn't she lie beneath him like a statue instead of writhing and moaning with pleasure?

Ross sighed, closed his eyes, and pulled Gillian into the curve of his body, seeking the solace of sleep. He had just started to doze when someone pounded on the door. Spitting out a curse, Ross eased away from Gillian, crept across the chamber, and opened the door.

"What does a man have to do to earn his rest?" he hissed when he saw Niall standing outside the door.

"I wouldna bother you if it wasna important," Niall replied. "There's trouble, Ross. I decided to ride out to check on the herd before I retired, and saw reivers making off with some of our livestock. I tried to stop them but there were too many. Since I wasna expecting trouble, I had gone out alone."

"Wait here," Ross said, mindful of his sleeping wife.

Turning back into the chamber, Ross pulled on his braies, stomped into his boots, and grabbed his shirt, jacket, and weapons before joining Niall.

"How many reivers were there? Did you recognize any of them?"

"I counted at least six, but there could have been more. You are nae going to like this, Ross, but they were MacKays."

"MacKays? Impossible, we have a truce."

"Truce or no, I recognized the plaid."

Ross belted on his claymore and dirk, threw on a jacket and headed down the stairs. "Wake the men. We might be able to catch up with them. Or at least follow their trail. I canna believe MacKay would break the truce."

"He had us right where he wanted us," Niall said, "unsuspecting and unaware."

Twenty minutes later, Ross led a party of men through the gates and into the dark night. They rode to the winter pasture at the foot of the nearby hills. As Ross had expected, the reivers were gone, and with them a dozen or more cows.

"We'll follow their tracks," Ross said as he studied the signs on the soft ground in the moonlight. "They canna have gotten too far."

They found their missing cows a few miles away. Apparently the reivers weren't expecting to be chased and had given up their prize rather than tangle with angry MacKennas. If Niall hadn't ridden out to check on the herd, the thieves would have escaped, and they might never have gotten their cows back.

But that was not all Ross learned when he found the missing cows. He also found a piece of MacKay plaid caught on a nearby bush. Cursing MacKay for his trickery, Ross rode home in a rage. This treachery would not go unpunished. After he renounced his MacKay wife and returned her bag and baggage to her father, the feud would resume. So much for peace.

Chapter Seven

Ross dismounted in front of the keep, issued a few curt orders to Gordo, and stormed inside just as the sun rose over the nearby hills. Those unlucky enough to be in the hall when he entered scattered at the sight of his glowering features and clenched fists.

"Tell Hanna to have food on the table in thirty minutes," he called in passing to one of the men setting up tables for the morning repast.

Then he stormed up the stairs to the solar and burst into the bedchamber. Stomping to the bed, he pulled the covers off of Gillian and barked, "Get up!"

Gillian blinked awake, saw Ross standing over her, and smiled. How could she not smile after all the pleasure he'd given her? It had been a most extraordinary night, one she wasn't likely to forget anytime soon. She stretched sinuously, recalling the erotic delight Ross evoked with his hands and mouth and other manly parts of his body.

"Get up, Gillian," Ross repeated in a voice that was curiously lacking in feeling or compassion.

Gillian sat up, pulling the sheet high to cover her nakedness. "What is it, Ross? Has something happened? You look so . . . so angry."

"Anger doesna begin to describe how I feel," he spat. Curling his fingers around her arm, he yanked her out of bed. "Meet me in the hall in thirty minutes. Doona be late. And wear your heavy cloak; 'tis cold outside. I'll send Alice to pack your trunk."

Gillian gaped at him. "Pack my trunk? Are we going somewhere?"

"Aye, I'm taking you to Braeburn."

Gillian's face lit up, and she clapped her hands. "We're going to Braeburn for a visit? Why did you nae say so? I'll be ready, Ross. You willna have to wait for me. It will be wonderful to see Da and my brothers again."

Ross sent her a strange look but said naught as he nodded curtly and retraced his steps to the hall. His mood hadn't lightened when Gillian joined him thirty minutes later. In fact, the tension in the hall was so thick she could have cut it with a knife. Obviously something had happened that she was not privy to. From the animosity directed at her, Gillian could conclude only that the problem involved her or her clan.

Gillian knew for certain she was the target of the hostility when a servant set a bowl of porridge in front of her instead of her usual plate of eggs.

"What is this about, MacKenna?" Gillian demanded to know. "Why does everyone look angry at me? What have I done to deserve such animosity from your clansmen?"

"Doona try to tell me you didna know," Ross hissed. "Your father had this planned from the beginning."

"What are you talking about?"

"Reivers attempted to steal our cows last night. They were MacKays. The feud has officially ended. Our herd wasna guarded as it would have been had we not agreed to a truce. A truce, ha!" Ross repeated.

Gillian's mouth dropped open. "Nay, Da wouldna break the truce. He came to you with the peace offer, do you nae remember? Why would Da ask for a truce if he intended to break it?"

"To catch us off guard, and he almost succeeded, but he didna get away with our cows. Thanks to Niall, we discovered your father's treachery in time to catch up with the thieves. They left the cows and ran off like cowards when they heard us coming after them."

"I doona ken why you think Da did this. He promoted our marriage to cement the truce. Da wouldna betray me in such a manner."

"Would he not? He knew I would return you to Braeburn once the truce was broken. I was the one betrayed, by both you and the MacKay. You knew this would happen—doona deny it."

"I admit I knew the truce wouldna last, but I thought it would be broken by a MacKenna."

"Finish your porridge. I canna wait to rid Ravenscraig of a viper."

"If I had my sword, I would run you through," Gillian retorted.

"We tried that once before," Ross replied, "and it didna end well for you, if you recall."

"What makes you think my father broke the truce? What proof do you have that MacKays were the thieves you chased?"

Ross reached into his jacket pocket and retrieved a square of cloth. "What does this look like?"

Gillian stared at the piece of MacKay plaid. "What does that signify?"

"I found it caught on a bush near my stolen cows."

"So? It could have been there a long time. You are jumping to conclusions, MacKenna."

"I think not. Are you ready to leave?"

Gillian stood and pulled her cloak over her shoulders. "Let's go. I canna wait to see your face when Da proves you a liar."

Both Silver and Ross's horse were waiting outside in the courtyard. A horse cart loaded with her trunk was pulled up beside them. A stable lad sat on the driver's bench, waiting for directions.

When Ross made no attempt to help Gillian into the saddle, Gordo materialized to help her. Then Ross trotted off, and Gillian urged Silver to follow. The cart lumbered into place behind them. Ross remained detached as Gillian rode beside him; he made no attempt at conversation. Gillian could tell he was fuming inside, and that most of his anger was directed at her.

Gillian was relieved when, several hours later, she saw Braeburn's tower rising up through the frosty mist swirling over the moors. She was chilled to the bone and couldn't wait to feel the warmth of her father's hearth.

The gate was open, and they rode through.

"Would the gate be open if a MacKay had broken the truce?" Gillian taunted. Ross glared at her but said naught. "Nay, the gate would be closed for fear of retaliation."

They reined in before the keep. A lad ran up to take their reins. Gillian slid off Silver without Ross's help and mounted the stairs. She charged into the hall with Ross hard on her heels.

Tearlach MacKay turned at the sound, a welcoming smile curving his lips. "Daughter, 'tis glad I am to see you." He held out his arms, and Gillian ran into them.

"Oh, Da, I have missed you," Gillian said into the burly expanse of his chest.

Tearlach held her away from him, his face a mask of concern. "What is it, lass?" He slanted a hard look at Ross. "What have you done to her, MacKenna?"

"I've done naught but bring your daughter home to her treacherous father," Ross bit out. "You broke the truce, MacKay. I no longer want any MacKay under my roof, so I've brought the viper back to you."

"The devil you say!" MacKay roared. "I didna break the truce. What makes you think I did?"

"Reivers attempted to steal my cows last night. We chased them off before they could disappear into the hills with my livestock."

"What has that got to do with me? I pledged an end to the feud in good faith. Neither I nor any of my men would break that truce once the pledge was given."

Ross reached into his pocket and retrieved the square of plaid. "I found this on a bush near my cows. 'Tis the MacKenna plaid, is it not?"

Tearlach examined the plaid closely. "Aye, what of it?"

"What of it!" Ross spat. " 'Tis as clear as day. You or one of yours raided my herd last night."

"What's amiss, Da?"

Gillian spun around at the sound of her brother Murdoc's voice. Both he and Nab had just entered the hall. "Lads, the MacKenna has accused the MacKays of breaking the truce."

"What nonsense is this, MacKenna?" Murdoc challenged. "We gave our word. Why would we break the truce when we are planning a celebration? I am to be wed in three days. We were going to have an invitation carried to you today."

"You're getting married, Murdoc?" Gillian exclaimed. "That's wonderful! We all love Mary."

Murdoc grinned. "Not as much as I do."

"All this talk of weddings doesna solve the problem at hand," Ross charged. "Someone tried to steal our cows. If it wasna you, then who was it?"

"I doona know," Tearlach said.

"I doona believe you," Ross spat. "The proof is in the plaid I hold in my hand."

Murdoc picked up the piece of plaid and held it up. "This wee bit of cloth—is that all the proof you have?"

" 'Tis enough."

Murdoc rubbed the material between his thumb and forefinger and handed it to Nab to inspect. "Bah, our weavers didna weave this flimsy stuff," Nab claimed.

Gillian snatched the square of cloth from Nab's fingers and gave it a more thorough examination. "Nab is right," she concurred. "This didna come from our looms." She threw it into Ross's face. "So much for your proof, MacKenna. If you will excuse me, I'm going up to my chamber. Please have my trunk carried up as soon as it is brought in."

All three men watched Gillian walk off. Once she was out of sight, Tearlach gave Ross an ungentle shove. "You've gone and done it now, MacKenna. Gillian isna one to forgive and forget."

"So I've noticed," Ross said dryly.

"Come sit by the fire. We need to talk," Tearlach invited.

"Verra well, but I'm still not convinced your clansmen didna raid my land."

Tearlach turned to his sons. "Look into it, lads, while MacKenna and I chat. Question everyone, those who left the keep last night and those in the village with access to horses."

"I doona trust the word of a MacKay," Ross growled.

"You are trying my patience, son-in-law. Now then, what did you expect to gain by returning Gillian to Braeburn?"

"I canna abide betrayal."

"And you think my Gillian betrayed you."

"It crossed my mind," Ross bit out. "The raid could have been planned well before our marriage, in which case Gillian would have had knowledge of it."

"You are wrong, dead wrong. Do you think I would give my daughter to you, knowing you might harm her if I were behind the raid? Nay, make no mistake: I love my lass well, MacKenna. I also ken how she thinks. I wish you luck in making your apology to her."

"Do you swear you werena behind the raid?" Ross asked, searching Tearlach's eyes for a hint of truth.

"I swear on the grave of my Maudie, Gillian's mother. I didna break the truce. And I am willing to speak for my sons and kinsmen."

Ross slumped against the back of his chair. "Who else would dare such a thing?"

"I doona know. But as long as you and Gillian are here, you may as well stay for the wedding. We can try to solve the mystery together during the festivities. Besides, Gillian needs time to cool off. She may not want to return to Ravenscraig with you. You werena kind to the lass, MacKenna."

"I didna hurt her," Ross said.

"Mayhap not physically." Tearlach sighed heavily.

"Ah, well, Gillian is your problem, lad. I'm sure you'll find a way to get back in her good graces."

Tearlach waved a servant over and ordered whiskey for him and his guest. When it arrived, Tearlach tossed it back neat while Ross sipped his, a thoughtful look on his face as he contemplated this latest turn of events. If MacKay wasn't behind the raid, who was? Who wanted the truce broken? Ross expressed his thoughts to Tearlach.

Tearlach shook his head. "I doona ken, lad. My clansmen and allies are aware that the feud ended with the wedding between you and Gillian. Everyone agreed to honor the truce."

"Everyone except Angus Sinclair, I'd wager."

"Ah, well, Angus," Tearlach said. "He could have had Gillian if he'd spoken up sooner. While we always assumed Sinclair and Gillian would wed, no formal declaration had been made nor betrothal papers signed." He shrugged expansively. "Sinclair declared himself too late."

Ross asked the question he had been dreading: "Did Gillian love Sinclair?"

"We both ken that women are capricious creatures, lad. They are in love with the word *love*. I suppose she fancied herself enamored of Sinclair."

"I found them together on the moors one day. I doona know if the meeting had been prearranged or not, but Sinclair was trying to convince Gillian to run off with him."

Tearlach's shaggy brows shot upward. "But she didna, did she? That should tell you something."

Ross's voice hardened. "It told me that I arrived in time to prevent Gillian from leaving with Sinclair."

"Are you dissatisfied with your marriage, MacKenna? I know Gillian can be a handful, but . . ."

Ross gave a rueful laugh. "Handful? Is that what you call her?" He sobered, sipped his whiskey, and considered MacKay's original question. Was he really dissatisfied with his marriage?

In bed, he and Gillian were equals. She responded enthusiastically to his lovemaking and followed no matter where he led. She was his flame, beautiful, spirited, and bright. Thus far he had been able to avoid being consumed by her fiery spirit. Unfortunately, taming her was going to take a great deal more time and effort.

"I canna truthfully say I am dissatisfied with the marriage," Ross admitted. " 'Twould help if Gillian wasna so prickly. She seems to resent me and my kinsmen. She is verra slow to put aside the feud."

"Ah, well, there is naught I can do about her attitude; her behavior is no longer my concern. You are her husband; she is your problem now."

Ross sought to change the subject. His headstrong wife wasn't his only problem. "The Sinclairs are your allies. Is there a reason the Sinclair chieftain would want the truce broken? Gillian is no longer available. You ken the raiders tried to make it look like the MacKays broke the truce, do you nae?"

"Aye, I ken and I doona like it. But I canna lay the blame on Sinclair without proof. If he is behind the raid, I doona ken why."

"Without a confession, we have no proof," Ross said sourly. He tossed back the rest of his whiskey and rose.

"Where are you going?"

"Home."

"I hoped you and Gillian would stay for Murdoc's wedding."

"We'll be back in plenty of time for the ceremony. We are nae properly dressed for a wedding."

"Aye, well, if you say so. The wedding will commence in three days at the hour of sext. Plan to stay the night or longer, if you wish."

"Verra well. I'll go fetch Gillian."

"Her chamber is on the second floor, first door on the right. Good luck," Tearlach ventured, chuckling to himself.

Ross found Gillian's chamber easily enough, but when he tried the latch, he discovered the door locked against him. "Gillian, open the door."

"Go away, MacKenna."

"I'm ready to leave, Gillian, and you're coming with me. I am satisfied that your father had naught to do with the theft of my cows."

"I'm not going anywhere with you, MacKenna."

"Gillian, be reasonable."

"How can I be reasonable when you dragged me out of bed, called me a viper, and accused me of betraying you? I am where I belong. Go away and leave me alone."

"You are my wife, Gillian."

"To my everlasting regret," Gillian shot back.

"Open the door!" Ross ordered. "I doona enjoy talking to a piece of wood."

"And I doona enjoy talking to an arrogant wretch who calls himself a warrior."

"I *am* a warrior!" Ross thundered.

The door opened. A fuming Gillian stood on the threshold, wearing braies and wielding a sword. "Prove it," she spat. "Prove you are a warrior," she demanded, raising her sword in a challenge.

Once Ross's anger subsided, he attempted a conciliatory manner. "You ken I doona fight women, do you nae?"

"I ken, but I intend to change your mind. If I win, you will return to Ravenscraig alone and I will live out the rest of my days at Braeburn. If you win, I will accompany you to Ravenscraig peaceably."

"Put down the sword, lass. You ken you canna win. Your brother is taking a wife soon. There will be no place for you in the keep; you will become a burden to your family."

"This is my home. There will always be a place here for me. Besides, you doona trust me, and your kinsmen hate me. I prefer to remain where I am loved and trusted."

She thrust her sword forward, forcing Ross to back up. "You forget one thing, Gillian. We are married. I can force you to return to Ravenscraig and neither your father nor brothers would dare say me nay."

"Take up your sword, MacKenna. Doona be a coward. Fight me for my right to direct my own fate."

"I promised your father I wouldna harm you. If I take up a sword against you, you would lose the battle and mayhap die. Is that what you want, wife?"

"What I want is to be treated with respect and dignity. There is naught between us but mistrust."

A slow grin curved Ross's lips. "You are wrong, lass. We are good together in bed. Have I not proved that to you?"

The sword wavered in Gillian's hands but did not lower. Ross thought she looked adorably distraught. He did not doubt, however, that she would run him through if he continued to provoke her. But would she actually aim to kill? He rather doubted it, but wasn't willing to take that chance. He waited for the opportunity to disarm her without hurting her. As for drawing his sword against her, he simply wouldn't do it.

"Doona treat me like a frail female, MacKenna, for it willna work."

"You realize, do you nae, that if you leave my home and protection, the truce will be broken? 'Twas part of the agreement between me and your father."

Gillian seemed to mull that over. Ross thought she had never looked more beautiful or desirable. The flame that was her spirit burned bright.

"If we make a private agreement to duel for my freedom, it will have naught to do with the truce."

Ross was beginning to grow angry. "Forget it, Gillian. You're coming home with me, and that's final. Drop the sword."

Gillian really didn't want to hurt Ross, but she could not give in. If she returned meekly home with Ross, what would stop him from accusing her of betrayal another time and dragging her to Braeburn again? She couldn't bear the ridicule. This had to be settled here and now. One way or another.

"Nay, MacKenna. Fight me or let me stay where I willna be accused of betrayal at the slightest provocation."

Gillian was more than a little surprised when Ross drew his sword. "Verra well. We will take this outside."

"You're going to fight me?"

"'Tis what you want, so we might as well get on with it."

"Aye. Aye," she repeated more forcefully.

"After you," Ross said, indicating that she should precede him down the stairs.

Gillian didn't trust him. "Nay, after you."

Ross shrugged, turned, and proceeded down the

stairs. "You wouldna take advantage of me while my back is turned, would you?" he taunted.

Affronted, Gillian gave a huff of disgust. "I amna an assassin. Keep walking, MacKenna."

Tearlach, Murdoc, and Nab were in the hall, talking to several of their kinsmen. Conversation ceased when they saw Ross and Gillian walking toward the front door with swords drawn.

"What's this?" Tearlach asked, reaching for his own weapon. "Is there an enemy within?"

"I'm going to fight MacKenna for the right to remain at Braeburn, Da," Gillian said.

All eyes swung to Ross. "Is that right, MacKenna?"

Ross shrugged. " 'Tis what Gillian wants."

"Are you daft, lass? You are no match for a Highland warrior. Did you learn naught from your last encounter with MacKenna?"

"This is my life, Da. Doona question my motives or belittle my skill."

"Be reasonable, Gillian," Murdoc pleaded. "Challenging your husband will gain you naught. And you, MacKenna, are you eager to do grave injury to your wife?"

"I promised your father I wouldna hurt your sister, Murdoc, and I intend to keep my promise."

"MacKenna canna hurt me," Gillian claimed. "I willna let him. You and I crossed swords in practice many times, Murdoc, and you didna hurt me, not once."

"Da would have thrashed him if he did," Nab interjected. "Be sensible, Gillian. Stop this now lest you live to regret it. No one, neither Da nor I, can stop MacKenna from punishing you for this folly if he so chooses."

Gillian sent Ross a sidelong glance. He didn't seem particularly angry. He appeared calm, far too calm for her peace of mind. She squared her shoulders and marched out the door. If she didn't show him the error of his ways she would never earn his respect.

"Are you coming, MacKenna?" she threw over her shoulder.

"Nay, but I hope to verra soon," he said, tongue in cheek.

Behind her, Gillian heard her father and brothers chuckle. Her face reddened until it matched the color of her hair.

Tearlach caught up with Ross. "Surely you're not going to fight the lass, are you?"

Ross pulled away. "If I doona, she will think me a coward. If naught else, this will teach Gillian a lesson. Fear not, MacKay; Gillian will come out of this unscathed."

"I pray you are right, MacKenna," Tearlach warned. "For if my lass is harmed . . ." His sentence trailed off, but his meaning was clear.

"Have our horses saddled and Gillian's trunk loaded in the cart," Ross said in an aside to Murdoc. "I'm taking Gillian home to Ravenscraig as soon as this is finished."

Gillian halted in the courtyard just short of the gate, where there was sufficient room for maneuvering. Then she took a fighter's stance and whirled to challenge Ross. He ambled toward her, seemingly unfazed as he watched her through narrowed lids.

"Make your move, Gillian, but be sure your heart is in it before you attack me."

"Of course my heart is in it," Gillian shot back. "You embarrassed me in front of your kinsmen. You called me a traitor, a viper, and other hurtful names. You jumped to conclusions without proof and dragged me to Braeburn in shame. You care naught for me, MacKenna. Not that I expected more from you. We are enemies, forced to wed to save our clans."

"We are enemies no longer, lass. You could be carrying my bairn."

Gillian lowered her sword a little, confusion marring her smooth brow.

" 'Tis possible, you ken?" He made a slashing motion with his sword. "Would you risk the life of our bairn to satisfy your pride?"

Gillian hesitated. She truly didn't believe there was a bairn growing inside her, but that brief moment of hesitation nearly undid her. Ross lunged for her sword. Regaining her wits, she whirled away.

"Doona even think it, MacKenna."

She tightened her grasp on the sword hilt and thrust it forward. She had initiated the fight; now she waited for Ross to retaliate so the battle could begin in earnest. Ross sidestepped Gillian's thrust easily and made no move to engage her. Gillian thrust again. She didn't want to kill Ross, but she had no compunction about nicking his skin and drawing a wee bit of blood. Her pride demanded that she make an effort to punish him for shaming her.

Angry and frustrated, Gillian began to stalk Ross, willing him to stand still so she could gain satisfaction. But the pompous ass kept evading her blade. Then, like a streak of lightning, Ross made his move. When Gillian responded, Ross whipped his sword upward, catching the hilt of Gillian's blade. With a twist of his wrist, Gillian's sword flew into the air. It landed near Nab. He calmly picked it up and handed it to Tearlach.

" 'Tis done, lass," Tearlach said. "Go home with your husband."

When Gillian looked as if she were going to protest, Ross reminded her of their pact. "I disarmed you with little effort. 'Tis time you acknowledged that I am the better swordsman."

"Mind your husband," Tearlach advised. "Return to Ravenscraig and give him an heir or two."

Before Gillian realized what Ross intended, he scooped her into his arms and deposited her onto the back of her horse. "We will return for the wedding, MacKay. Count on it. Meanwhile, learn what you can about the reivers, and I shall do the same."

"Are you going to let him do this, Da?" Gillian pleaded. "What about you?" she cried, turning to her brothers. "Help me!"

Murdoc and Nab were laughing so hard, Gillian would have bashed them with a weapon if one had been available. The final indignity occurred when Ross refused to hand over Silver's reins to her. He led her mount as if she were a disobedient child in need of chastising.

"If I canna handle my own horse, let me ride in the cart with my trunk," Gillian said.

Ross's answer was to knee his horse into a gallop, forcing Silver to keep up. The fact that she was able to remain in the saddle was a testament to Gillian's superb horsemanship.

Gillian was cold, hungry, and exhausted by the time they reached Ravenscraig a good three hours later. A light snow had begun to fall, and the wind had risen. Gillian looked forward to warming herself before the hearth, even if it was MacKenna's hearth.

Gordo met them at the door. "Why did you bring her back, lad?"

"I was wrong, Uncle. MacKay wasna behind the raid."

"How can you be sure?"

119

"Let's just say that sufficient proof existed to exonerate the MacKays. By the way, we're invited to a wedding. Murdoc MacKay is marrying his sweetheart."

Ross lifted Gillian to the ground and guided her up the stairs into the warmth of the hall. Gillian headed straight for the fire blazing cheerfully in the hearth.

"Bring food and drink to my chamber," Ross said to a passing servant.

Gillian was aware that everyone was staring at her, and not in a good way. "They hate me," she said when Ross joined her.

As if aware of the animosity aimed at Gillian, Ross held up his hand for silence. "I was wrong," he announced. "The MacKays didna break the truce; nor was my lady responsible in any way for the raid. Gillian is my wife, and I willna have her treated with anything but respect. Is that clear?"

Gillian heard a scattering of *ayes* that were half-hearted at best.

"Only a fool would believe a MacKay," Seana snarled, sashaying up to join them. "You are thinking with your cock, Ross MacKenna. Mayhap when you've had your fill of the red-haired witch you will listen to your head and toss her out on her arse."

Gillian had had all she could take of Seana's insults. In fact, this day had been one disaster after another. She had to retaliate or burst. Hauling back her arm, she swung at Seana. Her fist connected with Seana's jaw, sending her sprawling at Ross's feet.

Stunned, Ross looked first at Gillian and then at Seana, who was just beginning to stir. Holding back his laughter, Ross seized Gillian's waist, flung her over his shoulder like a sack of wheat, and headed toward the stairs, one hand planted firmly on her curvy bottom.

Chapter Eight

"What do you think you're doing?" Gillian demanded when Ross set her on her feet in their bedchamber. "I am perfectly capable of walking up the stairs on my own."

Ross grinned. "Are you capable of walking away from Seana without killing her?"

"That's a different matter. She may have started this brawl, but I'm willing to finish it."

"Forget Seana. Do you recall what I said about drawing a sword on me the last time you attempted it?"

Gillian sent him a wary look. "You said I would be sorry."

"Are you?"

She raised her chin. "Not yet."

Ross reached for her. She tried to sidle away, but he was too fast for her. "Every instinct tells me you deserve to be punished."

Her chin rose even higher. "Go ahead, if you dare."

"Your father and brothers wouldna stop me."

"Nay, they wouldna," Gillian acknowledged, sounding not at all repentant.

"I have never raised a hand to a woman. Nor do I make a habit of engaging in swordplay with one. You, my spirited wife, have made me rethink my position."

Gillian blinked. "What are you going to do?"

Winding a lock of flame-bright hair around his fist, he pulled her face close, until their noses were touching. "What do you think I *should* do? If you were me, what mode of punishment would you advise?"

Gillian forced a smile. "Were I you, I would congratulate you for showing spirit in face of adversity. Few wives have the courage to protect themselves against brutal husbands."

Ross's brows flew together. "You think me brutal?"

Gillian could not lie. "I . . . Nay, you have shown considerable restraint for a man of your sort."

"This keeps getting better and better," Ross growled, clearly not amused. "What sort am I, pray tell?"

Gillian stared directly into his blue eyes; she couldn't have looked away even if she'd wanted to. "You are a MacKenna; does that answer your question? We wouldna have wed had circumstances not demanded it of us."

His mouth was nearly touching hers when he said, "You are a MacKenna now, too, Gillian. As badly as I want to beat you, I canna do it. I will, however, have your promise that you will never take up a sword against me again."

"Does that include a dirk?" Gillian asked sweetly.

"Let me rephrase that. Your promise encompasses all weapons, including your fists, which you just proved can be dangerous. My clansmen will think me weak if I doona break your habit of wielding weapons. They already think me pathetic for not beating you."

A smile kicked up a corner of Gillian's lush mouth.

"Gillian."

"Oh, verra well, I promise . . . but only until you do something that warrants my taking up a weapon."

"*Gillian.*"

"Doona scold me, MacKenna. A woman must have the means to defend herself."

Ross sighed. "We'll discuss this later."

"What are you going to do now?"

"We will sup first, and then I'm going below to repair the damage you did with your fist."

"Seana deserved it."

Ross's lips twitched. "Aye, she did."

"Are you laughing at me, MacKenna?"

"Och, can you blame me? You are one of a kind, lass." He let her hair slip through his fingers, mesmerized by the flow of living flame that cascaded over his hand.

"I am going to kiss you," Ross whispered scant moments before his mouth clamped over hers.

Gillian felt the fervor of his kiss clear down to her toes. Resisting something she found so enjoyable was impossible. She leaned into his hard body and kissed him back. She knew Ross would have taken the kiss to the ultimate conclusion had a timid knock not sounded on the door.

Ross sighed regretfully. "That will be our food." He set her aside and opened the door to Alice and her cousin Annie, each carrying a tray.

"Set the food on the table," Gillian said over the rumbling of her stomach.

Ross pulled a chair up for Gillian and one for himself. Then he joined her at the table.

"There's water heating in the kitchen for Gillian's bath," Alice said before she and Annie departed. Gillian smiled her thanks.

They ate ravenously: cock-a-leekie soup, slices of leftover boiled beef, root vegetables, and thick slices of bread slathered with butter. Once he had eaten his fill, Ross slid his chair back and rose.

"I'll leave you to your bath while I go below and try to placate Seana."

"Why do you even bother?" Gillian huffed.

"For many reasons. My kinsmen were angry with you earlier today. I need to make sure they understand you had naught to do with the raid."

Ross took his leave of her when the tub and water bearers arrived. He descended the stairs, wondering what had taken place during his absence. He found a knot of people gathered around Seana. He forced his way through until he reached her side. She was holding a wet cloth to her cheek and chin. When she saw Ross, she removed the cloth, revealing a purple bruise.

"See what that traitorous witch did to me?" Seana screeched.

"Gillian is no traitor." He raised his voice so all could hear him. "Though I have already said this, I will say it again: No MacKay was responsible for the raid. My wife isna a traitor."

Seana raised tear-filled eyes to him. "The redheaded witch hurt me, and you allowed it."

Ross sighed. "You should have held your tongue, woman. I doona blame Gillian for retaliating. 'Tis time you left Ravenscraig, Seana." He looked around. "Where is Niall?"

Niall stepped forward. "I am here, Ross."

"Will you escort Seana to her father's keep tomorrow? She has insulted my wife one time too many."

"I doona want to leave, Ross," Seana said, pouting. "I've made my home at Ravenscraig. My father's new wife is relieved to be rid of me and willna welcome me back."

"Nevertheless . . ."

"I want to wed the lass, Ross," Niall said. "Seana means well. I will make her behave. Doona send her away."

"Och, Niall, are you certain you want that kind of responsibility? I doona think Seana would fit in here. She and Gillian doona get along."

"I can handle Seana; I promise."

Ross could not deny his kinsman, even though he feared Niall didn't realize what he was getting into. Then again, marriage might be exactly what Seana needed to silence her acid tongue. He considered the match for a moment and arrived at a better solution.

"Would you consider handfasting, Niall?"

Niall thought about it and nodded. "If that will convince you I am serious, Seana and I will handfast for a year and a day."

"Will you take Niall for your handfast husband, Seana?" Ross asked. "Can you be a faithful and dutiful wife for a year and a day?"

Seana slid Niall a sidelong glance. "Can we live at Ravenscraig?"

Niall turned to Ross. "What say you, Ross?"

" 'Tis against my better judgment, but if you can control Seana, then I suppose you can both live here. But at the first sign of trouble, I will ask you to take Seana elsewhere."

"Agreed," Niall said.

Ross's sweeping glance encompassed everyone in the hall. "Hear this," he proclaimed loudly. "If anyone insults my bride, he or she will earn my wrath. Neither my wife nor her family was responsible for the raid. I swear I will get to the bottom of this. Both MacKay and I want peace between our clans."

Turning on his heel, Ross headed toward the stairs and almost ran over Gizela. "Doona sneak up on me like that, Gizela. How can I help you?"

"Beware of the viper, laird."

Ross stiffened. "Are you referring to my wife?"

"The viper, laird, send her away."

"Send who away? Nay, doona tell me. 'Tis difficult to believe anything you say. Have you no one to heal?"

"I can give you a charm to win your wife's heart, laird. She is nae too happy with you just now."

"First you call her a viper and then you wish to help me win her heart. Make up your mind."

Gizela looked startled. "You misheard me, laird. I go now to prepare the charm."

"Forget it," Ross called after her as she scurried off. He continued up the stairs, shaking his head. Gizela's words were mostly puzzles no one could solve. He didn't know why he even bothered.

To Ross's regret, Gillian was sleeping when he entered the bedchamber. She appeared so deeply asleep he didn't attempt to awaken her. He spied the tub set up before the hearth and tested the water. It was still warm, and he hadn't bathed yet. He undressed, climbed into the tub, and made good use of the soap. Because the water was cooling rapidly, he didn't linger. He left the tub, used Gillian's discarded towel to dry himself, and climbed into bed beside her.

She was warm and soft and oh, so tempting. And she smelled heavenly. His arm stole around her waist, and he pulled her into the curve of his body. She sighed but didn't open her eyes. Would she be angry if he awakened her? he wondered. He wanted her. Ross didn't understand his constant need for his reluctant bride. Even though she reviled him and considered him an enemy, her response to his lovemaking was anything but reserved.

Gillian was an enthusiastic lover, a fact Ross thoroughly appreciated and very much enjoyed. Though she claimed to prefer Angus Sinclair, she wasn't a wee bit reticent about responding to him. The woman was an enigma, one Ross hadn't been able to figure out yet. Of course, he hadn't helped his cause by jumping to conclusions about her kinsmen. The raid was another puzzling, potentially disastrous situation, one he hoped to solve before his clansmen clamored for the feud to resume.

The feel of Gillian resting warm and supple in his arms distracted Ross's thoughts, making him painfully aware of his erection. He inched closer to her, felt himself lengthen and thicken, and pressed the head of his engorged cock into the hot crevice between her thighs.

Ross tried to sleep, but his body was too tense, too needy. Still, he resisted waking her. But naught could stop him from exploring her lush curves, inhaling the arousing scent of her. His hand settled on her knee, and then moved upward, over the smooth expanse of her thigh and the gentle curve of her hip.

Though Ross knew he should stop, he couldn't. His wandering hand found her breast. He cupped it, toying with her nipple. He smiled when he felt the tip harden and elongate. He squeezed gently. Did she realize she was responding to his touch without conscious knowledge?

A soft gasp warned Ross that Gillian had awakened. "What are you doing?"

"You're awake."

"I am now. Go to sleep. Mayhap you're not as tired as I am."

He flexed his hips, his erection probing relentlessly against the soft hollow between her thighs. "I want you, lass."

"Nay, MacKenna, I am angry with you. I want naught to do with you."

"I doona believe you."

He turned her on her back so he could reach her mouth. Then he kissed her. At first her lips remained tightly closed, hard and unyielding. He probed them gently with his tongue, then more firmly, until they parted beneath his. Groaning, he entered the warm cavern, tasting her sweetness even as he knew that her mind had yet to accept him.

"Surrender, Gillian," Ross whispered against her lips. "Your flame burns brightly; only I can douse the fire smoldering inside you. I will chase the flame until you yield."

Gillian said naught as he kissed a burning path along her cheekbone, down her slender throat to her breast, where her nipple begged for his attention. He heard her moan when he took the tender morsel into his mouth and suckled. She arched the fluid curve of her back, panting softly.

"Do you yield to me, love?"

"I . . . am . . . not . . . your . . . love."

Her actions denied her words as her arms crept around him, pulling him closer. She rose against him, pressing her breast more firmly into his mouth. Pleased with her response, Ross alternated between one breast and the other, suckling her nipples into hard points. When she began writhing beneath him, his mouth left her breasts, kissing a trail of fire down her taut stomach to the patch of fiery hair at the juncture of her thighs.

"Ross."

Though his name was no more than a sigh on her lips, Ross accepted it as her surrender.

"Aye, love, I ken what you want."

He parted her tender nether lips with his fingers; she was hot and slick, and they slid inside on a cushion of honeyed dew. He moved them in and out until he felt her body grow taut, felt the tension coil inside her, felt her headlong rush to completion. She cried out in protest when he withdrew his fingers, then sighed with pleasure when he placed his mouth where his fingers had been.

He aroused her slowly, adeptly, his tongue teasing then darting inside, only to retreat and begin anew. She grasped his head between her hands, holding him in place while he continued his sweet torture. When he felt her start to shatter, he crawled up her body and shoved his aching cock inside her, burying himself deep as she spasmed around him.

Then he began to thrust in and out, faster, harder, deeper. The firestorm within her reignited, intensified; he heard her moan, felt her slick passage clench around him, stirring him to greater heights. He exploded in a rush of hot seed as she climaxed a second time. A long while passed before Ross could breathe, let alone move. Gillian must have felt trapped beneath his weight, for he felt her push against his chest. Only then did he summon the energy to lift himself off her.

Gillian rolled away from Ross, too disgusted with her easy surrender to face him. He had but to touch her and she yielded. Had she no pride? How could her body betray her when her mind rejected him utterly? He had shamed her before his clansmen, who distrusted and disliked her because she was a MacKay.

He touched her arm. "Gillian, are you all right?"

"Aye. Are you happy now that you got what you wanted?"

"I made us both happy. Go to sleep, lass."

"Not yet, MacKenna. Tell me what happened belowstairs. Are your kinsmen still angry at me?"

"I spoke with them. They ken that your kinsmen are nae to blame for the raid. I suspect you will find them more respectful than they have been in the past."

She rose up on her elbow. "What about Seana? Did you send her away?"

A log in the grate sparked, briefly illuminating his face. His frown told her what she wanted to know. "I canna believe you let her stay," Gillian scolded. "Unless"—she bit her bottom lip—"you intend to bed her yourself. I willna stand for it, MacKenna. You have shamed me enough."

She started to leave the bed, but Ross stopped her by wrapping his arms around her. "Och, lass, I doona want Seana. She is handfasted to Niall. I couldna turn them both out."

"I heard naught of a handfasting."

"It happened when I returned to the hall. I asked Niall to escort Seana to her father's keep. He asked permission to handfast with her instead."

"You shouldna have allowed it. Seana is a troublemaker. She still wants you. Think you handfasting with Niall will keep her happy and out of trouble?"

"Niall is a braw lad, capable of controlling his woman. Now go to sleep. Tomorrow we will prepare for our return to Braeburn to attend your brother's wedding."

A large group of MacKennas left Ravenscraig two days later shortly after daybreak. A small number of men were left behind to defend the tower against attack, though in truth none was expected. Gillian and Ross rode at the head of the contingent, which included Gordo, Niall, and Seana.

They arrived at Braeburn a few hours later, in time to join a prewedding celebration. Even amid the air of jubilation, Ross felt a stirring of disquiet, as if something unexpected was about to happen. He prowled the hall but could find naught amiss. He raised a tankard of ale with a group of MacKays, impressed with their friendliness and camaraderie. This wouldn't be possible if the clans were still feuding.

Ross caught sight of Gillian across the crowded hall, talking and laughing with a group of her kinswomen. Naught seemed amiss there. He spied Gordo and made his way to him, stopping along the way to congratulate Murdoc on his upcoming nuptials.

"What think you, Uncle?" Ross asked when he reached Gordo.

" 'Tis a fine gathering of former enemies," Gordo said dryly. He slanted a glance at his nephew. "What's amiss? You look troubled."

"I doona know, Gordo. I canna put my finger on it. All seems well, but I amna convinced. Have you seen a Sinclair in the crowd?"

Gordo glanced slowly about the hall, trying to identify the different plaids. "Nay, I see no Sinclairs, but that doesna mean they are nae here."

Tearlach MacKay strode up and clapped Ross on the back. "I see you've succeeded in making peace with my daughter, son-in-law."

"It wasna easy," Ross admitted. "Gillian's temper is a fearsome thing."

Tearlach chuckled. "That it is. 'Tis glad I am to see you both. Bringing our clansmen together like this will go a long way to ensure peace between future generations. I want Murdoc's bairns to live without fear. I ken not all Highland clans feel the same, but mayhap a lasting peace between the MacKays and MacKennas will inspire others to follow our example."

Ross nodded agreement. "Are all your allies expected to attend the celebration?"

"Aye."

"What about the Sinclairs? I doona see any of them in the hall."

"Angus sent word that he and his clansmen would arrive in time for the ceremony tomorrow."

When Ross merely grunted, Tearlach moved on.

Gordo searched Ross's face for several heartbeats before asking, "What are you thinking, lad?"

"I doona trust Sinclair. If he doesna show up tomorrow, I'm thinking we should head back to Ravenscraig instead of lingering here to celebrate, as we originally planned."

"Whatever you decide is fine with me, Ross. I learned long ago to trust your judgment."

As it happened, Angus Sinclair arrived with a small group of his kinsmen the following morning, well before the ceremony was to begin. Ross was standing beside Gillian as he watched Sinclair wade into the crowd before being swallowed up by the solid mass of humanity waiting to proceed to the kirk.

"I need a heavier shawl," Gillian remarked as a blast of cold air rolled in through the open door. "Wait here, Ross. I willna be long."

Ross wasn't going anywhere. He was too intent on keeping an eye on Sinclair, though he had no idea where the man had disappeared to. "Hurry," Ross said. "The procession to the kirk is about to begin."

"Go on without me if I'm not back," Gillian said. "I'll join you at the kirk."

Gillian hurried off to her chamber. She found her heavy plaid shawl where she had left it and exchanged it for the lighter-weight one she was wearing. When she heard the door open and shut behind her, she smiled and turned, expecting to see an impatient Ross.

"Angus! What are you doing here?"

"I need to talk to you. When I saw you go up to your chamber, I followed."

More than a little angry, Gillian snapped, "Make it fast, Angus. Ross is waiting for me."

"He left for the kirk with the others. We are quite alone."

A frisson of apprehension slid down her spine. "This isna right. We shouldna be alone in my bedchamber. You can tell me what you wish to say on the way to the kirk." She reached for the door latch.

Angus was there before her. "Are you happy, Gillian?"

"Happy enough," Gillian admitted. "What is this about?"

"We cared for each other, lass. 'Twas me you wanted to wed; me you *should* have wed."

"We canna change what happened, Angus. I am

133

wed to Ross now; there is naught either of us can do about it."

"You're wrong, Gillian. There is a great deal I can do about it. You can come with me now. According to the agreement between your father and MacKenna, if you leave your husband, the feud will resume."

"I doona ken why you wish to sabotage the truce."

"And I doona ken why you wish to live with the enemy. I am willing to have you even if MacKenna had you first."

"I canna do it, Angus. 'Tis true I wanted to wed you; why did you nae speak up sooner? Now I have spoken my vows. I am legally joined to Ross; naught will change that."

"How can you give your body to the enemy? How can you endure the shame?"

Ross's lovemaking wasn't difficult to endure, Gillian thought, smiling inwardly. It was pure magic. As for shame, if her father and brothers felt no shame dealing with Ross MacKenna, then why should she? Besides, she had begun to realize there was more to Ross than his mighty sword arm and skill as a warrior. It was difficult to think of Ross as an enemy when he had been inside her body, giving her more pleasure than she could bear.

"There is no shame to be had in the marriage bed," Gillian maintained.

"Do you enjoy kissing the MacKenna, Gillian?"

Gillian merely stared at him.

"Let me show you how a real man kisses."

Though Gillian knew what Angus intended, she was unarmed and defenseless. Snagging her around the waist, he dragged her against him and claimed her mouth with ruthless determination. His lips were demanding, hard, nearly painfully so. He backed her toward the bed. She resisted; he persisted. His tongue demanded entrance to her mouth, but she stubbornly refused to open.

The back of her knees hit the edge of the bed. She went down heavily, taking all of his weight as he followed her down. She felt him tugging her skirts upward and pounded him on the back. When she opened her mouth to scream, he thrust his tongue down her throat. She retaliated by clamping down hard with her teeth. He jerked back and cursed.

"Give over, Gillian. You know you want me."

She pushed against him. "Why are you doing this, Angus?"

Both looked up when the door burst open. "What in the hell is going on here?" Ross snarled.

Angus leaped to his feet. "It should be obvious, MacKenna. Gillian and I arranged this meeting. She doesna want you. 'Twas always me she wanted."

Gillian scooted off the bed, so angry with Angus she wanted to take up her sword and run him through. Then she looked into Ross's face and lost the ability to speak. She had never seen him like this. The stark planes of his face were rigid with rage, his hands clenched into fists, his eyes cold and flat.

"Ross . . . I—"

"What do you have to say for yourself, Gillian?" Ross asked through clenched teeth.

"I didna invite Angus to my chamber."

Ross skewered Sinclair with a look that would have felled a man with a conscience. "Is what Gillian said true, Sinclair?"

"Gillian never wanted to wed you, MacKenna," Sinclair confided. "She and I had an understanding. I would have wed her had you not interfered. She invited me up here. I could deny her naught."

"You lie!" Gillian cried. "Doona believe him, Ross."

"Get out!" Ross ordered, pointing Sinclair toward the door.

Once they were alone, Gillian said, "He is lying, Ross; I swear it."

Gillian shivered beneath his cool regard. "We will discuss this later, Gillian. We're late. We must leave for the kirk immediately." He found her plaid, wrapped it about her shoulders, and escorted her from the chamber.

Tearlach was waiting for them at the kirk. "Where have you been?" he admonished. "We held the ceremony for you."

"We were unavoidably detained," Ross explained as he guided Gillian to the pew reserved for family.

Gillian was quick to note that Angus was sitting in the kirk with other members of his clan. Moments later Murdoc's bonny bride appeared and the wedding commenced. Ross remained blessedly mute, though his expression was no less fierce. Did he really believe she had invited Angus to her chamber?

The ceremony was brief but meaningful. Gillian shed tears of happiness for Murdoc. For the first time since the truce, she realized how much peace meant to her family. Because of the constant fighting, her brothers had deliberately refrained from taking brides, lest they be killed in one of the frequent battles with the MacKennas and leave their wives widows. Now, mayhap Ramsey and Nab would consider marrying and settling down, too.

The celebration continued in Braeburn's great hall. After a meal that seemed to drag on forever, the tables were cleared so dancing could begin.

Ross had never felt jealousy before and scarcely recognized his reaction to the scene in Gillian's bedroom. He had always known that she preferred Angus Sinclair to him, but he had hoped she would settle into their marriage without too many regrets. From what he had observed earlier in her chamber, she still yearned for Sinclair.

Ross glanced around the hall, noting that Sinclair was speaking earnestly to Seana. Where was Niall? He angled a look at Gillian, surprised to see her staring at Sinclair and Seana, too.

"I didna know they were friends," Gillian remarked, gesturing toward the couple.

"Neither did I, although 'tisna odd. Clan McHamish is neutral, friends to both Clan MacKay and Clan MacKenna. They have never taken sides."

The commotion in the hall grew more intense as the tables were pushed against the wall and people crowded around the bride and groom to offer congratulations and words of advice.

"We need to talk about what happened in your chamber earlier," Ross said. "If we leave now, our absence willna be noticed."

Gillian stared at Ross for the space of two heartbeats and then nodded. Ross had difficulty looking away from the mesmerizing depths of her emerald-green eyes. They sucked him in and would have devoured him if he hadn't found the strength to turn away.

"Come," he said, guiding her from the hall. No one seemed to notice them slip away and mount the stairs to Gillian's old chamber.

The moment Ross closed the door, Gillian rounded on him. "I didna invite Angus into my chamber. You accuse me falsely, MacKenna."

"I've accused you of naught . . . yet." He glanced at the mussed bed, his expression brittle with disgust. "Please explain why you and Sinclair were rolling around on the bed like animals in heat."

"If I had my sword, I would run you through for that remark. Any fool could see Angus was attacking me and I was resisting."

Ross could do naught but stare at her; she was magnificent in her fury. No flame burned brighter than Gillian. She almost made him forget he wanted to take her to task for inviting Sinclair's attention.

"Tell me what happened," he demanded.

Gillian slanted him a dismissive look. "I doona need to explain myself. If you refuse to believe me, 'tis your loss." She turned away.

"Oh, no, I need more than that, Gillian. Did you invite Sinclair into your chamber?"

She gave an exasperated huff. "Are you deaf? I already told you I didna."

"Are you saying he tried to force himself on you?"

"Are you daft as well as deaf, MacKenna? Of course he did, and that's all I'm going to say on the subject."

"If you are telling the truth, Sinclair will be made to pay for his insult to you."

Turning on his heel, he strode toward the door.

"Wait! What are you going to do?"

"Doona overset yourself, lass. 'Tis none of your concern. I will take care of Sinclair."

"Do naught to end the truce. 'Tis what Angus wants."

Ross spun around to face her. "Did he tell you that?"

"Not in so many words, but it was implied."

"Why? What does he hope to gain if the feud resumes?"

"I doona know."

Ross sent her a hard look. "Then 'tis up to me to find out."

With a lethal glint in his eyes and his hands clenched into fists, Ross stormed out.

Chapter Nine

The wedding celebration in the hall had become a noisy, drunken revelry. Though the bride and groom had disappeared, the festivities continued without them. Ross's anger still raged as he entered the hall and glanced about for Angus Sinclair. He saw the object of his animosity standing with Seana's father, Douglas McHamish, on the periphery of the crowd, and strode purposefully toward him.

Ross knew the moment Sinclair saw him, for Sinclair stiffened and assumed a confrontational stance.

"I'd like a private word with you, Sinclair," Ross bit out.

"I've been expecting you, MacKenna," Sinclair sneered. "There is an alcove nearby where we won't be interrupted."

His eyes cold and flat, his mouth turned down, Ross followed Sinclair around the perimeter of the hall and down a hallway, where he found a sparsely furnished alcove that held only a small table, two chairs, and a narrow sideboard.

"Have your say, MacKenna," Sinclair challenged. "I've naught to hide."

"You attacked my wife," Ross charged. "Tell me why I shouldna kill you."

"I entered Gillian's chamber at her behest." He sent Ross a sly smile. "Mayhap she wanted a real man in her bed."

Ross's temper hung by a slim thread. Another remark like that and it would snap.

"Gillian denies she invited you to her chamber."

"Aye, I ken why she would. She's afraid of you, MacKenna. Gillian wanted me long before you came into the picture."

"You think Gillian is afraid of me?" Ross snorted in disbelief. "Ha! My wife fears naught. If you knew her at all, you wouldna make such a foolish statement. Gillian said you wanted the feud to resume. I want to know why."

"Gillian misheard me. Surely you ken she was a reluctant bride. She didna want the truce; 'twas her father's idea."

Ross sent Sinclair a grim smile. "If you had any idea how much passion resides in Gillian's body, you wouldna have waited so long to claim her. She is magnificent, Sinclair. But Gillian's passion is mine alone. If you so much as look crosswise at her, I will kill you."

Sinclair did not appear intimidated despite Ross's threats. "If Gillian wants me badly enough, we will find a way for us to be together."

Sinclair's cockiness was more than enough to snap Ross's control. He seemed so sure of himself that Ross began to doubt Gillian. Had she lied to him about inviting Sinclair into her bedchamber? Had she fed him naught but lies? Ross had one more question to ask Sinclair before he beat the man to a bloody pulp.

"Gillian hasna been out of my sight since our arrival at Braeburn. When, pray tell, did she invite you to her bedchamber? Think carefully before you answer, Sinclair, for your life depends upon your reply."

"Ha! It should be obvious to you," Sinclair sneered. "When Gillian returned to her bedchamber before the procession to the kirk, she looked back and sent me a look that could be mistaken for naught but an invitation."

"You lie!" Ross shouted as he lunged for Sinclair. Though Sinclair could be telling the truth, Ross preferred not to believe it.

Ross had but a few pounds and a few inches on Sinclair, but rage made Ross the stronger man. They struggled violently, knocking over the chairs in the process and falling against the table. It splintered beneath their combined weight and broke apart. Finally Ross got the upper hand. Pressing his forearm against Sinclair's throat, Ross backed him against the wall.

"Tell me why you are working to destroy the truce."

Sinclair, unable to speak because of the pressure against his neck, merely shook his head.

"Admit you lied about Gillian inviting you to her bedchamber."

Naught emerged from Sinclair's throat but a gagging sound. Ross was too incensed to realize he was slowly choking Sinclair to death.

"What in God's name is going on in here?" Tearlach cried from the doorway. "We could hear the ruckus from the hall. MacKenna, release Sinclair before you kill him."

"The bastard attacked your daughter in her bedchamber," Ross bit out.

Tearlach skewered Sinclair with a look. "Is that true, Sinclair?"

His eyes bulging, unable to do more than make gurgling sounds, Sinclair tried to pry Ross's forearm away from his throat.

"Release him, MacKenna!" Tearlach demanded. "Let him speak."

Ross heard Tearlach's order through a red haze. He wanted to kill Sinclair; he truly did. But little by little he released the pressure and stepped away. Sinclair slumped against the wall and slid down.

"He tried to kill me," Sinclair croaked hoarsely.

"Did you attack my daughter?" Tearlach asked.

"Nay, Gillian invited me to her bedchamber."

"Gillian denies it," Ross growled. "He was forcing her when I burst into the chamber. If I hadna arrived in time . . ."

"I know my daughter, Sinclair, and she is no liar. I wouldna blame MacKenna if he killed you, but you are nae important enough to destroy the truce."

"Ask Sinclair why he wants the feud to resume," Ross prodded. "He hinted as much to Gillian."

Sinclair stared past Ross and Tearlach, his gaze stopping at the door. Both men turned to see what he was looking at.

"I thought I told you to remain in your chamber," Ross barked.

Gillian's gaze took in all three men. "I had to know what was going on down here."

"If I hadna stepped in, Ross would have killed Sinclair," Tearlach explained. "Tell me true, lass, did you invite Sinclair to your bedchamber?"

Gillian slanted a quick glance at Ross before answering. "Nay, Da, I didna. I doona know why Angus is lying."

" 'Tis not as though you are happy in your marriage," Sinclair snarled. "The look you gave me was all the invitation I needed to follow you to your chamber."

Tearlach ignored his outburst. "Did Sinclair say he wanted the feud to resume, daughter?"

"Not in so many words, but he hinted at it."

"I refuse to allow the truce to be broken over jealousy," Tearlach declared. "Gillian is wed to the MacKenna, and you, Sinclair, have no place in her life. Since I am inclined to believe my daughter, I think it best for all concerned that you and your kinsmen leave. I will countenance no more trouble in my home during this happy time.

"As for you, MacKenna, there will be no killing, do you ken? I want my future grandchildren to live in peace, and I am sure you and Gillian want the same."

"We do," Ross acknowledged, "but I canna promise to hold the peace if Sinclair continues to provoke my anger. He refuses to accept that Gillian is wed and no longer his for the taking."

"Is that your last word, MacKay? Are you banishing me from your home?" Sinclair asked.

"Aye, for the time being, Sinclair. Peace must be maintained."

"Verra well," Sinclair spat, slanting Ross a venomous look. "But when MacKenna breaks the truce and you need my help, you will pay hell to get it." He rose unsteadily to his feet and staggered off.

"You should have let me kill him," Ross groused. "He is not finished making trouble for us, I fear."

Tearlach shook his head. "I doona ken what Sinclair is about. He could have had Gillian anytime he wanted, but he waited until it was too late. He has no one but himself to blame."

"Do you ken his reasons for wanting the truce to end?" Ross asked.

"I canna believe he would jeopardize the peace. His clan has as much to gain by peaceful coexistence as we do."

"Angus does naught without a reason," Gillian volunteered. "If he thinks I would have him after what he did today, he is sadly mistaken."

Ross stared at her. "What are you saying, lass?"

Gillian looked her husband straight in the eye. "Angus isna the man I thought he was. I am glad I didna marry him. While I doona know what he is planning, it canna be good."

A smile played at the corners of Ross's mouth. He was glad he hadn't killed the bastard. If he had, he might never have gotten such an admission from Gillian.

"I will be ready for whatever he plans," Ross said. He turned to address Tearlach. "If I were you, I would watch Angus Sinclair closely."

"Aye, I ken," Tearlach acknowledged. "I'd best return to the hall. I want to see Sinclair and his kinsmen on their way."

Ross and Gillian left the alcove on Tearlach's heels. By mutual consent they made their way through the revelers in the hall, up the stairs, and to their bedchamber. The moment Ross closed the door behind them, he pulled Gillian into his arms and kissed her until she was breathless.

"I am glad you didna kill him," Gillian said when he allowed her to breathe again. "Da wants this truce more than anything."

"What about you, lass? There was a time you called me murderer, a time you would rather run me through than wed me. You told me often enough 'twas Sinclair you wanted."

"I canna go on hating you, Ross. 'Tis true I wanted Angus, and that I blamed you for my brothers' deaths, but 'tis likely you are going to be the father of my children, so 'tis time I realized that I must accept our marriage."

That wasn't exactly what Ross wanted to hear, but it would do for now. For the first time he felt that their marriage had a chance to survive and flourish. More existed between them than simple passion.

Ross, Gillian, and the kinsmen accompanying them left Braeburn two days later, even though the revelers continued to celebrate Murdoc's wedding. Murdoc and his bride had departed the day following their wedding to spend time in Inverness. Nab and Ramsey planned to leave the next day for Edinburgh, where they intended to spend the winter enjoying big-city life while Tearlach and Murdoc minded the keep in their absence.

The return journey to Ravenscraig proved uneventful. Not that Ross was expecting trouble. For the first time in generations, peace reigned in this part of the Highlands. And if Ross had anything to do with it, Clan MacKenna and Clan MacKay would suffer no more raids or battle deaths.

His people fell into their winter routine after Ross's return to Ravenscraig. Crops were stored, wood was brought in and piled up to fuel the many fireplaces, meat was salted, and preserves were made of the last of the fruit taken from the trees in the orchard.

During the following days, Ross and Gillian seemed to have begun feeling comfortable with each other. Ross could scarcely wait for nightfall so he could make love to Gillian. Her response to his lovemaking had him eagerly anticipating the moment they could mount the stairs together and shut the door on the world.

The weather, though cold, wasn't snowy. During the lull, Ross decided to go to Wick to purchase staples and supplies to last them through the winter months, when travel was difficult if not impossible. He asked Donald and Niall to accompany him in the cart to transport the supplies back to the keep.

After a particularly satisfying bout of lovemaking, Ross told Gillian about his plans to leave two days hence, weather permitting.

"Make a list of foodstuffs you think we may need to survive the winter," Ross said.

"May I go with you?" Gillian asked.

"Not this time; mayhap in the spring, when the weather is more predictable."

"I'll confer with Donald and Hanna and have my list ready before you depart."

Ross intended to gather Gillian into his arms and sleep, but his good intentions flew out the window when Gillian settled her soft curves into his body and sighed. The moment his hands found her breasts, he knew he had to have her again. His unaccountable need for his wife perplexed him. The more he had her, the more he wanted her. Did Gillian feel the same way? he wondered. She never refused him, so mayhap she wanted him as badly as he wanted her.

He slid his hands down her stomach and over her hips to the warm place between legs. Gillian turned her head and stared at him.

"Ross?"

"I canna seem to get enough of you, lass."

147

"But we just . . ."

"Aye."

He thrust his fingers inside her, working them slowly, diligently, while kissing her, thrusting his tongue in and out of her mouth in imitation of what he wanted to do below. When Gillian began pushing her hips against his hand, he removed his fingers, moved over her, and shoved his throbbing cock inside her.

Their second mating was fast and furious. Ross and Gillian reached their peak within seconds of each other.

Gillian couldn't believe how easily Ross had aroused her after their first mating. Though she didn't want to appear as insatiable as Ross, she was always eager to go where he led. In fact, she no longer thought of Ross as the enemy. Their relationship had become too intimate to maintain a semblance of animosity. What did she feel for Ross besides sexual attraction? she wondered. What did Ross feel for her?

Had a truce not been declared, Gillian would never have met Ross, let alone wed him. Somehow that thought was discomfiting. She would have wed Angus and considered herself lucky to have him for a husband. The thought of spending the rest of her life with Angus no longer seemed attractive to her.

Gillian sighed, wondering what that said about the woman who had once wielded a sword against Ross MacKenna. She fell asleep before the answer arrived.

The following day Gizela confronted Gillian in the hall. "Doona let him go, lass," the old woman said, gripping Gillian's arm so hard, Gillian knew she would bear a mark on her tender skin.

"Whatever are you talking about, Gizela?"

"The laird. He rides into danger."

Gillian wished she had more patience with Gizela, but she had a great deal to do before Ross left on the morrow. "I doona have time for this, Gizela."

"Doona let him go," Gizela insisted, her expression earnest.

"Why? What kind of danger? Does someone mean Ross harm?"

"Aye, didna I just say so? Warn him, lady. He doesna listen to me."

When Gizela turned to leave, Gillian held her back. "Wait. Who means Ross harm?"

Just then Seana sashayed across the hall. "That one," Gizela said, pointing a bony finger at Seana.

"Doona be silly," Gillian chided. "If Seana wishes anyone harm, 'tis me."

"Och, that she does."

Gillian took her eyes off Gizela for a moment to watch Seana, and when she looked back, the old woman had scooted off and disappeared. Exasperated, Gillian shook her head. She should know better than to listen to anything Gizela said, yet. . . . yet . . . How could she discount a threat to Ross? She couldn't. She hurried off to find her husband.

Gillian found Ross in the small chamber off the hall he used to conduct business. Niall was with him.

"Are you busy, Ross?" she asked as she poked her head into the chamber.

"I was just leaving," Niall said, rising, "unless Ross has something else to add to our discussion."

Ross waved him off. "I canna think of anything. If you decide not to accompany me to Wick, I will understand. The journey isna dangerous, but you are my heir, and mayhap 'tis best that you remain at Ravenscraig in case something unforeseen happens to me."

"Ross!" Gillian exclaimed. "Naught will happen to you."

Niall laughed. "Your lady wife is right, Ross. Gordo is here to see to things, and since I have business in Wick, I wish to accompany you."

Niall departed. Gillian stared at Ross, recalling Gizela's warning. Did Ross have a premonition of danger? Was that why he'd tried to convince Niall to remain at Ravenscraig?"

"Is something wrong, Gillian?" Ross asked.

"I didna know Niall was your heir."

"He is until we have a son." He searched her face. "What is it? You appear upset."

"I just spoke with Gizela."

"Is that all? You know better than to heed anything Gizela says."

"She asked me to warn you," Gillian persisted. "She said you shouldna go to Wick, that someone wishes you harm."

Ross laughed. "Are you worried about me?" He rose and stalked toward her. "I can take care of myself, lass. Besides, there is naught to worry about. The journey to Wick is neither long nor dangerous."

"Do you never heed Gizela's warnings?"

"Who can understand her? Her warnings are vague and unpredictable. Who did she say wished me harm?"

Gillian bit her lip, wondering if she should tell Ross. Now that she thought about it, it seemed unlikely that Seana wished Ross harm. Seana wanted Ross, had always wanted him. She would gain naught by his death.

"You're right," she agreed. "Gizela's warning was too vague to be taken seriously. Just promise me you will be alert for danger."

Reaching out, Ross pulled her against him. "Doona worry, Gillian. I am always careful, but this time there is nae need to worry."

Then he kissed her, making Gillian forget Gizela's warning, forget Seana, and forget even her reason for seeking Ross in the first place.

Two days later, Ross, Donald, and Niall left for Wick. They expected to be gone two, mayhap three days. Gillian tried to keep to her routine during Ross's absence. She set some women to rendering fat from the hog they had butchered and salted, and others to making candles to burn during the long winter nights to come. She conferred with Hanna about meals and busied herself counting bed linens.

While all this activity was going on, everyone but Seana offered to lend a hand. Gillian avoided the haughty woman as often as possible, but sometimes their meeting was unavoidable. Two days after Ross left, Seana confronted Gillian in the hall.

"When do you expect Ross to return?" Seana asked.

Gillian glanced out the window, noting that the sun had already set. "Probably tomorrow. If he were arriving today he would have already been here. Why are you asking about Ross instead of Niall?"

Seana bristled. "I was referring to all three men. Tomorrow," she repeated. "Excuse me; I just recalled something important I must do."

Gillian stared after Seana as she hurried off. The woman was a thorn in her side. Though Seana had done naught to rouse suspicion, Gillian couldn't forget

Gizela's warning. Since Seana hadn't left the keep since the men's departure, Gillian saw no reason for alarm. Ross was right when he said Gizela thrived on predicting doom and death.

The cart was loaded with all the items Ross had purchased in Wick and ready to roll three days after he and his kinsmen left Ravenscraig. Though Ross had wanted to return home a day earlier, it had taken longer than he'd expected to find all the items they needed. After breaking his fast that morning, Ross had decided to ride ahead and let the slower cart follow at its own pace.

Ross couldn't believe how much he had missed Gillian. During the past three days she had never been far from his thoughts. Her flaming hair and responsive body haunted his dreams. Considering theirs had been an arranged marriage neither he nor Gillian wanted, Ross had become inordinately fond of his feisty wife. He had to chuckle every time he recalled her attempt to run him through with her sword during that final battle between Clan MacKay and Clan MacKenna.

The situation would have been laughable if Gillian hadn't been so serious in her endeavor to skewer him. The experience had taught him never to underestimate a woman wielding a sword.

Ross's thoughts of Gillian eased the monotony of his long ride to Ravenscraig. Before he realized it he was at the halfway mark in his journey, with the cart still some distance behind him. If he hadn't been so distracted by his thoughts, he would have seen riders approaching him from the west. They were nearly upon him before he became aware of their presence. When he recognized their plaid, he stopped to await them.

"What brings you so far from home?" Ross asked when the leader approached him. "Are you traveling to Wick for supplies?"

When the leader did naught but stare at him, Ross asked, "What is it, man? Is aught amiss?"

Stunned, Ross scarcely had time to twist aside as the man pulled his sword from the sheath he carried on his back and thrust it without provocation into Ross's flesh. Though the assailant had aimed for Ross's gut, his sword wavered at the last minute and found a home in Ross's right side.

As the leader withdrew his sword, Ross gasped out, "Why?"

Then he slid from the saddle onto the frozen ground. The attacker cast one last glance at Ross, turned his mount, and led his men away, leaving Ross to die on the cold ground, his life's blood pooling beneath him.

Gillian had planned a grand feast for Ross's homecoming. Though she didn't know precisely when he would return, she expected him today, and had been lingering in the hall so she could be the first to greet him. Thus, she wasn't surprised when she heard the cart roll up to the front entrance. She ran to the door and flung it open, shivering in the blast of cold air that struck her. Apprehension sliced through her when she saw a riderless horse tethered to the rear of the cart.

"Fetch Gizela!" Niall shouted as he jumped from the cart. " 'Tis Ross; he's been hurt. Send men to help carry him inside."

"I am here," Gizela said. "I have already summoned help. Why didna you nae heed me, lass?" she hissed to Gillian.

Gillian had no time to wonder why Gizela had been so near at hand. She gave an agonized cry and ran out to the wagon, ignoring the cold that penetrated to her bones. Gordo was close on her heels.

"Och, nay!" she cried, nearly collapsing when she saw Ross lying in the bed of the cart with supplies piled around him and blood pooling beneath him. "What happened? He isna dead, is he?"

The thought that Ross might be dead sent her heart spiraling out of control. Ross couldn't be dead! He was too strong, too vital. Who would want him dead?

"Get out of the way," Gordo ordered as men arrived to carry Ross into the keep.

"Be careful," Gillian admonished. "Doona hurt him. How did it happen, Niall?"

"We doona know," Niall answered with marked impatience. "Ross was anxious to return home and rode on ahead. We followed in the cart some distance behind. We doona know when or how it happened. When we came upon him, he was lying on the ground, bleeding from his wound."

"What kind of wound, and where is it?" Gillian demanded, following close behind the men carrying Ross into the keep and up the stairs to the solar.

Niall sent her a cursory glance, as if her questions were annoying. "He suffered a grievous wound, lady. Someone thrust a sword into his side."

"Who would do such a thing?"

"Ross is the only one who can tell us that," Niall answered darkly. "When we find out, he will be avenged."

They had reached the solar. Ross was lowered gently to the bed. With Gordo's help, Gillian began tearing off his clothing to inspect the wound. When she finally bared his torso, she let out an involuntary cry. The wound was jagged and ugly, blood still oozing from it. And his body was cold, so very cold.

"He's freezing!" Gillian exclaimed. "Bring more blankets, lots of them."

"Move away," Gizela said, gently pushing Gillian and Gordo aside. "I canna treat the laird with you hovering over him."

Reluctantly Gillian moved aside, wringing her hands in despair. Ross's breathing was shallow, his skin pale, his lips blue. He looked more dead than alive.

"Can you save him?" Gillian whispered.

"All I can do is try, lass." She glanced over her shoulder at the people crowding into the chamber. "Get out, all of you. The laird's wife will assist me. Bring hot water and clean cloths," she ordered Alice, who hovered nearby, wringing her hands.

When Ross's kinsmen lingered, Gizela said, "Get out, all of you; you too, Gordo!" The room cleared. "Close the door, lass."

Gillian obeyed, then returned to Ross's bedside. "What can I do to help? How bad is it? Will he live?"

"God's will be done," Gizela intoned piously.

Alice arrived with a basin of hot water and a stack of clean cloths. She placed them on a nearby table and departed. Gillian watched anxiously as Gizela carefully probed and then cleaned the wound with hot water and sprinkled dill seeds directly into the gaping gash.

"Thread the needle for me, lass; my eyes are nae as sharp as they used to be."

Gillian searched for the items in Gizela's medicinal basket. Her hands were visibly shaking when she attempted to push the thread through the eye of the needle, but she finally succeeded. Gizela snatched it from her fingers.

"His skin is so cold," Gillian complained. "He must have lain on the frozen ground a long time."

"You can thank God for that," Gizela answered. "The cold thickened his blood, keeping him from bleeding to death."

Gillian winced as the needle pierced Ross's flesh, but Ross didn't seem to notice; he didn't even stir. "Did the sword pierce anything vital?" she asked fearfully.

"I doona think so, but it was close."

Gizela tied off the last of the many stitches and reached for a jar of salve.

"What is that?" Gillian asked.

"Yarrow salve—it promotes healing." She picked up several clean cloths and made a thick pad, placing it directly on the wound. Then she tore the rest into strips to wrap around Ross's torso. "Lift him, lass, while I bind the bandage into place."

Ross was deadweight in her arms as Gillian lifted his torso off the bed. Gizela worked fast, and moments later she instructed Gillian to lower Ross and cover him.

"Stay with him while I go to the kitchen to make an infusion of mandrake root. If we can get it down him, it will put him into a deep sleep and dull his pain."

Gillian nodded, unable to speak past the lump in her throat. Ross couldn't die. She wouldn't let him. Reaching out, she pushed a strand of dark hair from his forehead, and then she stroked his cheek. If only he could tell her who had done this to him.

She kissed his cold lips and spoke softly in his ear. "Ross, can you hear me?"

No answer was forthcoming.

"Ross, please, tell me what happened. Who did this to you?"

Miraculously, Ross opened his eyes. They were dimmed with pain and confusion.

"You are safe, Ross," Gillian crooned, tears streaming down her cheeks. "Gizela will take care of you. Can you tell me who did this to you?"

Ross stared at her. His mouth moved, as if there were something he wanted to say but he couldn't quite get the words out. Gillian leaned close. "Try, Ross, please. Tell me who hurt you."

He gasped out a word. Stunned, Gillian strained closer, waiting for him to speak again, to repeat the name. His eyes closed and he gasped the name on a sigh. Though Gillian had heard the same name on his lips twice, she couldn't credit it. And she didn't dare repeat it until Ross awakened and confirmed what she'd heard.

A short time later, Gizela returned with the narcotic, and together they managed to dribble enough down Ross's throat to put him into a deep sleep. Until he awoke again, there was nothing Gillian could do but wait.

Chapter Ten

Ross hovered between life and death while Gizela worked whatever magic she was capable of to keep him from crossing over into the world of perpetual darkness. The entire hall was in mourning, and prayers were being offered up daily for the laird's recovery.

Gillian rarely stirred from Ross's bedside. She slept little and ate even less. If she was aware of the animosity drifting up from the hall, she made no mention of it. Four days after the attack upon Ross, Gizela entered the chamber and ordered Gillian to eat and rest.

"I canna leave him, Gizela. What if he should die while I am gone? I need to be with him."

"Ross willna die, lass," Gizela said with confidence.

Gillian looked up, her eyes filled with hope for the first time in days. "Are you sure? He still hasna awakened."

"Sleep is the best healer. The laird's wound isna infected; I am confident he will survive."

Gillian wished she could be as convinced as Gizela.

"Go, lass," Gizela urged. "Eat something first. I will sit

with the laird while you are gone. When you return, you can rest on the cot Alice has made up in the corner."

"You will call me if there is a change in his condition?"

"Aye, I will send word if the laird awakens."

Reluctantly, Gillian left the chamber. As she descended the stairs to the hall, angry voices drifted up to her. She had no idea what the argument was about until she walked into the chamber. Absolute silence reigned as everyone turned to stare at her.

"The laird . . ." Gordo began, barely above a whisper.

"He lives," Gillian said.

"No thanks to you," Seana spat. "The laird lies near death because of you and your kinsmen. Everyone kens your part in the attack upon Ross."

Lack of sleep had taken its toll upon Gillian, making her wonder if she had heard right. "What are you saying? How could you hold me responsible for something of which I had no knowledge? When Ross awakens, he will tell you the truth."

"We know the truth," an angry voice called out. Others in the hall voiced their agreement.

"You have betrayed the MacKennas," Seana snarled. "The laird's death rests upon your head."

"Ross willna die!" Gillian cried. "Gizela has said so."

"That old hag kens naught," Seana scoffed. "Gillian should be sent back to Braeburn, where she belongs. When Niall becomes laird, he will seek revenge for Ross's death."

"Why do you keep insisting that Ross will die?" Gillian demanded. "My husband is very much alive."

"He hasna stirred in four days," Niall reminded her. "Many believe our laird willna awaken."

" 'Tis true," Seana affirmed. "The old witch who

159

claims to possess healing powers canna be trusted. She is crazy in the head."

"You can argue about this all you like," Gillian replied, her voice rising. "But I refuse to believe Ross will die."

"Leave the lass alone," Gordo ordered. "She is distraught and worried about her husband."

Nodding her thanks to Gordo, Gillian turned abruptly and headed for the kitchen, leaving the anger and dissention behind, though she could still hear Seana raging against her. What made Seana think she had harmed Ross? Why did Ross's people believe it was her kinsmen who'd tried to kill him? She had to admit the unprovoked attack was mystifying, but she hoped the mystery would be resolved once Ross awakened. She didn't for one moment believe her father capable of such treachery.

Hanna gave Gillian a narrow-eyed glance when Gillian entered the kitchen. "Do you ken what they are saying about you?"

"Do you believe what they are saying, Hanna? Your opinion means a great deal to me."

"Did you conspire to harm our laird?"

"Nay, I didna; nor are my kinsmen responsible. Da wouldna break the truce in such a cowardly manner."

Hanna searched Gillian's face and nodded, obviously satisfied with her answer. "Alice swore you were innocent, but Seana has roused everyone's anger to a fever pitch. She has Laird Ross already in his grave and Niall proclaimed the new laird. She insisted you werena satisfied in your marriage and wished the laird ill so you could wed Angus Sinclair."

Gillian dropped into a chair, exhaustion etching her features. "I was nowhere near Ross when he was attacked. And I wouldna have Angus on a silver platter. They blame me unjustly."

"Seana said you sent a message to Braeburn, informing your clan about Laird Ross's travel plans so they could attack him upon the road."

"Did Seana produce the messenger or confirm that a message had been sent by me?"

"She said she'd spoken to the lad who carried the message to Braeburn. He was from the village, but Donald couldna find him when he went to investigate Seana's claim."

"Seana lies," Gillian said tiredly. "I canna think about this now. I promised Gizela I would eat something before I returned to Ross's bedside."

"Then eat you shall," Hanna said. "I made a tasty venison stew for the evening meal, and you can be the first to sample it."

She filled a bowl with the savory concoction and placed it before Gillian with a slab of bread, thickly spread with butter. Gillian ate mechanically, tasting little of what went into her mouth. Her mind wandered back to the name Ross had spoken before falling unconscious. What did it mean? Had he given her the name of the man who had attacked him? Though her mind was whirling with possibilities, she had no right to point a finger without proof. No one but Ross could accuse his attacker.

Gillian finished her meal, thanked Hanna, and rose. "I must return to Ross," she said.

"Doona let the rabble in the hall rattle you, lass," Hanna advised. "Seana is a troublemaker. I pray Niall has the good sense not to listen to her."

Her head held high, Gillian returned to the hall and headed for the staircase.

"There she is!" Seana cried, pointing a finger at Gillian. "Doona let her return to the laird's bedside. Mayhap she and the old witch are planning to hasten Ross's death."

"How dare you!" Gillian gasped, whipping around. "You have no reason to accuse me or Gizela of treachery. The fact that Ross is alive is due to Gizela's skill."

"The MacKay lassie is right," Gordo argued. "Say what you want about Gizela's strange mumblings, but never accuse her of wishing my nephew harm."

"Send the MacKay wench to Braeburn!" Seana shouted.

"Aye, return her to her father," others chimed in.

"Seana, you are being too harsh," Gordo protested. "We have no proof of Gillian's guilt. Ross will tell us the truth of it when he awakens."

"*If* he awakens," Seana charged. She turned to Niall. "As acting laird, you have the power to send Gillian away."

"As long as Ross lives, I have no power to banish his wife," Niall objected. "I have faith Ross will awaken soon and name his enemy."

Niall didn't see the look Seana sent him, but Gillian did. If looks could kill, Niall would be dead. Gillian shuddered and turned away. Protesting her innocence was a waste of time and energy. Only Ross knew the truth, and until he could speak, it would remain a mystery.

Ross was still unconscious when Gillian returned to his bedside. Gizela was bending over him, inspecting his wound. "Has it festered?" Gillian asked fearfully. "Is he feverish?"

"The wound is red and raw and he is a mite warm,

but I doona think his fever will spike. You should rest. Alice put fresh linens on the cot while you supped."

"Gizela, tell me true. Do Ross's kinsmen hold me responsible for the attack upon him? Do they hold my clan responsible?"

"I didna want to tell you, for I knew it would upset you," the old woman said. " 'Tis the McHamish wench's doing. Did I nae warn you about her? She had a scheme in mind when she handfasted with Niall."

Curious, Gillian asked, "What scheme?"

Gizela's eyes clouded over. "There will be difficult times, but the flame will prevail. Search for the proof, lass, for the truth will prevail."

Gizela's vague reply annoyed Gillian. "What does that mean?"

Gizela shuddered. "You must seek the truth."

"I doona—"

"Get some rest, Gillian, lass. The difficult times I spoke of are near at hand."

Sensing that she would get naught more from Gizela this night, Gillian cast one last glance at Ross and lay down on the cot. She fell asleep the moment she laid her head on the pillow.

Someone was shaking her. Gillian awoke to harsh voices and light stabbing against her eyelids. Immediately alert, she rose on her elbow and stared up at Alice. "What is it? Is Ross . . . ?"

"Naught has changed with the laird," Alice said. "Gordo wishes to speak with you. He said 'tis urgent."

Gillian rose shakily to her feet. She took several steps toward the bed before Gordo appeared in front of her.

"What is it, Gordo? Why are you looking at me like that?"

"My kinsmen want you gone. 'Tis none of my doing, Gillian; believe me. But I fear for your life if you doona leave now. Talk is getting ugly below. With no one else to blame, your kinsmen are the likely suspects. I want to keep you safe for Ross's sake."

"This is all Seana's doing," Gillian bit out. "If she hadna put ideas in people's heads, no one would blame me for harming Ross. I am innocent, Gordo; I swear it."

"I believe you, lass," Gordo agreed. "But I am sending you away to keep you from harm. Your horse is saddled, and Hanna has prepared provisions for your journey. The weather is not too harsh yet; you should have no problem reaching Braeburn. We willna ken the truth until Ross can speak."

"You're forcing me to leave?" Gillian cried. "Nay, I need to be with Ross. No one can care for him as well as I can."

"You will kill him," Seana said from the doorway. "Leave now, while you are still able."

"I willna let the laird die, mistress," Gizela said from Ross's bedside.

"And I will help care for him," Alice promised.

Ross groaned and began to thrash. Gillian pushed Gordo aside and raced to his bedside. "Ross, can you hear me?"

Ross mumbled something indecipherable and stared blankly up at her. "He's awake!" Gillian cried.

"Nay, lass, he sees naught," Gizela assured her.

"Come away, Gillian," Gordo said, easing her away from the bed. "You must leave before the threats against you are put into action. 'Tis for your own good."

"Go, lassie," Gizela urged. "Remember what I said, and do what must be done to find the proof."

"What are you babbling about, Gizela?" Seana asked. "We've heard enough of your crazed muttering."

"I'll fetch your fur-lined cloak and the bag I packed for you, mistress," Alice said as she went to the wardrobe for the items.

"You packed my bag?" Gillian asked, stunned.

"I had no choice. Gordo ordered it. You will need this," Alice said as she handed Gillian her sword. Immediately Gillian strapped the sheath across her body so that the sword rested between her shoulder blades.

Then Alice placed the cloak around Gillian's shoulders and thrust a purse into her hand. Inside were the coins Tearlach MacKay had given her for a wedding gift.

"I'll carry the bag out for you and fetch the provisions for your journey from the kitchen."

"I'm not leaving Ross," Gillian insisted.

"*I* value your life, even if you doona," Gordo said kindly.

"You have a strange way of showing it," Gillian shot back.

"I but wish to protect you. I ken my nephew is inordinately fond of you."

Gillian sent a pleading look toward Gizela. The healer's eyes were downcast. She could expect no help from that quarter.

She tore her eyes away from the bed, where Ross now lay still as death, and slowly walked to the door. Abruptly she turned. "Take care of him, Gizela. Doona let Seana near him. She wishes him ill."

"Nay, Gillian, you misjudge Seana," Gordo said. "She is a MacKenna now."

When Gillian glanced at Gizela, she read confirmation of Seana's guilt in the healer's rheumy eyes and knew Gizela would protect Ross.

Gillian paused and glanced over her shoulder as Ravenscraig's gate closed firmly behind her. Briefly she wondered if she had been wise to decline Gordo's offer to escort her to Braeburn. Then she felt her sword resting against her back and knew she would be all right.

"I wish you Godspeed and a safe journey home," Gordo called to her through the gate.

"Will you keep me informed of Ross's progress?" Gillian asked.

"When Ross recovers enough to tell us what happened, we will let you know."

A sob clogged Gillian's throat as she nodded her understanding. Gordo's promise wasn't much, but it was all she had. She reined Silver toward Braeburn, shivering beneath her cloak. She worried that her father was going to demand satisfaction from Clan MacKenna when he learned she had been forced from Ravenscraig, and that lives would be lost. Knowing Tearlach, he wouldn't let the insult go unpunished. She feared a battle was brewing, and she didn't know how to stop it.

Gillian had traveled but a short distance when Gizela's parting words began to penetrate through the thick fog of her brain. Gizela had told her to find proof of her innocence. It never occurred to Gillian that her father might be responsible for wounding Ross. Tearlach MacKay was a man of his word. Once he agreed to a truce, he would never break it. He would wish no harm to his daughter's husband.

Gillian pulled on Silver's reins. The mare stomped to a stop and pawed the frozen ground. Gillian realized she couldn't return to Braeburn. Not yet, anyway. She had to find out if the name Ross had spoken in his delirium had been that of his assailant. She was the only one who had heard the name, the only one who could prove both her innocence and that of Clan MacKay.

Her mind made up, Gillian reined Silver in a different direction. Though she would have a great distance to travel, it had to be done.

Shivering beneath her fur-lined cloak, the hood pulled low over her brow, Gillian stopped once shortly after midday to eat the food Hanna had prepared, and to rest her horse. Though it was cold, there was no sleet or snow, allowing Gillian to continue throughout the afternoon. She knew the way to her destination, for she'd visited the small fortress a time or two with her family. When she reached the small village of Halkirk, she knew she could travel no farther this day and must find a place to stay. The wind had picked up; very few people were out on the street at this time of day. Most would be tucked up snug and warm in their cottages with their families. The church bell began chiming vespers as she rode down the deserted street, looking for an inn.

The main thoroughfare held naught but a few shops that had already closed for the night. Cold and weary, Gillian felt as if she carried the world on her shoulders; so much depended on her. With no place to stay, she urged her valiant mare forward, noting with alarm that the wind had picked up, and large, fluffy snowflakes were drifting down from the sky.

Just when she feared she would freeze to death before reaching her destination, she saw a lad crossing the street and hailed him. He stopped and waited for her to reach him.

"Are you lost, lady?" he asked.

"I'm in need of lodging for the night," Gillian explained. "Is there an inn hereabouts?"

"Nay, we are but a small village, but my granny Maddie sometimes takes in stranded travelers."

Relief washed through Gillian. "Can you take me there? I will pay whatever she asks."

"Follow me, lady," the lad said as he sprinted down the street. At the edge of town he turned down a lane that led to a tidy cottage with a light burning in the window. "This is Granny Maddie's cottage," the lad said.

Gillian dismounted. "My mare needs food and water. She has carried me a long way."

"I can tend your mare, lady. Granny Maddie has a lean-to behind the house. She'll be nice and cozy there."

Gillian fished out a coin from her purse and tossed it to the boy. "Rub her down well, please."

The lad looked at the silver in his hand and grinned. "Doona worry none, lady; I will take good care of your mare. Leave everything to me. I'll give her a measure of oats, if it pleases you."

"Yes, that will be fine," Gillian said as she removed her bag tied to the saddle. "What is your name, lad?"

"Duncan McHamish."

"Thank you for your help, Duncan McHamish."

The boy touched his forelock and led Silver away. Gillian approached the cottage and knocked on the door. A small dumpling of a woman with rosy cheeks and white hair answered the summons.

"Your grandson told me you might be able to put me up for the night," Gillian said through chattering teeth.

"Would that be Duncan?" Maddie asked. Gillian nodded. Maddie motioned Gillian inside. "Come in, lassie, so I can shut the door. I am Maddie McHamish and you are . . . ?"

"Gillian MacKay," she answered, purposely using her maiden name now that she was among the allies of her clan. "Mayhap you know my father, Tearlach."

"Not personally, but I've heard of him. Have you traveled a great distance?" When Gillian nodded, she went on. "You poor wee thing, you must be cold and hungry." She glanced past Gillian into the growing darkness. "Are you alone?"

"Aye, I hope that doesna make a difference."

"Nay, it doesna. Sit yourself by the fire while I fix you something to eat. I have a small room off the kitchen that should serve you nicely, and I'll build up the fire in the hearth so it will be warm and cozy."

"I can pay for my lodging and food," Gillian said.

"I doona require payment, but your coin will be welcome," Maddie said as she led a shivering Gillian to the hearth and pulled up a bench for her to sit on.

"Shall I take your cloak?" Maddie asked.

Warmed by the fire, Gillian nodded, forgetting that she carried her sword in a sheath strapped to her back.

"Oh, my," Maddie said. "I see you are armed."

Gillian removed the sword and leaned it against the hearth. "I never go anywhere unarmed."

"There's hot water in the kettle on the hob over the hearth. Mayhap you want to wash your hands and face before you eat."

"I'd like that," Gillian replied.

Maddie found a cracked bowl, poured water from the kettle into it, and retrieved a clean cloth from a cupboard. "There's cold water in the bucket on the sink. Use what you need, lass, while I dish out your supper."

Gillian busied herself at the sink as delicious odors wafted to her from the food Maddie was ladling into a bowl. After she finished washing, she approached the scarred oaken table, which had been bleached nearly white, and sat down.

"The fare is plain but filling," Maddie said as she placed a bowl of thick mutton-and-barley stew in front of her guest. Maddie hummed to herself as she cut thick slices of bread and fetched butter from a cupboard.

Gillian tucked into the meal, sighing blissfully as the hot stew warmed her stomach. "This is delicious." She bit off a hunk of bread and chewed thoughtfully. "Are you related to Douglas McHamish and his daughter, Seana?"

Maddie chuckled. "Everyone hereabouts is related in some way to the McHamish. Do you plan on visiting McHamish Keep?"

"Aye. I ken 'tis close, but I couldna continue farther tonight; I've traveled too far today in the cold."

"The castle is an hour ride from here, but you look too done-in to continue, lassie. You'll sleep comfortably tonight. I keep the room made up for travelers in need of shelter. I enjoy the company." She picked up a candlestick. "Follow me, Gillian MacKay."

Gillian retrieved her bag and followed Maddie to a small alcove off the kitchen. It was furnished with a narrow bed—piled high with blankets—a chair, and a nightstand. Maddie set the candle down on the nightstand.

" 'Tisna fancy, but at least you will be warm and dry. There's a chamber pot under the bed. Sleep as late as you like."

"Thank you, Maddie. You have been most kind."

After Maddie left, Gillian undressed and climbed into bed. She was so weary, she fell instantly asleep.

She awoke the next morning after a deep, dreamless sleep to the sound of movement in the tiny kitchen.

As much as Gillian hated to leave the warm bed, she knew she should depart before she lost her nerve. If she could prove the McHamish was the renegade who had attacked Ross, he would be made to pay.

"Did I wake you?" Maddie asked when a short time later Gillian entered the kitchen carrying her bag.

"Nay, 'twas time I was up and on my way."

"Sit down and break your fast with me and Duncan, Gillian MacKay. Only a poor host would send a guest away hungry."

Gillian noticed the lad standing near the hearth and smiled at him. "Good morning, Duncan."

Duncan touched his forelock and smiled back. "Good morning, lady. I'll saddle your wee mare when you're ready to leave."

Gillian moved to the table and sat down. Duncan joined her. Gillian wasn't about to leave without breaking her fast. She had no idea when or where her next meal would come from. Mayhap she wouldn't be alive to see another meal. Besides, she couldn't resist the platter of eggs and ham, fresh bread, and hot tea Maddie placed before her.

"Dig in, lassie," Maddie said as she joined Gillian and Duncan at the table.

The food was delicious, and among them they cleaned the platter.

" 'Tis time I was off," Gillian said.

"I'll fetch your mare," Duncan said, ducking through the door.

Gillian reached into the purse attached to her waist, removed two silver coins, and handed them to Maddie.

"Oh, nay, lassie, 'tis too much," Maddie demurred.

"You saved my life, Maddie McHamish. If anything, 'tis not enough."

Maddie accepted the coins and fetched Gillian's fur-lined cloak as Gillian buckled the sheath and sword across her body.

"Will I see you again, Gillian MacKay?"

"I doubt it, Maddie."

"Then God go with you, lassie."

Gillian opened the door, pulling her cloak tight about her as a blast of cold air took her breath away. Silver was already saddled and waiting; Duncan handed her the reins and gave her a boost up.

"Do you need directions?" Maddie asked from the front door.

"Nay, I know the way. I thank you most kindly, Maddie McHamish."

Gillian wondered what Maddie would have done if she'd known Gillian was on her way to accuse her kinsman of a terrible crime. She probably would have turned her out in the cold to freeze to death. Gillian sighed. If McHamish was responsible for wounding Ross and leaving him to die, then he deserved punishment. For all she knew, Ross could be dead by now. That thought firmed her resolve to learn the truth.

After more than an hour of slogging through light snow, Gillian saw McHamish Keep sitting atop a hill across the glen. She urged Silver onward, not surprised to find the portcullis closed and armed men stationed atop the wall walk.

"What do you want, lady?" a man armed with bow and quiver called down to her.

"I wish to speak with Douglas McHamish. Open the gate."

"Who are you?"

"Gillian MacKay. Ask your laird if he is afraid to face a woman."

The man disappeared. Gillian huddled in her cloak as she waited, her patience hanging by a slim thread. Did McHamish intend to keep her outside until she froze to death? Apparently not, for moments later she saw Douglas McHamish himself striding through the bailey toward the gate.

"What do you want, Gillian MacKay?" McHamish asked warily.

"I've come a long way to see you. Are you nae going to invite me inside to warm myself by your fire?"

Gillian knew McHamish would comply. Hospitality was sacred in the Highlands. It was unthinkable that McHamish would deny a guest entry. McHamish nodded to the gatekeeper, and the portcullis was slowly cranked open. Gillian urged Silver through the opening. A lad ran up to take the reins from her.

"Follow me," McHamish said, turning abruptly toward the keep.

McHamish Keep was small compared to Braeburn

and Ravenscraig, but the inside was attractive and fragrant with the scent of fresh pine rushes. McHamish's second wife, a haughty blond, swished over to greet her. McHamish made the introductions.

After a cursory glance at Gillian's flaming hair, Eileen McHamish asked, "What brings you to us on a raw day like this, Gillian MacKay?"

Gillian thought Eileen's manner a bit chilly. "I but wish a private word with your husband."

Eileen's eyebrows arched upward. "Did you nae wed the MacKenna? Where is your husband?"

Slicing an accusatory glance at the McHamish, Gillian said, "Ross is . . . presently indisposed."

Eileen frowned. "Your business must be important to warrant traveling alone. Will you warm yourself by the fire and have a bite to eat?"

Gillian shook her head. "Nay, my business canna wait." She turned to McHamish. "I would speak with you in private."

The wary look she had noticed earlier had not left McHamish's eyes.

"Shall I take Gillian MacKay to the solar?" Eileen asked. "No one will bother us there."

"What I have to say is for McHamish's ears alone," Gillian said, earning a scowl from Eileen.

When his wife started to protest, McHamish said, "Verra well, lass, but I doona know what we might have to discuss."

Gillian felt Eileen's eyes boring into her back as she followed McHamish up the winding staircase; she prayed she wasn't about to accuse a man falsely. Had Ross really spoken the name in his delirium, or had he said something entirely different? Nay, she had heard the name clearly. Squaring her shoulders, she formed in her mind the words she wished to say.

McHamish motioned Gillian toward a bench before the hearth. Gillian shook her head.

"A dram of whiskey, then?"

Gillian shook her head again. Mustering her courage, she asked, "Did you attack my husband? Did you run him through with your sword? You must have caught him unaware, for I see no mark from his sword on you."

McHamish remained silent a long time. Then he seemed to collapse inward, his stance less confident. "He isna dead, then?"

"Damn you to everlasting hell!" Gillian shouted as she threw off her cloak and pulled her sword from its sheath in one smooth motion. "You didna kill Ross, but even as we speak, he lies near death." She waved her sword threateningly before McHamish's face. "How could you? What reason did you have to run him through and leave him to die on the frozen ground? What did Ross ever do to you?"

"Put your sword away," McHamish ordered. "I was in a rage and sought revenge after Angus Sinclair informed me of Ross MacKenna's insult to my daughter."

Gillian thrust her sword toward McHamish's gut. McHamish whirled away, surprisingly agile for a man her father's age. "What lies did Angus tell you?"

"Step back and I'll tell you, though I doubt they were lies," McHamish added.

Gillian retreated a step, but did not let her guard down.

"Go ahead and speak, though your excuses will make no difference. Ross did naught to Seana."

"According to Sinclair, MacKenna tossed Seana aside like dirty laundry when he wed you. And that was after he forced her to whore for him. Then he gave her to one of his rough kinsman, a man who beats her regularly. Seana sent me a message that she isna happy in her handfast marriage, but MacKenna willna let her leave Ravenscraig. I did what was necessary to avenge my daughter's honor."

Shocked, Gillian lowered her sword a little. "You were a fool to listen to Angus Sinclair. Both he and your daughter are liars. They conspired together to do Ross harm. Angus hates Ross and wishes him ill, and he used you to do his bidding without risking his own neck."

McHamish sputtered indignantly. "Are you accusing my daughter of treachery?"

"Aye, I am. Arm yourself, Douglas McHamish. Unlike you, I willna hail you as a friend and skewer you with my sword when you least expect it, as you did to Ross."

McHamish drew himself up to his full height. "Are you daft? I canna fight a woman."

"Fight or die," Gillian challenged.

Chapter Eleven

Douglas McHamish spread his arms. "I amna armed, lass."

Gillian glanced about the solar, saw McHamish's sword leaning against the hearth, and motioned to it with her head. "Fetch your weapon, McHamish."

McHamish lowered his arms, clearly reluctant to engage Gillian in battle. "I willna. Run me though if you wish, but doona expect me to fight a woman."

"Why not? You attacked a man who considered you a friend, a man unaware of your vicious intent. Take up your sword!" Gillian repeated, unwilling to listen to any more lame excuses.

McHamish shook his head. "If what you say about Seana and Sinclair is true, then I have been sorely misled by my own daughter and the Sinclair chieftain. Kill me if you wish—I will do naught to stop you."

Gillian's sword wavered. Killing McHamish would solve naught if Angus Sinclair and Seana were the culprits.

"If you think it will help, I will go to Ravenscraig, explain what happened and why, and bring my daughter home, if I am allowed to leave alive," McHamish added. "I acted out of anger and shame before I had time to analyze the situation fully." His expression hardened. "Angus Sinclair has much to answer for."

Startled, Gillian asked, "You would go to Ravenscraig and confess?"

"Aye, the Highland code demands it of me. I ken now that my unprovoked attack upon the MacKenna laird was a despicable act. It shames me to think I have been duped by my own daughter and her accomplice."

Gillian couldn't kill a man who had been made a fool of, a man who expressed sorrow for being led astray and acting impulsively. Though McHamish had wielded the sword that wounded Ross, Angus Sinclair was the real culprit, and Sinclair must be the one to pay with his life.

"I willna kill you, Douglas McHamish. I shall let Ross and his kinsmen decide your punishment. But Angus Sinclair willna escape so easily; this I vow."

"What are you going to do, lass?"

"What I intended to do when I left Ravenscraig: kill the man responsible for harming Ross." She turned to leave.

"Wait! You are but one woman. I should be the one to challenge Sinclair for the lies he told me, and for my wounding and mayhap killing a man I considered a friend."

"Nay," Gillian replied. "Justice would best be served if you went to Ravenscraig and told Niall and Gordo exactly what you've told me. If they continue to blame my father, I fear the blood feud between our clans will resume. 'Tis what Sinclair wants, you know, though I doona ken why."

McHamish bowed his head. "I will do as you ask, Gillian MacKay. If the MacKenna spares my life, I will be grateful. If not, I will die knowing I did the right thing. As for Seana, even though she has sinned grievously against the MacKinna laird, I pray she begs forgiveness and is allowed to live."

Gillian nodded curtly, turned on her heel, and strode off, purpose etched on her beautiful features. Without a backward glance she marched down the stairs and out the door, ignoring Eileen, who followed her to the door.

"Are you leaving already, Gillian MacKay? I'm sure Douglas would want you to partake of our hospitality. We are about to sit down to our midday meal. Will you join us?"

Gillian stopped just short of the door. She had no food to eat on her journey to Sinclair's stronghold, which she estimated would take at least four hours to reach, longer if the weather turned nasty. She glanced out the window and saw that snow was beginning to fall. If she was caught in a blizzard, she would never make it to her destination. And above all else, she wanted to kill Angus Sinclair.

"You canna leave now, lass," McHamish advised as he came up to join his wife. "Darkness arrives early this time of year; you could be stranded on the road in a blizzard. Bide the night with us. I doona want your death on my conscience."

"Verra well. I will sup with you, but I still intend to leave today, if the weather allows."

The weather did not allow. Gillian was forced to spend the day in idle pursuits with McHamish's wife. As the light waned, Gillian stood at the window and watched in despair as the wind rose and snow swirled in aimless patterns. Though she was desperately anxious to leave, she was forced to accept McHamish's invitation to spend the night.

After the evening meal, Elaine led Gillian to a tiny, cheerless chamber with a listless fire burning in the hearth. Elaine held the door open for Gillian and followed her inside, carefully closing the door behind her.

"What business did you have with my husband?" she asked bluntly. "Pray, tell me it has naught to do with my stepdaughter. Seana is a shameless hussy, and I doona want her to return. My husband's keep is more peaceful since she left us."

"Seana is Niall MacKenna's handfast wife," Gillian stated. "Nevertheless, my visit has a great deal to do with Seana. I think your husband should be the one to tell you what he did in the name of justice, misguided though he was."

"I knew Seana would bring grief to Douglas," Elaine wailed, wringing her hands. "Good sleep, Gillian MacKay. I will see that you are provided with food for your journey when you leave."

Gillian slept little that night. Despite his words of repentance, she did not entirely trust McHamish after what he had done to Ross. She kept her sword close at hand and slept in her clothing. During the long night, Gillian heard the wind subside, and she hoped the snow had ceased as well.

Gillian awoke shortly after dawn, performed simple ablutions, and went down to the hall. McHamish was up and waiting for her. The first thing Gillian did was walk to the window and peer outside. A murky daylight had chased away the lingering darkness, revealing snow upon the ground but no wind to speak of. She turned back to McHamish.

"I will leave as soon as I break my fast."

"I assumed as much, and asked Cook to prepare food for your journey. I will be leaving for Ravenscraig myself in a few days, after I see to my affairs here. Doona do anything foolish, lass. I ken you consider yourself a warrior, but you are still a woman. Think you MacKenna will appreciate your risking your life for him?"

"My life is my own to risk," Gillian said tartly. "I am a skilled swordsman; avenging Ross is something I must do to win Clan MacKenna's respect."

A serving woman entered the hall with bowls of steaming porridge. Though Gillian made a face, she forced herself to eat, knowing the gruel would fortify her for the difficult day ahead.

Gillian was surprised and very happy when she saw the sun peeping out from behind a cloud. It was a good omen. McHamish sent her on her way with a sack of food and a warning to be wary of Sinclair.

"Beware, lass. If Sinclair could convince me to kill the MacKenna, he is capable of almost anything," McHamish cautioned.

"You think because I am a woman he will take advantage of me?"

Mchamish had the grace to flush. "In part, lass, but also because he is crafty and without morals."

"I can take care of myself. You havena changed your mind about going to Ravenscraig and confessing your crime, have you?"

"Nay, lass, I havena. Your mare is saddled and waiting outside for you."

A serving girl approached with a sack of food, which Gillian tucked under her arm. "Good-bye, Douglas McHamish. I hope Clan MacKenna treats you with more kindness than they treated me. I canna attest to their willingness to listen to you, for you harmed their laird; they may slay you before they hear you out."

McHamish inclined his head. "I accept that I did wrong and that Highland justice will prevail."

Gillian nodded and took her leave. "Good luck," she threw over her shoulder.

Gillian knew she had hours of hard riding ahead of her. But thoughts of Ross lying pale and helpless in what might be his deathbed spurred her on. Killing the man responsible for hurting Ross had become an obsession.

When had she stopped thinking of Ross as the enemy? Gillian wondered. When had love replaced hatred? The realization that she loved Ross MacKenna was so stunning, she brought Silver to a halt to contemplate what she had just learned about herself.

Did Ross return her love? Once she killed Angus Sinclair, Ross would know the full extent of her feelings for him.

Gillian resumed her journey, stopping only to eat and to rest her horse at midday. She reached the Sinclair stronghold an hour before dusk. She rode through the gate without being challenged. Apparently Sinclair was not expecting trouble. She continued on across the bailey and dismounted before the front entrance. It was an unpretentious keep built on a lesser scale than Ravenscraig and Braeburn. It wasn't even as large as McHamish Keep. In the not-too-distant past, Gillian had been anxious to wed Angus and become mistress of Angus's home. Until her conversation with

McHamish, she had never imagined Angus being capable of such evildoings. What did he hope to gain by killing Ross? Or seeing the feud resume?

Gillian lifted the large brass knocker shaped like a lion's head and banged on the door. Angus himself opened it.

"Gillian, what are you doing here?" Angus asked. His expression held a wariness that Gillian would have sworn was guilt. "Have you finally decided to leave your husband?"

"I ken what you did, Angus," Gillian said as she pushed past Sinclair.

Sinclair closed the door behind her. "Mayhap it would help if you told me what you're referring to."

"I spoke with Douglas McHamish."

Angus stiffened. "I doona ken what you are trying to tell me."

"Ross lies near death at Ravenscraig."

A sly smirk curved Angus's lips. "Which of his enemies finally did the deed?"

Gillian threw off her cloak and pulled her sword from its sheath. "You tell me, Angus. Why did you incite McHamish to attack Ross?"

"Is that what McHamish told you?"

"Aye, and I believe him. You and Seana conspired together at my brother's wedding feast to end Ross's life. But you failed. He was still alive when I left Ravenscraig."

"You didna leave Ravenscraig; you were forced to go. I was told MacKenna's kinsmen blame Clan MacKay for the attack upon their laird."

"How do you know? Has Seana has been in touch with you?"

Angus laughed. "Aye, she has been a font of information. MacKenna got what he deserved for stealing my intended bride. The feud never should have ended. Once Ross is dead, the fighting will resume, and your father will see the wisdom of giving you to me."

"What wisdom? I doona ken your thinking. How will Ross's death help you and Seana?"

"Seana will become mistress of Ravenscraig and wife to the new laird. 'Twas all she ever wanted. As for me, one day you will ken what it is I desire, but now is not the time. You are here—'tis all that matters. Put away your sword, lass, afore you hurt yourself."

Gillian raised her weapon. "I am going to kill you, Angus Sinclair."

"My hands are clean, Gillian. No one can blame me for attacking your husband. Even if MacKenna has the wits to name his killer before he dies, it willna be me."

"McHamish wouldna have attacked Ross if you and Seana hadna goaded him into it."

Gillian jabbed Angus's shoulder with the tip of her sword, drawing blood. Angus cursed and leaped backward. Immediately two kinsmen rushed to his defense.

"Coward!" Gillian taunted. "Are you afraid to defend yourself? Do you need help subduing a mere woman?"

"My sword," Angus said.

One of Angus's kinsmen tossed him a sword. He caught it handily and used it to push aside Gillian's weapon. "I doona want to hurt my intended wife, lass. My future depends upon our marriage."

"I will never become your wife," Gillian spat. She raised her sword and leaped forward.

Sinclair seemed surprised at the fierceness of Gillian's attack. Frantically he parried her savage thrusts. His shock at her expertise was evidenced in his deep scowl and by his eagerness to retreat from the sharp point of Gillian's sword.

"Stop it, Gillian!" Angus spat. "Stop it, I say!"

Gillian ignored him, for she knew he finally realized he was fighting for his life. Though Angus was larger, stronger, and his sword heavier, Gillian was fast, accurate, and determined. She silently rejoiced when she saw sweat break out on Angus's forehead. Even though it might mean her death, Gillian was determined to kill Angus Sinclair. Never had she wanted anything so badly.

Angus danced away and glanced at the blood flowing down his arm, where Gillian's sword had pierced his flesh. "This is madness, Gillian. I doona want to kill you. Desist now or suffer the consequences."

"Kill me if you can, Angus. If Ross dies, I have naught to live for."

Angus skipped away from a particularly brutal thrust that could have slit his gullet. "This is ridiculous. Seize her!"

Angus's guard was down. Gillian was preparing to lunge forward to deliver the lethal blow when she was seized from behind, her arms pinned at her sides and her sword plucked from her hand. Though she fought hard to escape, two of Angus's kinsmen held her fast.

"Now then," Angus said, wiping sweat from his forehead, "we will see who has the upper hand. Sinclair Keep was to be your home at one time; I hope you enjoy your stay here."

"I amna staying," Gillian proclaimed. "Only a coward refuses a challenge. Do you fear me so much that you had to call for help?"

Angus looked as if he wanted to strike her. His fists

were clenched, his eyes dark with anger. "I fear no woman, Gillian MacKay. I need you alive; killing you would serve naught."

"I doona ken your meaning. What will keeping me here against my will gain you? I am wed to another man."

Angus grinned. "MacKenna is a dead man. If he isna dead yet, he will be soon, with a wee bit of help from a friend."

"Are you suggesting one of Ross's kinsmen would harm him? No one but Niall would gain from his death, and Niall would never harm Ross. I'd stake my life on it."

Angus said naught. Gillian gasped; it suddenly occurred to her to whom Angus was referring. "Seana! You two are working hand in hand to end Ross's life. Ross's death will make her mistress of Ravenscraig."

"Lock my intended wife in the tower," Angus ordered. When Gillian started to protest, Angus said, "Fear not, Gillian; the tower chamber is comfortably furnished. I'm sure you will enjoy your stay there."

Ravenscraig Castle

Gizela refused to allow Seana inside Ross's chamber without supervision. Though Niall questioned her motives, the healer adamantly refused to back down. When Gizela wasn't in attendance, Alice took her place.

The day after Gillian had been forcibly evicted from Ravenscraig, Ross awakened, his memory still confused as to the events that had caused the pain he was feeling. Though he had called out for Gillian time and again, he knew instinctively that the hand soothing his hot brow did not belong to his wife.

When the haze cleared from Ross's eyes, he looked for Gillian, but saw Gizela instead. His mouth was so dry he had difficulty finding moisture to wet his tongue so he could speak.

"What . . . happened?"

"So you finally decided to join the living." Gizela cackled. "What do you remember?"

"Naught. Have . . . I been . . . drugged?"

"Only enough to ease your pain. Infection came despite my best efforts to prevent it."

"Gillian . . ."

Before Gizela could answer, Ross's eyes closed and he drifted off to sleep—a healthy sleep this time, not the death-like state from which he had just emerged. Patting Ross's cheek, Gizela left the chamber to tell Ross's kinsmen that their laird had awakened and would recover. It had been touch-and-go for a while, and even Gizela had begun to doubt her healing skills. But she no longer doubted. Ross would live and bring Gillian back to Ravenscraig, where she belonged.

Seana met Gizela on the stairs. "What is the rush, old woman? Has the laird finally met his maker? Am I the new mistress of Ravenscraig?"

"If that is your hope, then I am the bearer of bad news. Our laird lives and will recover. He awakened and spoke to me just moments ago. Move aside. The laird's kinsmen must be told."

Seana and Angus had planned Ross's demise carefully. Since it appeared that he was going to live, Seana hurried to her chamber to prepare another method guaranteed to bring Ross to a quick end.

Seana wasn't ignorant when it came to herbs and poisons. She knew that certain household poisons could kill a man if given in hefty doses. She had filched a small bottle of arsenic used to kill rodents from Hanna's store of poisons and hidden it in the chamber she shared with Niall. She retrieved it now and tucked it into her pocket, waiting for the right moment to use it. She and Angus Sinclair deserved to get what they both desired.

When Seana entered Ross's chamber, she found Niall, Gordo, and several others crowded around the bed. Cursing her rotten luck, she joined Niall at Ross's bedside.

"I heard Ross has awakened," she said to her husband.

"Aye, Gizela said he spoke to her."

Seana went still. "What did he say?"

Gizela must have heard, for she turned to glare at Seana. "Are you worried what he might say, lady?"

Seana shrugged. "Like everyone else, I was hoping Ross would name his assailant."

"He will," Gizela promised, her eyes glowing with a knowledge no one else possessed. "Mayhap you had best prepare for that day."

Niall sent his wife a narrow-eyed look. "What does Gizela mean, Seana?"

"The healer speaks nonsense. Pay her no heed, husband. I am sure Ross will tell us who tried to kill him."

Gizela turned to address Niall. "Will you ask Hanna to prepare a rich beef broth for Laird Ross?"

"Aye," Niall said as he wheeled about and left.

"The laird needs his rest," Gizela said, shooing everyone from the chamber. "I will summon you when he awakens again."

Ross's worried kinsmen filed out of the chamber. Seana hurried to catch up with Niall.

"You have other things to do, husband. Let me fetch the broth for Ross."

Unaware of his wife's duplicitous plans, Niall readily agreed. The kitchen was a woman's province, and foreign to him.

Hanna had heard about Ross's awakening and had already begun preparing beef broth when Seana entered the kitchen. After Seana relayed Gizela's message, Hanna said, "Tell Gizela I will carry the broth up to Laird Ross when it is ready."

"I'll take it up," Seana offered. "There is no reason for you to climb all those stairs when my legs are younger and stronger than yours."

Suspecting naught, Hanna nodded. "Sit down and wait. It shouldna be long."

The wait, though short, was too long for Seana. The sooner Ross got the poison, the quicker Niall would become laird of Clan MacKenna, and she the mistress of all she beheld. Seana smiled as Hanna ladled the broth into a bowl. Its rich, deep red suited Seana's purposes perfectly. The arsenic would be undetectable.

Hanna set the bowl of steaming broth and a spoon on a tray and handed it to Seana. Seana turned and started down the long passageway to the hall. Glancing about to make sure she was alone, she reached into her pocket and removed the small bottle of poison. Balancing the tray in one hand, she removed the stopper and quickly poured the poison into the broth, stirring it with the spoon to blend it in. If she couldn't have Ross, no one else would.

Seana continued on to Ross's chamber. "It's about

time," Gizela snapped when Seana entered the sick-room with the broth.

"Has Ross awakened?" Seana asked as she set the tray on the bedside table.

"Nay, but I am certain he will awaken soon. Now that his mind is clear, he will be able to name his assailant."

"Shall I feed him the broth?" Seana asked, all innocence and concern.

Gizela's eyes narrowed. "You doona fool me, lass. The devil in your eyes gives you away."

Seana backed off. "I doona ken what you mean."

"Leave me. I doona need your help."

Seana turned to leave, but before she exited the chamber, she glanced over her shoulder and saw Gizela pick up the bowl and spoon and bend over Ross.

Everything was working out just as she'd planned. The old crone would be blamed for Ross's death; no one would suspect Niall's wife.

Gizela waited until Seana left the chamber and closed the door behind her before turning her attention to the broth. She stared into the bowl, examining the contents closely. Then she held it to her nose and sniffed.

When Seana had entered the chamber with the broth, Gizela had seen a black aura surrounding her and realized she was up to no good. Her visions of late had been filled with warnings. She knew intuitively that someone in the keep wished the laird ill.

As Gizela stared into the broth, an image began to form. She saw a hand, a woman's hand, emptying a foreign substance into the broth. Her eyes flared angrily when comprehension dawned. Not one drop of this vile brew, she vowed, would pass the laird's lips. She carried the bowl to the window, opened the sash, and spilled the contents onto the rocks below. Then she pitched the empty bowl and spoon after it.

A few minutes later Alice entered with an armful of clean linen. "Mama wants to know if Laird Ross ate the broth."

Without telling her why, Gizela asked Alice to fetch another bowl. "Bring it yourself, lass," the healer said. "Doona let anyone else touch it."

Alice sent her a puzzled look. "Was something wrong with the first bowl Mama sent up?"

" 'Twas the bearer of the broth I didna trust. Do as I say, lass. Laird Ross is awakening and needs nourishment."

Alice hurried off. She returned a few minutes later with a fresh bowl of broth and a clean spoon. Gizela stared at the contents several long moments before nodding acceptance.

"Laird Ross canna be left alone," she told Alice. "He must be watched over closely and protected from those who wish him harm."

"Does someone in the keep wish Laird Ross harm?" Alice asked, clearly aghast at the thought.

"Aye. Until he is aware of what is going on around him, he is not to be left alone with Seana. Will you help me keep him safe?"

Alice squared her shoulders. "You can trust me, Gizela. I will keep the laird safe for Gillian."

"Gillian . . ."

"The laird speaks," Alice said in a hushed voice.

"Where is . . . my . . . wife?"

"You will see her soon, laddie," Gizela soothed. "You must eat if you wish to regain your strength. Hanna made a tasty beef broth for you." She dipped the spoon into the untainted broth and brought it to Ross's lips. "Open your mouth, laird. The broth will strengthen your blood."

Dutifully, Ross opened his mouth. He didn't realize how hungry he was until the liquid rolled down his throat to his empty stomach. To Gizela's obvious delight, he finished the broth to the last drop.

Gizela set the bowl down and stared into his eyes. "What are you . . . staring at?" he asked. "I amna . . . going to die . . . if that's what you are . . . worried about." His voice was becoming stronger with each word he spoke, his mind more lucid.

"Of course you are nae going to die, laird. Alice and I will see that you stay well."

Ross frowned as he considered her words. "Something is wrong. What are you keeping from me, Gizela?"

"Do you recall what happened to you?"

"I hurt," Ross said, touching the bandage over his wound. His brow wrinkled as he tried to recall.

"Tell me what you remember," Gizela urged.

"Wick," he muttered. "I remember going to Wick to purchase supplies. I rode ahead of the cart on the return to Ravenscraig, and . . ."

"And . . . ?" Gizela prodded.

Ross shook his head. "I canna remember."

"The answer will come to you, laddie. Give it time. Shall I give you something for pain?"

Ross closed his eyes. "No more laudanum. My head is still fuzzy, and I am verra tired. Tell Gillian I wish to see her when I awaken."

"Stay with him, Alice," Gizela said. "There are things I need to do while the laird sleeps."

Alice pulled up a chair and sat at Ross's bedside. "No one will hurt Laird Ross; that I promise," she said.

Gizela nodded and left. The moment she entered

the hall, Seana began to wail, "He's dead! Ross is dead!"

His face a mask of horror, Nial stared at Gizela. "Is it true, Gizela? Is Ross dead?"

Gizela aimed a fierce look at Seana. "Why would you think Laird Ross is dead, lass? He lives and is beginning to recall what happened to him."

"Did . . . did he drink the broth I brought?"

"Aye, every drop, and asked for more. I predict he will be up and around verra soon."

"Are you sure? Verra sure?"

"Aye, no thanks to you." The accusation hung in the air like autumn smoke.

"Are you accusing Seana of something?" Niall asked.

A fierce light appeared in Gizela's eyes. "The truth will come out. Evil doesna go unpunished." After uttering those cryptic words, Gizela made her way to the kitchen.

"Doona listen to that old hag, Niall," Seana said soothingly. "She shouldna be left alone with Ross. I will sit with him if it pleases you."

"It doesna please *me*," Gordo spoke up. "I will sit with Ross myself."

Niall searched Seana's face, his expression puzzled. "What is Gizela talking about, wife? What made you think Ross was dead?"

"I wouldna put it past Gizela to give him a potion to end his life," Seana insisted. "How do we know what she is feeding him?"

"Gizela has no reason to harm Ross. No one here does."

"Aye, you are right," Seana acquiesced. "Forgive me for accusing her falsely."

Niall nodded and walked away. Seana waited until he was out of sight before hurrying to her chamber and packing a bag with her belongings. She didn't know why the poison hadn't worked, but once Ross remembered that her father had attacked him, he would put two and two together and realize that she was in some way involved. It might not be tomorrow or the next day, but when he remembered, she wanted to be far away from here.

Seana knew the only place she would be welcome was Sinclair Keep. Donning her warmest cloak, she left the hall, telling no one but a servant that the day was so fair she'd decided to ride to the village.

While Seana made a stealthy escape, Gizela was in the kitchen questioning Hanna about the rat poison she kept in the storage cabinet. When Hanna went to fetch it, she found it had disappeared.

Chapter Twelve

Ross awakened the following day with a clear mind. He saw Alice dozing in a chair beside the bed and frowned. Where was Gillian? He distinctly recalled asking for her, and couldn't understand why she seemed to be avoiding him. When he tried to sit up, Alice awakened and went to him.

"How are you feeling?" she asked anxiously.

"Better. Will you fetch Gillian for me, please?"

Alice gave him a strange look, then turned and hurried off. Ross didn't think much about her reaction until Gordo, Niall, and Gizela entered the chamber.

"Something is wrong," Ross guessed from Gillian's mysterious absence.

"Do you recall who attacked you?" Niall asked.

"Of course I remember, now that my mind is clear of drugs," he answered, sending a reproachful look toward Gizela.

" 'Twas for your own good," Gizela muttered.

"We held off storming Braeburn Castle until you awakened," Niall explained. "But we are prepared to leave the moment you give the word." He shook his head. "I doona understand why MacKay broke the truce, or why he tried to kill you."

Ross sent him a startled look. "Whatever made you think MacKay was responsible?"

Glaring at Niall and Gordo, Gizela mumbled, "Men act impulsively; women search for the truth."

"Who else would want you dead, Ross?" Niall asked, ignoring Gizela.

"Tearlach MacKay wasna responsible for attacking me," Ross said. "The man who hailed me as a friend and betrayed me was Douglas McHamish."

A strangled gasp escaped from Gordo's throat. "Nay! McHamish has no quarrel with Clan MacKenna."

"I saw him with my own eyes, Uncle," Ross insisted, letting his head fall back against the pillow. "There was bloodlust in his eyes. He wanted me dead."

"For what reason?" Gordo asked.

"Mayhap you should question Seana about that," Ross replied. "But first, tell me why my wife isna at my side, where she belongs."

Niall cleared his throat while Gordo stared down at his feet. Neither man seemed willing to provide an answer.

"Gillian isna at Ravenscraig," Gizela said in a voice that left no doubt about her feelings on the matter.

"She's gone?" Ross gasped. He tried to rise but lacked the strength. "Why would she leave me while I lay near death?"

Though Ross could think of many reasons why Gillian might leave him, none of them was comforting. Anticipating his death, had she fled into the arms of Angus Sinclair, the man she had really wanted to wed?

Did she hate Ross so much that she couldn't wait for him to die before leaving Ravenscraig?

"They sent her away," Gizela said, pointing a bony finger at Niall and Gordo. "Seana spoke out against Gillian. She accused Clan MacKay of trying to kill you, laird."

He rounded on his kinsmen. "And you believed Seana?"

"W-we thought . . ." Niall stammered.

"What did you think?" Ross gritted out from between clenched teeth.

"It wasna Niall's decision alone," Gordo added. "Everyone believed MacKay was responsible and began to look upon Gillian as the enemy."

"We had no choice but to order her to leave," Niall said.

"Niall is right," Gordo confirmed. "Gillian didna want to go, but I advised her to return to Braeburn when things became ugly. I feared for the lass's life and wanted to keep her safe for you."

"I canna believe you forced my wife to leave her home!" Ross berated. "How long has she been gone?"

"Three days. You opened your eyes and spoke shortly after she left but were in no condition to name your assailant. This is the first day you've been coherent."

"You were wrong to force Gillian to leave," Ross declared. "You should have been questioning Seana's loyalty, not Gillian's. Fetch Seana, Niall. Gizela, bring me something to eat, something more substantial than the gruel you've been feeding me."

Though Gizela hurried off to do Ross's bidding, Niall did not immediately leave; he merely shuffled his feet, looking uncomfortable.

"I did what I thought best at the time," Gordo said. "I knew MacKay would protect Gillian, and I talked the others into waiting until you were able to name your attacker before rushing off to lay siege to Braeburn."

"I will take your word about the seriousness of the situation," Ross admitted grudgingly. "If I find Seana is responsible in any way for her father's unprovoked attack, she will be punished."

"As she should be," Gordo agreed.

"Go to Braeburn and fetch Gillian, Uncle. Tell her I want her to return home."

"What about McHamish?"

Ross's expression darkened. "I will get to the bottom of this as soon as I am able. There has to be a reason for McHamish's unprovoked attack."

Gordo took his leave. Ross glanced at Niall, his eyebrows raised in question. "Why are you still here? Did I nae just ask you to fetch your wife?"

Niall shifted nervously. "Seana is gone, Ross. I havena seen her since yesterday. She's not at Ravenscraig; no one except a servant saw her leave."

"Once the laird awakened, Seana realized she couldna stay without implicating herself in the plot against your life," Gizela said as she swept into the chamber. She set the tray she carried on the bedside table. "She tried to kill you by placing poison in your broth. I saw it in a vision and threw out the tainted soup before it passed your lips."

"Seana would never poison Ross," Niall scoffed. "She isna evil."

"Are you sure, Gizela?" Ross asked.

"Verra sure."

"But why? At one time she hoped to become my wife and mistress of Ravenscraig. I knew she was angry when I wed Gillian, but murder?"

"Think about it, laird. Who would gain from your death?" Gizela hinted as she uncovered the tray.

"Gizela is old and senile. Doona listen to her," Niall said disparagingly.

Ross sighed. "Leave me, both of you. I am hungry and tired and need to think. Send Gillian to me when she returns."

Niall looked as if he wished to say more, but left, as Ross had ordered.

Propped up by pillows, Ross partook ravenously of beef-and-barley stew, fresh bread, and ale. Once he had eaten his fill, he decided to test his legs. He rose unsteadily, tottered a moment, and then regained his footing. Though he was still weak and in a good bit of pain, he was a strong man and expected to recover quickly.

He managed to use the chamber pot without help and then staggered back to bed. He wasn't ready to sleep yet; he had too much to think about. Seana had agreed to handfast with Niall with little complaint, and, recalling Gizela's words, Ross now wondered about her willingness. Though his mind was still a bit foggy from the drugs Gizela had fed him, the answer came to him: Niall was next in line to become laird of Clan MacKenna if Ross died without an heir. Had Niall conspired with Seana? Did Niall wish to become laird badly enough to end his life?

Nay, Ross refused to believe his cousin guilty of betrayal. If Seana had conspired with anyone, it was her father. But even that didn't make sense. To his knowledge,

Douglas McHamish had no reason to wish him ill. Yet McHamish had attacked him with the intent to kill.

Ross didn't doubt that Seana had convinced his kinsmen Clan MacKay was responsible for the attack. And she probably would have blamed Gizela if he had died after eating the poisoned broth.

Ross closed his eyes, the pain behind his eyes growing. Gillian was gone because his kinsmen had sent her away. Knowing Gillian, she had probably been livid, and he couldn't blame her if she refused to return.

Ross finally slept. He awakened later that afternoon and ate a hearty evening meal. Despite lingering pain from his wound, he felt his strength returning. Gordo arrived before bedtime to report his findings to Ross.

"Where is Gillian?" Ross wanted to know the moment Gordo entered his chamber. "Did she refuse to leave Braeburn? I canna blame her, but I swear I'll make it up to the lass."

Ross was surprised when Tearlach MacKay followed Gordo through the door. "My daughter isna at Braeburn," MacKay said. "Nor did I ken you had been wounded."

Ross reared up in bed, his mind clear despite the pain caused by his sudden movement. "What do you mean, she isna at Braeburn? Where else would she go?"

"That's what I would like to know, MacKenna," Tearlach growled.

"Think you she sought refuge with Sinclair?" Ross asked. "She wanted Sinclair from the beginning."

"The lass sought vengeance," Gizela muttered.

"Gizela, I didna see you enter," Ross said, spying the old woman standing in a dark corner of the chamber. "What did you say?"

"The lass sought vengeance," Gizela repeated.

"That doesna make sense." Tearlach snorted. "Tell us what you know, old woman."

"Ask the laird. He kenned the truth and spoke the name in his delirium."

Frustrated by Gizela's vagueness, Ross said, "I know naught." Then his brows rose as comprehension dawned. "Think you I spoke McHamish's name to my wife in my delirium?"

"Douglas McHamish?" Tearlach asked. "What has he got to do with all this?"

"McHamish is the man who tried to end my life," Ross explained. "I doona ken why, but the man came at me with his sword when I greeted him as a friend."

"I will go to McHamish and fetch my daughter," Tearlach vowed.

"Not without me," Ross said. "We will leave at first light. Gordo, can our lads be ready that soon?"

"You canna go, laird," Gizela insisted. "You willna be able to sit a horse and could do yourself serious harm. You need more time to mend."

"The healer is right," Tearlach agreed. "McHamish isna my enemy. If he had a reason for wanting you dead, I will drag the answer from him."

"You canna go alone," Ross said. "Take some of the lads with you."

"Aye," Tearlach agreed. "We'll leave at first light."

The men left. Ross found himself alone with Gizela. "I know most people think you daft, Gizela, but I ken better now. Tell me what you know about my wife. Did she seek out McHamish because of me? Though she fancies herself a fierce warrior, she is still a woman with only a woman's strength. Can you 'see' aught, Gizela? I may not believe in pixies and elves, but I am beginning to believe you have certain powers."

Gizela closed her eyes, and when she finally opened them they appeared eerily incandescent. Though her expression was vague, her words cut through the silence like a sharp knife.

"The flame no longer burns at Ravenscraig." Ross opened his mouth to speak, but Gizela raised her hand to stop him. "Your lady is with Sinclair."

Ross wanted to howl. "Gillian is with Sinclair? Why would she go to him?"

The mist in Gizela's eyes cleared, and she seemed to look through Ross without seeing him. Then she turned abruptly and fled.

"Gizela, wait! Tell me more."

Ross staggered from bed to follow. Cursing roundly, he stumbled toward the stairs, hoping to find Gizela in the hall below, but the corridor was strangely deserted.

He met Alice at the top of the steps.

"Is there something you need, laird?" Alice asked.

"Did you see which way Gizela went?"

Alice gave him a strange look. "I didna see Gizela."

"Fetch her for me."

"Shall I help you back to bed first?"

"Nay, I doona need help."

Ross stumbled back to his chamber. He walked across the room and back to test his strength. Though his knees were still wobbly, he knew it wouldn't be long before he could sit a horse.

When neither Gizela nor Alice returned, Ross poured himself a mug of ale from a pitcher Gizela had left for him earlier and sought his bed. Before he fell asleep, his thoughts turned to his fierce bride with the flaming hair and a spirit to match. When had he come to care for her? How had she found her way into his heart in so short a time?

* * *

"Wake up, laird. MacKay has returned."

Ross opened his eyes to a weak winter sun shining through the window. Gizela was shaking him. He blinked several times until Gizela's wrinkled face came into focus. "What did you say?"

"MacKay has returned."

"What time is it? Have I slept long?"

"I put laudanum in your ale. You slept through the night; 'tis nearly noon."

Ross seared her with a furious glare. "You drugged me again!"

Gizela showed little remorse. "Sleep is the best healer. Alice is fetching something for you to eat."

"Where is MacKay? Is Gillian with him?"

"The MacKay laird is partaking of the midday meal in the hall. He will tell you what you want to know."

"I will join him. Fetch someone to help me dress. Gillian deserves an apology from me."

"I doona think—"

"Say no more, Gizela. I am going, and that's final."

Ross swung his legs over the side of the bed and stood. He took a few steps, pleased by his progress. When Gizela continued to stand there, he growled, "Go!"

Gizela scooted from the chamber as Ross went in search of his clothing. Donald arrived a few minutes later, took one look at Ross, and smiled.

"'Tis good to see you up and about, laird. We all feared for your life."

"I couldna remain in bed a minute longer. There is too much to be done. Help me with my braies and shirt. I am anxious to see Gillian. We all owe her an apology."

Donald sent him a contrite look. "I ken we jumped

to the wrong conclusions about the MacKay lass, but we were too worried about you to think clearly."

"For the first time in my life I amna proud of what my kinsmen did," Ross allowed. "But I intend to right the wrong that was done to Gillian."

Ross buttoned his shirt over his bandaged torso and headed toward the door. "Lead the way, Donald; I am ready to resume my duties as laird of Clan MacKenna."

Though it was slow going, Ross managed to navigate the spiral staircase with naught but a steadying hand from Donald. When he entered the hall, everyone stood up and cheered. Ross failed to locate Gillian when he scanned the hall, but he did see MacKay sitting at the high table. His steps slow but steady, Ross joined MacKay. Though it was difficult to admit, it felt good to sit after the long trek down the stairs. But Ross's mind was on more important matters than pain and weakness.

"Where is Gillian? Did you bring her back with you?"

MacKay sighed heavily. "She wasna with McHamish."

Ross shot from his chair. "What are you saying? Where is she? She couldna have disappeared into thin air. If McHamish has harmed her, I will kill him with my bare hands."

"Sit down, MacKenna, and listen to what I tell you. 'Tis a strange story, but it makes sense when one considers Gillian's fiery nature. My daughter arrived at McHamish's keep with every intention of killing him."

"Did she? Kill him, I mean?"

MacKay snorted. "I have no doubt she would have if McHamish hadna explained some things to her."

"What things?" Ross roared. "Doona keep me in suspense."

"Sit down, lad. Fill your plate and eat while I talk. You look like you could use a good meal."

Ross had to admit he was hungry. Broth and gruel did little to fill a grown man's stomach. He filled his plate from platters of meat, potatoes, and root vegetables, buttered a slice of thick bread, and began to eat. But he had a hard time swallowing. How could he eat when he knew naught of Gillian's fate?

MacKey cleared his throat. "When Gillian was driven from Ravenscraig, she went directly to McHamish Keep and accused him of attempted murder. She challenged him, but McHamish refused to fight a woman."

"I'm surprised Gillian didna run him through," Ross muttered.

"So am I, but McHamish explained that his rage at you had been fueled by Angus Sinclair and his own daughter. He was so angry, he could think of naught but killing you for making his daughter your whore. He believed you forced her to become your leman and then abandoned her."

"I should have insisted that Seana return to her father's keep before I wed Gillian," Ross reflected. "But Niall wanted her, and she seemed willing enough. Did you find Seana with McHamish?"

"Nay, McHamish swore he hadna seen Seana since Murdoc's wedding. He didna even know she had left Ravenscraig. Seana and Sinclair conspired against you and brought McHamish into it when Sinclair told him that you had cast Seana aside and forced her to handfast with your cousin, a coldhearted man who treated her cruelly."

"Niall? Coldhearted and cruel? Bah! Not bloody likely!"

"According to McHamish, Gillian set him straight.

Apparently my daughter felt McHamish had been deceived and gave him the benefit of the doubt. He told me he'd been planning to confess all to you, but his wife begged him to stay with her a little longer."

Ross nearly choked on his mouthful of food. "Think you Gillian went after Sinclair?"

" 'Tis what McHamish says."

"Sinclair is without scruples; he has no conscience. What did he hope to accomplish by goading McHamish to act against me? I doona understand."

MacKay shook his head. "Nor do I. At one time I considered Angus Sinclair the perfect mate for my daughter. I would have wed her to him had I not called a truce between our clans, and had he not delayed in signing the betrothal contract."

"We've heard naught from Gillian. What do you think that means?" Ross asked.

MacKay searched Ross's face. "I am worried, MacKenna. I doona ken what has happened to my lass."

Ross's face hardened. "I will confront Sinclair first and take care of McHamish later. Go home, MacKay. Gillian is my responsibility. I vow I will bring Gillian home to Ravenscraig, safe and sound. Although my kinsmen sent her from Ravenscraig without my knowledge, the guilt is still mine."

MacKay stood. "Send word if you need me."

Ross watched MacKay leave the hall. The thought that Gillian was with Sinclair made Ross's gut clench. Gillian might have been set on vengeance, but Sinclair was too sly and conniving for Ross's liking. Then again, Gillian might have gone to Sinclair for succor. That thought set Ross's teeth on edge.

Ross was smart enough to know that Sinclair wanted him dead so he could have Gillian, but deep in his heart Ross knew there had to be more to it than that, a deep, dark reason that no one was aware of. Ross intended to learn that reason if he had to choke it out of Sinclair.

Seana gave him another reason to worry. Where was she? If she hadn't gone home to her father's keep, where had she gone? There was but one answer, and it didn't take a genius to figure it out. Only one person would welcome Seana, and that was Angus Sinclair. What kind of mischief were they plotting?

Gillian paced the tower chamber, searching fruitlessly for a way to escape. As Angus had promised, the chamber was comfortable and she had not been harmed. But she was a prisoner, left to languish in solitude—too much solitude, with far too many empty hours to fret, to wonder if Ross was dead or alive. Though her heart told her he still lived, she needed more proof than woman's intuition.

Gillian was looking out the tiny window at the rocks below when the door opened and Angus entered the chamber. She whirled, scowling at the man she had come to despise.

"There is no escape, Gillian. You will fall to your death on the rocks below if you attempt to jump out the window."

"I will keep that as an option," Gillian sneered. "I prefer, however, to wait for Ross to come for me. It will be interesting to see what punishment he will devise for you."

Sinclair frowned and pointed to a three-legged stool. "Sit down, lass. There's something I must tell you."

Gillian resisted only a moment before plopping

down onto the stool. She was too curious to defy Angus. "Verra well, what do you wish to tell me?"

"Ross MacKenna is dead," he lied. "He passed away two days ago. Good riddance, I say."

Gillian leaped from her stool and flew at Sinclair, flailing at him with her fists. "Nay, you lie! Ross isna dead! I can feel him in my heart."

Angus captured her wrists and pushed her away. "You love the bastard! How could you? I thought you loved me, that you were forced to wed MacKenna."

"I didna know what love was until I met Ross. I admit I hated him at first, but that was before I really knew him."

"He killed your brothers."

"I don't know that Ross was the one who slew them. Anyone could have killed them in the heat of battle. I now realize that seeking a truce was the right thing to do. The killing has stopped; my surviving brothers will live to wed and have children."

He shoved her away. She stumbled backward and clutched the edge of the table to keep her balance.

"That will change when the feud resumes," Sinclair said.

Gillian caught her breath. "Why is that important to you?"

Angus started to answer but caught himself in time. He appeared surprised when Gillian whirled on him and asked, "Who told you Ross is dead? I doona believe you."

"Ross MacKenna lives," a voice announced from the doorway.

"Damn you, Seana, when will you learn to keep your mouth shut?" Angus shouted.

"What are you doing here, Seana?" Gillian wondered aloud.

"Gizela discovered what I had done, so I left while I was still able."

Gillian sent Angus a smug look. "I knew you were lying. Ross and his kinsmen should be arriving at your gates verra soon."

"I wouldna be too sure of that, Gillian MacKay," Seana replied. "Ross is in no condition to leave his bed. And his kinsmen are nae fond of you. Mayhap Ross is glad to be rid of you."

Mayhap Seana was right, but Gillian would have to hear it from Ross's lips before she believed it. "Let me go to Ross, Angus. You have no right to hold me against my will. As long as Ross lives, I am still wed to him. Your plans have gone awry—admit it."

"I admit naught. If MacKenna is lucid and recovering, he kens who attacked him and will be making plans to slay his enemy. Meanwhile, let him think you are at Braeburn."

"Ross will send men to Braeburn for me when he learns what his kinsmen have done."

"It will take time for MacKenna to recuperate, let alone figure out where you went and go after McHamish. Mayhap he will kill McHamish before McHamish implicates me."

"And mayhap he will listen to McHamish, just as I did."

"She's right, Angus," Seana mused. "Ross MacKenna doesna kill indiscriminately. He will listen to my father. He will want to know what he did to earn Father's enmity. You must prepare for an attack."

"The MacKays and MacKennas are allies now," Gillian reminded him. "You are doomed. Together they will annihilate you. You canna hope to defend your keep against their combined strength."

Gillian silently rejoiced. She believed Angus had no choice but to release her.

"I am smarter than both your father and MacKenna."

Gillian felt cold fingers of fear creep up her spine. "What are you going to do?"

A sly look flitted across Sinclair's face. "I admit that MacKenna will find his way here eventually. When he arrives, you will tell him you came to me of your own free will, that you prefer me to him. According to the terms of the truce, if you leave Ravenscraig of your own free will, the feud will resume."

Resentment tinged Gillian's words. "I didna leave of my own free will!"

"You will tell MacKenna that you sought refuge with me because I am the only one who offered you comfort. You will convince him that you wish to remain with me. If you do not, I will order my men to loose their arrows at him as soon as he approaches the keep," Angus said with a smirk. "His kinsmen will consider the truce broken, which is precisely what I want. MacKenna will be dead, and both clans will eventually annihilate each other, until there is no male heir to take your father's place as Laird of Clan MacKay. Only you will survive."

Curiosity tugged at Gillian. "Why should that matter to you?"

Angus sent her a feral grin. "Figure it out, Gillian." He turned to Seana. "Come, Seana, let us leave Gillian to ponder her life as my future wife."

Gillian paced the tiny tower chamber, Angus's words ringing in her head. She didn't doubt for a minute that Angus would kill Ross if she didn't do as he asked. And now that Angus knew she loved Ross, he had a powerful weapon to use against her.

Gillian's dilemma, as she saw it, was to lie to Ross or let him die at the gates of Sinclair Keep. Time lengthened as she contemplated Angus's duplicity and how badly she had misjudged his character. When Seana entered the tower chamber with Gillian's supper, Gillian was surprised so many hours had passed.

Seana set the tray on the small table, and when she didn't leave, Gillian asked, "Have you come to gloat?"

"It does my heart good to see you thus. It wouldna have come to this if you hadna wed Ross. I should be the mistress of Ravenscraig."

"Why rehash the past? You are handfasted to Niall. Niall is a good man; you should have been the kind of wife he deserves."

Seana lowered her voice so that the guard could not hear. "Niall isna Ross." She shrugged. "'Tis too late now. I can never return to Ravenscraig after what I did."

Gillian went still. "What did you do?"

"It scarcely matters, since naught came of it. Suffice it to say I am no longer welcome there." She circled Gillian slowly, her face mottled with envy. "And now Angus has his sights set on you. But doona mistake his motives. He cares naught for you."

"If that's what you came to tell me, you are wasting your time. I already figured that out. I canna believe my family didna ken Angus's evil nature long ago."

Seana leaned in close. "Mayhap I can help you."

"You wish to help me?" Gillian asked incredulously. "Why?"

A guard, standing near the door, cleared his throat. "Time to leave, mistress."

Without a word of explanation, Seana spun on her

heel and exited behind the guard. Gillian sat down hard on the stool. What did Seana mean? Did she really want to help her? It seemed unlikely. Gillian knew Seana too well. The other woman did naught unless it served her own purpose.

Gillian sighed wearily. This was all her fault. She had acted impulsively. Instead of thinking things through after being forced to leave Ravenscraig, she had rushed forth to avenge Ross, and look where it had gotten her.

In more trouble than she had ever faced before.

Chapter Thirteen

Ross's recuperation was nothing less than a miracle. Gizela's salves and herbal concoctions had given energy to Ross's body at the same time they healed his wound. Three days later, though lacking his full strength, Ross pronounced himself ready to confront Sinclair and bring his wife back to Ravenscraig. He needed to tell Gillian that, had he known what his kinsmen intended, she would have never been sent away.

As Ross pulled on his padded leather vest and armed himself, he worried constantly about Gillian. If she had succeeded in killing Angus Sinclair, why hadn't anyone carried the message to Ravenscraig? If Gillian had failed, wouldn't she have fled to Braeburn? He clenched his fists. If Sinclair had hurt Gillian, he was a dead man. His face set in harsh lines, Ross strapped on his claymore and dirk, flung his plaid over his shoulders for warmth, and strode into the hall to join his clansmen.

Ross nodded in satisfaction when he was greeted by twenty armed men, all of whom had vowed to right the wrong they had done Gillian by accusing her unjustly. Dawn was just breaking when Ross led his clansmen out the door into the cold, crisp air. Their horses pawed the snow-covered ground; gusts of warm air turned frosty as they exhaled. A glance at the bruised, sullen sky convinced Ross that the sun would not make an appearance on this raw winter day.

They rode without stopping until the modest towers of Sinclair Keep came into view. Ross halted his clansmen well out of arrow range, but close enough to be seen and heard by the men patrolling the wall walk.

Cupping his hands around his mouth, Ross shouted, "Inform Sinclair, if he is still alive, that Ross MacKenna is here, and that I've come for my wife."

Ross saw men scurrying atop the wall walk and wondered whether Sinclair would show himself. He didn't have long to wait. Ross spat out a curse when he noted that Sinclair seemed in good health.

"Where is my wife?" Ross shouted.

"What makes you think she is here?"

"Doona take me for a fool, Sinclair. I know what you and Seana did, how you gulled McHamish into believing his daughter was being mistreated. I also know Gillian came here after she left McHamish Keep. Where is she? What have you done to her?"

"Gillian is in good health, MacKenna. You have the right of it—she did come here. But not for the reason you seem to think. She came here for comfort and succor after your kinsmen forced her to leave Ravenscraig."

"That wasna my doing, and well you know it."

"Gillian doesna want you, MacKenna. She came to me. I welcomed her in my home and in my bed."

Ross felt his heart thud painfully against his chest. "I doona believe you. What have you done to her?"

"I did naught but show her kindness. Unlike your kinsmen, mine welcomed her."

Ross dismounted and approached the wall. "I will believe that when I hear it from Gillian's own lips. She kens the consequences should she leave me, and I doona believe she wants war."

"Verra well, MacKenna, have it your way. I'll fetch Gillian so she can tell you in person how she feels."

Niall and Gordo dismounted and joined Ross. "Doona trust him," Gordo warned. "Gillian's own father believed she intended to kill Sinclair. Why would she fall into his arms and his bed? Unless, of course," Gordo mused, "McHamish lied to MacKay."

Ross wouldn't know what to believe until he spoke with Gillian.

Gillian looked expectantly toward the door when she heard the key turning in the lock. She reared back when the door banged open and Angus appeared in the opening.

"He's here," Angus snarled. "The man has amazing recuperative powers."

Gillian's heart soared. Ross was alive and well. Thank God for Gizela and her healing powers. Her hopes quickly deflated, however, when she realized that Ross was in grave danger.

"The time has come to express your love for me, and to let your husband know you doona wish to be with him."

"Angus," Gillian pleaded, "doona do this. Death and destruction are sure to follow."

"Aye, I'm counting on it. Your brothers will return to Braeburn, and the feud will resume. You've already lost two brothers—only three more to go."

Gillian sucked in her breath. "You're mad!"

Angus smirked. "*Ambitious* is a more fitting word." He grasped her wrist. "Come, 'tis time to declare your love for me to your husband."

Gillian raised her chin to a defiant angle. "You canna make me do it."

Angus shrugged. "It wouldna be difficult to order my archers to put an end to his life. I have but to give the signal to my kinsmen. One way or another, the feud *will* resume. It makes no difference to me whether or not Ross MacKenna leads his clansmen into battle."

Fear thudded through Gillian. What choice did she have? She would say anything to save Ross's life. Once Ross was out of danger, she would figure out a way to thwart Angus and his nefarious plans.

"Verra well, I will lie to save Ross's life. But I doubt he will believe me."

"For his sake, you had best make him believe whatever you tell him. Enough talk—MacKenna awaits you."

Gillian preceded Angus down three flights of stairs to the hall and out the front door. But instead of leading her to the wall walk, he guided her to the portcullis. Her heart nearly burst with love when she heard Ross call her name. How could she do what Angus demanded of her? She answered her own question: She had to if she wished Ross to live.

"Are you all right, lass?" Ross called.

Fearing that he was too close to Angus's archers, Gillian warned, "Stay where you are, Ross."

"Is Sinclair holding you prisoner?"

"Nay, I am here of my own free will. Your kinsmen sent me away. There was nowhere else I wished to be."

"That was not my doing, Gillian. I was unconscious

and couldna stop them. They realize their mistake now and wish to apologize."

When Gillian couldn't find the words to answer, Angus hissed, "Speak up. Convince him."

"I doona want you, Ross. I never wanted you. I was forced to wed you against my wishes. 'Tis Angus I want. 'Tis Angus I've always wanted and should have wed."

"I could have sworn Gillian cared for you, lad," Gordo said, "but I was wrong. You heard her. Let us go. You doona need the lass."

"I doona trust Sinclair. Look at Gillian, Gordo. She looks . . . Her expression isna natural."

"Ross, did you hear me?" Gillian shouted. "I wish to stay with the man I love."

Ross winced. Her repudiation of their fledging relationship hurt more than he cared to admit. "Didna McHamish explain that Sinclair goaded him into attacking me?"

Gillian swallowed hard. "I didna believe McHamish. Angus wouldna encourage an unprovoked attack. McHamish lies."

"Not bloody likely," Ross said darkly. He tried again. "You know what will happen if you refuse to return to Ravenscraig with me, do you nae?"

Now it was Gillian's turn to wince. "Aye, I know the consequences, but I must follow my heart."

Angus's arm snaked around Gillian's waist as he whispered in her ear, "Nice touch. If I didna know the truth, I would believe you myself."

"Our clans will fight until no one is left standing. Is that what you want?" Ross challenged. "Your brothers and father could die."

"Nay, I . . ." Gillian stifled a cry when Angus's hand

tightened painfully on her arm. "Just go away and leave us in peace, Ross."

Determination hardened Ross's features. "I refuse to allow your selfish disregard for your family to end the hard-won truce that both clans sought." He started forward. "You are coming home with me."

Angus gave a barely discernible signal to his archers, who immediately readied their bows. Nearly frantic with fear, Gillian cried, "Doona come any closer, Ross." Then she flung herself into Angus's arms and kissed him.

"Well-done," Angus murmured against her lips. Then he kissed her back, nearly gagging her with his tongue as he thrust it into her mouth.

Gillian wanted to spit out his taste, to wash out her mouth, but she forced herself to accept his kiss as well as his hand on her breast. Whatever it took to save Ross's life, she would do. But once Ross left, she would kill Angus if he ever touched her in that way again.

Angus broke off the kiss. "Listen to the lass, MacKenna. Accept that we are lovers and let the feud resume. My kinsmen and I will fight beside the MacKays, just as we always have."

As if he hadn't heard, Ross drew his claymore and continued walking toward the gate. Angus nodded to one of his archers, who immediately raised his bow and pulled back the string. Gordo, who had been watching the wall walk closely, yelled a warning and pushed Ross aside. The arrow missed Ross by scant inches. Gordo pulled Ross back toward the main body of his men.

"She's not worth it, lad. 'Tis obvious you misjudged the MacKay lass. She was just waiting for the chance to betray you. Come away. Send for MacKay and discuss this latest development with him. The peace terms were agreed upon by both clans. If you decide they have been broken and the feud should resume, then so be it. We will answer the call to arms."

When Ross had seen Sinclair place his hands on Gillian, he wanted to howl in outrage. And when Gillian kissed the other man, he had been ready to scale the wall and kill Sinclair first and then his faithless wife. The arrow that narrowly missed him drove home what Ross had known for some time: Sinclair wanted him dead. Had his kinsmen been right all along? Had Gillian helped Sinclair plan his death?

Reluctantly Ross turned away and mounted his horse. He would waste no more time on the woman who had betrayed him. He never wanted to see the flame-haired witch again.

Gillian felt Angus's fingers tighten on her arm as Ross turned and rode away. She wanted to call him back, to beg him not to leave her, but she couldn't live with being responsible for Ross's death.

But Angus hadn't won yet. She would find a way to foil his plans and return to Ravenscraig, to the man she loved.

"You were wise to send MacKenna away," Angus sneered as he caressed her arms.

Gillian pulled herself free from his loathsome embrace. "Never touch me again!" she spat. Her fierceness must have startled him, for he removed his hand. "I canna bear your hands on me."

"Get used to it," Angus snarled. "When we wed, you *will* give me an heir."

A hint of malice tinged Gillian's chilling words. "Mayhap you willna live to touch me again."

Angus seemed taken aback by her venom. "Gillian," he cajoled, "we were betrothed; at one time you were eager to wed me."

"I am wed to Ross, Angus. There is no way those bonds can be broken short of—"

". . . death," Angus finished. "Exactly. I am a patient man. I can wait." He grinned. "I doona think it will be too long a wait."

He grasped her arm and began pulling her back toward the keep. Gillian's teeth were chattering in the cold air, and she didn't resist. Her day would come, and when it did, she would be ready.

Seana met them at the door. "That went well," she gloated. "Ross's expression when you caressed his wife was priceless. He deserved that and more for abandoning me and wedding MacKay's daughter."

Angus pushed Seana aside. "Move, woman; make room for my future wife."

Seana followed them into the hall. "I doona ken why you still want the MacKay wench after MacKenna used her."

"I intend to wed Gillian after her husband's demise."

Seana sidled up to him. "Why do you want an unwilling woman when you can have me? We both know Niall willna want me back in his life. You and I are two of a kind. Your keep would be well managed if you wed me."

Angus let his gaze rove over her. "You are good between the sheets, Seana, but you would bring naught to me in marriage. 'Tis likely your father has already disowned you. But mayhap I will keep you as my leman."

Gillian watched Seana's face closely. Her sour expression told Gillian that Angus's words did not sit well with her. Did Seana now hope to wed a chieftain, since she'd failed to find a laird for herself?

"You are welcome to Angus," Gillian said, sniffing in disdain. "I already have a husband; I doona need another."

Seana stared at Gillian, her eyes narrowed. Tossing a glance at Sinclair, she turned and left in a fury.

"You and Seana are perfect for each other, Angus," Gillian ventured. "You are wasting your time on me. I loathe you."

Angus gave her a violent shove. "We'll see about that. Up the stairs with you. You will reside in the tower until my plans come to fruition. Meanwhile, prepare yourself for a visit from me tonight. 'Tis time I availed myself of your charms."

Gillian rounded on him. "Over my dead body."

Angus sent her a disparaging look. "You are unarmed and at my mercy. You will submit to my will, for you have no other choice. Besides," he gloated, "your husband already thinks we are lovers."

He gave her another shove toward the stairs. Since Gillian had no choice but to obey, she started up the winding staircase, her thoughts spinning wildly out of control. In a moment of desperation she considered turning abruptly and plowing into Angus, sending him hurtling down the stairs. She almost put that thought into action, until she considered that Angus might pull her down with him. She flattened her hand over her stomach. She had missed her woman's time and had begun to suspect that she was carrying Ross's heir. She could not dare risk harming her bairn.

When she aimed a sidelong glance at Angus over her shoulder, he growled, "Doona even think it."

Sighing, Gillian continued up the stairs. When they reached the tower, Angus opened the door, shoved her inside the chamber, and slammed the door behind her. She heard the key turn in the lock and Angus say, "Mayhap going without your supper will make you more amenable to my advances."

"Not bloody likely," Gillian muttered beneath her breath.

Gillian stared at the closed door, wishing she were a wisp of smoke that could slide under the door to freedom. She sat down on the narrow bed, rested her elbows on her knees, and cupped her chin with her hands.

Try though she might, she failed to understand the logic behind Angus's actions. She knew he wanted Ross dead, but why did he want the feud to resume? None of it made sense. Even if Ross died, she still had a father and three brothers to defend her honor. Surely not all of them would die in battle. What made Angus so certain her entire family would perish?

The supper hour came and went. Gillian began seriously to consider ways to thwart Angus's unwanted attention. Without a weapon, she had no hope. But as long as she possessed determination and will, she would defend herself as best she could. She would make sure Angus understood that bedding her would be akin to bedding a wildcat.

The cruel reality of darkness followed close on the heels of twilight. Gillian stared at the door, inwardly preparing for Angus's entrance. Though she nearly went mad waiting, the delay gave her an opportunity to form a plan of sorts. She wouldn't submit easily. Mayhap Angus would lose interest and seek Seana's bed instead.

Refusing to let sleep claim her, Gillian remained awake and alert. The candle had burned down to a stub when she heard the door latch rattle. She stiffened and rose to meet Angus, determined to stand on her own two feet instead of cowering like a weakling.

The door opened, but the figure that slipped inside was not Angus.

"Seana! I thought you were Angus. What are you doing here?"

Seana smiled thinly. "Angus is dicing, drinking, and bragging to his kinsmen about bedding Laird Ross's wife. We doona have much time."

"Time for what?"

"I've come to set you free."

Stunned, Gillian stared at Seana as if she had just grown horns. "Liar. You doona like me. Did Angus send you to torment me?"

"Forget Angus. You are a distraction to him. I want Angus for myself, and that willna happen as long as you remain here. I am no longer welcome at Ravenscraig after what I did. I have no home, for my father willna allow me to return."

"What did you do?"

"It doesna matter now. But if I canna have Ross, Angus will do. He may not be an important laird like Ross, but he is a chieftain. Once Angus beds you, he willna turn to me again."

"I willna let Angus bed me," Gillian vowed. "I want naught to do with him."

"Then you will be pleased to be free of him."

"Aye, verra pleased." Gillian narrowed her eyes. "But why not just kill me? Why are you offering me freedom?"

"Your death wouldna endear me to Angus. He would know immediately that I was responsible."

"Angus will still punish you if I disappear. He will guess you were involved."

"Think you I am stupid?" She walked to the window and flung open the shutters that Gillian had closed against the cold. "You are going to leap to your death."

A look of horror appeared on Gillian's face. "You are mad. I may be desperate, but not desperate enough to leap to my death."

"No one will die. Rip off a portion of your gown."

"What?"

Impatience colored her words. "Hurry! Angus will tire of dicing soon, and his thoughts will turn to bedding you."

Curious but still wary, Gillian ripped the hem of her gown and handed it to Seana. She watched curiously as Seana walked to the window and tossed the material through the opening. Gillian ran to the window and watched the cloth flutter down and land close to the riverbank on the rocks below.

"That should do it," Seana said. "Angus will think you leaped to your death and that your body was carried out to sea. Follow me."

"Where are we going?"

"There's another set of stairs that leads to the kitchens. Servants sometimes use them. I'll show you to the postern gate, where a horse is waiting for you. The horse willna be your own, for that would ruin the ruse. 'Tis a horse I purchased for you in the village earlier today. Here," she said, pulling off her cloak and handing it to Gillian. "Wear this."

"How will we leave without being seen by the guards?"

"There is no guard at the door. Angus no longer saw any need. The door to the tower is locked from the outside, so he thought there was no way you could escape." She crept out the door and motioned for Gillian to follow. The moment Gillian cleared the door, Seana closed and locked it.

"This way," Seana whispered. "The servants are abed. We shouldna encounter anyone about in the kitchen."

Seana located the staircase and led the way down the narrow passage lit by wall sconces. When they reached the bottom, Seana stepped into the kitchen, looked around, and motioned for Gillian to follow.

The cavernous kitchen was deserted, just as Seana had predicted. Gillian followed her out the door and into the dark garden.

"Is there a guard at the postern gate?" Gillian whispered as they made their way through the frosty night air.

"Aye, but you need not worry about him. He should be sleeping soundly. I slipped a sleeping draft in his ale before he went on duty."

"You've thought of everything," Gillian muttered.

"I am naught but thorough when my sights are set on something I want. Angus may suspect, but no proof exists that would point to me."

Snow crunched beneath their feet as Seana led Gillian through the cold winter night to the postern gate. Gillian stopped abruptly when she saw a guard leaning against the wall. He appeared to be sleeping soundly, if his snoring was any indication.

Ignoring him, Seana found the latch and swung the gate open. Gillian froze at the squeal of rusty hinges and then relaxed when the guard remained oblivious. Gillian stepped out through the gate and spied the horse, its reins tethered beneath a rock.

"I want my sword," Gillian said, turning back to Seana.

"I couldna steal one and had no coin to buy one. Mayhap you willna need a weapon. Braeburn isna far. But you must hurry. The guard will awaken soon, and I want to be in the hall when Angus decides to join you in the tower."

Fearing that Seana was up to some kind of trickery, Gillian pulled the reins from beneath the rock, flung herself atop the horse, and galloped off into the darkness.

Seana shut and latched the gate and returned to the keep the same way she had left. From the kitchen she entered the hall and seated herself beside the hearth, where Angus could see her. Quietly, she picked up a piece of embroidery she had left there earlier. If she were lucky, Angus wouldn't realize she had left while he and his kinsmen caroused.

A short time later Angus rose and stretched. "Enough," he said, failing to keep the excitement from his voice. " 'Tis time I showed my future wife that I am more of a man than the MacKenna laird."

A loud cheer rose from his companions, along with lewd words of advice. Angus noticed Seana and strutted over to her, staggering slightly. "Have you been here long?"

"Aye, you were too interested in dicing and drinking to notice me. You doona have to go to Gillian, you ken. While I am eager to please you, I doubt Gillian will welcome you."

Angus puffed out his chest. "Bedding Gillian has naught to do with you and me. She was meant to be mine, and I shall have her, even if I have to force her. Mayhap her husband will set her aside after we become lovers. If that happens, the feud will continue and Braeburn will be mine."

"I doona ken how Braeburn will be yours. Gillian

has three living brothers and a father. They would have to die before Braeburn would fall to Gillian."

Angus's eyes gleamed with malice. "They will die; I will make sure of it."

Because their minds worked in the same way, Seana understood immediately what Angus planned. "You intend to kill them yourself."

Angus shrugged. "Men die in battle. Who is to say who killed whom?"

Admiration glowed in Seana's eyes. "We think alike, Angus Sinclair."

Angus sent her a puzzled look and strode off. Seana calmly picked up the piece of embroidery she had been working on and, smiling savagely, pierced the cloth with the needle.

Seana heard Angus's howl of outrage filtering down from the upper reaches of the keep, and her smile widened. A few minutes later Angus came bounding down the stairs, his face white as a sheet. She jumped from her chair.

"Angus, what's wrong?"

"The bitch has killed herself!" he shrieked as he flew out the door. "Follow me," he called to his kinsmen, who were staring at him as if he had lost his mind. To a man, they rushed out after him.

An hour passed before the lot of them returned. Angus stumbled to the hearth and subsided into a chair, looking defeated.

"What happened?" Seana asked innocently. "How did Gillian kill herself? She had no weapon. What did you expect to find outside?"

Someone handed Angus a mug of ale. His hands shook as he brought it to his mouth and drank deeply. "She leaped to her death," he said shakily. "We found a piece of her gown caught on the rocks below. She must have fallen into the river and been swept out to sea. We didna look farther downstream, for the fall alone would have killed her."

He grasped Seana's hand. "I didna want the lass to die, Seana. I wanted to wed her. I wouldna have believed it of her if I hadna seen the proof for myself." He shook his head. "Gone. Everything I have done to secure my future died with Gillian. What am I going to tell the MacKay?"

Seana made soothing noises as she reached out to Angus. "You still have me, Angus. Come to bed—let me comfort you."

Confused and broken, his plan in ruins, Angus rose and followed Seana up the stairs to his bedchamber.

Gillian couldn't believe Seana had freed her, despite the fact that her motives had been selfish. She kept glancing behind her, waiting for the sound of Angus's men hunting her down. The horse she rode was neither young nor fast, and the night was dark and moonless. How she hated to leave Silver behind. But she counted herself fortunate not to be afoot.

Seana had been wrong, however, when she assumed that Gillian would go to her father at Braeburn. Nay, she would return to Ravenscraig and Ross. She knew he was angry with her, and prayed he wouldn't send her away. If he still desired peace between their clans, he had no choice but to let her remain with him. She desperately hoped he would understand why she had lied about being Angus's lover and realize she had sent him away to save his life.

Gillian picked her way across sweeping moorland made treacherous by a dark sky raining icy pellets down upon her. She was cold, so very cold. How she wished she had her plaid to keep her warm. The thin cloak Seana had given her did naught to keep out the wind. Still, she pushed onward, too numb with cold to realize that snow had begun to fall from the sullen sky, or that she was just scant miles from Ravenscraig.

Shivering uncontrollably, Gillian bent low over her horse's withers, clutching its mane with stiff fingers to keep from falling from the saddle. When she heard a horn cut through the silence, she glanced up, stunned to see Ravenscraig Tower looming before her. When she tried to call out, naught but a loud croak issued forth. Two large tears ran down her cheeks, followed by another and another. They froze on her face.

Gillian closed her eyes; she was tired, so very tired. Her hands and feet had lost all sense of feeling long ago. Her hold on the horse's mane loosened, and she started to fall. The frozen ground came up to meet her and she knew no more.

Chapter Fourteen

Ross rolled out of bed in a foul mood. Returning to Ravenscraig without Gillian had left a bad taste in his mouth, even though it had been Gillian's choice to remain with her lover. Ross shook his head to clear it of unwanted thoughts. Until he decided what was to be done about the situation, he didn't want to think about Gillian.

Ross washed in icy water, shaved, dressed, and descended to the hall to break his fast. His bleak features and stormy expression must have warned everyone away, for Gordo merely nodded to him and returned his attention to his food. The assembly in the hall turned deathly quiet, until Ross lifted his mug of ale and drank deeply. Then the babble of voices resumed.

Ross knew he wasn't fit company right now, and wondered if he ever would be again. A knife had been thrust into his heart and he was still bleeding. The problem, as he saw it, was whether he should fight for his wife or disavow her. According to the terms of the truce, if Gillian refused to return to his keep, the feud would resume. The good Lord knew their marriage had had a rocky beginning. Perhaps they were just two people who should never have wed.

"Forget her, lad," Gordo advised when Ross continued to stare into his bowl of porridge without tasting it. "No woman is worth such anguish."

Ross sent him a stony glare. "Go to hell, Uncle."

Gordo shrugged and resumed eating. As for Ross, his appetite had fled. If it weren't so cold and blustery outside, he could work out his frustrations in swordplay. Mayhap he could organize wrestling matches in the hall and take on anyone willing to accept his challenge. Anything was better than sitting in the keep with naught to do but mull over past mistakes.

Forcing himself to forget his faithless wife, Ross began to eat, tasting naught but sawdust.

"We have visitors," Gordo announced at the sound of a horn. "Who would venture out so early on such a day as this?"

Ross could not bring himself to care. When Gizela hobbled up and pulled on his sleeve, Ross shooed her away. He didn't want to hear anything Gizela had to say.

Gizela was not so easily disuaded. "Heed me, laird; the flame has returned. She has need of you."

"Go away, old woman. I am in no mood to listen to your blather."

Ross knew Gizela referred to Gillian as the flame because of her red hair, but he didn't want to hear anything concerning his wife.

"She lies near death, Laird Ross. We must act quickly."

"Gillian is with Sinclair," Ross spat. "Never mention her name to me again."

Gizela shook her gray head. "Have you no faith in your wife?"

Truly angry now, Ross shoved Gizela aside. "Go away! How can I have faith in a woman who prefers another man's bed?"

"You must believe, laird," Gizela persisted. "Do you wish her dead?"

Ross winced. Did he want Gillian dead? Nay, never that. "What are you trying to tell me? What makes you think Gillian needs me?"

Gizela's eyes clouded over as she gazed toward the front door. She appeared to have gone into a trance. Then she let out a shriek and ran out of the hall.

Ross leaped to his feet so quickly, his chair tumbled backward. "What in God's name is wrong with her?"

"Best we follow her," Gordo said, rising. "Gizela wouldna act this way if something out the ordinary hadna happened."

Rousing himself from his apathy, Ross followed Gordo out the door. He felt the cold bite deep into his bones as he and Gordo raced through the bailey close on Gizela's heels. If the old woman felt the cold, she didn't show it as she raced toward the gate.

"What is it?" Ross called up to a man on the wall walk.

"Someone is at the gate. I was on my way to fetch you."

"Open the portcullis," Ross shouted when he heard Gizela screeching.

The healer was the first one through. Ross and Gordo were right behind her. Ross saw Gizela fall to her knees beside a crumpled figure lying on the ground.

"Can you see who it is?" Ross asked Gordo.

"Nay, but we had better find out. Gizela seems distraught."

Intuition told Ross whom he would find long before he saw her flame-red hair fanned out across a blanket of new-fallen snow. It reminded him of blood, and he shuddered.

" 'Tis Gillian," Gordo said as Ross bent to scoop his wife into his arms. "What devil brought her to Ravenscraig?"

"She hovers near death," Gizela cried. "We must hurry."

"Leave her," Gordo advised. "The world will be well rid of her. It will save you from having to kill her yourself."

"Nay!" Gizela screamed as she flew at Gordo, her tiny fists flailing impotently against Gordo's chest. "Fool! All men are fools!"

"Easy, Gizela," Ross soothed. "I willna let Gillian die here on the cold ground."

So saying, he carried her into the keep and up the stairs to the solar; her flaming hair trailed over his arm. He remembered how much he enjoyed running his fingers though her silken tresses as he placed Gillian on the bed. "Build up the fire, Gordo."

Her fragile skin was white, bloodless, and so cold Ross feared they had found her too late. He picked up one of her hands and chafed it between his own, cursing beneath his breath. Why had Gillian ventured out in naught but a thin cloak with no gloves to protect her hands?

"Leave," Gizela ordered. "I will care for my lady. Send Alice to me with my medicinal chest."

"I amna leaving," Ross maintained.

Eyes blazing, Gizela rounded on him. "Nay! You wish my lady ill. Take your uncle and go."

Gordo grasped his arm and pulled him from the chamber. "Come away, lad. She's in God's hands now. If her punishment is death, then so be it."

Ross knew Gordo was right. Gillian had betrayed

him, mayhap even conspired to end his life. Still, he didn't want her death on his conscience. Furthermore, there were too many unanswered questions that would die with her. Why had Gillian abandoned her lover's bed? What had prompted her to leave Sinclair, ill-prepared to face the elements? Winters were harsh in the Highlands, and well she knew it.

Ross found Alice and relayed Gizela's request, but instead of returning to the hall, he went to the stables to inspect the horse Gillian had ridden to Ravenscraig. The poor mare had been ridden hard and was nearly done-in. She was also long in the tooth and somewhat malnourished. Why hadn't Gillian ridden Silver? Naught made sense. He left the mare in good hands and returned to the keep.

Ross subsided into a chair before the hearth, staring into the dancing flames. If Gillian lived, he knew he would never feel the same about her. She had slept with another man, mayhap carried another man's bairn. According to the law, he could kill her if he wished. But that would mean decades, mayhap centuries of feuding and killing. Tearlach MacKay would not take the slaying of his only daughter lightly. Nor could Ross bring himself to kill or physically harm a woman.

Gillian could never be trusted again; that was a given. But returning her to Braeburn would likely also mean the resumption of the feud, assuming, of course, that Gillian would live.

Niall joined Ross and sat down. "What is the MacKay lass doing here?"

"I doona ken. She is in no condition to talk."

"Will she live?"

" 'Tis in God's hands."

"Gillian deserves punishment, but . . . you willna hurt her, will you?"

Ross sent Niall a disgusted look. "You know me better than that, Niall. If Gillian lives, I will probably return her to Braeburn. Never again will I allow her in my bed or give her free reign of my keep."

Both men stretched their legs toward the heat, lost in their own thoughts. When Alice approached Ross a short time later and whispered into his ear, Ross sloughed off his apathy and climbed the stairs to the solar.

Assisted by Alice, Gizela worked feverishly to warm Gillian's chilled body. Buckets of warm water had been carried to the solar and poured into a tub, but neither woman was strong enough to carry Gillian from bed to bath. And so Gizela had relented and sent for Ross.

Ross swept into the chamber and came to an abrupt halt when he saw Gillian lying on the bed. Though her eyes were open, Ross realized she was aware of naught that was going on around her. Her face now held a wee bit of color, probably due to Gizela's ministrations, but she was still too pale.

"Well," Gizela snapped as she whipped the blanket off Gillian. "What are you waiting for? Lift the lass into the tub."

Ross froze. The sight of Gillian's body shouldn't have affected him so strongly. Though he had seen her nude countless times, he never tired of looking at his warrior wife. Her body was sleekly muscled, not soft like most women's, yet her womanly curves were not lacking. He focused his gaze on her face, hardening his heart against the provocative lure of her charms.

Ignoring the tightening in his loins, he lifted Gillian

into his arms and placed her in the tub of hot water. Gizela pushed him aside and knelt to tend to her charge.

"Stay close," Gizela told Ross. "I'll need you to carry her back to bed."

Ross watched a moment, and then retreated a few steps.

"Can you hear me, lass?" Gizela asked as she sponged Gillian with warm water.

Though Ross listened closely for Gillian's response, he didn't hear the words she murmured.

"Will she be all right?" Alice asked anxiously.

"Aye, though it was close. Fetch me some broth from the kitchen and ask someone to bring up a few bricks to heat in the hearth. Once Gillian is back in bed, we will wrap her in blankets and place hot bricks around her."

After Alice hurried off, Ross joined Gizela beside the tub. He sucked in a startled breath when Gillian moved her head and stared at him.

"Ross . . ." she murmured.

"Aye. How do you feel?"

"Cold. Did I make it to Ravenscraig, then?"

"We found you on the ground outside the gate. Why did you leave your lover?"

"Not now," Gizela warned. "Wrap the lass in the blanket warming on the hearthstone and carry her back to bed."

Ross did as he was told, trying to ignore how good Gillian felt in his arms and failing miserably. He grew hard, silently cursing his lust for the red-haired warrior woman lying helplessly in his arms. His lust retreated when he heard her teeth chatter and felt her shivering; she clung to him as if he were a lifeline.

This wouldn't do at all, Ross thought as he placed

Gillian on the bed. He shouldn't feel anything but disgust and resentment. "Why is she still shivering? Can you do naught to stop it?"

Alice returned with the broth. Donald followed close behind, carrying several bricks, which he placed on the hearthstone to warm.

"Broth and warm bricks; there is naught more I can do," Gizela said. Her gaze slid over Ross, as if assessing his worth. "There is something *you* can do, laird. Wait here while I try to get some broth down the lass."

Working together, Alice and Gizela managed to get Gillian to swallow a few spoonfuls of broth. But she was shivering so hard much of it spilled on the cloth Alice had tucked under her chin.

"Take the bowl away, Alice," Gizela ordered. "I will summon you if I have need of you."

Once Alice left, Gizela turned a thoughtful gaze on Ross. "Are you willing to do what is necessary to save your wife?"

Ross glanced at the bed. It was literally shaking from Gillian's violent shivering. "I will do what I can as long as you ken that the lass means naught to me. I reject her as my wife."

Gizela narrowed her eyes. "You will rue those words, Ross MacKenna." For some unknown reason, her voice sent chills down Ross's back.

"Let me worry about that. What is it you wish me to do?"

"Take off your braies and shirt and climb into bed. Warm the lass with your body heat. You are the only one who can rekindle the flame."

Ross drew back as if struck. "Climb into bed with Gillian? Nay, I canna. I have renounced her. She has sinned grievously against me."

"Your faith in your wife disappoints me, laird," Gizela chastised. She waved him away. "Take your ill-humor and leave. Tell Alice to send up more blankets. If we doona warm her soon, I fear for her life."

Despite his hostility toward Gillian, Ross couldn't let her die. He began unbuttoning his shirt as he strode to the bed.

Gizela took one look at Ross's strained features and slipped from the chamber, closing the door behind her.

Ross finished undressing, pulled back the covers, and slid into bed beside Gillian. His arms went around her as he settled her against his warmth. The coldness of her body shocked him. How could anyone be that cold and still live? He chafed her back and arms, willing warmth into them. He heard her sigh and felt her burrow more deeply into the curve of his body.

"Ross," she whimpered. "I thought I'd never see you again."

Ross's mouth flattened. She sounded as if she cared, but he knew her words to be false. The sickness in his gut increased each time she whispered his name and snuggled against him, seeking his heat.

Despite Ross's resolve, his body reacted violently. Gritting his teeth, he turned his thoughts away from his arousal and forced himself to remember Sinclair's hands on Gillian, his boasting that he and Gillian were lovers.

"Ross, I'm sorry," Gillian muttered. "I didna mean it. I didna . . ." Her voice faltered as she drifted off to sleep.

Hardening his heart, Ross endured the torture until Gillian stopped shivering and settled down to sleep. Then he retreated from the scorching flames that tempted him and climbed out of bed. For a long moment he stared at her, his eyes drinking in the evocative line of her nape, the splendor of her curves. Cursing, he pulled on his clothing with amazing speed and fled. Holding Gillian in his arms had been the most difficult thing he had ever done. Her betrayal had utterly devastated him.

Gizela met him when he returned to the hall. "She is all yours now," Ross growled.

"The flame is yours alone; she always was and always will be your destiny. She belonged to you since the day she was born."

"Enough! I will hear no more nonsense about flame and destiny. See to her, Gizela. The sooner she recovers, the sooner I can return her to her father."

Muttering to herself, Gizela hobbled off.

"How does the lass fare?" Gordo asked as he handed Ross a mug of ale.

"Well enough."

"Has she said aught about . . . ?"

"Leave off, Gordo. We all know that happened, and that's the end of it. As soon as weather permits, I want you to carry a message to Tearlach MacKay. 'Tis time he came to fetch his daughter."

"That will mean—"

"I *know* what it means," Ross said before Gordo could finish the sentence. " 'Tis the way it has to be. 'Twas a bad bargain to begin with."

Gillian slept through the day and night. She awakened the next morning wrapped in a cozy cocoon of toasty blankets and surrounded by the warmth of the fire dancing in the hearth. She raised her head and looked for Ross. His side of the bed was cold, as if he hadn't lain beside her. But she knew he had. The remembered heat of his body still warmed her.

Ross understood and had forgiven her.

Gillian smiled, recalling that wonderful moment when Ross had climbed into bed and taken her into his arms. She was still smiling when Alice entered the chamber and opened the drapes, letting in a stream of weak winter light. Alice glanced at Gillian and grinned.

"You're looking better, Gillian. Gizela said you were lucky you didna suffer far worse than mild frostbite. You'll not lose any fingers or toes."

"I feel better," Gillian said, scooting up in bed to rest her shoulders against the headboard. "Where is Ross?"

Refusing to look at Gillian, Alice busied herself with straightening the chamber. "Gizela said you should stay abed until your strength returns."

"What is it, Alice? What are you keeping from me?"

" 'Tisna for me to say, Gillian." She headed toward the door. "I'll fetch your breakfast."

"Alice . . ."

But it was too late; Alice had already scooted out the door. What was going on? Gillian wondered. Surely Ross wouldn't have climbed into bed with her if he hadn't understood why she had pretented to disavow their marriage? Her relief was palpable when Gizela shuffled into the chamber.

"Alice said you were awake and alert," Gizela said.

"Thanks to you, I'm sure. I feared I wouldna make it to Ravenscraig. Where is Ross?"

"Ah, lass, I doona know how to tell you this."

"Tell me what? Is something wrong with Ross? Has he been injured or—"

"Nay, lass, the laird is well."

"Then what—"

"The laird has told me naught, but I ken the mood in

the keep and doona like it. I fear it doesna bode well for you, Gillian."

The blood froze in Gillian's veins. She had fought against tremendous odds to return to Ravenscraig, almost freezing to death in the process. How could Ross turn away from her?

"I must think on this," Gillian said with a sigh. She glanced up at Gizela, her face intent. "Are you sure I am . . . well?"

Gizela gazed placidly back at her. "The bairn survived your ordeal."

"What? I wasna sure I carried Ross's bairn."

Gizela merely nodded her head. If Gillian had ever doubted Gizela's powers, she no longer did. "Are you sure, Gizela?"

"Aye. I looked into your eyes and saw the son you will give our laird."

"A son? How can you ken such a thing?"

"I ken many things." She stared deep into Gillian's eyes, as if delving into her very soul. "You doona intend to tell him, do you?"

Gillian shook her head. "I canna. Not while he harbors ill-will toward me. If he doesna ken what I did to save his life, he doesna deserve to know about the bairn. Will you tell Ross I wish to see him?"

"Aye, lass, but I amna sure he will come."

Gizela departed. She found Ross in the hall with some of the lads, discussing the weather and loss of livestock during the most recent storm. She pulled on his sleeve.

"Laird Ross, your lady wishes to speak with you."

Ross turned and scowled at Gizela. "I have more important things to do."

Gizela pulled him off to the side. "Mayhap you

should set your bitterness aside and listen to your lady."

Annoyance darkened Ross's brow. "I have naught to say to Gillian." He turned away.

"Doona deny the flame, for she fills your heart, whether or not you wish to admit it."

"Stop that flame nonsense," Ross growled. "Gillian is naught but a woman, with a woman's weakness and a woman's foibles. I thought she was different; I thought she had a warrior's heart, but I was mistaken. She betrayed me."

He pushed the old woman aside. "Doona pester me, woman."

"What should I tell Gillian?"

"Tell her naught, for she deserves naught from me."

"The loss will be yours," Gizela warned. "More than you know or can imagine."

Ross paid her no heed as he wrapped himself in his plaid and accompanied his kinsmen out the door into the biting cold.

Gillian picked at the food Alice had brought her with little appetite. After Ross had refused to see her, she had never felt more alone in her life. But she wasn't about to be ignored by him. As soon as she was on her feet, which she expected to be very soon, she intended to fight back, to right the injustice done to her and find her way back into Ross's heart.

Gillian remained in bed but one more day. She arose the following morning at her usual time, dressed warmly, and wrapped herself in her plaid. Then she descended the stairs and entered the hall with her head held high. She had done no wrong.

The weather had broken, and the sun now pierced

the windows, reaching into the dark corners of the hall. Gillian heard a collective gasp as she took her place at the high table beside Ross. Ross looked up from his bowl of porridge and glared at her.

"What are you doing here?"

"Breaking my fast. Have you an objection?"

"Aye, I doona break bread with those who betray my trust." Deliberately he rose and moved to another table, taking his bowl and spoon with him.

Gillian swallowed hard. Once she found her voice, she said loudly enough for all to hear, "Your kinsmen sent me away for no reason. I was unjustly tried and found guilty."

No one answered; no one even looked at her. Ross continued eating, though his expression gave Gillian the impression that his porridge tasted foul. Abruptly he pushed back his chair, gained his feet, and walked away. The hall emptied soon after, leaving Gillian alone and friendless. She waited for someone to serve her, and when no one did, she rose and walked into the kitchen.

Hanna greeted her warily. "Are you hungry, lass?"

"Do you believe I betrayed Ross, Hanna?"

"I doona know what to believe. The story I heard from the lads doesna bode well for you. Did you really tell Laird Ross that you love Angus Sinclair? I didna want to believe it, but Gordo assured me it was true."

"No one knows the real story, Hanna, and Ross refuses to listen."

"If you swear you didna betray Ross, I will believe you."

"I swear I didna betray Ross," Gillian said solemnly. "I wish Ross would listen to my explanation."

Hanna grinned. "I knew you wouldna play Ross

false. Sit down while I fix your favorite, eggs and ham, and some slices of toasted bread."

Gillian was too hungry to pass up such a grand breakfast. She opted for warm milk instead of ale and sipped it while Hanna prepared her food. After she had sated her hunger, she returned to the solar to plot a way back into Ross's heart.

For the next few days, Gillian languished in near isolation, ignored by everyone but Alice, Gizela, and Hanna. Ross avoided her like the plague. But Gillian didn't let that stop her. She had learned where Ross slept. If Ross wouldn't come to her, she would go to him. She would make him listen to her even if she had to tie him to the bed to do it.

Ross breathed a sigh of relief when Tearlach MacKay finally answered his summons and arrived at Ravenscraig. MacKay charged into the hall, stomped the snow off his boots, and bellowed, "Where is your laird?"

Ross got to his feet and strode forth to greet his father-in-law.

"What happened, MacKenna? Do you need my help extracting my daughter from Sinclair's clutches? I offered to ride with you, but you said Gillian was your responsibility, that you would rescue her without my assistance. What went awry, lad?"

Ross squared his shoulders. "I have bad news, MacKay. Sit down by the fire while we talk."

MacKay stiffened. "Has Sinclair hurt my lass? I will tear him limb from limb."

Ross guided MacKay to the hearth and pulled out a chair for him. The older man sat but remained wary.

His voice rose on a note of panic. "Where is Gillian? Do not tell me you left her with Sinclair!"

"Gillian abides at Ravenscraig . . . for now."

MacKay visibly relaxed, although his eyes remained narrowed with what could only be described as suspicion. "Mayhap you should explain why I am here, lad."

Ross took a deep breath and related everything that had happened, including how Gillian had abandoned their marriage and taken Sinclair for a lover. When he finished, the taste in his mouth had turned as sour as his disposition.

"Let me get this straight," MacKay said slowly. "We both kenned that Gillian sought out Sinclair to kill him. Why in God's good name would you think they had become lovers?"

"I but repeat the words she spoke to me. Ask anyone who was there."

"And you believed her?" MacKay shook his head. "You doona know Gillian if you think she betrayed you with Sinclair." He assumed a thoughtful look. "What is Gillian doing at Ravenscraig? Apparently she didna remain with Sinclair."

"She showed up at our gate four days ago," Ross explained.

"You opened your gates to her?"

"I did, MacKay, but only because I didna wish her death on my conscience. She had traveled from Sinclair Keep in a snowstorm, wearing but a thin cloak to ward off the cold. If I hadna let her in she would have frozen to death."

"Did she tell you why she left Sinclair after she refused to return to Ravenscraig with you? Was she being held prisoner? Do you know the facts?"

"I know all I need to know. I summoned you to take your daughter back to Braeburn with you. No one wants her here."

A stubborn streak as wide as his daughter's suddenly asserted itself in Tearlach MacKay. "If I have the right of it, your kinsmen judged Gillian wrongly and sent her away while you were unconscious."

"Ross nodded."

"And McHamish told me she left his keep with the intention of killing Sinclair, am I correct?"

Again Ross nodded.

"But no matter what she told you, she *did* return, did she nae?"

"You're not going to change my mind, MacKenna," Ross maintained.

"Are you anxious to resume the feud, then?"

"Gillian broke the truce when she refused to leave Sinclair."

"One could say you broke the truce when your kinsmen forced Gillian to leave your keep."

"We are at a stalemate, then. Take Gillian and let the feud resume."

MacKay rose, looking down his nose at Ross. "Bloodshed isna the answer. Gillian was forced to leave Ravenscraig and then returned of her own free will. The terms of the truce havena been broken. Gillian is yours, Ross MacKenna, for better or worse. I suggest you calm yourself and listen to her explanation."

He resumed his seat. "Fetch ale and food for me and my men. 'Tis a long way back to Braeburn. And tell my lass I want to speak with her."

"I amna your servant, MacKay," Ross snapped as he motioned to a servant and relayed MacKay's needs. "I doona want to spill blood any more than you do, and I promise to honor the truce if you take Gillian back to Braeburn with you."

"Och, you are a coward, MacKenna. I never thought I would see the day a mere lass would defeat you."

Ross leaped to his feet and reached for his claymore, which, of course, he didn't carry inside his own home. "You go too far, MacKay. Truce or nay, you are treading on dangerous ground."

MacKay sighed. "Verra well, I will say no more. As soon as I sup and see my lass, I'll be on my way. You're going to have to find a way to settle this on your own, MacKenna. I wash my hands of the whole business."

"Da!" Gillian cried from the doorway. "Alice said you were here."

MacKay held out his arms, and Gillian flew into them. "What mischief have you gotten into now, daughter?" he whispered into her ear. "Your husband told me an incredible story"

With a snort of disgust, Ross whirled and stomped off.

"Did you tell MacKenna that you loved Sinclair and wished to stay with him?"

"Aye," Gillian readily admitted. "Unfortunately the foolish man believed me." She proceeded to explain everything that had happened after she'd left McHamish.

"You were always impulsive, Gillian, but attempting murder after you were forced to leave Ravenscraig tops everything. What in God's good name made you think you could kill those responsible for attacking MacKenna? You are but a woman. You were fortunate McHamish refused to accept your challenge, but challenging Sinclair in his own keep was stupid. You couldna have been thinking rationally."

Gillian shot a glance at Ross's departing back. "Ross lay near death, I could think of naught but revenge."

MacKay sighed. "MacKenna wants me to take you back to Braeburn with me. I canna fix this, lass. You're on your own."

Gillian's chin notched upward. "I amna leaving Ravenscraig."

MacKay nodded. "I assumed as much. That's why I refused MacKenna's request. You're too much like me to surrender." He rose. "Now hug your old da so I can leave."

Chapter Fifteen

Ross wasn't on hand to bid MacKay farewell. He was too angry to think clearly and had sought refuge in the stables. He had wanted Gillian gone, but MacKay had outwitted him. Though he was loath to admit it, the old fox was right: Gillian had been forced to leave Ravenscraig and had returned. The truce had not been broken. But that didn't satisfy Ross. He would never trust Gillian again. No one wanted her here; why didn't she realize her life would be miserable if she remained?

"Why is the lass still here?" Gordo asked when he found Ross in the stables.

"MacKay insisted Gillian hadna broken the terms of the truce because she was forced to leave and then returned of her own free will. I did everything I could to convince him to take her to Braeburn with him, but the wily old fox outwitted me."

Gordo shook his head. "Och, what a coil, lad. Gillian must know she isna welcome."

"Aye, she knows. I no longer share her bed."

Gordo stroked his chin. "Has Gillian offered an explanation? We all heard her say she was Sinclair's leman."

Ross's face hardened. "She could explain away until doomsday and I wouldna believe her."

"Ross! I know you are avoiding me, but I'd like to speak with you."

Ross bit back a curse when Gillian, wrapped to her ears in her plaid, entered the stables.

"That's my signal to leave," Gordo muttered.

"Stay, Uncle."

"Nay, this is between you and the MacKay lass," he said as he darted past Gillian and out the door.

"We need to talk," Gillian said once they were alone. "Since you insist on avoiding me, I decided to come to you."

"We have naught to say to each other," Ross bit out.

"First, thank you for saving my life. You could have let me die outside your gate."

"I wouldna let an animal die in the snow like that."

Gillian shuddered and pulled her plaid closer around her. His voice was as frigid as a winter night. Thawing him wasn't going to be easy. He had already tried and convicted her.

"I truly did intend to kill Angus Sinclair when I set out for his keep, but I made a serious mistake in thinking I could do it alone."

Ross turned away. "No explanations are necessary. Naught can justify the fact that you became Sinclair's leman. Return to the keep; 'tis cold out here."

Exasperation colored her words. "Why do you refuse to listen to me? Why must you be so stubborn?"

"Some things canna be explained nor forgiven."

"Verra well, think what you will. I willna, however, be driven from my home. I belong at Ravenscraig, at your side, in your bed, mistress of your keep."

"You will never, ever take your place in my bed again," Ross replied. "Now, I have duties to perform. You are still recovering, and 'tis best you return to the keep, where it is warm and dry."

"Doona think you can ignore me forever, Ross MacKenna, for I willna allow it. And if you take a le-man, I will make you verra, verra sorry," she added as she whirled on her heel and stormed off.

Gillian was still fuming when she entered the hall. If Ross refused to listen to her, how could she ever get back in his good graces? She settled into a chair before the hearth and stared thoughtfully into the flames. She could be as stubborn as Ross, and she was not about to let him ignore her. She had been ready to die for Ross, and she had to find a way to make him aware of the sacrifices she had made on his behalf.

The weather turned again. It snowed for days; the wind howled, and frost covered the windows. Inside, games were played, men diced, women sewed or embroidered, and musicians brought out their instruments and played for the enjoyment of those who had no musical skills. People gathered around storytellers of an evening, enthralled by tales of heroism and past battles.

During those long evenings, Gillian sat in the hall with the others, yet felt isolated because she was ignored. After a few days of people walking circles around her, Gillian decided she had had enough and planned a night Ross wasn't likely to forget anytime soon.

As people began drifting off to their beds one blustery evening, Gillian returned to her chamber. When Alice arrived to help her get ready for bed, Gillian requested a tub and water to be brought up for a bath. She waited with bated breath until Alice relayed her wishes to the kitchen, fearing that her request would be denied. To her surprise, a tub promptly arrived and was filled in due time while Alice built up the fire and brought towels and soap.

Gillian luxuriated in the bath until the water grew cool. Then she stepped into a warm towel and let Alice dry her. After she dismissed her maid, she rubbed fragrant cream Gizela had made up for her into her skin and studied herself in the mirror, noting that while her pregnancy was scarcely noticeable, her breasts were larger. Shivering in the cool air, she pulled on her warmest bed robe and slippers and sat down before the fire to brush her hair dry.

Gillian's mind raced. What if her plan failed and Ross rejected her? How could she continue to live in such a hostile environment? Would her bairn be accepted? Or would he be ignored by everyone, including his father? Gillian refused to contemplate failure. But of one thing she was certain: She would return to Braeburn if Ross refused to accept their bairn. At least there her babe would be loved and protected by her father and brothers.

Gillian inhaled sharply and rose when she heard the church bells chime matins. It was midnight, the darkest part of the night, when everyone in the keep would be sleeping. It was time. Gillian opened the door, pleased to find the corridor outside her chamber deserted. Cautiously she made her way through the chill air and up the stairs to Ross's chamber on the floor above the solar. She had learned from Alice where Ross slept. Dragging in a sustaining breath, Gillian eased the door open.

The only light in the small chamber came from the hearth. The room held welcome warmth after the cold bite of the drafty corridor. Gillian slipped through the door and closed it behind her. The well-oiled hinges did not betray her presence.

Gillian glanced toward the bed. The curtains were drawn. She offered a quick prayer that Ross was alone in his bed. She crept on tiptoe to the bed, dropped her robe, and kicked off her slippers. Shivering without the protection of clothing, she parted the curtains and slid beneath the covers.

Ross didn't awaken. He was lying on his side, facing away from her. Her hands itched to touch him, and they did, roaming freely over his warm, naked body. She heard Ross moan and smiled. While his mind might reject her, his body welcomed her. He rolled over on his back. She slid one hand downward, over the hardening length of his manhood, caressing lower to cup the sac beneath.

Gillian gasped as Ross awoke and grasped her wrist in a bruising grip. With his other hand he pushed aside the bed curtains, admitting feeble light from the hearth.

He murmured her name, his voice a low growl in his throat. "Gillian."

"Aye, did you expect someone else?"

"I thought I made it clear I doona want you in my bed." He shoved the covers down and started to rise.

Gillian wasn't about to let him up until he'd heard everything she had to say. Nimbly, she rose up and straddled him. "You're not going anywhere, Ross MacKenna."

"Are you so hungry for a man between your legs that you'd go where you're not wanted?"

Anger ate at the edges of her brain. *Arrogant* and *impossibly dense* were the only words she could think of at the moment to describe Ross. "I want only you, Ross, no one else. Why do you nae believe me?"

Ross raised his hands to push her off of him and had the bad fortune to make contact with her breasts—full, wonderfully warm, and firm breasts with ripe, cherry-red nipples. And she smelled delicious. Did she know what she was doing to him? She was naked; he'd realized it the moment she had climbed on top of him. He felt branded by the hot wetness of her sex pressing against his loins.

"Gillian," he gasped in a strangled voice. "You have to leave. We will talk in the morning."

"I'm not leaving, Ross." She stretched out over him, so they were breast to breast, hip to hip, sex to sex.

Ross felt himself spinning into a turbulent whirlpool of sensations. And when she lifted herself slightly and kissed him, he nearly exploded.

Ross tried not to return Gillian's kiss. Tried to remain motionless and uninvolved, but he was no statue made of stone. To his credit, he kept his lips tightly closed. But he couldn't control his randy cock. Half-heartedly, he tried to lift her off of him, but she clung tenaciously. Never had he felt so weak and ineffectual.

"I doona want you, Gillian. You're embarrassing yourself by forcing my response."

She curled her fingers around his arousal. "Deny it all you wish, but your body doesna lie. I am your wife, Ross. I didna betray you. I sought revenge against those who had hurt you."

Ross gave a bitter laugh. "I doona call sleeping with the enemy revenge."

"I didna sleep with Angus. I lied to save your life. He would have killed you had I not sent you away."

"Bah! Think you I canna take care of myself? You shouldna have taken up the sword in my defense, if that's what you did. I am still not convinced of it. Explain how Sinclair convinced you to bed him instead of kill him?"

"Damn you, Ross! What can I say to convince you of my innocence? I have been judged harshly. You canna deny I was driven away by your kinsmen after being unjustly accused of trying to harm you. I am through talking; 'tis time for action."

Rising up on her knees, she positioned herself over his sex and took him inside her. His hard, smooth length slid deep. Ross groaned as her sheath tightened around him. He fought a battle to control his need to move, to drive hard and deep inside her, and lost as he surrendered to the velvet heat and slick wetness of her feminine core. He watched her feverishly, sweat popping out on his forehead as her hips rose and fell, taking all of him.

"What . . . do . . . you hope to . . . gain from . . . this?" he bit out from between clenched teeth.

"Be quiet and let our bodies do the talking."

"It willna . . . work." Ross gasped. "But I willna turn down a whore who accosts me in my own bed."

He saw Gillian wince and immediately wished his words back. How could the flame-haired witch incite such fury in him? How could he love and hate a woman at the same time? How could he want to empty himself inside her so badly that he shook from the need? A smile curved his lips. If Gillian wanted sex, he would give her sex—wild, mindless sex.

His arms went around her, and he turned with her until she was trapped beneath him.

"Wha . . . ! What are you doing?"

"Giving you what you want. Just so you doona make too much of it, I want you to ken this means naught to me. I am giving you no more than I would a leman who came to my bed to pleasure me."

He gripped her hips, lifted her slightly, and thrust deep and hard. His rhythm was fast and relentless. His speed increased until his furious strokes were pressing her into the mattress. He felt her writhing beneath him and abruptly pulled out. She screamed in protest. He bent to her breasts, sucking her swollen nipples into his mouth.

"Ross . . ."

"Is this what you want, Gillian?" He fought a difficult battle to gain the upper hand. Temptation didn't whisper; it roared.

"I want *you*, Ross. Not a man without a heart or soul."

"You want my lust, and so you shall have it."

He trapped her breasts between his hands, returning his mouth to her nipples, scraping his teeth against them, creating heat and flames with his lashing tongue. If this was punishment, Gillian no longer cared. If she and Ross could find pleasure in bed, how long would it be before he realized he had misjudged her, that she was but an innocent victim?

Gillian ached to have him back inside her. She raised her hips, inviting him, tempting him, needing him. Ross ignored her plea as he slid down her body, spread her with his fingers, and found her with his mouth. Gillian cried out.

"Ross, please!"

He didn't even glance up at her as he tortured her with his tongue, gliding in and out of her wetness, lapping and teasing, until she felt herself spinning out of control. Gillian felt the first wave of orgasm start at her toes, swelling as it swept through her, stealing her wits, her senses, rising ever upward into a shattering climax.

Before she had time to recover, Ross rose up, lifted her hips high, and thrust inside her. Instinctively she wrapped her ankles around his back. She looked into his eyes just as a bursting spark from the hearth offered a glimpse of dark fire igniting beneath his lashes. Before she could grasp the meaning behind the brief glance into his soul, Ross grasped her hips and thrust forcefully inside her, pounding relentlessly, driving her to the brink of madness. She lowered her lids, surrendering to Ross's mastery, to the magic flowing between them. She sensed him watching her as she writhed beneath him, a faint smile curving his lips.

Her senses unraveled. She tried to breathe as he sank deep, withdrew, sank deeper. Grasping his head, she brought his lips to hers, forcing a kiss he seemed reluctant to give. But it mattered not to Gillian, for the torrent of release roared through her. On a wave of inconceivable pleasure, she was flung to the pinnacle of ecstasy, suspended for one incredibly intense moment, and then released to float to earth in a silken cocoon of bliss.

Dimly she heard Ross shout and felt him collapse on top of her. She lay limply beneath him, unable to move, to think, to wonder if this would lead to reconciliation. She didn't have long to wait. Ross lifted himself up and off of her. He lay beside her, unmoving, one arm raised to cover his eyes.

"Ross, that—"

". . . changes naught. Doona read too much into this, Gillian. You came to me; I didna invite you. You wanted sex; I gave you sex."

"You know it was more than that. I lo—"

He lowered his arm and glared at her. "Nay, doona say it."

"Verra well, but there is something else you need to know."

"I doona want to hear that either. You can leave now. You got what you came for."

Gillian fought tears with anger. Anger she could handle; tears she could not. Weakness wasn't something the MacKays were noted for. She shoved herself off the bed, pulled on her hastily discarded bed robe, and stepped into her slippers.

"Deny me if you wish, Ross, but doona take me for a coward. You canna drive me away again. One day you will realize how wrong you are about me."

Her head held high, Gillian made a regal exit.

The moment the door closed behind her, Ross hit the pillow with his fist again and again, cursing his weakness for letting Gillian get to him. He should have been able to deny her, deny himself as well, and send her on her way.

Vaguely he wondered what she had wanted to tell him. Had he been right in refusing to listen? He didn't know what she could tell him that would ease the situation between them. The day she had slept with Sinclair, the bonds of matrimony had been broken.

Though a wee voice of doubt whispered inside him, Ross effectively silenced it. Gillian had admitted her guilt, after all. Still, Tearlach MacKay believed his daughter innocent, was quite adamant about it. Was Ross wrong to condemn Gillian without hearing her out?

The answer still hadn't arrived when dawn's gray fingers peeled the night away. More confused than ever, Ross rose and readied himself to face the day. He groaned aloud when he opened the door and found Gizela loitering in the corridor.

"What do you want?" he asked, steeling himself against the sharp edge of her tongue.

"The flame will prevail in the end. Naught you can do will dim her light."

"Is that all?"

"Nay, laird, I have come to warn you."

Ross's patience began to wear thin. "Warn me about what?"

"I doona know yet, but danger comes as surely as I am standing here."

Ross brushed past her. "Be sure to let me know when it gets here." His sarcasm was sharp and cutting. Gizela appeared to take no offense, for she merely shook her head, *tsk*ed loudly, and hobbled off.

Despite his apparent detachment, Gizela's words worried Ross more than he cared to admit. The old woman had the "sight," and like most Scotsmen, he was superstitious about such things. But until the danger arrived, and he knew from whence it came, he had no weapon to use against it.

Ross joined his kinsmen in the hall and took his seat at the high table. He was quick to notice that Gillian was absent. He frowned. Had he been too rough on her last night?

"What are you frowning about, cousin?" Niall asked as he joined Ross.

Ross forced a smile. "'Tis still snowing," he said, avoiding the question. "Mayhap we can organize swordplay and wrestling in the hall. I grow weary of dicing."

"I will see to it." Niall hesitated a moment, then said, "I miss Seana. If she returned, I would forgive her."

"She tried to poison me."

"We have only Gizela's word," Niall protested. "How did she know the broth was poisoned? How could anyone know?"

"Seana disappeared; that alone was an admission of guilt."

"I doona see it that way, Ross. Mayhap she chose to leave rather than be accused unjustly."

"McHamish told the MacKay that Seana and Sinclair plotted together to kill me."

"We have only MacKay's word. You didna speak directly to McHamish. I canna believe Seana could betray me, betray us. Would you let her return if I promised to keep her out of trouble?"

"The question is moot, for no one knows where Seana has gone. MacKay said she isna at her father's keep."

"Seana abides with Angus Sinclair."

Both men spun around to see Gillian standing behind them. "Is that true?" Ross asked.

"Aye, if you had listened to my explanation, you would have known. She fled there after she left Ravenscraig. She plans to wed Angus."

"What?" Niall spat. "You lie! Seana is wed to me."

"She is your handfast wife. After a year and a day she can wed whomever she pleases," Gillian replied. "She kens the truth about what happened to me at Sinclair

Keep, for she is the one who released me from the tower."

Ross stared at Gillian, trying to decide whether she lied or spoke true. He had naught but the word of a MacKay, a mortal enemy of Clan MacKenna until their marriage united the clans. And since Seana wasn't here to corroborate her story, Ross felt disinclined to believe it.

"Can you prove you were Sinclair's prisoner and not his lover?" Ross demanded.

"I wouldna lie to you."

"So you say," Ross muttered, returning his attention to his porridge.

Gillian plopped down in a chair. She took one look at the porridge in Ross's bowl and turned as white as a new snowfall. She rose abruptly and rushed from the hall. Ross stared after her, wondering if she had finally realized he was never going to believe her lies.

Gillian returned a quarter hour later looking perfectly normal, as if nothing had happened. She sank into a chair and asked a servant for dry toasted bread.

Gillian had been feeling so well, she'd been surprised when a sudden queasiness overwhelmed her and she'd had to run from the hall. She no longer doubted that she carried Ross's bairn—a bairn he didn't deserve. The signs of her pregnancy were beginning to be evident. How long could she keep her condition a secret? More important, did she want to remain at Ravenscraig? The only place she would be truly welcome was Braeburn.

Gillian chose not to invade Ross's chamber again. The harsh Highland winter had settled over the land. The holy days of the Christmas season were hard upon them. But celebrations were at a minimum, for concern over the survival of their livestock during these harsh winter days was on everyone's mind.

On a morning that promised to be free of snow, Ross gathered his kinsmen for a foray into the valley to rescue cows mired in deep snow and to distribute feed. Gillian watched them leave with deep foreboding. Though she couldn't name what bothered her, she knew intuitively that something would change when the men returned. She asked Alice to fetch Gizela and returned to the solar.

"Are you ill?" Gizela asked when she entered Gillian's chamber. "Is it the bairn?"

Gillian touched her stomach, still flat beneath her gown. "Nay. I feel . . . I canna explain it. Something bad is about to happen."

Gizela nodded wisely. "You are right, lass. Evil returns to Ravencraig."

Gillian's breath caught in her throat. "What kind of evil?"

Gizela muttered incoherently about wickedness invading the keep. "Watch your back, lass."

Gizela wove back and forth a moment, then turned and hobbled out the door.

"Gizela, wait! You've told me naught."

"I've told you a great deal," she said as she disappeared into the dark recesses of the corridor.

At times like this, Gillian believed that although Gizela might have the 'sight,' she spoke in riddles.

As they sat down to the midday meal, it began snowing again, and still Ross hadn't returned. Gillian tried to eat, but the smell of cooked food nauseated her.

She asked for clear broth. Hanna brought it out herself, a worried look on her face.

"You look peaked, Gillian. Are you ill?"

"I amna ill, Hanna." She leaned close to one of the three women who had befriended her at Ravenscraig and said, "I am carrying Ross's bairn, but you mustna tell him."

Hanna clapped her hands. "A bairn! It has been a long time since Ravenscraig has celebrated a birth."

"Promise you will keep my secret until I tell Ross," Gillian pleaded. "And if he continues to ignore me, I may return to Braeburn and never tell him."

"Och, lass, the man is a ninny. Doona worry; I will say naught until you release me from my promise. Does Alice know?"

"Nay, but I will tell her. I canna hide my condition from her much longer. She has sharp eyes."

"Enjoy your broth, lass. I'll send out some crackers. Mayhap they will aid your digestion."

The broth and crackers helped, and Gillian felt better for telling Hanna about her condition. Of course, Gizela knew, but talking to her was like talking to someone who was lost in her own world, one that few people understood.

Gillian remained in her chamber the rest of the day. She didn't leave until Alice arrived to tell her the evening meal was being served. Gillian stepped into the corridor, aware of a commotion taking place below in the hall. She hurried down the stairs, her heart pounding with dread. Something was amiss, and she feared what she would find. A bone-deep chill reached her first. Then she noticed that the doors had been thrown wide, admitting men, wind, and blowing snow.

Niall emerged from their midst carrying a woman, her lashes white with snow and her lips blue. Memories overwhelmed Gillian as she recalled her own narrow escape from an icy grave. When she rushed forward to offer her help, a clawlike hand gripped her arm.

"Stay, lass; she brings naught but trouble."

"Let me go, Gizela. Go fetch your medicinal chest. The woman has need of our help."

Gillian brushed off Gizela's hand and rushed toward the woman being held so tenderly in Niall's arms. She stopped abruptly, her mouth open in shock. She knew now what Gizela meant, for the woman being carried into the keep was Seana.

"What is *she* doing here?" Gillian demanded.

"We found her out on the moor," Ross explained. "Her horse was about done-in, and she had become disoriented in the snowstorm."

"Why bring her here?"

"Ravenscraig was the nearest shelter. What would you have us do, leave her to freeze to death?"

Gillian's eyes flashed with anger. "Have you forgotten that the woman tried to poison you?"

Seana seemed to come alive in Niall's arms. "Nay, you accuse me unjustly." At her direction, Niall set her on her feet. Though she wobbled a bit, she seemed none the worse for wear. "I wouldna harm Ross."

"Then why did you flee instead of staying and defending yourself?"

"I heard Gizela accuse me of trying to poison Ross and feared for my life."

"Why did you nae return home instead of seeking succor from Angus Sinclair?" Gillian demanded.

"My stepmother wouldna welcome me. You have no

right to accuse me when you are the one who sought comfort in Sinclair's bed."

Gillian knew she had to explain what had really happened, and she turned to Ross. "I never bedded Sinclair. On the contrary, I charged him with plotting your death and challenged him to defend himself.

"I was so angry I didna consider the consequences. I would have skewered Angus with my sword had he not called upon his men to disarm and capture me when he realized he wasna skilled enough to win. He imprisoned me in the tower. I would still be there is Seana hadna freed me. She had plans of her own for Angus, and my presence in his keep was hindering them."

Seana sent Gillian an incredulous look. "You are a diligent liar, Gillian. To my knowledge, you were never Angus Sinclair's prisoner. You were his lover. I wasna aware of a challenge. You seemed happy enough with Angus once you became his leman."

"If I was so happy, why did I leave?" Gillian shot back.

Seana shrugged. "Mayhap you tired of Angus. Mayhap you found he isna a particularly gifted lover."

"Is that why you left?" Gillian shot back.

Seana cuddled closer against Niall, smiling adoringly up at him. "Nay, I realized I was wrong to flee Ravenscraig and missed Niall."

"And you dare to call me a liar." Gillian snorted.

"Enough!" Ross growled, putting an end to the heated debate. "Did you or did you not put poison in my broth, Seana?"

"Nay, I didna, Ross. Why would I want you dead? At one time we meant a great deal to each other."

"Did you and Sinclair goad your father into trying to kill me?"

"Who told you such a thing?"

"Your own father told the MacKay."

"And you believed the MacKay? Och, he is as devious as his daughter. MacKay proposed the truce to lull you into a false belief that peace would prevail. I believe you will find that Tearlach MacKay is behind the attack upon your life, and that his daughter was aware of his deceit."

"My father is an honorable man," Gillian said with quiet dignity. "He is the one who wanted peace in the beginning. Besides, he wasna in the keep when Gizela discovered the poisoned broth."

"You were here," Seana maintained. "Besides, Gizela could have been mistaken. She has never liked me. How did she know the broth was poisoned? Did she taste it? Did anyone die?"

"Take Seana to your chamber, Niall. I have heard more than enough about this matter," Ross ordered.

"Can Seana stay, Ross?" Niall asked. "She is in no condition right now to travel to her father's keep."

"She can stay until I sort this through."

So saying, Ross strode off. Seana sent Gillian a smug look as Niall escorted her to his chamber.

Gillian sank down into a chair. Did Ross actually believe Seana? Obviously he was more willing to believe his former leman than he was his own wife. Things between her and Ross had deteriorated to the point that Gillian reconsidered her determination to remain with her husband. Seana was a dangerous woman, one too treacherous to trust.

Chapter Sixteen

The snow continued, the wind howled, and travel was still hazardous. Gillian realized that even if Ross planned to question McHamish about his daughter, the harsh weather prevented him from doing so. Furthermore, she seriously doubted that Niall could keep Seana from causing trouble at Ravenscraig.

As people began drifting off to bed, Gillian rose and climbed the stairs to her chamber. She seemed to be more tired than usual these days. She found Alice waiting for her when she arrived.

"You look out of sorts, my lady," Alice said as she helped Gillian undress. "I canna blame you. Gizela says that Seana brings naught but trouble to the household."

"Aye, the woman is a menace. I wonder why she left Angus Sinclair," she mused as Alice slid a night rail over her head and helped her into a warm bed robe.

"Mama and I will try to keep an eye on her, but it isna possible to ken her every move."

"Thank you, Alice. You and your mother have been good friends to me. I doona know what I would do without you. Go seek your own bed now. I am tired and intend to retire."

"Shall I brush out your hair first?"

"Nay, I will do it myself."

"Sleep well, my lady," Alice said as she slipped out of the chamber and shut the door behind her.

Gillian picked up the brush, sat before the hearth, and began the soothing strokes that always helped her to relax her. She yawned and looked longingly at the bed. It was time. She had just finished the last stroke of the brush when the door opened and a woman stepped through. At first Gillian thought Alice had returned, and smiled, thinking her maid had come to see if she needed anything before she retired for the night. The smile slipped from her face when Seana stepped from the shadows into the circle of light.

Gillian leaped to her feet, wishing she had her claymore handy. "What do you want? You should be with your husband."

"Niall returned to the hall to drink with some of the lads. I told him I was exhausted and needed to recover from my ordeal."

"If you are ailing, what are you doing here?"

Seana stalked forward. She didn't stop until she was scant steps away from Gillian. "I should have let you rot in that tower chamber," Seana charged. "Naught turned out as I planned. Angus was furious with me. He believed I forced you to jump from the tower and sent me away."

"I am sorry your plans didna work out, but you canna blame me for that."

"Who am I to blame if not you? Releasing you from the tower was a mistake I will regret the rest of my life. You have Ross, while I have no one."

"You have Niall. He cares for you even though you care naught for him."

"Niall is a fool. He could be laird if he were man enough to wrest the reins of leadership from Ross. It would have been so easy when Ross lay near death."

"Niall is loyal to Ross; he would never betray his cousin. Not everyone is conniving and evil-minded like you."

Seana growled and took a menacing step closer to Gillian. Gillian reached back and grasped the handle of the water pitcher behind her.

"Doona even think about it, Seana. Your problems are of your own making. I suggest you return to Niall's chamber and consider your sins. Niall willna let you harm Ross; that I can promise. 'Twould be to your advantage to be a good wife to your husband."

"Doona tell me what to do, Gillian MacKay. It seems to me you have more to worry about than I do. No one wants you here. I heard you and Ross doona even share a bed. You should return to Braeburn, where you will be safe."

Gillian narrowed her eyes. "Safe from whom?"

Seana turned and strolled toward the door. "I'll let you figure that out for yourself," she threw over her shoulder.

An icy chill traveled down Gillian's spine as Seana disappeared through the door. Gizela had been right: A viper slithered among them. A viper named Seana. Gillian knew she had to watch her back if she hoped to live to deliver her bairn. Mayhap Seana's suggestion was a good one. Mayhap she *should* return to Braeburn.

His nerves frayed, Ross paced his chamber. He had a strange feeling that something unanticipated was going to happen. He recalled Gizela's warning and wondered if bringing Seana to Ravenscraig was inviting disaster to the clan. Gillian had leveled serious charges against Seana. Should he believe them?

Ross paced to the window and gazed out. Had he made a mistake in allowing Seana to remain at Ravenscraig? He didn't know what to think. He couldn't have let Seana freeze to death in the raging storm, any more than he could have allowed Gillian to die in the same manner.

Despite everything he knew or suspected about Seana, he had no proof of any wrongdoing. Nevertheless, he was uneasy about the situation at hand. If Seana had tried to poison him, he needed to be on his guard. He also needed to put aside some of his anger and listen to what Gillian had to say.

His mind made up, Ross picked up a candlestick, left his dreary chamber, and strode briskly down the stairs to the solar. He stopped before Gillian's chamber and rapped lightly on the door. When no answer was forthcoming, he pushed the door open and entered. Apparently Gillian had already retired, for the curtains had been drawn around the bed. He set the candlestick down, parted the curtains, and poked his head inside.

"Gillian, are you awake?"

Gillian stirred beneath the covers and opened her eyes. When she saw Ross standing over her, she sat up and rubbed her eyes. "I am now. What do you want, Ross?"

Ross sat down on the edge of the bed. "I wish to speak to you."

"About what?"

Ross gazed into her sleep-flushed face and nearly

lost the ability to breathe. Her disheveled red hair surrounded her face in living fire, and he drank in the vision like a man who badly needed to quench his thirst. His gaze shifted lower. Were her breasts fuller? Were her nipples, clearly visible beneath the fine lawn of her night rail, larger than normal?

As if recognizing his sudden interest in her body, Gillian pulled the blanket up to her chin. "Tell me what you want, Ross."

Ross shifted his gaze away from her tempting body and cleared his throat. "I came in search of the truth."

"I told you the truth, but you refused to believe me."

"Tell me again. You and Seana gave me verra different versions of the same story."

Shrugging, Gillian said, "What's the use, Ross? You have believed naught I've said thus far."

"Can you provide proof that Seana and Sinclair plotted against me?"

"Nay, I canna. I have naught but McHamish's word to back me up."

"I intend to question McHamish as soon as the weather breaks. Meanwhile, I doona know what to expect from Seana. If she is guilty, she may attempt treachery again."

"I kenned it before you did," Gillian replied. "Watch your back, Ross. Now, if that's all you came to say, I bid you good night."

Ross reached out to sweep a lock of Gillian's hair from her forehead. The shock that traveled through his arm at that contact stunned him. She must have felt it too, for her eyes widened and she jerked away from his touch. Though Ross knew he should leave, his body refused to obey. His body wanted—demanded—more than a simple touch.

Cupping her face, he lowered his head and kissed her. He meant for it to be a fleeting taste, a simple touching of lips to indulge his craving. He should have known he wouldn't be satisfied with a mere taste, and that his craving would intensify until there was no turning back.

He deepened the kiss, his tongue thrusting past her lips, delving deep into the sweet warmth of her mouth. He hadn't realized how much he had missed her taste until he was inside her mouth, exploring as he wanted to explore another, more intimate part of her anatomy.

When she didn't kiss him back, he raised his head and stared into her eyes. He knew the question she wished to ask before she voiced it.

"Why, Ross? Why are you doing this?"

"Because I canna help myself."

He raised his body over hers and slowly lowered it, trapping her between him and the mattress. He grasped her hands, holding them above her head while he continued kissing her. When Gillian didn't protest, he released her arms, raised the hem of her night rail, and lifted it up and off. Then he lavished wet kisses on her breasts and nipples, laving them with his tongue until she moaned approval.

He felt her body relax beneath his, felt her lips soften as her arms came around him. She tugged at his clothes. He obliged her by rising and quickly shedding his shirt and braies. As naked as she, he crouched between her legs and nudged the opening of her sex with the blunt tip of his cock.

"Nay," she murmured, pushing him away. He thought she meant to deny him despite her initial acceptance, and started to rise. He had too much pride to force her.

"Stay," she softly whispered as she rose up and straddled him. "I'm not yet finished with you." Slowly she slid down his body. A groan escaped him as her hands roamed down his thighs and grasped his cock. When she lowered her head and touched her lips to his erection, his heart nearly burst from his chest. He clutched the bedding as she stroked him with her tongue, kissing his length and then slowly encasing him in the heat of her mouth.

Ross roared and arched so violently, Gillian started to topple off him. Watching her give him pleasure had taken more control than he possessed. Heaven couldn't be this sweet. He caught her in his arms and pressed her into the mattress beneath him.

Kneeling above her, he fought the need to plow into her and drive himself to completion. After she'd pleased him in such an extraordinary manner, he wanted to give her the kind of pleasure she deserved. Whether she was guilty of betrayal or nay, he still wanted this woman, this flame who had burned her way into his soul.

He lowered his body onto hers and kissed her. Gillian matched his kiss with an intensity that left him breathless. He could wait no longer. Shifting his hips, he impaled her. A fierce ecstasy he couldn't ever recall experiencing before overwhelmed him. He brushed soft kisses along her throat, catching a nipple in his mouth and suckling, savoring the sounds of pleasure and encouragement whispering past her lips.

Driven by a need so strong he could no longer deny it, he began thrusting and withdrawing again and again into the scalding inferno between her thighs. He grunted his approval when she wrapped her legs about his hips and met his pounding loins with sweet violence.

Gillian felt her world spin out of control as Ross filled her again and again. As she neared the crest, she could think of naught but reaching paradise with Ross. Then her thought process ceased as her muscles clenched around him. Unbearable sensation filled her as scorching fire melded pain and ecstasy into a breath-stealing climax. She heard Ross cry out, felt the explosion of his seed, and then she knew no more.

Gillian didn't hear Ross's soft curse as he pulled out of her and collapsed on the bed. Nor did she see his fierce expression as he left the bed. She had already fallen asleep.

Ross returned to his own dismal chamber in a daze. He had wanted desperately to stay with Gillian, to share her bed and to know that her warm body would be beside him when he awoke in the night. Though he wanted to believe everything she had told him, he needed time to think, to make a decision that would be right for both of them.

Weary of the snow that kept him confined, of circumstances that made his life a living hell, Ross blew out the candle, shed his clothing, and climbed into bed. Small hands groped him. He reared up, immediately aware that he wasn't alone. The woman in bed with him was naked and relentless in her pursuit of his body.

"I came to you as soon as Niall fell asleep," Seana murmured against Ross's ear. "I learned you're not sharing Gillian's bed and didna want you to be lonely. I ken how to please you, Ross."

Ross leaped out of bed, fumbled for a flint, and lit the candle he had doused moments earlier. "Go back to your husband, Seana. I have no need of you, not tonight, not ever."

Seana didn't bother covering her breasts as she sat up in bed. "Since when have you become a monk? How long have you been without a woman?"

Ross had no intention of answering. Instead, he found Seana's night rail on the floor and thrust it at her. Seana gave the night rail a scornful glance and waved it away.

"Never say you intend to remain faithful to a woman who has betrayed you. I was there, Ross. I saw Gillian and Angus wallow in lust while you hovered near death."

" 'Tis your word against Gillian's," Ross replied.

Ross's patience dangled by a slim thread. He was nearly convinced that he had been wrong about Gillian, that everyone had been wrong except Gizela. Seana was not above lying; nor would she shy away from using poison to gain her own selfish ends.

"Och, 'tis not like you to trust the daughter of your enemy."

"Your father tried to kill me. Would that not make you my enemy?"

"Nay. Blame Angus Sinclair. He told my father false-hoods about my treatment at Ravenscraig, forcing Da to defend my honor."

Ross snorted. "You have no honor, Seana McHamish. Leave this chamber before I have to throw you out."

Seana must have realized that Ross meant what he said, for she slid out of bed, grabbed her night rail from his outstretched hand, and shrugged into it.

"Are you sure you want me to leave?" she asked, rubbing her thinly clad body against him.

He pushed her away, strode to the door, and held it open. "Verra sure. Good sleep, Seana."

Sending him a look of loathing, Seana stormed out

the door. Ross closed and locked it behind her. Though he returned to bed, sleep did not come easily. He thought of Gillian and how badly his callous treatment of her must have hurt. Even though he'd publicly rejected her, he hadn't been able to control his raging lust for her. He was beginning to think that lust wasn't all he felt for his flame-haired wife.

The longer Ross thought about Gillian, the more something about her bothered him. If he hadn't been so needful, he might have recognized what it was about her that troubled him. If he had stayed with her instead of fleeing her bed like a coward, he might have satisfied the curiosity that now plagued him. But he had been so confused about his feelings, he wasn't ready yet to face Gillian in the light of day. And mayhap he was only imagining things.

Gillian awoke the following morning to sunshine. A smile curved her lips. No matter how much Ross tried to deny it, he wanted her, not just for a night but forever. He might even love her. Though she'd been disappointed to wake up alone, she knew Ross often rose earlier than she did. She'd wanted to wake up in Ross's arms. She frowned, unable to recall when exactly he had left her bed. No matter—they had a lifetime together.

Alice scratched on the door and entered the chamber. "Good morning, my lady. The snow has ceased for the time being, and the sun is shining. 'Tis amazing how a little sunshine can lift one's spirits."

"Indeed, sometimes little things can change one's outlook on life." Gillian smiled; making love with Ross was no little thing. "Help me dress, Alice."

"Are you hungry?"

"Famished."

" 'Tis a good sign that your bairn is thriving." Alice grinned. "My mother told me."

Gillian spread a hand over her stomach, gently fondling the barely discernible bump. Though it was too early to feel him move, she knew he was there. Ross's bairn. Would Ross be happy to learn he would soon become a father? Gillian wished she had told him about the bairn last night, but she had been so exhausted, she fell asleep. When she had awakened, Ross was gone.

Gillian dressed carefully in a dark green gown with sage-green trimming. Alice cinched a belt of gold links loosely around her hips and dressed her hair in a becoming style. Then Gillian wrapped herself in her plaid for added warmth. She wanted to look her best for Ross. After last night she had high hopes for their marriage and wished to win acceptance from his kinsmen.

Gillian left her chamber while Alice remained behind to straighten up. Gillian's mood was confident as she descended the stairs and entered the hall. She scanned the chamber for Ross, and when she didn't see him she joined Gordo at the high table.

"Good morning," she said cheerfully. "Where has Ross gotten himself off to this morning?"

Gordo sent her a strange look. "Ross has left Ravenscraig."

"Left? Where did he go?"

" 'Twas such a fine day, he decided to pay a call on McHamish. Niall and a few of the lads accompanied him. He'll likely be gone two or three days. He left me in charge of the keep."

Gillian felt a knot form in the pit of her stomach. Ross's visit to McHamish meant that he hadn't believed her explanation. Her heart sank. All her hopes for their future flew out the window. Had last night meant naught to Ross? Did he believe naught she had told him? Apparently not, else he would have saved himself a trip to McHamish Keep.

"Did Ross leave a message for me?"

"None that I know of. His leaving was rather sudden. He wanted to take advantage of the good weather."

Gillian managed a smile for the serving girl who placed a plate of eggs and ham in front of her. But when she swallowed the first bite, the food sank like a rock in her stomach. Her gut roiled, and nausea rose up to choke her. She excused herself and rushed from the hall. She barely made it to the garderobe, where she lost the meager contents of her stomach.

She was still trembling as she walked to her chamber. Suddenly she stopped and glanced around her. She had the strange sensation that she was being watched, yet the corridor was empty.

"If that's you, Gizela, show yourself," Gillian said.

When Gizela failed to appear, Gillian decided she was imagining things and continued on to her chamber. Alice smiled at her when she entered, but her smile changed to concern when she saw Gillian's pale face.

"Are you ill, my lady?" Alice asked solicitously.

"My breakfast didna agree with me, Alice. 'Tis naught to worry about. Mayhap I'll lie down for a while and take my midday meal in my chamber."

"Can I bring you anything?"

"A piece of dry toasted bread might help settle my stomach."

Alice helped Gillian out of her gown and into bed before she left. Gillian closed her eyes and reviewed in her mind everything Ross had said and done last night. He'd said naught about visiting the McHamish today. She consoled herself with the knowledge that no one had known there would be a break in the weather.

Still, Ross wouldn't leave in unpredictable weather unless he believed she had lied about her reasons for being with Angus Sinclair and sought to question McHamish about it.

Gillian's weary mind shut down as sleep claimed her. She slept until midafternoon and awoke hungry. She found the toasted bread Alice had left, along with two bannocks, and ate every bite, deciding it would hold her until the evening meal. Donning her chamber robe, Gillian remained in her room the rest of the day, finally dressing when Alice arrived shortly before the evening meal.

When Gillian left her chamber, she again felt as if she were being watched. Hackles rose on the back of her neck as she proceeded toward the stairs. Did someone wish her harm? Did the anxiety she was experiencing have anything to do with her pregnancy? She'd have to ask Gizela about it the next time she saw her. Gillian gave a sigh of relief when she reached the hall and was safely seated beside Gordo.

Another tense moment arrived when Seana made a belated appearance and seated herself on the other side of Gordo. But since Seana didn't attempt to converse with her, Gillian relaxed and enjoyed her meal without the digestive discomfort she had suffered early that morning. Since Gillian saw no softening toward her from Ross's kinsmen, she excused herself immediately after she had eaten. She felt Seana's narrowed gaze follow her from the hall and hastened her steps. She didn't sleep well that night.

Since breakfast was nearly always a disaster for

Gillian's newly delicate digestion, she chose not to show her discomfort in front of Ross's kinsmen and ate both breakfast and the midday meal in her chamber the next two days. By dinnertime she was usually ready to venture down to the hall to sup.

However, the sensation of being watched, of some unknown danger threatening her, did not disappear. If anything, it increased. But today of all days Gillian was determined to sup in the hall, for Gordo had told her that he expected Ross to return in time for the evening meal.

After an absence of several days, Gizela showed up in Gillian's chamber as Alice was helping her dress that evening.

"Where have you been?" Gillian asked. "I havena see you for days, and I wanted to seek your advice."

"I'm sorry, lass, but a woman in the village was having a hard time giving birth. I was summoned the day the laird left and didna return until I was certain the bairn would live. Heed me well, lass, for I bring a warning."

Gillian forgot her own misgivings when she heard Gizela's words. "What kind of warning?"

"You are in grave danger. 'Ware the darkness."

"What is that supposed to mean?"

Gizela closed her eyes. "I see darkness; I see danger; I see someone trying to snuff out the flame."

"You are frightening Gillian," Alice chided. "Go away, Gizela. Bring your doom and gloom to someone else."

"The laird returns tonight," Gizela said as she hobbled off.

"Pay her no heed, Gillian," Alice soothed. She peered closely at Gillian. "Gizela has upset you. Forget her. Go down and greet the laird."

Wearing her best gown and wrapped warmly in her plaid, Gillian left her chamber in a state of high anticipation. Now that Ross had learned the truth from McHamish, he would have no reason to accuse her of being unfaithful.

The first thing Gillian noticed was the noise wafting up the staircase. Then she recognized Ross's voice. The next thing she became aware of was the lack of light in the corridor. The torch in the wall sconce was unlit. She made a mental note to tell Donald as she paused at the top of the winding stone staircase.

Then she heard a whisper of sound behind her, and Gizela's warning hit her hard. She sensed danger, smelled it in the air, saw it in the shifting shadows around her. Before she could react, she felt something slam into her back. She swayed precariously and then lost her balance. As she hurtled headlong down the stairs, she screamed and crossed her arms over her stomach to protect her bairn.

Meanwhile, below in the hall, Ross warmed himself beside the hearth, telling Gordo about his conversation with McHamish. He had scarcely begun speaking when Gizela appeared beside him and tugged on his sleeve. He tried to shake her off, but she clung tenaciously.

"Hurry, laird," she pleaded. "If you doona come now, you will be too late to save the flame and the spark that grows within her."

"I am speaking to my kinsman, Gizela. I will make time for you later."

"The time is now, laird," Gizela persisted. "If you tarry a moment longer, it will be too late to save them."

Ross's temper flared. "Gizela, I—"

"Mayhap you should see what she wants," Gordo

suggested. "She looks distraught. We can continue our conversation later."

Ross sighed and nodded. "Lead the way, Gizela. There had better be a good reason for this."

Gizela made no reply as she flew from the hall. As he neared the bottom of the staircase he heard an ungodly scream, and knew immediately that Gillian was in trouble. Pushing Gizela aside, he bounded up the stairs, taking them three at a time. When he saw Gillian falling toward him, he braced himself and caught her in his arms.

Though she had tumbled down but a few steps from the top landing before he had scooped her into his arms, Ross feared she might be badly hurt. But his concern now was to keep himself steady so that he wouldn't stumble backward with Gillian.

Suddenly Gordo and Donald were at his back, their hands keeping him upright as he fought for balance.

"Steady, lad. We heard a scream and came as fast as we could," Gordo explained. "What happened?"

"I doona know yet." He looked down at Gillian. Her face was white, drained of all color, and her eyes were closed. "She's in no condition to talk right now. You can let go, Uncle. I'm steady enough to carry Gillian to our chamber now. Where is Gizela? I want to thank her."

"She wasna on the staircase," Gordo said. "Mayhap the old crone isna barmy after all. Do you need help?"

"I can manage, but fetch Alice, and see if you can find Gizela. Gillian will have need of them."

His balance restored, Ross continued up the stairs. His concern grew when Gillian clutched her stomach and groaned.

"Are you hurt, lass?" Ross asked anxiously.

Gillian opened her eyes. Ross noted that they were

glazed with pain and shock. "The bairn," she whispered. Her words were barely audible; Ross thought he had misheard her.

Ross was not surprised when he found Gizela waiting for him in the bedchamber. The healer always seemed to turn up when she was needed. "Put her on the bed," Gizela ordered. "Be careful, laird; she is verra delicate."

Ross placed Gillian in the center of the bed and stepped aside. He'd allow Gizela to examine Gillian, but he wasn't going to leave her. He watched in consternation as Gizela gently prodded Gillian's stomach and carefully felt her limbs for broken bones while speaking softly to her. Ross neither heard what she was saying nor Gillian's replies. Gizela clucked her tongue when she felt the bump on Gillian's forehead.

Impatience rode Ross. "Well?" he asked.

"By God's grace there are no broken bones, though she might have suffered a concussion. Time will tell."

Ross allowed himself to breathe, until he noticed Gizela's grave expression. He pulled her aside, far enough away so Gillian couldn't hear them. "What is it? Tell me what's wrong."

"There is a chance she might lose the bairn."

"Bairn? What bairn?"

"Didna Gillian tell you?"

There were no words to express his feelings, so he simply shook his head.

He glanced over at Gillian, saw that her eyes were open, and returned to her bedside. Gizela followed.

Gillian's eyes darted between Ross and Gizela, finally settling on Gizela. "My bairn, is he all right?"

"He clings tenaciously to life, lass," Gizela replied. "I will prepare an herbal tea to help keep him safe within you."

She hastened from the chamber, leaving Ross alone with Gillian.

"You took a nasty fall," he said. His gaze shifted from her face to her stomach. "Thank God you didna break any bones."

"I didna fall. I was pushed."

"God's bones! Who would do such a thing? Tell me and I will see him punished."

"I canna say, for the attack came from behind," Gillian said shakily. "I thank God you arrived when you did."

"Nay, thank Gizela. Are you sure you didna trip on the hem of your gown?"

"I didna trip."

His expression hardened. "If someone pushed you, I will find and punish the culprit." He gazed into her eyes, his own troubled. "Why did you nae tell me?"

Gillian knew what he was asking. "You werena ready to hear it."

A long silence ensued. When he finally spoke, his voice was harsher than he intended. "Is the bairn mine?"

Gillian paled. "If I had my sword, I would run you through for that."

Ross wanted to call back his words the moment they had left his lips. He knew not what devil made him accuse her unjustly. Having spoken to McHamish, he knew Gillian had indeed meant to kill Sinclair.

"Forgive me, my love."

No answer was forthcoming; Gillian had lost consciousness.

Chapter Seventeen

Ross began chafing Gillian's wrists and softly calling her name. What had he done to her? After learning he was to become a father, he had deliberately insulted her. He was a witless fool. How could he treat the woman he loved in such a vile manner?

All the breath was sucked out of him. Did he love Gillian? God in heaven, was it possible? He hadn't truly realized it until he had nearly lost her. Life without his warrior wife would be unbearably boring. It was true—Gillian had found a place in his heart against all odds, and if she forgave him, he would be forever grateful.

Ross breathed a sigh of relief when Gizela returned with the herbal tea she had brewed for Gillian. Alice followed, carrying a basin filled with melting snow and clean cloths.

"She isna responding," Ross explained on a rising note of panic. He couldn't lose Gillian now. "What's the matter with her?"

"She's unconscious but alive, laird. I've brought

snow for her head wound. The cold water should bring the swelling down."

She dipped a cloth in the icy crystals, wrung it out, and placed it on the lump growing on Gillian's forehead. Then Gizela and Alice moved together to disrobe the unconscious woman.

"Gillian may have bruises that need treating with yarrow salve. Stand aside, laird."

Ross refused to budge. "I will assist Gizela, Alice. You can fetch a night rail for my wife."

Without waiting for Gizela's permission, Ross carefully began removing Gillian's clothing, wincing in sympathy as each new bruise was uncovered.

" 'Tis not so bad," Gizela said as she spread a thick layer of salve on Gillian's bruised right shoulder, right hip, and scraped knee, then covered them with bandages. "I'm more concerned about the bairn than the bruises."

Ross's thoughts ran amok as he helped Gizela pull over Gillian's head the night rail Alice had fetched. Why hadn't Gillian told him about the bairn?

"Gillian, can you hear me?" Ross asked anxiously. "Doona leave me, lass."

Gillian opened her eyes. They were focused, and she seemed alert. Gizela nodded, apparently satisfied with her response. "No concussion, laird. Now all we have to worry about is keeping the bairn inside her, where it belongs." She reached for the steaming mug of tea and brought it to Gillian's lips. "Drink, lass. 'Tis a special brew to keep you from miscarrying."

Gillian slid a glance at Ross, opened her mouth as if to say something, but was stopped when Gizela brought the mug of tea to her lips, forcing her to drink. When the mug was empty, she lay back and closed her eyes.

"Why is she so pale?" Ross asked Gizela.

"Och, you would be pale too if you had just had the fright of your life. Doona fret, laird. The flame burns bright inside the lass. All will be well." She bustled toward the door. "You can find me in the kitchen brewing more tea if you need me. Come, Alice; Laird Ross needs a moment alone with his lady."

Ross nodded his thanks and approached the bed. He picked up Gillian's limp hand in his and willed her to open her eyes. He wanted to more know about their bairn. How long had she known, and why hadn't she told him?

Gillian opened her eyes. "Ross . . ."

"Aye, sweeting, I'm here. Will you tell me about our bairn?"

"Go away, Ross. I'm too angry to talk to you, and I need to conserve my energy. If you wish to be helpful, find out who pushed me down the stairs."

"Forgive my cruel words, lass," Ross begged. "I spoke without thinking. I know you didna betray me, and I promise that the man or woman who pushed you will be severely punished."

Ross couldn't blame Gillian for wanting him out of her sight, and silently vowed to make things right between them. If Gillian didn't return his love, he'd find a way to woo her.

Gillian turned her head away, refusing to look at him.

Regret rode Ross mercilessly. He sighed heavily, aware that now wasn't the best time to bare his heart to Gillian. "Verra well, lass, I will leave you to your rest and fetch Alice to sit with you."

Ross didn't have to look far for Alice. She was waiting in the corridor outside the door. She slipped into the chamber as soon as Ross left.

His heart heavy, Ross descended the stairs. A hush fell over the hall when he entered. He strode directly toward a bench where Gordo and Niall sat, their heads together in quiet conversation.

"How does the lass fare?" Gordo asked.

"Gizela thinks she'll be fine. She's treated Gillian's bruises and the bump on her head and . . ." His sentence fell off.

"What is it, lad?" Gordo asked. "Is aught amiss?"

"Gillian could lose the bairn she is carrying."

"You're going to be a father?" Niall asked enthusiastically. "Why did you nae tell us?"

"I didna know until a few minutes ago. I'm as surprised as you are." He sank down beside them. Someone brought him a tankard of ale. He frowned into it a moment before taking a healthy gulp.

"There's more, isn't there?" Gordo prodded.

"Gillian said someone pushed her down the stairs."

"Who would do such a . . ." Niall's words stuttered to a halt as several men burst into the hall in a swirl of cold wind.

Ross groaned when he recognized Tearlach MacKay, accompanied by his heir and several kinsmen. What a time for Gillian's father to pay a visit, Ross lamented. MacKay's thunderous expression did not bode well for Ross.

"You bastard!" MacKay roared as he reached for his sword and waved it menacingly in Ross's face. "My wee lass is dead and 'tis all your fault! Draw your weapon, MacKenna."

Stunned, Ross made no move in his own defense. MacKay would have cut him down if Gizela hadn't stepped between them. "Your lass isna dead, Tearlach MacKay."

MacKay stopped in his tracks, his sword still held at the ready. He waved Gizela aside and glared at Ross. "Gillian is alive?"

"Aye, a bit bruised, but alive. Why would you think she is dead?"

"Angus Sinclair sent word of Gillian's death to Braeburn." He scratched his head in bewilderment. "I knew Gillian was at Ravenscraig, but it didna occur to me to wonder how Sinclair was in possession of such information. I was too upset to think clearly." His narrow-eyed glance pierced Ross. "I kenned you were angry with Gillian, and that you tried to repudiate your marriage and send her away. When I received Sinclair's message I naturally assumed you were responsible for her death."

"I would never hurt Gillian," Ross declared. "I admit I was angry at her, but have since learned Gillian didna lie. 'Tis true she challenged Sinclair after she learned he and Seana had goaded McHamish into attacking me. Sinclair actually believes Gillian is dead. He thinks she leaped from the tower to her death," Ross continued. "News travels slowly in the winter when fierce storms make travel impossible."

"Clan Sinclair is no longer my ally," MacKay proclaimed. "Come spring I will deal with Angus. Where is my daughter? She isna here to greet me."

Ross cleared his throat. "Gillian took a wee fall down the stairs today, but doona fear; she suffered naught but a few bruises and bumps."

MacKay sent Ross a venomous look, but it was Murdoc who reacted first. "If you canna take care of my sister, we will take her home to Braeburn."

"Aye," Tearlach agreed, glaring at Ross.

"You're not taking my wife anywhere," Ross warned.

"Last time we spoke, you were more than eager to be rid of her."

"Things have changed since last we spoke."

"I want to see my daughter."

"I will take you to her," Ross said. "You can see for yourself that she is alive and well."

Gillian heard the sounds of a commotion wafting up from the hall and wondered what was happening. Had Ross found out who had pushed her? Gillian suspected Seana, but proving it was going to be difficult, for there were no witnesses. Her thoughts ended abruptly when the door opened, admitting Ross, her father, and her brother Murdoc. Her family had never been more welcome, especially after Ross's hurtful rejection of their bairn. Even though Ross had apologized, she wasn't sure she could forgive him.

"Da! Murdoc!" she cried, wishing she could rise from bed for a proper welcome. But Gizela had forbidden her to leave her bed until the danger of miscarriage was past. "What brings you to Ravenscraig?"

His eyes tearing up, Tearlach rushed to Gillian's bedside. "Ah, lass, 'tis happy I am to see you alive and well."

Gillian frowned. "Why would I not be? I but fell down a few stairs. A wee accident. Gizela has predicted a full recovery."

Tearlach searched her face and frowned. "That fearsome lump on your head doesna look like a wee accident to me. You're pale as a ghost, lass. Why the circles under your eyes? Has your husband been mistreating you? I should have fetched you home when MacKenna begged me to take you away."

Gillian's winced and aimed a heated glance at Ross. "Ross didna hurt me, Da."

"Leave us, MacKenna; I wish to speak to Gillian alone. Murdoc can stay."

"Now, see here, MacKay," Ross complained, "you canna order me about in my own home."

Tired of listening to their bickering, Gillian said, "Go away, Ross. I wish to speak in private with my family."

"Gillian, I doona think—" Ross began.

"That's the problem, Ross. You never think."

Ross started to speak, closed his mouth, and stomped out of the chamber. MacKay pulled a chair up to the bed and sat down.

"Why does Sinclair believe you are dead, lass? He sent word to me of your death, and I came as soon as I could to learn the truth for myself."

"Apparently Angus still believes I leaped to my death from the tower. He must not have learned I am at Ravenscraig, alive and well."

"You doona look well. What is wrong? I ken you fell down the stairs, but there's more to it than that, I vow."

Gillian sighed heavily. "Seana McHamish is here. Ross let her return to Ravenscraig. She claimed I lied to Ross, that the real reason I went to Sinclair Keep was to become Angus's lover. Ross believed her. But then, little by little, Ross began to change, giving me hope that he was beginning to love me a wee bit."

" 'Tis not difficult to imagine. You are a lovable lass when you doona have a sword in your hand," Murdoc observed wryly. "So what happened?"

"I didna fall accidentally. I was pushed."

MacKay half rose from his chair. "Pushed? MacKenna said naught about your being pushed. Name the bastard who did it."

"I doona believe it was any of Ross's kinsmen. I suspect Seana McHamish of pushing me, but I have no proof."

"I will take care of the slut," Murdoc promised.

"She's Niall MacKenna's handfast wife. Touch her and the feud will resume. Is that what you want?"

"If it's the only way to rid the world of a menace, then aye," Murdoc growled.

"Nay, I doona want to see another of my sons die by the sword," MacKay said thoughtfully. "How long before you can travel, lass? It looks like the weather will hold another day or two. We can make a bed in a cart, cover you with furs, and take you back to Braeburn, where you will be safe."

Gillian silently debated telling her father about the bairn she carried, ultimately deciding it was something he should know. "I'm carrying Ross's bairn, Da. Gizela doesna think my fall has harmed me or my bairn, so mayhap traveling willna hurt me."

"That settles it," MacKay resolved. "We're taking you home. You canna afford to suffer any more accidents. Ross MacKenna isna capable of protecting you."

"I doubt Ross will allow me to leave," Gillian replied.

"Aye, he will," Murdoc vowed, "after Da and I speak to him."

Tearlach rose. "Rest, lass. You need to be strong for our journey tomorrow. We can take Gizela with us, if it pleases you."

"Mary would welcome you with open arms," Murdoc added. "I'm to be a father myself come summer."

Gillian smiled. MacKay beamed. "It seems I'm to be blessed with grandchildren." He rose to leave.

"Da, wait. Say naught to Ross. Let me tell him I'm leaving. It will cause less trouble between the clans if it comes from me."

"Verra well, lass, but doona think I'll back down about this. You're leaving with me and Murdoc no matter what MacKenna says."

Tearlach and Murdoc left the chamber. Tearlach didn't have far to look for Ross. He was pacing the corridor outside the door.

"Gillian wants to speak to you," MacKay said. "Murdoc and I will wait for you below in the hall."

Gillian silently pondered the words she would say to Ross. Though she didn't want the feud to resume, she and her bairn needed to be safe.

"Your father said you wanted to speak to me," Ross said, sinking into the chair Tearlach had just vacated. "I'm glad. I wanted a moment alone with you. Once again I ask your forgiveness, Gillian. I never doubted the bairn was mine. It was thoughtless—nay, cruel of me to suggest otherwise."

The light in Gillian's eyes dimmed. "I canna begin to describe the hurt I suffered when you denied our bairn."

He looked so utterly miserable that Gillian's heart began to soften. "I ken you visited McHamish. What did you learn?"

"He confirmed everything you told me. Truth to tell, I kenned you hadna lied about what happened at Sinclair Keep even before I spoke with McHamish."

"Yet you *did* leave," Gillian charged. "My word wasna enough for you. You chose to believe Seana's version of what happened. I thought making love the night before you left was a new beginning for us. I thought . . . Never mind; naught matters now. When you denied our bairn, you denied me."

"Forgive me, lass. I burned with jealousy. I hated the idea that you preferred Sinclair to me."

Ross was jealous? Mayhap she should let him suffer a wee bit more. "I doona know if I can. Sending Seana away would be a good start toward healing our marriage. I am convinced she pushed me down the stairs."

"If I send Seana away, Niall will leave with her. I canna bear to part with the cousin I depend upon and love dearly. But," he amended, "if Seana is responsible for your accident, I will gladly send her away, and I'm sure Niall will agree with me."

"If Seana remains while you investigate, I amna safe at Ravenscraig. Da wants to take me to Braeburn, and I've agreed to go with him."

Ross leaped to his feet. "I already told your father nay. I willna allow you to leave. You carry my bairn. Think you I canna take care of you?"

"You havena done so thus far, Ross. Seana's next attempt on my life might succeed."

Ross sighed heavily. "Verra well, you give me no choice. I will send Seana away immediately. I will do whatever it takes to keep you from leaving me."

"Nay, I ken how well you love Niall. 'Tis best that I return to Braeburn while you investigate."

Ross stared deep into the emerald depths of her eyes. "How do I know you will return?"

Gillian refused to look at him. A thorough search of her heart found love but not forgiveness. Until that happened—if it happened—'twas best that she return to Braeburn.

"That depends on many things, Ross. When you denied our bairn, you killed something inside me. Though I can defend myself with a sword, I doona ken how to protect my heart against your cruel words."

Ross could tell his arguments were having little effect on Gillian. He had all but fallen on his knees before her and had been rejected. The only thing left was to declare his love for her, and right now she was too angry and hurt to listen. "I doona want to tire you. We will speak of this later."

Ross was angry at himself, angry at Gillian, and angry at the predicament in which he found himself. Though he wasn't accustomed to groveling, he had done so and been rejected. Because he knew he was upsetting Gillian, he took himself off.

MacKay was waiting for him in the hall. "Did Gillian tell you she is returning to Braeburn with us?"

"Aye, she did, but I didna give her leave to go. She is in no condition to travel."

"The weather is still holding. We can pad a cart with furs and bundle her up. My daughter's life is in danger as long as she remains at Ravenscraig."

Ross turned on him. "Nay, Gillian belongs at Ravenscraig. She's carrying my bairn; I am her husband. 'Tis my responsibility to take care of her."

MacKay turned belligerent. His son and his kinsmen, noting their laird's confrontational stance, rallied to him, presenting a united front.

"I doona wish to fight you, MacKay, but you have no legal say over your daughter. I am her husband and will do whatever is necessary to keep her at Ravenscraig."

They stood nose to nose, neither man willing to give an inch. The tension intensified as Ross's kinsmen reached for their weapons.

Gizela appeared out of nowhere. With little concern for her own safety, she inserted herself between the two powerful lairds, glaring at each man in turn.

"Your argument is pointless," she chided. "Gillian canna travel. If you wish the bairn to remain safe within her, she must remain in bed until I give her leave to rise."

"My lass isna safe here," MacKay charged, pushing Gizela aside. "She belongs at Braeburn, where she can be protected."

"You insult me, MacKay. Gillian will remain at Ravenscraig under my protection," Ross growled, taking a menacing step toward MacKay. "Naught you say will change my mind."

With surprising strength, Gizela shoved the two men apart. "There is another solution," Gizela said. "If you canna take Gillian away from the danger, send the danger away from Gillian. Laird Ross has already decided to send Seana McHamish away."

MacKay seemed to relax. "Aye, the solution makes sense. I will personally provide men to escort Seana McHamish to her father's keep."

Niall leaped to his feet, hands clenched at his sides. "You have no reason to send my wife away, Ross. She has done naught. I refuse to believe she is a danger to Gillian."

"Gillian was *pushed* down the stairs, Niall. She didna fall," Ross explained. With slow deliberation he searched each face in the hall, beginning with Gordo and continuing until he had looked every man in the eye. "Tell me, Niall, which one of my kinsmen would commit such an evil deed."

"None of us would hurt your wife, even though there were times we didna trust her," Gordo said.

"That doesna mean Seana did it," Niall exclaimed. "She isna evil."

"Where *is* Seana, Niall?"

"I am here, Ross," Seana said, pushing through the circle of MacKay and MacKenna clansmen.

"Did you push Gillian down the stairs?" Niall asked.

"Nay, I am innocent."

Gizela snorted. "So you say. Did you know Gillian is carrying the laird's heir?"

"No one knew, not even Ross," Niall argued, pulling Seana close.

Seana smiled up at Niall. "Mayhap Gillian is lying about being pushed. Mayhap she wanted the laird's sympathy."

"Enough!" MacKay shouted. "This isna solving the problem." He rounded on Ross. "What say you, Ross MacKenna?"

Ross didn't doubt Gillian. If she said someone had pushed her, then she was pushed. Furthermore, he'd stake his life on his kinsmen's innocence. His every instinct pointed to Seana. Though he loved his cousin well, he couldn't in good conscience allow Seana to remain at Ravenscraig. Why couldn't Niall see Seana for what she was?

"I'm sorry, Niall. I promised Gillian that I would send Seana away. I canna risk the lives of my wife and bairn."

"If she goes, I go with her," Niall bit out.

"So be it. 'Tis your choice, not mine. I love you too well to send you away."

"Where will you go?" Mackay asked. "McHamish willna welcome his daughter in his keep after the part she played in his attack upon your cousin. He is deeply ashamed of attacking MacKenna."

"Aye, 'tis true," Ross agreed. "I spoke with McHamish myself. Neither he nor his wife wants Seana to return to their keep. McHamish's wife is carrying his bairn, and she doesna trust Seana."

"We will leave in the morning and seek shelter with one of my kinsmen," Niall said. "But 'tis only a temporary solution. I will learn the truth for myself and act accordingly. If Seana is guilty of evil deeds, I will disavow her."

Ross's relief was palpable when he returned to the solar and found Gillian asleep. It wasn't going to be easy telling her she would not be leaving with her father.

Another fear was that Niall wouldn't heed his advice where Seana was concerned. Ross knew Niall was too bewitched by Seana to take her evil nature seriously. Seana knew too much about poisons and potions to be trusted. Afraid that Seana might try to harm Gillian before she left, Ross had decided to stay close to Gillian himself until Seana had left Ravenscraig.

Ross threw some wood on the dying fire, undressed, and climbed into bed beside his slumbering wife. Just lying next to her lush, warm body again was pure heaven. The moment his arms went around her, she sighed and cuddled into the curve of his body. Exhausted from the turmoil of the past several days, Ross fell deeply asleep.

He arose the next morning before Gillian awakened and hurried below to bid MacKay and Niall farewell. Niall and Seana hadn't appeared yet when Ross entered the hall.

"Good morrow," MacKay said. "We have broken our fast, and our horses await us in the courtyard. Your cousin and Seana havena appeared yet. We are waiting to make sure they leave before we return to Braeburn. I doona trust the McHamish lass."

A niggling feeling of dread crept down Ross's spine. Intuition told him that all was not as it should be. "Nor do I. I will send someone to fetch them."

He searched the hall for Donald, saw him, and beckoned to him. Donald had taken no more than a few steps when Niall staggered drunkenly into the hall.

"Where is she?" Niall gasped, falling heavily against Ross.

Ross supported his cousin in his arms. "What has Seana done to you?" Ross cried. No answer was forthcoming. Several kinsmen ran up to help ease Niall onto a bench.

"Fetch Gizela," Ross ordered.

"I am here, laird," Gizela said, appearing at his side.

"What is wrong with my cousin?"

"Stand aside. Give me room to examine him."

Ross backed up, motioning everyone else out of the way. Gizela pulled back Niall's eyelids, clucking her tongue as his eyes rolled back in his head. She checked the color of his skin, examined his fingernails, and smelled his breath.

"He's been dosed with valerian, a strong tranquilizer. He probably imbibed it last night, most likely in his wine. I doona believe he drank enough to kill him, else he would already be dead."

"Where is that witch he married?" MacKay roared.

"Donald, instigate a search of the keep. Gordo, check the stable. See if any horses are missing. And then speak to the keeper of the gate. I asked that the gates be opened early this morning in preparation for MacKay's and Niall's departure. I have a feeling Seana may have left Ravenscraig. She is verra good at disappearing."

"Good riddance," Gizela muttered. "I saw Seana fleeing in a vision. I was on my way to tell you of my vision when Niall staggered into the hall."

"Do you know where she went, Gizela?" Ross asked.

Gizela nodded solemnly. "Aye, but Angus Sinclair willna welcome her."

"She went to Sinclair? Again? I should have known."

Gordo and Donald returned to report their findings

a short time later. "Seana is nowhere in the keep," Donald said.

"One horse is missing from the stable, and the gatekeeper saw a rider leave shortly before dawn," Gordo reported. "It was dark. He couldna see clearly and didna think it was important enough to report."

"Och, I care not where the woman went," MacKay retorted. "I'll be on my way, MacKenna. It looks like the weather is about to turn, and I dare not tarry. I hope we are rid of Seana McHamish for good. As for Sinclair, 'tis time he was taught a lesson. In the spring I intend to lay siege to his keep and present it to one of my sons when he weds." He glanced at the slumbering Niall. "I hope your kinsman survives."

"Farewell, Tearlach MacKay. Come spring we will take on Sinclair together. Doona worry about Gillian or Niall. Gizela is the finest healer in all the Highlands."

MacKay's party took their leave. Ross saw Niall safely back in bed before returning to the solar and Gillian.

Gillian was sitting up in bed when Ross entered the bedchamber. She looked sleepy-eyed and deliciously disheveled. He approached the bed and sat down on the edge.

"Why is Alice not here to help me dress?" Gillian asked. "If I know my father, he is impatient to leave, and I amna ready."

"Alice isna coming to help you dress, sweeting. You canna leave your bed today. You are to keep to your bed until Gizela says you are ready to leave it."

"I feel fine," Gillian maintained, wincing as she tried to scoot up against the headboard. "Has Da agreed to wait until Gizela pronounces me able to travel?"

"You are not returning to Braeburn—not now, not ever."

"But last night you said—"

"I never agreed to your leaving. You just assumed I had."

"Did you send Seana away? You ken I canna stay as long as she is a threat to me and my bairn."

"I said I would send her away, did I nae? Think you I would allow anyone to hurt you and my bairn? Seana is gone. She and Niall were supposed to leave Ravenscraig this morning."

"I'm surprised Niall would let her go."

"Seana sneaked off early this morning. She drugged Niall so he couldna stop her. I should have kenned she would disappear, since she's done the same before."

"Is Niall all right?"

"Gizela said he'll be fine. A jug of drugged wine was found in his bedchamber."

"Where could Seana have gone? I doubt her father will welcome her return."

"I agree. Your father and I share the opinion that Seana has returned to Sinclair."

Gillian mulled over this surprising turn of events before speaking. "Be that as it may, Ross, I would feel more comfortable at Braeburn."

Frustrated, Ross ran his fingers through his thick, dark hair. "Tell me what to do to make things better between us. Jealousy made me say things I will regret the rest of my life. When I learned about the bairn, I saw Angus Sinclair's face and recalled that he was the man you claimed to love, the man you'd hoped to wed."

"Angus didna touch me. If he had, I would have found a way to kill him."

Ross grinned. "Why do I find that so easy to believe? I ken your skill with a sword and your cunning and your courage. Just thinking about you with another man makes me daft. I care deeply for you, Gillian."

Gillian gave her head a vigorous shake. "You care for me? What is that supposed to mean?"

Reaching out, he gently brushed a strand of flaming hair away from her cheek. Now was the time to tell Gillian that he loved her. Whether she believed him or not made little difference. This was something he had to do. "Do you nae ken what I'm trying to tell you?"

Gillian pushed his hand away. "I amna good at guessing games. Mayhap you should tell me what you are trying to say."

Gillian's nerves were shredded raw by the time he answered her question. "I amna a man given to fancy words, or one to spout poetry; I can only state plainly and truthfully what is in my heart."

"What is your heart telling you, Ross?"

Ross took a deep breath and said, "I love you, Gillian MacKay." The breath whooshed out of him. "There, I said it."

When Gillian opened her mouth to speak, he held up his hand. "Nay, say naught. I ken you are nae well and need time to heal, so I willna push for a response. I ken you doona return my love, but I am willing to wait."

Gillian could hold her tongue no longer. "Why did you nae tell me you loved me before you learned I was carrying your bairn? 'Tis not me you love, Ross. 'Tis the bairn that's growing inside me."

"You're wrong, lass. I love both of you. I've denied my feelings for you too long. You've become a part of me, a part I canna bear to live without. There is something about you that calls to something in me. Something compelling, something I've finally figured out. I love you, Gillian MacKay."

Denial rode Gillian hard. Why hadn't Ross said anything before now? All the times he had turned away from her, had distrusted her, were difficult to forget. Not too long ago he had begged her father to take her away, had been eager to abandon their marriage. Her head began to ache.

"Please leave. I'm weary."

Ross rose. "Gizela will have my hide if I tire you. I should check on Niall anyway. Please doona reject my love, lass. All I ask is that you give me a chance to prove how I feel."

Gillian nodded jerkily, then clutched her head. "I canna think right now. Send Gizela to me."

Ross bent and gently kissed the purple knot on her forehead. "I didna intend to distress you. I'll fetch Gizela immediately."

Gillian breathed a sigh of relief as the door closed behind Ross. Too many thoughts ran through her head. Ross's kinsmen didn't like her, his former leman had tried to kill her, and then Ross had stunned her by saying he loved her. No wonder her head ached.

Gillian loved Ross so deeply, it seemed like a miracle that he returned her love.

The problem, as Gillian saw it, was that she didn't believe in miracles.

Chapter Eighteen

Sinclair Keep

An agitated Angus Sinclair paced back and forth before Seana McHamish, ranting and raving, stopping periodically to stab a stubby finger at her.

"Why did you nae send word to me that Gillian was alive? I canna believe you let me believe the lass was dead. Did you arrange her escape and lie to me about it?"

No answer was forthcoming.

"I shouldna have opened my gates to you," Angus raged. "I should have let you find a more welcoming shelter. Blast and damn! I sent a message to the MacKay, informing him that his daughter was dead."

"I didna set Gillian free," Seana lied. "If she escaped, one of your kinsmen was responsible. I didna know she was alive until I returned to Ravenscraig."

Her lies fell on deaf ears. "You ruined everything. All my scheming, all my plans were for naught. Now Braeburn will never be mine. After years of preparing, of making things work my way, all is lost to me."

"You are a fool, Angus Sinclair. The MacKay still has three male heirs in line to inherit Braeburn. I fail to ken how keeping the MacKenna's wife in your tower would aid your plans. She isna free to wed you."

"Nay, you are the fool, Seana McHamish. You ken naught about my plans. The terms of the truce state that the feud would resume if Gillian abandoned MacKenna and her marriage. I made sure MacKenna and his kinsmen heard Gillian state her wish to leave him."

"I ken you wanted the feud to resume, but I dinna ken why. How would it benefit you?"

Exasperated, Angus dug his fingers through his hair. "Are you dense? When men die in the heat of battle, no one kens whose sword slays whom. Two of MacKay's sons fell on the battlefield. The other three would have died, too, had the feud continued, and then MacKay himself would perish. I would then become laird of Braeburn through my marriage to Gillian.

"But MacKay had to seek peace and wed his daughter to MacKenna." Disgust colored his words. "Gillian and Braeburn were lost to me, unless Gillian left MacKenna or MacKenna died. When she was forced from Ravenscraig, I was presented with the perfect opportunity to make my dream come true. And then you betrayed me and set her free. Even worse, you made me believe Gillian was dead."

"You accuse me falsely," Seana insisted, unwilling to admit her guilt. "Even if Gillian wasna set free, you couldna wed her. She has a living husband, and you canna predict that MacKay and his sons would die."

A crafty smile curved Angus's lips. "None of them would have lived long once the clans took up their swords and resumed the feud."

Seana gasped as comprehension dawned. "*You* killed MacKay's sons! Had the fighting continued, you intended to kill the MacKay and his surviving sons."

Angus shrugged. " 'Tis no worse than what you tried to do to MacKenna. Unfortunately your poison failed to kill the bastard. I had to take matters into my own hands or lose everything."

Angus paced away from Seana and then spun around, his expression grim. "Did you flee to Ravenscraig after you left here?"

Seana nodded.

"Why did you leave? Whom did you try to kill this time?"

Seana grimaced. "Doona think you are better than I am, Angus Sinclair. I but gave Gillian a wee shove down the stairs, but the wench has more luck than sense. Had Ross not stopped her downward plunge, she might have tumbled all the way to the bottom and broken her neck."

"You pushed Gillian down the stairs?"

"I hate her," Seana spat. "She is the reason I lost Ross. She prevented me from fulfilling my dreams. I wanted to be mistress of Ravenscraig. I wanted Ross MacKenna, but he banished me from Ravenscraig. Fleeing seemed a better choice than letting Niall take me where I didna want to go."

"I wonder what MacKay thought when he received my message. I hoped he would hold MacKenna responsible for Gillian's death. Had I known Gillian was alive and at Ravenscraig, I wouldna have sent the message to MacKay. Because of you, I have signed my own death warrant. By now Gillian has told her husband and father what really happened to her, how I held her prisoner and forced her to deny her marriage and lie to MacKenna. I'm as good as dead."

"What will you do?"

Angus's encompassing look took in the rank rushes on the floor, the aging, drafty hall, and the indefensible wooden curtain wall, and gave a scornful snort. "Sinclair Keep holds no fond memories for me. I havena tended to the upkeep, for I assumed I would be living at Braeburn one day."

"We could wed and start anew in the Lowlands," Seana suggested.

"You expect *me* to wed *you*, a woman whose own father doesna want her?" Angus sneered. "Nay, I have other plans. I intend to flee, but not with you. I am in possession of a good sword arm and will offer my services to the king and make my living as a mercenary. Those of my kinsmen who wish to accompany me can do so. I care not what you do, Seana McHamish."

Seana grasped his arm. "You intend to abandon me? I have done naught to gain your enmity. What will I do? Where will I go?"

"You are the cause of all my problems. Think you I believe you had naught to do with Gillian's escape? I amna stupid. If you came here seeking succor, you came to the wrong place. I plan to gather what valuables remain in the keep and leave while the weather still holds. You may do as you damn well please."

Turning on his heel, Angus left to consult with his kinsmen. Seana stared after him with searing hatred. What was she to do now?

Ravenscraig Tower

Ross rarely left Gillian alone after her close call with death, though Gillian didn't seem to welcome his company. Gizela had insisted that Gillian remain in bed several days following her mishap. Though Ross knew little about medicine, he made sure Gillian followed Gizela's orders. When all seemed well with the bairn a sennight after her fall, Gillian was allowed to leave her bed.

She had just finished dressing when Ross entered the bedchamber and roared a protest. "What are you doing out of bed? Are you deliberately trying to harm our bairn?"

Gillian gave an exasperated snort. "Leave off, Ross. Gizela gave me permission to get out of bed. My bairn and I are both fine. I fully intend to carry him to term."

Ross sent Gillian a skeptical look. "I suppose if Gizela has pronounced you well, then I shouldna protest," he relented. "I'll escort you down to the hall to break your fast."

"I can see myself down, thank you."

Ross shook his head. "Gillian, lass, why are you still angry with me? Did I nae bare my heart to you? Did I nae send Seana away, as you requested?"

Gillian sighed heavily. "Aye, you did, Ross, but I canna forgive you for denying our bairn. You should have kenned I was lying when I told you Angus and I had become lovers."

Ross pushed an impatient hand through his thick hair. "I amna a mind reader. 'Tis past time you forgave me. I want us to be a family, sweeting. I want to go to bed with you at night and wake up with you in my arms in the morning."

Gillian refused to meet his gaze. Unwilling to let the gap between them widen, Ross reached for her, pulling her gently into his embrace. "Mayhap you will believe this."

He lowered his mouth and kissed her. Rather than fight him, Gillian wanted to cleave to him, to become his love, his life, but her pride kept getting in the way. And logic argued that a man did not declare his love for a woman he had once considered an enemy. Ross wanted his bairn, not her.

To Gillian's disquiet, Ross's kisses affected her as they always did, leaving her craving more. It seemed like forever since she had been in his arms this way. Of their own accord her arms lifted and twined around his neck. With a soft growl of triumph, he brought her closer, held her tighter, enveloping her in the heat of his warrior's body. His kisses grew desperate, deepened, as his hands roamed freely over her back and bottom.

Despite her body's response to Ross's attempt to arouse her, Gillian resisted his seduction. She would know when her heart found the forgiveness Ross requested, and it wasn't now. Removing her arms from his neck and placing her hands against his chest, she pushed him away. Dropping his arms, Ross stepped back. She could tell it pained him to stop, but she wasn't ready yet to let him make love to her.

"Forgive me, lass. You are newly recovered from your fall. I had no right to press myself on you. But heed me well: I willna give up on you."

Gillian had little doubt that Ross was right. How could she resist a man who had declared his love so sweetly? But meanwhile, it wouldn't hurt him to suffer a wee bit of rejection.

Gillian knew she would allow Ross in her bed again, but she intended to speak to Gizela about her readiness to make love after her fall. She would do naught to harm her bairn.

Ross escorted Gillian to the hall. To Gillian's surprise and delight, she received a warm welcome from Ross's kinsmen. Everything that had happened in the past seemed to have been forgotten in the light of the news that Gillian was carrying their laird's heir.

Both Gordo and Niall were already in their places at the high table. They rose when Gillian entered the hall and stood until she was seated.

"You're looking well, lass," Gordo said. "Ross has been worried sick over you."

"He was worried about the bairn," Gillian maintained.

"Mayhap, though I doubt the bairn was his only concern."

Niall cleared his throat. "Gillian, do you really believe Seana pushed you down the stairs?"

Gillian looked at Niall, saw the devastation Seana had wrought, and wished she had the answer Niall sought. "Aye, Niall. As much as it pains me to admit it. Seana isna the woman you thought you knew. She is evil. She tried to poison Ross, and she drugged you. 'Tis time you opened your eyes to her true nature."

"Thank you for being truthful. I fancied myself in love with Seana. I thought my love could change her, but apparently I was wrong."

"You are better off without Seana," Ross said. "I regret my past association with her, for she brought naught but trouble to Ravenscraig."

"Amen," Gordo added.

Gillian ate her meal in silence. Hanna had gone out of the way to please her, tempting her delicate digestion with her favorite foods. To Gillian's relief, everything stayed down.

"I've neglected my duties of late," Ross said after he had eaten his fill. "Some of the lads and I intend to inspect the livestock today. Will you be all right? I'm leaving Gordo in charge of the keep during my absence."

"I'm fine, Ross, truly. Alice and I will be counting linen and inspecting stores today."

Ross frowned. "Doona overdo it your first day out of bed." Before he left, he lifted her chin and kissed her mouth.

Ross didn't leave the keep immediately. While Niall and the others were saddling the horses and loading sacks of feed, Ross went in search of Gizela. He found her in the stillroom, grinding roots and herbs she used for medicinal purposes.

"There you are, Gizela," Ross greeted her.

Gizela studied Ross through eyes brimming with intelligence and mystery. "Aye, laird, I was expecting you, and have an answer to your question."

Ross stopped in his tracks, astonished by her words. "You ken what I want?"

"Aye, laird, I do. Gillian is healed and her bairn is safely entrenched within her. If she wishes it, you may return to her bed and love her without fear of harming her or your son."

Ross never blushed, was rarely embarrassed, yet he could feel his cheeks heating now. Then something Gizela had said captured his attention. "I'm going to have a son?"

"Aye, didna Gillian tell you?"

"Nay, Gillian is angry with me."

"Her anger wanes, laird."

"You know this?"

"I know many things."

"Tell me how I can earn Gillian's love."

Gizela's sagging features eased as her lips turned up into a smile. "You canna gain her love, laird."

Ross's heart plummeted. "Are you saying Gillian will never love me?"

"Nay, laird, I am saying you already have her love. Go now and leave me to my work."

Ross's laughter followed him out the door and into the cold, crisp air. Gillian loved him. Now all he had to do was get her to admit it.

Lingering over her breakfast, Gillian conversed briefly with Gordo. She gasped in surprise when he asked, "Why are you tormenting the lad, Gillian? Any fool can see he loves you. I admit I didna think your marriage would work, but you and my nephew are matched in strength and stubbornness. I ken you love him but are too stubborn to admit it."

Gillian swallowed hard. Was she that easy to read? "Is it so obvious?"

"It is to me, and I'm sure others ken it as well. Are you nae pleased about the bairn you're carrying?"

"I am thrilled about the bairn, Gordo. 'Tis Ross I amna pleased with." She hesitated, then said, "He questioned whether the bairn is his. I find it difficult to forgive him."

"Och, the man is a fool. I know his careless words hurt you, but you canna blame him. I, too, heard you proclaim that you and Sinclair were lovers. I wasna the only witness when you renounced Ross and your marriage."

"I explained my reasons for lying to Ross. I did it to save his life. He should have kenned I was lying."

"Will you ever forgive him, lass?"

"Mayhap, after he has suffered a wee bit more." She rose. "If you'll excuse me, I need to confer with Gizela."

Gillian left the hall in a thoughtful mood. Had Ross suffered enough? Was it time to tell him she loved him? Mayhap she should end Ross's misery and let him make love to her—after she consulted with Gizela, of course.

Gillian located Gizela in the stillroom. She greeted the healer warmly. If not for Gizela, neither she nor Ross would be alive today.

Gizela turned at her greeting. "If people doona stop interrupting me, I will be forced to neglect my work. Are you unwell, lass?"

"I am well, and so is my bairn, thanks to you, Gizela. I have a question to ask of you."

"In truth, I was expecting you, so I will save you the trouble of asking your question and give you my answer. 'Tis time to forgive your husband. Your marriage was written in the stars long before you were born. Welcome the laird into your bed, lass. Naught he can do will harm you. Your bairn willna leave your body until the appointed time. Go now; can you nae see I am busy?"

Suppressing a smile, Gillian left the stillroom. Though most people thought Gizela a wee bit daft, her psychic powers were uncanny. Gillian didn't doubt Gizela's word. She believed her bairn was in no danger and that she would carry it to term, because the healer had said so.

She also knew it was time to heal her marriage, for her heart demanded it of her. She and Ross had started out as enemies and suffered through countless trials and tribulations to be together. The time had come to make things right between them.

The day flew by as Gillian went about her duties.

The linens were counted and the stores inspected. Everything was in good order. Gillian spoke to Hanna about preparing a special meal that evening and serving it to her and Ross in the solar. They would dine alone tonight, with naught to distract them.

Gillian ordered a bath and soaked in the tub until the water cooled. Afterward, Alice brushed out her hair and helped her into a filmy night rail and chamber robe. Then she ordered the tub emptied and refilled with clean water for Ross.

After Alice and the servants left, Gillian walked to the window and watched the snow fall, her mind stumbling over the words she wanted to say to Ross tonight. After long minutes of silent contemplation, she decided to say whatever was in her heart.

Ross entered the hall in a rush of cold air and blowing snow. He stomped the snow from his boots and headed for the hearth to warm his bones. He and the lads had had a busy day. They had rescued several head of cattle from snowdrifts, rounded up a few lost sheep, and delivered feed so the livestock wouldn't starve.

Ross was warming his backside when he noticed that Gillian wasn't in the hall. Disappointment rode him; he had hoped his wife would be on hand to greet him. Disappointment turned to concern. Had Gillian taxed her strength her first day out of bed?

He strode to the staircase; Alice met him on the bottom landing. "Your lady is waiting for you in the solar, laird."

Gillian was waiting for him? Had he heard aright? Though Ross had no idea what to expect, he took the stairs two at a time. He burst into the solar, his gaze searching the chamber for his wife. The first thing he saw was a tub of steaming water sitting before the hearth.

"Gillian? Alice said . . ."

His words fell silent when Gillian turned away from the window and greeted him with a smile. "I'm glad you're home, Ross."

Ross felt as if the floor had dissolved beneath his feet. Gillian was dressed informally in night rail and robe, her long hair framing her face in a halo of living flame. What was she up to now? Didn't she know she was tormenting him?

"You must be frozen," Gillian said. "The bath is for you. Shall I help you disrobe?"

Gillian wanted to help him undress? He blinked. Had he heard aright? Had the cold frozen his brain? "Are you well, sweeting?"

Slowly Gillian walked toward Ross, her gaze intent upon his face. "I am verra well, thank you. Let me take your plaid. Your bathwater is growing cold."

Ross watched warily as Gillian removed the woolen plaid from his shoulders and helped him out of his jacket. When she undid the strings at the neck of his shirt and pulled it over his head, he felt his cock grow hard and his body clamor with desperate need. Seeing Gillian like this reminded him why she was the only woman he wanted, the woman he would protect and love the rest of his life. Was she finally willing to be a wife to him again? Was she ready to release him from his misery?

Words failed him as he pulled Gillian against him, letting her feel the thick ridge of his need. His heart thudded wildly when, instead of resisting, she melted into his embrace and raised her face for his kiss. Ross didn't hesitate. Lowering his head, he met her lips, savoring her sweet taste while his tongue ravished her tenderly. Something had changed Gillian, and he wasn't going to question it.

Long moments later Ross drew back, his voice hoarse with need as he whispered against her lips, "I want to love you, wife. My body aches for you."

"I want that too," Gillian breathed, "Bathe first. Then we can talk, and afterward we will make love."

"Or we can love first and then talk while I bathe," Ross suggested, as eager as a green boy to be inside his wife again, to feel her body writhe against his.

"We have a lifetime to love," Gillian replied.

A lifetime; the word was music to Ross's ears. "Then I had best get on with the bathing." He chuckled.

Ross finished disrobing and climbed into the tub. Gillian knelt behind him, rubbed soap on a cloth, and began scrubbing his back. When she moved around to his chest, Ross's cock jerked upright in reaction. He didn't know how much of this sweet torment he could stand.

"Give me that," Ross said, snatching the cloth from her hand. "I had best wash myself. Fetch the drying cloth. I can wait no longer for my wife."

Gillian retrieved the drying cloth from the hearthstone and handed it to Ross. Smiling, he rose from the tub. Water streamed from his powerful body; his cock thrust upward from a nest of ebony curls. His face stark with unconcealed desire, he held out his arms so she could dry him.

Her hands shaking, Gillian ran the cloth over his warrior's body, loving the way it hardened beneath her touch. She had missed Ross, missed his body next to hers in bed, yearned for his kisses, his passion.

"What did I do to earn your forgiveness?" Ross asked. "Not that I'm complaining, mind you. This morn you were implacable and unforgiving. I was at my wit's end."

Gillian dropped the drying cloth and met his probing gaze. "We are nae enemies, Ross. Though my heart was sorely hurt, I realized that rejecting you wasna the answer. Before I could heal, I needed to forgive." She took a steadying breath. "I do love you, Ross, and I forgive you. I have loved you for a verra long time. My father must have kenned that we would suit before he proposed uniting our clans. But we needed to learn that for ourselves."

Ross closed his eyes to better savor her words. When he opened them, Gillian was smiling at him, her green eyes misty with unshed tears. "You are wise for your years, Gillian MacKay. I loved you as a warrior woman, but I love you better as the mother of my bairns."

"No more talk, Ross. Just love me. Almost dying has shown me that life is too short to waste on pettiness. You have apologized, and I believe you have suffered enough. I have suffered enough." She lifted her arms to him.

Groaning, Ross enfolded her in his embrace, bent his head, and kissed her, his fingers twining in her fiery hair to hold her head in place. He ravished her mouth until they were both breathless, and then he lowered her onto the fur rug before the hearth.

Trembling with need, he knelt beside her, untied the belt of her robe, and pulled it free. Then he rid her of her night rail, baring her glowing white flesh to his appreciative gaze. The gripping need inside him tightened. His breath came heavily as he kissed her mouth, her throat, her breasts. He wanted to devour her, every precious inch.

His voice vibrated hotly against the quivering flesh of her stomach as he said, "I want to taste you."

He stared into her eyes as his hands slid beneath her to cup the twin globes of her buttocks, his fingers slowly squeezing and kneading. The throbbing between her legs intensified; she arched violently when his thumbs parted her feminine folds, stroked, and slowly circled the tiny hidden nub of her sex.

"Ross . . ." The word died in her throat when Ross bent and pressed his mouth against her dewy cleft. A jolt of pleasure shot through her. Gasping, she went rigid.

Ross lifted his head and gazed at her so intently, Gillian felt scorched by it. She reached up and stroked his cheek. "I love you, Ross."

"I love you more, Gillian MacKay."

Spreading her thighs, he bent to her again and captured her sweet essence with his mouth. He licked her swollen flesh, holding her grinding hips in place as he laved her with his tongue, his mouth sucking softly in a heated kiss.

Gillian cried out, rising to meet the invading lash of his rough tongue as he teased, licked, and stabbed liquid flame inside her. Sensation overwhelmed her, ravished her senses. An exquisite pleasure so intense it bordered on pain shot through her. She convulsed as his tongue continued to flick in and out, piercing her with fire.

Tamping down his grinding need, Ross probed and nibbled to his heart's content. Her hot, sweet taste was intoxicating; her musky scent drove him wild. His body was ready to burst. He thrust his tongue deep inside her one last time and nearly lost control when she cried out, her hips thrusting up to meet his feasting mouth. Her climax released a primitive surge of love and lust inside him. Her cry of completion thrilled him. That he could satisfy his warrior woman so well was a sweet reward. That she could satisfy him so completely was even sweeter. He held her and kissed her as she writhed and twisted beneath him.

When the last tremor had passed, he tenderly placed a kiss on her stomach, marveling that his bairn could be growing within her slender body. "Are you all right, love? I didna harm the bairn, did I?"

Panting softly, Gillian said, "Our bairn is strong. Loving me willna hurt him."

That was all Ross needed to hear. He placed a final kiss against her moist center, stretched over her, and settled in the cradle of her hips. His pulse pounding, he sank slowly into her, using teeth-grinding caution lest he hurt her. Her thighs clenched around him in joyful welcome.

"Can you take all of me, lass? Are you sure it willna hurt you or our bairn?"

"I amna a fragile blossom, Ross."

Slowly, with great care, he penetrated her fully. He groaned and shuddered. She felt even better than she tasted.

His mouth settled over hers. Gillian tasted her scent on his lips and on his tongue. Her hands clutched at his broad back, and she writhed as he slid inside her. Her back arched, her eyes closing as her body caught fire again. She was only dimly aware of his voice murmuring love words against her mouth. This bold warrior of hers displayed his tender side as he told her he loved her, that he couldn't live without her.

She clung to him, frantic with need, with hunger, with a passion that matched his. Moments later the incredible tension exploded, her ragged cry of completion piercing the stillness.

Ross stiffened and clamped his teeth together, his eyes closing as pleasure, so raw and so primitive it nearly undid him, ripped through him. He shouted her name, his body clenching and shuddering as he poured himself into her.

Fearing he would crush her, Ross rose up on trembling arms and lifted his suddenly boneless body off and away. Once his strength returned, he rose, lifted her into his arms, and carried her to their bed.

"You must be cold," he said as he lay down beside her and pulled the covers up.

"I'm not cold." Gillian sighed, cuddling up against him. "I've never been warmer."

Ross gathered her in his arms, his hand resting on her stomach. "I vow that was as close as I will ever come to paradise."

There came a knock on the door. "That will be our supper," Gillian said. "I asked to have it brought to the solar. I didna want to share you with anyone tonight."

Ross left the bed and pulled on his braies before opening the door. Alice brushed past him, carrying a tray, her face wreathed in smiles. Ross pulled a table before the hearth and asked Alice to set out the food. She did as Ross bade, sending Gillian a knowing grin before she left the chamber.

"Did everyone in the keep know what you planned tonight?"

"Not everyone. Does it matter?"

"Nay, not when the outcome pleased me so well." He found her discarded robe and handed it to her, then pulled two chairs up to the table. "I doona know about you, but I am famished."

He seated Gillian and himself, then heaped two plates high with slices of roasted fowl, boiled potatoes, creamed onions, and stewed apples sweetened with honey from last summer's harvest.

Gillian ate ravenously, and when she finished, she leaned back in her chair and asked, "What are you going to do about Angus Sinclair? I know you're not going to let the matter rest."

Ross scowled. He didn't want Angus Sinclair to spoil their reconciliation. "Leave that to your father and me. We doona intend to let Sinclair escape punishment."

"What about Seana McHamish? Her evil shouldna go unpunished either."

"Doona worry, love. Seana McHamish willna hurt you again. But, aye, we will deal with her as well as Sinclair."

"Why can you nae tell me what—"

"Not now, lass. 'Tis off to bed with you. You need to rest, and I should speak with Gordo before retiring." He rounded the table and held his hand out to her.

She placed her hand in his and let him pull her to her feet. But once they reached the bed, she laughed up at him and pulled him down with her.

"A woman carrying a bairn can be verra temperamental. 'Tisna wise to deny her," she teased. "I amna tired, Ross. I would like us to love again, if you could manage it."

Ross threw back his head and laughed. "With you, once will never be enough."

Chapter Nineteen

Gillian welcomed the waning days of winter. Aside from feeling a wee bit more cumbersome due to the bairn growing inside her, she felt and looked well, her babe barely straining the front of her gown. And she had never been happier. Ross was the husband she had always longed for, her days were filled with moderate activity, and she had finally gained the respect of Ross's kinsmen.

As the sun began to grow warmer and blades of grass pushed through the melting snow, an air of expectancy prevailed throughout the keep. Gillian sensed Ross's restlessness and knew it had to do with Angus Sinclair. Highlanders were a vindictive lot, and Ross was no different. His thoughts never strayed far from Angus Sinclair and Seana McHamish and the retribution due them.

One night after a particularly mild day in early March, Ross slowly undressed Gillian and led her to their bed. Then he discarded his own clothing and proceeded to make sweet, slow love to her. His big hands were gentle as they caressed her swollen breasts and rounded stomach.

"You are lovelier now than when I first saw you, the day you faced me with a sword in your hand," Ross whispered against her lips.

"I am clumsy and ungainly," Gillian complained.

"In my eyes you are slim and beautiful. My bairn growing inside you doesna make you any less lovely. Gizela said it is safe to make love for some weeks yet."

Gillian laughed up at him. "You asked her?"

"Aye, I amna verra knowledgeable about such things. Gizela said you are strong and healthy, and that naught we do will harm our bairn."

Gillian pulled his hair, forcing his head down. "Then love me, husband. I doona want to waste time talking about it."

He caught her chin between his fingers and lifted her mouth to his, drawing the very breath from her lungs.

"I am too heavy for you," he said as he lifted her astride him. She opened her thighs and took him inside her. Her flaming hair fanned out over her shoulders and brushed the tips of her breasts enticingly as she rotated her hips and took him deeper.

"There has never been another lass like you," Ross murmured hoarsely. "You are all woman, but as courageous as any warrior known to me."

Their gazes met and clung as he moved inside her, blazing hot and intense. Raising his head, he took her nipple into his mouth, suckling her. His hands cupped her bottom, gently lifting her up and down his stiff cock. She was nearing the crest; he could tell by the increased rhythm of her breathing and the small cries escaping her throat. As she came apart in his arms, he watched the play of emotion on her lovely face, until he could contain himself no longer and spent himself inside her.

Later, as Gillian lay in his arms, she gazed up at him and asked, "Where has your mind gone? You left me after we made love."

"Your perceptiveness amazes me, lass. Has Gizela taught you how to read minds?"

"I know you, Ross. I can tell when your mind is elsewhere. What is bothering you?"

"I willna lie. 'Tis time I dealt with Sinclair and the McHamish lass. I sent a message to Douglas McHamish. I wanted to know if he had any objection to his daughter returning to his keep after I dealt with her and Sinclair."

"I sincerely doubt he wants Seana returned to him."

"Aye, I ken that, but Seana is his daughter, and I wanted him to know I am ready to seek retribution. I also sent for your father; 'tis time to plan Sinclair's punishment. Sinclair Keep isna easily defensible; it shouldna take long to roust the cur who hides within."

"Da is coming here?" Gillian asked, clearly excited about seeing her father again.

"Aye, I knew you would like to see him, so I asked him to come here instead of my going there."

Gillian rose up on her elbows and kissed Ross soundly on the lips. "I love you, Ross MacKenna. I bless the day my father offered me to you to seal the treaty. And I am verra happy I didna skewer you with my sword."

"That wouldna have been possible, lass of mine. 'Twill be a cold day in hell when a woman, even a warrior woman, bests Ross MacKenna at swordplay. Now go to sleep, sweet lass, lest I think you are nae tired enough to sleep and find other ways to wear you out."

"I amna tired, Ross," Gillian teased. "Mayhap you should show me those other ways."

Pulling her into his arms, Ross did exactly what he'd said he would. An hour later, both he and Gillian were sleeping soundly, arms and legs intertwined.

Tearlach MacKay arrived at Ravenscraig the next day with his usual bluster. He spied Gillian immediately and held his arms out to her. Gillian flew into them and breathed in his familiar scent. After a quick hug, he held her away from him and searched her face.

"You seem to be thriving, lass."

Ross joined them, placing a possessive arm around Gillian's waist. "Gillian and our bairn are well, MacKay, as you can plainly see. I'm glad you are here; we have plans to make."

"Where is Murdoc, Da?" Gillian asked. "Has Mary had her bairn yet?"

"Nay, but her time grows near. Murdoc didna want to leave her. But I didna come alone, lass."

Gillian glanced toward the door just as her brothers Ramsey and Nab entered the hall. "Ramsey, Nab!" she cried as the men rushed forth to greet her. "I thought you were in Edinburgh."

Ramsey and Nab hugged Gillian in turn. "Och, lass," Ramsey said, "town life and the king's court didna please us. 'Twas an adventure, to be sure, but crowded cities doona hold the appeal of pure air or the natural beauty of moors ablaze with purple heather below snow-topped mountains."

"Aye," Nab agreed. "We had our taste of the big city and are happy to be home."

"Tell them your news, Ramsey, lad," Tearlach urged.

"Shall we sit? Gillian tires easily these days," Ross

said as he led them to the hearth, where extra chairs had hurriedly been set in place for the visitors.

"Now," Ross said when each man had a tankard of ale in hand. "Tell us your news, Ramsey."

"I brought a wife home," Ramsey revealed. "A bonny lass with blue eyes and hair the color of a summer sunset."

Surprise colored Gillian's words. "Ramsey, you wed a Lowlander? I canna believe it of you."

"Judith was born in the Highlands, Gillian," Ramsey exclaimed. "She's been living in Edinburgh with her father. He has a position in the king's court. It was love at first sight for both of us."

"Why did you nae bring her here to meet us?" Gillian asked with a hint of disappointment.

Color rose in Ramsey's cheeks. "Judith is increasing and is often beset with sickness. I thought it best she not travel during the first stages of her pregnancy."

"I am thrice blessed," Tearlach bragged. "First our Mary will deliver and then Gillian, and not far behind, Judith." He sent Nab a sidelong glance. "Does that not give you the urge to find a wife, Nab, lad?"

"I will in my own good time, Da."

Tearlach straightened in his chair, all business now. "Your message said you were ready to roust Sinclair from his keep and exact retribution for the mischief he caused. As we agreed before, it will be a joint effort. Name the day you wish to begin the siege and my kinsmen and I will join you.

"Sinclair Keep is in shambles; he didna take care of it," Tearlach continued. "I chastised him about it often enough, but he didna seem to care." His expression grew thoughtful. "Mayhap he was waiting for Gillian's dowry to make repairs to his keep."

Ross made a harsh sound in his throat. "It matters not what he was waiting for. His punishment is long overdue."

"Aye," all three MacKay men agreed, raising their tankards as a sign of unity.

Ross, Tearlach, and their kin talked and drank and finally set a day to launch their siege. Since it would take a sennight to gather their kinsmen and see to their weapons, they mutually agreed to march to Sinclair Keep seven days hence.

"We will meet you at St. Tears Chapel," Tearlach said.

Their plans made, the MacKays joined the MacKennas for the noon meal and then took their leave. Gillian hated to see her family go, but knew there was a great deal that had to be done before they waged war against Angus Sinclair.

"Think you Angus is expecting a siege?" Gillian asked when they retired that night.

"I would assume so," Ross replied. He sent her a sharp look. "I ken you had tender feelings for the man at one time, but his evil deeds canna go unpunished."

"My tender feelings died the day I met you, my love. I will pray for your success and a safe return. I canna bear to lose another loved one."

"I doubt Sinclair will put up much of a fight. He is badly outnumbered. I wouldna be surprised if he surrenders without a fight when he sees the size of our army. Doona worry about it, Gillian; 'tisna good for the bairn. Naught will happen to me or your family, I promise."

There came a knock on the door. Ross went to open it. "Gizela, what do you here? Is aught amiss?"

"Naught is amiss, except . . ." She hesitated, then said, "I 'saw' Angus Sinclair dressed in battle gear."

Ross cursed. "He knows we are coming and is preparing to fight. I had hoped to avoid bloodshed."

"There willna be bloodshed, laird. Sinclair will die, but not by your hand."

"You do try my patience, Gizela." Ross sighed. "Please explain yourself."

"I can only tell you that I saw no blood on your hands."

She was gone before Ross could form his next question.

Ross shook his head. "I swear, that woman was put on this earth to bedevil me. I ken, however, that she is wise in many ways, so I willna dismiss her words out of hand."

The next day Ross received McHamish's answer to his message. He wrote that his wife had just given birth to a son, his heir, and they didn't want Seana to return to their household. Whatever punishment Ross devised for Seana was agreeable to McHamish.

The following days were busy ones for Ross. The entire keep was preparing to go to war. Ross appointed Gordo, despite his protest, as guardian of the keep in his absence, and left five men to guard Gillian and all he held dear.

Shortly after dawn on the appointed morning, Ross kissed Gillian good-bye and rode off with a company of twenty armed men. MacKay and an equal number of his kinsmen had already arrived when they reached St. Tears. Murdoc, MacKay's heir, had been left behind to guard Braeburn, but both Nab and Ramsey rode with their father. The combined forces continued on to Sinclair Keep.

The day was fine; traveling was easy and the sunshine welcome. The distance between St. Tears and Sinclair Keep was not great. The war party expected to reach their destination early in the afternoon and begin the siege immediately thereafter.

Ross called a halt on a rise overlooking Sinclair Keep to study the lay of the land. A strange silence prevailed. On a fine day such as this there should have been some movement in the courtyard, yet Ross saw no one. An air of abandonment hung heavy over the keep. Ross lifted his hand and motioned the war party forward. Tearlach MacKay joined him at the head of the column.

"What do you make of it, MacKenna?"

Ross eyed the keep cautiously, noting the lack of activity. Not one man was visible on the wall walk; not one horse was tethered in the courtyard. But what shocked Ross the most was the gate. It gaped open without a single guard in sight.

"'Tis odd that no one is about, and that the gate isna barred against us," he mused.

Ross called another halt just short of arrow range.

"The keep looks deserted," MacKay observed. "Think you Sinclair sets a trap for us?"

"He didna know when we were coming, so it doesna make sense. I'll ride a wee bit closer and see what happens."

Ross declined MacKay's offer to ride with him. If some treachery was afoot, he wanted to know what form it took before sending men into danger.

"If I reach the gate without mishap, you and the others can follow."

Ross spurred his horse. He had nearly reached the wooden curtain wall when a head popped up on the wall walk. But the man didn't hold a bow. Instead he waved a white flag attached to a pole.

"Where is Sinclair?" Ross called up to the man.

"Gone, Laird Ross. He fled with those of his kinsmen willing to follow him. They left naught behind but women, children, old men, and those of us who didna wish to leave the Highlands. The winter has been hard on us. The cotters are near to starving."

Ross turned in the saddle and beckoned his army forward. When they reached him, he led them through the gate and into the courtyard. Niall rode up beside him as an assortment of people crept timidly from the keep. The man who had waved the flag climbed down from the wall walk to join them.

"What do you make of this, Ross?" Niall asked.

"Sinclair has fled; that much is certain."

"I claim the keep and demesne for my son Ramsey," MacKay loudly proclaimed.

"Sinclair is your ally; 'tis within your right to claim Sinclair's holdings," Ross acknowledged.

"Hear me," MacKay said in a loud voice. "No one will be harmed. Repairs will be made to cottages; the curtain wall will be rebuilt with stone, and the keep refurbished. Food will be provided from my own stores. Who is in charge here?"

"That would be me, laird." The man holding the white flag stepped forward. "My name is Fergus."

"How long ago did Sinclair leave?"

"He fled just after Yuletide, laird, during the break in the weather. He left us with no weapons and only the food that he and his men couldna carry with them."

"Where did they go?"

"I can tell you that," a female voice announced.

Seana appeared in the open door of the keep. She

descended the steps and stopped before Ross. Ross was shocked. Why had Seana remained behind? Why hadn't Sinclair taken her with him?

Niall called Seana's name and reached for her. Ross grasped his cousin's arm in a firm grip. "Doona be a fool," Ross hissed. "Have you forgotten what Seana did to you, to me, to Gillian?"

Niall shook himself and stepped back, allowing Ross to deal with the woman he had once called wife.

"Verra well, Seana. Tell us where Sinclair went."

"Sinclair wanted to save his own skin when he learned Gillian was alive. He believed Gillian had leaped to her death from the tower and hoped to blame Ross for her untimely end. He intended to tell MacKay that Gillian became despondent when Ross rejected her and took her own life. When I told him Gillian was alive and at Ravenscraig, he feared reprisal. Coward that he was, he fled."

"Gillian would never take her own life," MacKay growled. "Besides, I kenned Gillian was safe at Ravenscraig after she escaped from Sinclair's tower. I saw her myself."

"But Angus didna ken that," Seana explained. "He truly believed Gillian had leaped to her death."

"Why did you let him believe such a thing?" Ross asked. "You are depraved as well as evil."

"I wanted Angus to wed me!" Seana spat. "As long as Gillian lived, that would never happen. And if I killed her, he would never forgive me. The best I could do was to help Gillian escape, make Sinclair believe she was dead, and get him to wed me before he learned the truth."

"How could you, Seana?" Niall accused. "You were wed to me."

"Our handfast marriage was a farce. I wed you under duress. I wanted a real marriage. I wanted to be mistress of a keep, even a keep such as this."

She sent Niall a scornful look. "Niall would never become laird because he isna ambitious enough to do what had to be done to make that happen."

"Kill me, you mean," Ross retorted.

Seana shrugged but said naught, confirming Ross's belief. Ross heard Niall groan and placed a bracing hand on his cousin's shoulder. Niall's spine stiffened, his expression proclaiming his fealty to Ross.

"You still havena told me where to find Sinclair."

"He fled to Edinburgh," Seana revealed. "He planned to enter the king's service as a mercenary." She scowled. "He refused to take me with him. He left me here to face a bleak winter alone, with scarcely enough food to sustain me and those who remained behind. I curse him a thousand times over. I hope he rots in hell."

"Amen," MacKay added. "Now we will never ken why he opposed a truce with the MacKennas."

"I can tell you," Seana said, "but I want something in return."

"You deserve naught!" Ross roared. "I rue the day you came into my life."

"I had a plan," Seana said, "but MacKay ruined it when he wed his daughter to you."

"And I couldna be more grateful," Ross replied. "Tell us why Sinclair wished the feud to continue."

"First tell me what my punishment is to be. Will you let me return to my father's keep?"

"Nay, your father doesna want you, and I canna blame him."

Seana blanched. "Are you going to kill me?"

"I admit the thought did enter my mind. But if you

tell us what we want to know, mayhap we will consider leniency."

Seana approached Niall and knelt awkwardly at his feet. "Niall, for what we once meant to each other, have mercy. I am still your wife. If you take me back, I promise to be a good wife to you."

The look on Niall's face was implacable. "You are no longer my handfast wife, Seana. I renounce you. I willna interfere with the punishment Ross and MacKay decide upon. May God forgive you, for I canna."

Seana, her demeanor anything but submissive, turned to confront Ross. "Verra well, I will tell you what you want to know if you promise not to slay me."

"I agree," Ross said. "You have naught to lose by telling the truth, and much to gain."

"Angus wanted the feud to continue until all MacKay's sons and the MacKay himself were slain in the feud. Then he intended to wed Gillian and claim Braeburn for himself."

"That doesna make sense," MacKay scoffed. "What made Sinclair believe my sons and I would die fighting MacKennas?"

Seana hesitated.

"Continue, Seana." Ross said,

"You've already lost two sons, MacKay," Seana said with sly innuendo. "What makes you think they were slain by a MacKenna?"

MacKay's brow furrowed. "Why would I think otherwise?"

"Think about it, Tearlach MacKay."

MacKay staggered under the weight of Seana's words. "Are you saying Sinclair killed my sons?"

"Aye, he admitted to the deed, and despaired when

the feud ended. He used various methods of mischief to convince the clans to take up their swords again."

"Doona forget your part in all this," Ross said sternly. "Your evil deeds deserve harsh punishment."

"You promised!" Seana cried.

"I but promised you would live, and so you shall. You will be escorted to St. Sithian's Abbey, where you will spend the rest of your life cloistered behind walls, shut away from the world. I sent word ahead to expect you."

Seana looked as if she wanted to bolt, but there was no place to run. Her legs crumpled beneath her and she fell to the ground, begging for mercy. Her pleas fell on deaf ears.

Ramsey MacKay pulled her roughly to her feet. "You doona deserve mercy," he snarled.

"We canna return home until things are settled here," Ross told him. "Lock her away someplace until we can deal with her."

He watched dispassionately as Ramsey led a sobbing Seana away. "Fergus, is there ale available to accommodate us? We will gladly share our food if your stores are depleted. We brought enough provisions to distribute to your kinsmen."

"We can supply the ale and will be happy to share your food. There are bedchambers available for you and the MacKay if you wish them. The others can bed down in the hall."

Ross nodded his thanks, then turned to Niall. "Have the lads take the provisions to the kitchen."

As the men left to take care of their horses and carry in the provisions, Ross led MacKay to the hearth, where both sank down onto benches. MacKay appeared shaken. Ross would have been shaken, too, if he had just learned Sinclair had deliberately and cold-heartedly killed his sons.

"I'm sorry, MacKay," Ross said. "Betrayal is a heavy burden to bear, especially when it involves the death of your own flesh and blood."

"If Sinclair were here, I would reach into his throat and pull his heart out with my bare hands. I lost two sons and would have lost all my bairns and my own life if I hadna sought peace."

"Sinclair is no longer a threat to us or our loved ones. We have put an end to years of feuding and are now allies."

"Sinclair still lives, but my sons are dead," MacKay said in a voice rife with despair. "If there is a just God, Sinclair will meet his Maker and be thrust into hell for his sins."

"Sinclair would be a fool to return to the Highlands," Ross predicted. "He has made too many enemies."

"He is a dead man if he does," MacKay swore. "I've decided to rename Sinclair's stronghold Wickhaven and place Ramsey in charge. Half my clansmen will remain to help him keep order, though I doubt anyone here will object. Once provisions, men, and arms reach Wickhaven from Braeburn, Ramsey can make something of the chaos Sinclair has left behind. Judith can join him as soon as all here is put to right."

Ross and his kinsmen remained at Wickhaven several days to make sure order was maintained, while MacKay took it upon himself to escort Seana to St. Sithian's.

Three days had passed since Ross had left to wage war on Sinclair. Gillian was in the solar sewing baby clothing with Alice when Gizela rushed into the chamber, her eyes wild and unfocused. Gillian looked up from her work and rose, her heart pounding with alarm. "What is amiss, Gizela? Is it Ross?"

Gizela shook her disheveled gray head. "Evil approaches Ravenscraig's gates. You must order the portcullis lowered at once, else all is lost."

"Who comes?"

Gizela's answer was forestalled when Gordo entered the solar, his confusion apparent. "Is Gizela here, Gillian? She said we must lower the portcullis as she raced by me just moments ago. I doona know what to make of it. Think you we should do as she says?"

"Och, 'tis too late!" Gizela cried, throwing up her hands as if to ward off evil. "'Tis up to you now, lass, for you are the only one who can defeat him."

"Gizela, what . . ." The words died in her throat as the sounds of clanking armor and loud voices drifted up from the hall.

Gordo didn't waste any more time in conversation as he turned and raced for the stairs. Lifting her skirts, Gillian followed as swiftly as she dared. Gordo reached the hall first. He skidded to a halt so fast, Gillian ran into him. He reached around to steady her as she gaped at the company of men wearing the king's colors over their mail. They were heavily armed and holding their weapons at the ready.

When their leader turned and grinned at Gillian, she had to hang on to Gordo to keep from falling. So many questions crowded her brain, she couldn't find the words to express them. What was Angus Sinclair doing here wearing the king's colors?

Gordo asked the question Gillian could not. "What do you here, Angus Sinclair?"

Angus strode forward, his gaze focused on Gillian. "I thought you dead, Gillian," he accused. "I believed you had jumped from my tower to your death. I didna know you were alive until Seana sought my protection after she fled Ravenscraig."

"Seana knew I wasna dead," Gillian replied. "She could have told you anytime she wished."

"Aye, but she chose not to tell me for reasons of her own. But her scheme didna work out as she wished."

"You are wearing the king's colors. Are you really in the king's service?"

"Aye, my kinsmen and I are mercenaries in the king's army. 'Twas the lesser of two evils."

"Why are you here?" Gordo asked.

Sinclair's smirk sent fingers of dread racing down Gillian's spine. "We are here on the king's business. Where is the MacKenna? Why is Ravenscraig so poorly defended? We rode through the portcullis without being challenged."

"Why would we challenge the king's soldiers?" Gordo replied. "Had we known it was you, you wouldna have been allowed to enter."

"My husband will return soon," Gillian asserted.

"Fortune is with me," Sinclair gloated. "I expected a fight, but for once everything is going my way. Hear me," he loudly proclaimed. "By the king's order, I hereby lay claim to Ravenscraig Tower."

Gillian stepped forwards. "You are a liar, Angus Sinclair. Show me the document bearing the king's seal and mayhap I will believe you."

Sinclair made no move to produce such a document. "It makes no difference whether or not such a document exists. Ravenscraig is now in my possession. How convenient for me that MacKenna isna here to challenge me. When he returns, we will be waiting for him. He will ride into our trap and die."

"How many men were left behind to defend the keep?" Gillian whispered to Gordo.

"Six, including myself. Ross saw no need to leave a large force behind, for we have no enemies."

"What are you whispering about?" Sinclair barked.

"There are men on the wall walk and others stationed within the keep to stop you from seizing that which is not yours and never will be," Gordo claimed.

Sinclair laughed. "MacKenna left behind but a handful of men. They have been captured and disarmed and are being led at swordpoint into the hall even as we speak."

The shuffle of feet brought Gillian spinning around in time to see five men being prodded into the hall. Her gasp of dismay brought another bark of laughter from Sinclair.

"Accept it, Gillian MacKay. I am your new lord and master."

"Never! You will rot in hell before I will be yours, Angus Sinclair!"

Chapter Twenty

"Doona rile the man, lass," Gordo warned as Sinclair took a menacing step toward Gillian.

Gillian held her ground. "Look at me, Angus Sinclair." She pressed the fullness of her gown against her stomach, delineating the swelling beneath. "I carry Ross's bairn. Do you still want me?"

The rage that had been simmering inside Sinclair burst forth. "Stupid bitch! 'Twas never you I wanted; 'twas Braeburn. I planned and schemed for the day I would claim you and become laird of Braeburn. Then the MacKay sued for peace, wed you to MacKenna, and all was lost to me. I decided to have Ravenscraig instead."

Gillian and Gordo exchanged puzzled looks. "You're mad," Gillian charged. "There is no way you could become laird of Braeburn. I have three living brothers and a father."

"Had the feud continued they all would have died, one by one, in the same manner in which your two brothers met their Maker," Sinclair said. "Why do you think I worked feverishly to sabotage the treaty? But naught worked. Without a feud, your father and brothers couldna die fighting MacKennas, and I couldna claim you and Braeburn."

"I doona ken," Gillian replied uneasily. She wasn't sure she wanted to understand.

"I didna expect you would. No one was smart enough to figure it out."

"Figure what out?" Gordo demanded. "Speak plainly, man."

Sinclair sneered at Ross's uncle. "Think you the MacKay lads fell beneath a MacKenna sword?"

Gillian gasped as comprehension dawned. Grief mingled with rage. "Duplicitous bastard! Traitor! You killed my brothers! You planned to slay my entire family and blame their deaths on the feud."

Sinclair shrugged. " 'Twas easily accomplished, until your father turned coward and sought peace. I wanted Braeburn—always have. When your father wed you to the enemy, new plans had to be made."

A stunned silence descended in the hall. Even Sinclair's kinsmen stared at their chieftain in dawning horror and disbelief. It was obvious from their reaction that Sinclair hadn't taken his kinsmen into his confidence. Highlanders were a proud lot. Attacking one's allies was unheard-of. Sinclair's actions broke the strict code of honor by which they lived.

Gillian was filled with a rage so intense, it could not be controlled. Angus Sinclair had cold-bloodedly killed two of her brothers and planned to kill her father and surviving brothers. Then he intended to wed her and claim Braeburn. Vengeance burned deep in her soul. Just seeing Angus's smirking face in front of her demanded retribution. She reached for her claymore, biting back a curse when she realized she hadn't carried a blade in months.

"The king will hear of your betrayal and punish you for your foul deeds," Gillian cried.

Sinclair laughed. "The king doesna care what happens in the Highlands. He has his hands full protecting his borders. Feuds are the least of his worries."

Something snapped inside Gillian. Beyond rage, she reached for her eating knife and launched herself at Sinclair. In the red haze that surrounded her, she heard Gordo call her name and felt his hand brush her gown in an effort to stop her. But Gillian was in no mood to be stopped. She moved swiftly and surely, scarcely aware of what she did as she plunged the knife into Sinclair's chest.

Sinclair fell to the floor, writhing in pain. "Kill her!" he screamed to his men. "Kill everyone. Let no MacKenna live."

To a man, the entire cadre stepped away from their fallen chieftain, as if distancing themselves from a traitor to the Highland code of honor. Gordo sprinted forward, seized Sinclair's sword, and prepared to defend Gillian. But it wasn't necessary. None of Sinclair's kinsmen raised his sword to Gillian. In fact, the five MacKennas who had been held at swordpoint broke free with little effort.

"Cowards!" Sinclair screamed. "I'm dead. She's killed me!"

"You'll live, much to my regret," Gillian said with icy disdain. "Had I a sword or a dirk instead of an eating knife, you *would* be dead. A well-deserved death, I might add. Even your own kinsmen hold you in contempt."

Gordo knelt beside Sinclair, holding him down as he examined his wound. "Aye, you'll live." He glanced up at Sinclair's kinsmen, who were milling around him. "Which one of you is Sinclair's lieutenant?"

A man stepped forward. "I am Robert Sinclair, Angus's lieutenant."

"Your chieftain is a traitor to his kinsmen and his allies, Robert Sinclair. He deserves to die. If you wish to return to Edinburgh, you and your kinsmen may leave."

"We are nae returning to Edinburgh," Robert said. "We doona like being mercenaries. We miss the Highlands."

"We want to return to our families," a warrior called out.

"Aye, we left them behind to follow Angus," Robert explained. " 'Twas wrong of us. We want to return to our homes, though they may be no more than hovels." He shook his head. "Angus convinced us that the king gave him Ravenscraig Tower, and that our lives would be better here."

Slowly Gillian emerged from the rage that had caused her to attack Angus Sinclair. Seeing that she still held the bloody eating knife she had plunged into Angus's chest, she dropped it and stepped away from the fallen man, wiping her hand on her gown.

"I doona ken what has become of your homes or families, for my husband and father left several days ago to lay siege to the keep. But I'm sure if you swear fealty to my father, you will be forgiven and allowed to dwell on your land in peace."

Two of Sinclair's kinsmen helped him to his feet.

"Leave him," Gordo cried. "Angus Sinclair must die!"

"Have mercy!" Angus begged. "If you let me return to Edinburgh, I promise to remain there until the end of my days."

"You dare beg for mercy?" Gillian spat. "Did you

show my dead brothers mercy? Nay, you killed them in cold blood. Had my eating knife been an inch longer, you would be dead."

"At least treat my wound," Sinclair begged. "I am in pain."

"Why? You're going to die anyway," Gordo said coldly.

"Make way," Gizela said, pushing through the crowd. She stopped before Gillian, holding her basket of medicines in front of her. "Leave Angus Sinclair to me, lady. I will take care of him."

Gillian looked into Gizela's eyes, understood what the healer was saying, and nodded. "Aye, I ken that you will, Gizela."

Gillian began shaking in the aftermath of all the violence, as if suddenly aware of what she had done. But she regretted naught. She would do it again, but the next time her aim would be true.

Alice rushed over to her and led her to a bench. "Mama is fetching something to calm you. Look at you; you are shaking like a leaf. Are you unwell?"

"Nay, I am well enough, albeit angrier than I have ever been in my life. My brothers are gone; naught will bring them back. But knowing that Angus Sinclair will pay for his crimes eases the hurt."

"Your father willna go easy on him," Alice predicted.

Gillian slid a knowing glance at Gizela. "Angus will die this day," she predicted. "Has Gizela finished treating him yet?"

Alice left Gillian briefly to check on Gizela's progress. "I saw Gizela sprinkle a white powder on Sinclair's wound. She is sewing him up as we speak," she reported when she returned.

"See that the rushes are changed. I want none of Angus Sinclair's blood in my keep," Gillian said weakly.

As the tension ebbed from her body, her stomach roiled and her head began to ache. She wanted Ross. She wanted her husband. She wanted to lie in his arms and feel his comfort surround her.

Hanna appeared with a mug of something hot and steaming. "You were verra brave, lass. 'Twas a great shock you just received. Drink this—it will calm you and soothe your bairn."

Gizela sidled up to Gillian as she sipped the potion. "'Tis done, lass. Angus Sinclair willna harm you or those you love again. He will breathe his last this day."

Gillian stared at Gizela. "Are you sure, verra sure? My eating knife did little damage."

Gizela's wise old eyes held a wealth of knowledge. "Trust me, lady; Angus Sinclair is a dead man."

"Thank you, Gizela."

Gillian turned away as Sinclair's kinsmen dragged him to his feet. They stood there, awaiting orders. Gordo strode toward her, his expression fiercely determined.

"I told Sinclair's kinsmen they may leave, Gillian, but their chieftain is to remain in our dungeon to await punishment."

"Let his kinsmen take him away," Gillian said tiredly.

"What? Nay! The man killed your brothers. Your father willna be pleased if I free him. The man deserves to die."

"Angus Sinclair *will* die, Gordo; doona doubt it. I doona want him to die in my keep. As for his kinsmen, they are innocent. They knew naught of Angus's duplicity. Their wives and children need them. If my father and Ross decide a different fate is in order, let them dole it out."

"Ross will skin me alive if I let Sinclair leave without the punishment he deserves," Gordo argued.

Gillian stared off into space. "Gizela has taken care of Angus in her own way."

"What is that supposed to mean?"

"I amna sure. Gizela said he is a dead man, and I believe her."

His mouth agape, Gordo stared at Gillian a full minute before turning on his heel and barking out an order. Moments later Sinclair's kinsmen dragged him out the door.

"Let me help you to bed, Gillian," Alice said. "You've had enough excitement for one day. I will bring a tray up to you later."

"I amna hungry."

"Mama will fix you something to tempt your appetite."

Though Gillian didn't want to appear weak, she was in shock and grieving as Alice helped her to the solar and settled her in bed.

Once Ross saw that Ramsey MacKay had everything under control at Wickhaven, he and his men left the keep and headed home. When they reached a crossroad, they spied riders approaching from the direction of Ravenscraig.

"Can you identify them?" Ross asked Niall.

Shading his eyes against the sun, Niall peered at the riders. "They're wearing the king's colors."

Ross raised his hand, halting his army. "We'll stop here and wait for them. If they're coming from Ravenscraig, I want to know the nature of their visit."

It took a good fifteen minutes for the riders to reach them. "They have the look of the Sinclairs about them," Donald muttered as he joined Ross and Niall. "Look there!" Niall cried, pointing to a horse bearing a body lying limply across its withers. "Who do you suppose that is?"

"Pass the word," Ross ordered. "No one is to draw a sword unless they threaten us." Ross searched the face of each Sinclair in turn and then glanced at the dead man draped over the horse's back.

Robert Sinclair rode forth to meet Ross.

"Who are you?" Ross asked.

"Robert Sinclair."

Ross spared Sinclair's uniform a scathing look. "Where do you think you're going? Have you been to Ravenscraig Tower?"

Robert's horse danced beneath him, as nervous as Robert appeared. "You may as well know, laird, for you will learn of it soon enough. Our chieftain is dead, and we are returning to Sinclair land and our families. We doona like being mercenaries."

Ross rode over to the dead body, lifted its head, saw it was Angus, and let it drop. "How did he die?"

" 'Tis a mystery. Something happened at Ravenscraig that we doona understand."

Ross's lips thinned. "Explain yourself. How did you gain entry to Ravenscraig? The walls are impregnable."

"We wear the king's colors, though we will be glad to be free of them. Even you wouldna dare deny the king's soldiers entry."

"That doesna explain your reason for visiting Ravenscraig, nor how Sinclair died."

" 'Tis difficult to explain, much less ken, Laird Ross. We followed our chieftain to Ravenscraig on the king's business, or so we were led to believe. Angus told us the king had awarded him stewardship of Ravenscraig Tower, and that our lives would improve if we followed him into battle. We were prepared to fight for Ravenscraig to better our lot, until we learned Angus had lied to us. He had no written order from the king."

"What happened?"

"Your lady is verra brave, Laird Ross. She challenged Angus to show her the document with the king's seal. Of course, he couldna. When Angus discovered you werena at Ravenscraig, he told your lady he intended to set a trap for you. He intended to kill you and your kinsmen as you rode into the bailey."

Ross smiled. "My lady is a true warrior woman. However, naught you've said thus far explains Sinclair's death."

He scratched his head. " 'Tis truly a mystery. Today we learned that Angus Sinclair betrayed his allies. We trusted him, until he bragged about killing the sons of our ally to further his own plans. When your lady heard Angus admit to killing her brothers, she plunged her eating knife into his chest. It didna appear to be a serious wound. Your healer treated him before we carried him off. Soon after we left Ravenscraig, however, he keeled over and died."

"Gillian stabbed Sinclair with her eating knife?" Ross repeated. He dismounted to take a closer look at the body.

"Your lady showed more courage than most men," Robert said admiringly. "Had she a sword in her hand, I swear she would have slain Angus where he stood. When Angus ordered us to kill her, none of us would obey him. Shamed by our chieftain's treachery, we surrendered our swords. Angus broke the code of the Highlands; he didna deserve our loyalty."

Ross felt Gillian's pain keenly. It must have been devastating to her to learn that Angus had killed her brothers. The shock could have dire consequences to a woman carrying a bairn.

"Gordo MacKenna wanted to imprison Angus in the dungeon," Robert continued, "but your lady told us to take him away. Gordo wasna happy with your lady's decision."

"I doona doubt it," Ross muttered, thinking that Gordo would have objected most strenuously. He was surprised Gordo hadn't killed Sinclair on the spot.

"Will you allow us to return to our homes and families?" Robert asked. "MacKay hasna harmed our wives and bairns, has he?"

"You should have thought of them before you went haring off with your chieftain. But rest easy; we doona wage war on women and bairns. Ramsey MacKay has taken stewardship of Sinclair Keep. He will need men to work his land and tend his cows. If you swear fealty to him, I am sure he will welcome you back. Your lot will be better with Ramsey MacKay than it would have been with Angus Sinclair. He cared naught for the welfare of his people."

"Sinclairs and MacKays are allies," Robert said. "We swore fealty to our overlord once, and we willna hesitate to do it again. Are we free to leave, Ross MacKenna?"

"Aye, but when next we meet, you had best be wearing plaid instead of the king's colors. Tell Ramsey what you told me, and mayhap he will allow you to remain on his land."

So saying, Ross turned his horse toward Ravenscraig and rode like the wind toward home and his wife. A wife he loved beyond reason, beyond his own life.

Niall and the others trailed behind him, unable to keep up with his furious pace.

The sun had disappeared behind the mountains, spreading shadows over the land when Ross rode through the portcullis into the inner bailey. He dismounted at the front steps, threw his reins to a young lad who had run up to greet him, and mounted the stairs two at a time. He burst into the hall as the tables were being laid for the evening meal.

"Where is my wife?" he shouted to no one in particular.

Gordo heard him and ran up to greet him. "You should have seen her, laddie. She was magnificent," Gordo said, beaming.

"I know all about it. I met the Sinclairs on the road. Angus is dead."

Gordo nodded. "That doesna surprise me, although he was verra much alive when he left here. I would have gone after him and seen to his demise if Gillian hadna persuaded me that I would be wasting my time. She kenned the traitor wouldna live long."

"Robert Sinclair told me that Angus died shortly after they left Ravenscraig. It was sudden and unexpected. Gillian was right, though I doona ken how or why. Where is she? Is she well?"

"Alice took her upstairs to rest. She appeared to be in shock. It wasna easy for her to hear Sinclair brag about killing her brothers. We havena seen her since she left the hall, but Alice assured us she is well, and that your bairn thrives."

The words were scarcely out of Gordo's mouth before Ross peeled away from him and raced up the stairs to the solar. He found Gillian sitting before the fire, wrapped in her MacKay plaid and staring into the flames. She seemed oblivious to her surroundings. Ross approached cautiously, so as not to frighten her. The breath caught in his throat when he saw silent tears streaming down her face.

"Gillian." He spoke her name softly. She turned her head and stared at him. At first he thought she didn't recognize him.

"He killed them, Ross," Gillian whispered. "He wanted to kill all of them, Da and my brothers. Afterward, he intended to wed me and claim Braeburn."

Ross lifted her into his arms, then sat in the chair she had just vacated and settled her on his lap, murmuring comforting words into her ear.

Her voice trembled as she said, "I wanted to kill Angus for what he did to my family. All this time I believed my brothers were slain by MacKennas. I hated you for it."

"Forget the past, sweet lass. We have the future ahead of us. A future where peace will reign in the valley and our children will know a life without bloodshed or feuds."

Gillian nestled in his arms, his warmth chasing away the coldness of reality. As long as she had Ross, all was right in her world. She couldn't bring her brothers back, but she could make sure the clans never had reason to feud again.

"Can you tell me what happened?"

Gillian took a deep breath and nodded. "We didna recognize Angus and his kinsmen at first; they wore the king's colors. The men you left behind to guard the keep believed the party was sent by the king and let them ride through the gate unchallenged. Gizela warned us to lower the portcullis but we acted too late.

"Angus was surprised to find you gone and the keep undefended. He was prepared to fight to claim Ravenscraig for himself. He immediately made plans to kill you and your party when you rode through the portcullis." She shuddered. "I must have gone a wee bit daft then, for I stabbed him with my eating knife. I didna hurt him badly, but I wanted to."

Ross's heart nearly stopped. "What if his men had turned on you? They could have slain you and our bairn."

"I'm sorry. I was too enraged to think past the horror of Angus's confession. As it turned out, Angus's kinsmen were as horrified as I by his treachery."

He feathered kisses on her lips. "I know. I met them on the road to Wickhaven."

She looked up at him. "Wickhaven?"

" 'Tis what your father renamed Sinclair Keep. He claimed ownership and left Ramsey in charge." He hesitated a moment, then said, "Angus Sinclair is dead."

Gillian didn't seem surprised. "Did you nae hear what I said?" he asked. "Sinclair is dead."

"Aye, I heard." She shrugged. "I doona wish to talk about Angus Sinclair."

Ross frowned but respected her wishes, rocking her gently in his lap.

"Do you want to hear about Seana McHamish's fate?" Ross asked.

Gillian nodded.

"We found her at Wickhaven. She fled there after she left Ravenscraig. She remained there because she had no place else to go after Sinclair refused to take her to Edinburgh with him. The keep and its people were in sad shape. Your father promised to supply provisions and whatever else is needed until Ramsey can bring order to the keep and land."

"You didna kill Seana, did you?"

"Nay, but in time she may wish she were dead. Your father escorted her to St. Sithian's Abbey. 'Tis a strict order; she will spend the rest of her days in prayer, behind walls from which there is no escape."

Ross kissed her then, cradling her in his arms like a child he needed to protect. Gillian melted into the kiss, into his warrior's body, drinking deeply of his vitality, his zest, growing stronger by the minute.

"I feel better already," Gillian said with a sigh when he broke off the kiss. "Seana is gone and Angus is dead, though Da willna be pleased to hear it. He would have wanted to exact his own brand of vengeance on Angus."

"Aye, I ken it. The way you stood up to Sinclair was verra brave, lass, though foolish for a woman in your condition. You saved us, you know. If you hadna gotten Sinclair to admit he killed your brothers, his kinsmen wouldna have turned against him."

"Bravery had naught to do with it," Gillian admitted. " 'Twas rage that drove me. Rage and the knowledge that Angus meant to kill you. I love you, Ross MacKenna. I canna imagine my life without you in it."

Ross's arms tightened around her. "That is something you need never worry about. You are mine, Gillian MacKay. And what is mine I keep. I love you, sweet lass."

A whisper of sound warned Ross that they were not alone. Immediately alert, he whipped his head around, surprised to see Gizela standing near the door.

"Gizela, what do you here?"

"Angus Sinclair is dead?"

"Aye, he is."

Gizela nodded complacently, satisfaction clearly visible in her fathomless eyes. " 'Tis as it should be."

Ross stared at her. Suddenly the pieces of the puzzle began to fall into place.

"What did you do to him, Gizela?" Ross asked.

"The man deserved to die," the healer said. "He couldna be allowed to live."

"MacKay was robbed of the right to punish Sinclair in his own way."

Gizela shrugged. " 'Twas better this way, neatly and quickly done, without fuss or bother. No great loss there. Think no more on it, laird. Attend your lady; she is your future."

She shuffled off, disappearing as mysteriously as she had come. "Gizela, wait! How did you do it?" Ross called. No answer was forthcoming.

"Let her go, Ross," Gillian said. "I knew Gizela didna intend for Angus to live. That's why I let his kinsmen take him away over Gordo's objection. I didna want him to die in my keep. We are well rid of him. Does it really matter how he died?"

"Aye, naught matters but you, sweet lass, and the future that is ours to live."

Ross rose to his feet, taking Gillian up with him. He carried her to their bed and showed her without words the true meaning of love.

Epilogue

On the day Gillian went into labor, the moors and hillsides were ablaze with purple heather; the scent of it filled the warm air and floated on gentle breezes. Members of Clan MacKay and Clan MacKenna were gathered in the hall to await the birth.

Abovestairs in her bedchamber, Gillian paced the floor, her contractions monitored closely by Gizela. Alice and Hanna were also present, preparing the chamber for the eagerly anticipated birth.

Gillian let out a groan as a particularly violent contraction brought a fine sheen of sweat to her forehead. This bairn couldn't be born soon enough to suit her. For the last month she hadn't walked; she'd waddled. She felt ungainly and unattractive despite Ross's assurance that she was just as beautiful to him now as she had ever been.

"Do you feel like you could push, lass?" Gizela asked.

"I feel that if I doona push this bairn out soon, I will

explode." Gillian gasped as another contraction gripped her. "How much longer do I have to walk? I've been pacing for hours. I doona know how much more of this I can take."

Gizela eyed Gillian's belly and guided her over to the bed. " 'Tis time to bring your bairn into the world. Lie down." She assisted Gillian into bed. "Alice, fetch the kettle of water heating on the hearthstone."

A flurry of activity followed Gizela's orders. Once the hot water had been poured into a bowl, Gizela washed her hands with strong soap and ordered the other ladies to do the same. Then she returned to the bed.

"Bear down when the next contraction comes, Gillian." She placed a hand on Gillian's stomach, felt the beginning of a strong contraction, and said, "Now, lass, push."

The pushing went on for the longest thirty minutes of Gillian's life. Thus far she had controlled her cries, but now it was no longer possible. She was hurting so much she didn't even realize she had screamed. She wanted Ross. If Ross were here with her, she would be braver. What silly rule said men didn't belong in the birthing room?

Gillian's piercing scream reached the hall. Ross leaped from his chair, uncertain what to do. Tearlach MacKay grasped his arm.

"Naught is amiss, lad. Take it from a man has who survived the births of five braw sons and a wee lassie. You'll have to wait it out as I did."

Ross subsided into his chair, wishing himself in the solar with Gillian. Why were men barred from witnessing the birthing when they were the ones responsible for their wives' travail? When Ross heard Gillian scream a second time, there was no holding him back. Shaking off MacKay's restraining hand, Ross took the stairs two at a time and burst into the bedchamber.

"Laird, this is no place for a man," Hanna admonished, trying to block his view of the bed.

"This is where I belong," Ross said, pushing past Hanna.

"Ross," Gillian said weakly. Her smile of welcome turned into a grimace of pain as she reached for his hand. He grasped it and held it tightly.

"What can I do to help, Gizela?"

"Birthing isna a pretty sight, laird. Are you sure you want to be here?"

"Just tell me what to do," Ross replied. "I canna bear to see Gillian suffer. Is it always like this?"

Gizela placed herself at the foot of the bed. " 'Tis an easy birth compared to some. Support your lady's back as she pushes your bairn out. It willna be long now. I can see his head. 'Tis as red as his mother's."

"Are you all right, Gillian, lass?" Ross asked as he gently lifted her head and shoulders and sat behind her to provide support.

"Push, lass," Gizela urged. "Doona hold back. Soon you will hold your son in your arms."

Gillian's face turned a mottled red as she labored to push her child into the world. With Ross supporting her and whispering encouragement into her ear, the pain became more bearable, enabling her to bear down more forcefully.

With a whoosh, the baby slid into Gizela's hands. Gizela held the perfectly formed boy up by his feet, gently slapped his bottom, and waited along with the others for the sound of life. Everyone breathed a sigh of relief when he let out a hearty wail of protest.

"You have a fine, braw laddie, laird," Gizela said as she handed the babe to Hanna. Hanna cleared his mouth and took him over to the washbasin to clean and wrap him in swaddling clothes.

The afterbirth was quickly delivered and carried off in a bowl by Alice. Ross gently laid Gillian down and sat on the edge of the bed.

"Are you all right, lass? It pains me to see you suffer."

Gillian blinked at him sleepily. " 'Twas worth it, Ross. Did you hear our son cry? He's going to be a strong warrior like his father."

"Or like his mother," Ross teased.

"I want to see him."

Hanna handed the babe to Ross, who placed him in Gillian's arms. The first thing Gillian did was unwrap him, count his tiny fingers and toes, and check for imperfections.

"He's perfect," Ross said wonderingly.

"What shall we name him?"

"Tavis, for your dead brother."

"Tavis Taren MacKenna," Gillian added.

" 'Tis time you left, laird," Gizela said. "Your lady is exhausted and needs rest. And we need to clean her and change the bedding so she will be presentable for visitors."

Ross rose and picked up his son, cradling him tenderly in his arms. After placing a kiss on Gillian's forehead, he carried the bairn from the chamber to show him off to his grandfather and uncles.

"Gillian has given me a fine, braw son," Ross exclaimed as he strode into the hall. "I present to you Tavis Taren MacKenna, future laird of Clan MacKenna."

Tearlach MacKay dashed away a tear as he inspected his new grandson, his second, since Murdoc's wife had given him a healthy grandson one month earlier.

After the child was inspected and admired by members of both clans, the celebration began. When the babe started to fuss, Ross quietly left the hall to return him to his mother.

Gillian watched through teary eyes as Ross brought their son to her. She held out her arms.

"You should be sleeping," Ross said, placing the bairn in Gillian's arms.

"I needed to see my bairn again before I could sleep," Gillian said as she cuddled the babe.

"I love you, Gillian," Ross murmured. "Thank you for our son."

No answer was forthcoming. Gillian had already fallen asleep, her arms curled around her son. But it didn't matter; she already knew Ross MacKenna's heart belonged to her, just as hers belonged to him.

AUTHOR'S NOTE

I hope you enjoyed the nonstop action and enduring love between Ross and Gillian. Though generations of enmity separated the two, it took love and mutual respect to finally bring an end to an ancient feud and unite two warring clans.

My next book, *The Price of Pleasure*, takes you to another time, another place. The story opens in a French prison called Devil's Chateau during Napoleon's rise to power. Hovering near death, Reed Harwood, spy extraordinaire, prays for death, but instead he is rescued and nursed back to health by the Black Widow, a woman rumored to buy prisoners for her own pleasure.

I don't want to give away any more of the story, but I promise you won't be disappointed with this sexy tale of love and denial, good versus evil, with, as always, a happy ending.

I love hearing from readers. I can be reached through e-mail at conmason@aol.com and by snail mail at P.O. Box 3471, Holiday, FL, 34692. Visit my Web site at www.conniemason.com for information about my new releases and to see my new book cover.

ATTENTION
BOOK LOVERS!

Can't get enough of your favorite **ROMANCE**?

Call **1-800-481-9191** to:

✳ order books,

✳ receive a **FREE** catalog,

✳ join our book clubs to **SAVE 30%!**

Open Mon.-Fri. 10 AM-9 PM EST

Visit **www.dorchesterpub.com**
for special offers and inside
information on the authors you love.

We accept Visa, MasterCard or Discover®.
LEISURE BOOKS ♥ LOVE SPELL